HUNTED

NEW YORK TIMES BESTSELLING AUTHOR

SUZANNE BROCKMANN

Previously published as *Love with the Proper Stranger*
and *Texas Prey*

PLEASE RECYCLE • THIS PRODUCT IS RECYCLABLE

Recycling programs
for this product may
not exist in your area.

ISBN-13: 978-1-335-40633-0

Hunted
First published as Love with the Proper Stranger in 1997.
This edition published in 2021.
Copyright © 1997 by Suzanne Brockmann

Texas Prey
First published in 2015. This edition published in 2021.
Copyright © 2015 by Barb Han

This edition published by arrangement with Harlequin Books S.A.

For questions and comments about the quality of this book, please contact us at CustomerService@Harlequin.com.

Harlequin Enterprises ULC
22 Adelaide St. West, 40th Floor
Toronto, Ontario M5H 4E3, Canada
www.Harlequin.com

Printed in U.S.A.

CONTENTS

Suzanne Brockmann is an award-winning author of more than fifty books and is widely recognized as one of the leading voices in romantic suspense. Her work has earned her repeated appearances on the *New York Times* bestseller list, as well as numerous awards, including Romance Writers of America's #1 Favorite Book of the Year and two RITA® Awards. Suzanne divides her time between Siesta Key and Boston. Visit her at suzannebrockmann.com.

Books by Suzanne Brockmann

Not Without Risk
Night Watch
Taylor's Temptation
Get Lucky
Identity: Unknown
The Admiral's Bride
Hawken's Heart
Harvard's Education

Visit the Author Profile page at
Harlequin.com for more titles.

LOVE
WITH THE
PROPER
STRANGER

Suzanne Brockmann

For Mary Gray, Kirsten McDonough, Sylvia Micalone and all of the other wonderful Workcamp volunteers who have allowed me to help raise a hammer and build houses alongside them, even if only in spirit.

Prologue

She laced his coffee with opium.

He wasn't supposed to drink coffee this late at night. The doctor had told him not to. But she knew how much it pleased him to cheat the doctor's rules just a little every now and then.

He smiled as she brought it to him, smiled again as he took a sip. He liked it sweet.

The opium wouldn't kill him. It was part of the ritual, part of the game. She'd given him enough to confuse him, enough to slow his wits, to keep him docile and in control as she prepared for her checkmate.

She kissed the top of his balding head and he smiled again, breathing a deep sigh of contentment—the king, relaxing after a hard day at the office, secure in his castle alongside his beautiful queen.

Tonight, this king would die.

* * *

Tony was breathing hard. John Miller could hear him clearly over the wire, his voice raspy and loud in the radio headset. Tony was breathing hard and Miller knew he was scared.

"Yeah, that's right. I'm FBI," Tony said, giving up his cover. Miller knew without a doubt that his partner and best friend was in serious, serious trouble. "And if you're as smart as your reputation says you are, Domino, then you'll order these goons to lay down their weapons and surrender to me."

Domino laughed. "I've got twenty men surrounding you, and you think I'm going to *surrender...?*"

"I've got more than twenty men on backup," Tony lied, as Miller keyed his radio.

"Where the *hell* is that backup?" Miller's usually unshakable control was nearing a breaking point. He'd been ordered to sit tight and wait here outside the warehouse until the choppers arrived in a show of force, but he couldn't wait any longer. He *wouldn't* wait.

"Jesus, John, didn't you get the word?" came Fred's scratchy voice over the radio. "The choppers have been rerouted—there's been an assassination attempt on the governor. It's code red, priority. You're on your own."

No choppers. No backup. Just Tony inside the warehouse, about to be executed by Alfonse Domino, and John Miller here, outside.

It was the one scenario Miller hadn't considered. It was the one scenario he wasn't ready for.

Miller grabbed the assault rifle from the floor of the van and ran toward the warehouse. He needed a miracle, but he didn't waste time praying. He knew full well that he—and Tony—didn't have a prayer.

* * *

"I quit."

The board of directors looked at her in stunned silence.

Marie Carver gazed back at the expressions of shock on the familiar faces and knew that those two little words she'd uttered had granted her freedom. It was that easy. That simple. She quit.

"I've made arrangements for my replacement," she told them, careful not to let her giddy laughter escape. She quit. Tomorrow she would *not* walk through the front doors and take the elevator up to her executive office on the penthouse floor. Tomorrow she would be in another place. Another city, another state. Maybe even another country. She passed around the hiring reports her secretary had typed up and bound neatly with cheery yellow covers. "I've done all the preliminary interviews and narrowed the candidates down to three—any one of which I myself would have utmost faith in as the new president of Carver Software."

All twelve members of the board starting talking at once.

Marie held up her hand. "Should you decide to hire an outside candidate," she said, "you would, of course, require my approval as the major stockholder of this company. But I think you'll be impressed with the choices I've given you here." She rapped the yellow-covered report with her knuckles. "I ask that you hold all of your questions until after you've read this. If any concerns remain unanswered, you can reach me at home until six o'clock this evening. After that, I'll remain in touch with my secretary, whom I've promoted to Executive Assistant." She smiled. "I appreciate your understanding, and will see you all at the next annual shareholders meeting."

She gathered up her briefcase and walked quickly out of the room.

The opium was working.

His pupils had retracted almost to a pinpoint and he was drooling slightly, blinking sleepily as he watched her dance.

This was the part she liked. This was where she showed him what he would never again have the chance to experience, to violate.

True, this one had been gentle. His soft, old hands had never struck her. He'd been careful not to hurt her. He'd given her expensive presents, fancy gifts. But the act itself would always be an act of violence, always despicable, always requiring punishment.

Capital punishment.

Her dress fell in a pool of silk at her feet, and she deftly stepped out of it. His eyes were glazed, but not enough to hide his hunger at the sight of her. He stretched one hand out toward her, but he didn't have the strength to reach her.

And still she danced, to the rhythm of the blood pounding through her veins, to the anticipation of the moment when he would gaze into her eyes and know without a doubt that he was a dead man.

Freedom.

It hit Marie like the coolness of the air that swept through the open door at the end of the hall. It felt fresh and clean, like that very spring breeze, bringing hope and life and renewal. Through that open door she could see her car, sitting out in the parking lot, ready for her escape.

"Mariah."

There was only one person on that board of directors who could slow her departure. Susan Kane. Aunt Susan. Marie turned, but kept moving, backward, down the hall.

Susan followed, her long, batik-patterned dress moving in the breeze, disapproval in her slate-blue eyes. "Mariah," she said again, calling Marie by her childhood nickname. "Obviously you've been planning this for some time."

Marie shook her head. "Only two weeks."

"I wish you had told me."

Marie stopped walking then, meeting the older woman's sternly unwavering gaze. "I couldn't," she said. "I didn't tell most of my own staff until this morning."

"Why?"

"The company doesn't need me anymore," Marie said. "It's been three years since the last layoffs. We've turned it around, Sue. Profits continue to rise—we're thriving. You know the numbers as well as I do."

"So take a vacation. Take a leave of absence. Sit back on your laurels and relax for a while."

Marie smiled ruefully. "That's part of my problem," she said. "I can't relax."

Susan's face softened, concern in her eyes. "Is your stomach still bothering you?"

"Among other things." Like, for instance, the fact that Marie was thirty-two years old and since her divorce four years ago, she had no life outside of the office. Like, the fact that she still worked long overtime hours to increase profits, to expand, to hire more people, even though the failing computer software company that her father's sudden fatal heart attack had thrust into her lap had long ago become a Fortune 500 business. Like, the fact that each morning she found herself walking into the new, fancy office building into which the company had recently moved, and she wondered, what exactly was the point? What purpose did she serve by being here, by stressing herself out enough to develop stomach ulcers over the mundane, day-to-day operation of this business?

One day she was going to wake up, and she was going to be sixty years old and still walking into that building, still going home much too late to that sad excuse for a condo, still living out of boxes that she *still* hadn't managed to unpack.

And she'd look at her life, and all those meaningless, wasted years would stretch back into her meaningless, wasted past.

Because the truth was, even though she'd dutifully gotten her degree in business as her father had wanted, Marie had never wanted to run this company.

Shoot, it had taken years before she'd admitted that to herself. As far as knowing what she really wanted to do, Marie honestly didn't have a clue. But there was something that she did know.

She wanted to do more than keep a multimillion-dollar corporation up and running. She wanted to have a sense of real purpose. She wanted to be able to look back on her life and feel proud—feel as if she'd truly made a difference.

She was considering running for office. She was also thinking about joining the peace corps. She had found a list a mile long of volunteer organizations that desperately needed man power—everything from accountants for the Salvation Army to hands-on, hammer-wielding home builders for Foundations for Families.

But before she could do anything, she had to handle her stress.

Step one was cutting herself off from this company—breaking her addiction to this job and the company's addiction to her. She was going to do it cold turkey.

The company would survive. Marie knew they'd survive. Any one of her three job candidates would bring a freshness and vitality to the job that she'd lacked for nearly two years now. Whether or not Marie would survive was a different story…

"Where are you going?" Susan asked.

"I don't know," Marie admitted. "I'm just going to take my camera and go. I read in a book about stress-reduction that I should take a few months and leave everything behind—including my name. This book recommended that I temporarily take on a new identity. Supposedly that'll help me distance myself from everything that's been causing my ulcers." She smiled. "I'm going to leave Marie Carver locked in my condo—along with all my doubts about my sanity and my worries that Carver Software will go into a nosedive the moment I leave town."

Susan pulled her in for a quick hug—an unusual display of affection. "The job will be yours again when you come back," the older woman whispered. "I'll make sure of that."

Marie pulled away, unable to answer. If she had her way, she'd never be back. If she had her way, Marie Carver and her damned ulcers would be gone forever.

* * *

She used the knife to cut off a lock of his hair.

He didn't have too much, just a light fringe of gray at the back of his head, but that didn't matter. It was the only thing of his that she would keep.

Besides the money.

He was handcuffed now. He'd let her do that willingly, thinking she was playing some new sex game, never suspecting he had only moments left to live.

But when she unsheathed the stiletto, there was a hint of consternation in his drug-glazed eyes.

"What are you doing?" he asked.

She shushed him with a kiss. He couldn't speak. He wasn't allowed to speak.

But he didn't know the rules. "Clarise?" he said, fear pushing past the opium, creeping into his voice, making it waver as she set the tip of the stiletto against his chest.

She felt a flash of regret.

Clarise. She liked that name a lot. It was a shame that she would only be Clarise for a few moments longer. She couldn't use that name again. And she wouldn't. She was too smart to make that mistake.

"This has gone far enough," he said, trying to hide his fear behind an air of authority. "Release me now, Clarise."

She smiled and leaned on the whisper-thin blade, sliding it deep into his heart, setting him forever free.

"Kill him."

Domino's order came before John Miller had reached the warehouse doors, and the gunshots—four of them in rapid sequence were amplified deafeningly through his headset.

Tony.

Tony was dead.

Miller knew it. He had no chance of saving his friend.

He had this tape, though, this tape of Domino giving the order to off a federal agent. He had enough evidence to put Domino on death row. Blasting his way through that warehouse door at twenty to one odds would only get himself killed, too.

He knew that as well as he knew his own heartbeat.

But the heart that was pounding in his chest wasn't beating with a recognizable rhythm. And the red cloud of rage that covered his eyes didn't obscure his vision, but rather made it sharper, clearer.

Tony was dead, and the son of a bitch who ordered it done was *not* going to make his escape in a power-boat, losing himself in South America, outside of the FBI's jurisdiction. No, Alfonse Domino was going to burn in hell.

Miller hit the warehouse door at full run, bringing his gun up and into position at his hip, shouting in rage at the sight of Tony's crumpled body lying on the cold, blood-soaked concrete, shooting the surprise off the faces of Alfonse Domino and his men.

She had her airline ticket all ready, under an assumed name, of course. A temporary name.

Jane Riley. Plain Jane. Plane Jane. The thought amused her and she smiled. But only briefly. She knew she had a noticeable smile, and right now she had no desire to be noticed.

Her hair was under a kerchief for the occasion, and

she wore a dowdy camel-colored jacket she'd picked up at a secondhand store downtown.

She took nothing of Clarise's with her. Nothing but the money and her collection. Nine locks of hair.

She traveled light, boarding the plane to Atlanta with only a tote bag that held several novels she'd picked up at the airport shop and two hundred thousand dollars in cash. The rest of the money was already in her Swiss bank account.

In Atlanta, she'd catch a train to who knows where. Maybe New York. Maybe Philadelphia.

She'd catch a show or two, take her time deciding exactly who she wanted to be. Then she'd get her hair cut and colored, shop for a new wardrobe to match her new personality, pick a new town in a new state, and start the game all over again.

And then she'd have ten locks of hair.

Chapter 1

John Miller's heart was pounding and his mouth was dry as he awoke with a start. He stood up fast, trying hard to get his bearings, reaching automatically for his gun.

"John, are you all right?"

Christ, he was in his office. He'd fallen asleep with his head on his desk, and now he was standing in his office, with his side arm drawn and his hands shaking.

And Daniel Tonaka was standing in the doorway watching him. Daniel was expressionless, as he often was. But he was gazing rather pointedly at Miller's weapon.

Miller reholstered his gun, then ran both hands across his face. "Yeah," he said. "Yeah, I'm fine. I just fell asleep—or something—for a second."

"Maybe you should go home and go to bed."

Bed. Yeah, right. Maybe in some other lifetime.

"You look like hell, man," Daniel continued.

Miller *felt* like hell. He needed a case to work on. As long as he was working, the dreams weren't so bad. It was this damned in-between time that was unbearable. "I just need some more coffee."

Daniel didn't say anything. He just looked at Miller. He was relatively new to the bureau—just a kid. He was hardly twenty-five years old, with a young handsome face, high cheekbones and deep brown, exotically shaped eyes that announced his part-Asian parentage. Those eyes held a wisdom that extended far beyond his tender years. And true to the wisdom in his eyes, the kid always knew when to hold his tongue.

Daniel Tonaka could say more with his silence and maybe a lift of one of his dark eyebrows than twenty other men could say if they talked all day.

Miller had had half a dozen new partners since Tony, but Daniel was the only one who had lasted for any length of time. Next week it would be, what? Seven months? The kid deserved some kind of award.

Miller knew quite well the reputation he had in the bureau. He was "The Robot." He was a machine, an automaton, letting nothing and no one get in the way of his investigation. He was capable of putting everyone around him into a deep freeze with a single laser-sharp look. Even before Tony had died, Miller had kept his emotions to himself, and he had to admit he'd played his cards even closer to his vest over the past few years.

He was aware of the speculation about his lack of close friends within the bureau, the whispered conversations that concluded he was incapable of emotion, devoid of compassion and humanity. After all, a man who so obviously didn't possess a heart and soul couldn't possibly feel.

Some of the younger agents would go well out of their way to avoid him. Hell, some of the *older* agents did the same. He was respected. With his record of arrests and successful investigations, he'd have to be. But he wasn't well liked.

Not that a robot would give a damn about that.

Daniel stepped farther into Miller's office. "Working on the Black Widow case?"

Miller nodded, gazing down at the open file on his desk. He'd been studying the photos and information from the latest in a string of connected murders before he'd fallen asleep.

And dreamed about Tony again.

He sat back down in his chair, grimacing at his stiff muscles. Christ, everything ached. Every part of him was sore. He desperately needed sleep, but the thought of going home to his apartment and sinking into his bed and closing his eyes was unbearable. The moment he closed his eyes, he'd be back outside that warehouse. He'd dream about the night that Tony died, and he'd watch it happen all over again. And for the four thousandth time, the choppers would never come. For the four thousandth time, Miller would arrive too late. For the four thousandth time, blowing Domino's ass straight to hell *still* wouldn't make up for the fact that Tony's brains were smeared across the concrete.

God, the stab of guilt and loss he felt was still so sharp, so piercing. Miller tried to push it away, to bury it deep inside, someplace from which it would never escape. He tried to put more distance between himself and this pain, these emotions. He could do it. He *would* do it. He was, after all, the robot.

Miller took a swig from a mug of now-cold coffee, trying to ignore the fact that his hand was still shaking. "The killer did her last victim about three months ago." The coffee tasted like something from a stable floor, but at least it moistened his mouth. "Which means she's probably preparing to make another go of it. She's out there somewhere, hunting down husband number eight. At least we think it's number eight. Maybe there've been more we just don't know about."

"What if she's decided she's rich enough?"

"She doesn't kill for the money." Miller picked up the picture of Randolph Powers, knife blade protruding from his chest as he gazed sightlessly from his seat at the dinner table. "She kills because she likes to." And she was getting ready to do it again. He knew it.

"I haven't had time to look at this file," Daniel admitted, sitting down on the other side of the desk, pulling the report toward him. "Are we sure this is the same woman?"

"Exact M.O. The victim was found in the dining room, cuffed to the chair, with the remains of dinner on the table." Miller ran his fingers through his hair. God, he had a headache. "Opium was found in his system in the autopsy. The entire house was wiped clean of fingerprints. The only photo was a wedding portrait—and the bride's veil was over her face. It's her."

Daniel skimmed the report. "According to this, Powers married a woman named Clarise Harris two and a half weeks prior to his death." He glanced up at Miller. "The honeymoon was barely over. Didn't she usually wait two or three months?"

Miller nodded, rummaging through his desk drawers for his bottle of aspirin. "She's getting impatient." Jackpot. Miller twisted off the aspirin bottle's cap—empty. "Damn. Tonaka, do you have any aspirin in your desk?"

"You don't need aspirin, man. You need sleep. Go home and go to bed."

"If I wanted free advice, I would've asked for it. I think what I asked for was aspirin."

The deadly look Miller gave Daniel was designed to freeze a man in his tracks.

But Daniel just smiled as he stood up. "You know, I really hope we're partners for a good long time, John, because I cannot for the life of me imitate that look. I've tried. I practice every night in my bathroom mirror, but…" He shook his head. "I just can't do it. You have a real God-given talent there. See you later."

Daniel closed the door on the way out and Miller just sat, staring after him, wishing…for what?

If the kid had been Tony, Miller might have told him about the nightmares, about the fact that he was too damn scared even to try to sleep. If the kid had been Tony, Miller might have told him that this morning when he'd gotten on the bathroom scale, he'd found he'd lost twenty pounds. Twenty pounds, just like that.

But Daniel Tonaka *wasn't* Tony.

Tony was gone. He'd been dead and gone for years. Years.

Miller reached for the phone. "Yeah, John Miller. Put me through to Captain Blake."

It was time to get down to real work on this Black Widow case. Maybe then he could get some damned sleep.

* * *

Garden Isle, Georgia, was the best kept secret among the jet set. The beaches were covered with soft white sand. The sky was blue and the ocean, although murky with mineral deposits, was clean. The town itself was quaint, with cobblestone streets and charming brick houses and window boxes that overflowed with brightly colored flowers. Most of the shops were exclusive, the restaurants trendy and four-star and outrageously expensive—except if you knew where to go.

And after two months on Garden Isle, Mariah Robinson knew exactly where to go to avoid the crowds. She loaded her camera and her beach bag into the front basket of her bike and headed toward the beach.

Not toward the quiet, windswept beach that was only several yards from her rental house, but rather toward the usually crowded, always happening beach next to the five-star resort.

Most of the time, she embraced the solitude, often reveling in the noise-dampening sound of the surf and the raucous calls of the seabirds. But today she felt social. Today, she *wanted* the crowds. Today, just on a whim, she wanted to use her camera to take photographs of people.

Today she was meeting her friend, Serena, for lunch at one of those very same four-star restaurants.

But she was more than an hour early, and she took her bike with her onto the sand. She set it gently on its side and spread her beach blanket alongside it. There was a reggae band playing in the tent next to the resort bar even this early in the morning, and the music floated out across the beach.

She sat in the sun, just watching the dynamics of the people around her.

Some sunbathers lay in chaise lounges, their noses buried in books. Others socialized, talking and flirting in large and small groups. Men and women in athletic gear ran up and down the miles of flat, hard sand at the edge of the water. Others walked or strolled. Still others paraded—clearly advertising their trim, tanned bodies, scantily clad in designer bathing suits.

Mariah took out her camera, focusing on a golden retriever running next to a muscular man in neon green running shorts. She loved dogs. In fact, now that she wasn't shut up in an office each day from dawn till dusk, she was thinking about getting one and—

"Fancy meeting you here this early."

Mariah looked up but the glare from the bright sun threw the face of the woman standing next to her into shadows. It didn't matter. The crisp English-accented voice was unmistakable.

"Hey," Mariah said, smiling as Serena sat down next to her on her blanket.

"I thought you'd sworn off the resort beach," Serena continued, looking at Mariah over the tops of her expensive sunglasses.

Serena Westford was older than Mariah had originally thought when they'd first met a few weeks ago—she was closer to forty than thirty, anyway. Her smile was young though. It was mercurial and charming, displaying perfect white teeth. Her hair was blond with wisps escaping from underneath the big straw hat she always wore, and her trim body was that of a twenty-four-year-old.

She was as cool and confident as she was beautiful.

She was everything Mariah wished she could be. Everything Marie Carver wished she could be, Mariah corrected herself. But Marie Carver had purposely been left behind in Phoenix, Arizona. Mariah Robinson was here in Georgia, and Mariah was happy with her life. She went with the flow, calm and relaxed. No worries. No problems. No stress. No jealousy.

Serena was wearing a black thong bathing suit, covered only by a diaphanous short wrap that fluttered about her buttocks and thighs in the ocean breeze, leaving only slightly more than nothing to the imagination. Despite the fact that Serena Westford was no longer a schoolgirl, she was one of the minuscule percentage of the population who actually looked *good* in a thong bikini.

Mariah let herself hate her friend—but only for a fraction of a second. So what if Mariah was destined never to wear a similarly styled bathing suit? So what if Mariah was the exact physical opposite of petite, slender, golden Serena? So what if Mariah was just over six feet tall, broad shouldered, large breasted and athletically built? So what if her hair was an unremarkable shade of brown curls, always messy and impossible to control? So what if her eyes were brown? Light brown, not that dark-as-midnight intriguing shade of brown, or cat green like Serena's.

Mariah was willing to bet that behind Serena Westford's cool, confident facade, there lurked a woman with a thousand screaming anxieties. She probably worked out two hours each day to maintain her youthful figure. She probably spent an equal amount of time on her hair and makeup. She was probably consumed with worries and stress, poor thing.

"I just came down here to violate the photographic rights of these unsuspecting beachgoers," Mariah told her friend, unable to hide a smile.

The two women had first met when Mariah took Serena's picture here on the resort beach. Serena had been less than happy about that and had demanded Mariah hand over the undeveloped film then and there. What could have been an antagonistic and adversarial relationship quickly changed to one of mutual respect as Serena explained that while in the peace corps, she'd spent a great deal of time with certain tribes in Africa who believed that being photographed was tantamount to having one's soul kidnapped.

Mariah had surrendered the film, and spent an entire afternoon listening to Serena's fascinating stories of her travels around the world as a volunteer humanitarian.

They'd talked about Mariah's work for Foundations for Families, too. Serena had mentioned she'd seen Mariah getting dropped off by the Triple F van in the evenings. And they'd talked about the grassroots organization that used volunteers to help build affordable homes for hardworking, low-income families. Mariah spent three or four days each week with a hammer in her hand, and she loved both the work and the sense of purpose it gave her.

"Hey, I got a package notice from the post office," Mariah told her friend. "I think it's my darkroom supplies. Any chance I can talk you into picking it up for me?"

"If you had a car, you could pick it up yourself."

"If I had a car, I would use it once a month, when a heavy package needed to be picked up at the post office."

"If you had a car, you wouldn't have to wait for that awful van to take you over to the mainland four times a week," Serena pointed out.

Mariah smiled. "I like taking the van."

Serena looked at her closely. "The driver *is* a real hunk."

"The driver is happily married to one of the Triple F site supervisors."

"Too bad."

Serena's sigh of regret was so heartfelt, Mariah had to laugh. "You know, Serena, not everyone in the world is husband hunting. I'm actually very happy all by myself."

Serena smiled. "Husband hunting," she repeated. "The biggest of the big game." She laughed. "I like that image. I wonder what gauge bullet I'd need to bring one down…"

Mariah gathered up her things. "Let's go have lunch."

She would know him when she saw him, but she simply hadn't seen him yet. He would have money. Lots of money. Enough so that when she asked for the funds for the down payment on a house, he wouldn't hesitate to give it directly to her. Enough so that he would open a checking account in her name—an account she would immediately start draining. She would transfer the money to dummy accounts out of state.

She had the system set up so that anyone following the paper trail would be stopped cold, left high and dry.

She'd sit on the cash for a week or two, then make the deposits into her Swiss bank accounts.

Three million dollars. She had three million dollars American already in her Swiss accounts.

Three million dollars, and nine locks of hair.

Yes, she'd know him when she saw him.

"Garden Isle, Georgia," the agent named Taylor said as he looked around the table from Daniel Tonaka to Pat Blake, the head of the FBI unit, and finally to John Miller. "It's her. The Black Widow killer. It's got to be."

He slid several enlarged black-and-white photos across the conference table, one toward Blake and the other toward Miller and Daniel. Miller sat forward slightly in his chair, picking it up and angling it away from the reflections of the overhead lights. He couldn't seem to hold it steady—his hands were shaking—and he quickly put it down on the table.

"She's going by the name Serena Westford," the young agent was saying. "She came out of nowhere. Her story is that she spent the past seven years in Europe—in Paris—but no one seems to know her over there. If she *was* living there, she wasn't paying taxes, that's for sure."

The photograph showed a woman moving rapidly, purposefully across a parking lot. She was wearing a hat and sunglasses, and her face was blurred.

Miller looked up. "What's your name again?"

The young man held his gaze only briefly. "Taylor. Steven Taylor."

"Couldn't you get a better picture than this, Taylor?"

"No, sir," he said. "We're lucky we even got this one. It was taken with a telephoto lens from the window of the resort. It's the best of about twenty that I managed to get at that time. Any other time I tried to take her picture, she somehow seemed to know there was a camera around and she covered herself almost completely. I have about five hundred perfect pictures where her face is nearly entirely obscured by enormous sunglasses or her hat. I have five hundred other perfect shots of the back of her head."

"Yet you're certain this woman is our Black Widow." Miller didn't hide his skepticism.

Daniel shifted in his seat. "I believe it's her, John. Hear him out."

Miller was usually unerringly accurate when it came to reading people. He knew for a fact that Patrick Blake disliked him despite his record of arrests. And he knew quite clearly that Steven Taylor was afraid of him. Oh, he was polite and respectful, but something about his stance told Miller clear as day that Taylor was going to request a transfer off this case now that he knew Miller was aboard.

Daniel Tonaka, on the other hand, had never been easy to read. He was unflappable, with a quirky sense of humor that surfaced at the most unexpected moments. As far as Miller could tell, Daniel treated every person with whom he came into contact with the same amount of courtesy and kindness. He treated everyone from a bag lady to the governor's wife with respect, always giving them his full attention.

Daniel had spoken up to say he had a hunch or a feeling about a suspect or a case only a handful of times, and all of those times he'd been right on target. But this time he'd used even stronger language. He *believed* Serena Westford was the Black Widow.

Miller looked expectantly at Steven Taylor, waiting for him to continue.

Taylor cleared his throat. "I, um, used the computer to search out the most likely locations the Widow would choose for her next target," the young man told him. "She prefers small towns with only one or two resorts nearby. I programmed the computer to ignore everything within two hundred miles of the places she either met or lived with her previous victims, and narrowed the list down to a hundred and twenty-three possibilities. From there, I accessed resort records and used a phone investigation to query the resort staff, searching for female guests under five feet two inches, traveling alone, staying for extended lengths of time.

"Frankly, there was a great deal of luck involved in finding Serena Westford. She'd arrived at the Garden Isle resort only two days prior to our call. When it became clear she was traveling under an alias, I went to Georgia myself to try to further identify the suspect." He shook his head ruefully. "But as you can see, in all of the pictures we have of the Black Widow, her face is covered."

"But her legs aren't," Daniel pointed out. "Steve got plenty of pictures of Serena Westford's legs."

"Her legs are visible in some of the other photos we found in the victims' houses," Taylor said. "We have no pictures of the Black Widow's face, but we have plenty of photos of her legs." He looked at Daniel and grinned. "Tonaka had the idea to take those pictures and *these* pictures and run a computer comparison. According to the computer, there's a ninety-eight percent chance that the Black Widow's legs and Serena Westford's legs are one and the same."

Miller glanced at Daniel. Damn, the kid was good at finding creative alternatives. "A computer match of legs won't hold up in a court of law as proof of identity," he commented.

"No kidding," Taylor said, quickly adding, "Sir. But it's enough to convince *me* that there should be a further investigation."

Miller passed the photograph to Captain Blake, and again his hands shook. The older man glanced at him, eyebrows slightly raised.

Miller turned back to Taylor. "Tell me more," he commanded.

"When Serena first arrived, she had traces of bruising beneath her eyes," Taylor continued. "I'd dare to speculate that that was from recent plastic surgery— probably a nose job to alter her appearance."

"We've been talking about the possibility of flying husband number seven's former housekeeper to Garden Isle," Pat Blake interrupted, "but if the Widow *has* had extensive plastic surgery, there's no way she could make a one hundred percent positive ID. I want no room for reasonable doubt. This one isn't going to walk away."

Miller nodded. What they needed was to catch the killer in the act.

"She's recently rented a beach house on Garden Isle," Taylor continued. "That's a clear indication that she's intending to stay, although at this point, I don't believe she's targeted her next victim. I've compiled a list of all of the people—both men and women—whom our suspect has had contact with over the past several weeks. Out of forty-seven people, twenty-eight have since left the island. They were there only on vacation, and they've gone home. Out of the other nineteen, one in particular stands out."

Taylor took a series of photos from his file, spreading them out on the table.

"Her name is Mariah Robinson," he said. "Or so

she says. According to our files, no such person exists. We've identified her as Marie Carver, former CEO of Carver Software out of Phoenix, Arizona."

Miller leaned forward to look at the photographs. One was of a tall young woman with shoulder-length dark hair, wearing a bathing-suit top and shorts, seated on a beach blanket. Another bikini-clad woman was sitting next to her, her face obscured by a huge straw hat.

The woman in the hat had to be Serena Westford. Her barely there bikini was designed to make blood pressures rise, yet it was the woman sitting next to her that drew Miller's eyes.

"Marie Carver—or Mariah Robinson as she calls herself—lives alone in a rented house on the island," Taylor continued. "She spends most of her time on a private beach taking nature photographs. She has a darkroom in her cottage. Every few days, she goes off island—I don't know where. I haven't had the opportunity yet to follow her. She and Serena seem pretty tight."

Mariah Robinson was more than tall, Miller realized. She was an Amazon—a goddess. She had to be only an inch or two shorter than his own six feet two inches. She was as tall as a man, but built entirely like a woman. Her breasts were full and generously proportioned to the rest of her body. Her hips were appropriately wide—enough so that she was probably self-conscious, hence the shorts. Her legs were impossibly long and well muscled.

Another picture caught her riding an ancient bicycle. She was going up a slight hill and standing above the seat, muscles straining in her legs, breasts tight against the cotton of her T-shirt.

Christ, what a body. There was so damned much of her.

Serena Westford was their Black Widow suspect. She had allegedly lured seven men to their deaths with her searing sexuality. She was a femme fatale in the most literal sense.

Yet it was this other woman, Mariah Robinson, who made Miller stand at attention. Of course, he'd always been a breast-and-leg man. And from what he could see from these pictures, she had more than enough of both. Enough for a man to sink into and lose himself in for a solid year or two.

God, what was wrong with him? He didn't usually have this kind of reaction to the female suspects in a case. Apparently, it had been too long since his last sexual encounter. Way too long. Back even before Daniel came on as his partner. Miller couldn't even remember when it was, or even whom he'd been with.

Maybe that was why he wasn't sleeping. Maybe he *would* finally be able to sleep if a woman was in bed with him. Maybe all he needed was a little sexual relief.

Except the reason he *hadn't* had sex since forever was because none of the women he'd met during that time had managed to turn him on.

Yet here he was, having a definite physical reaction from surveillance photos of a murderess's best friend, who also happened to be living under an alias. What the hell was wrong with him?

And wasn't it just his luck that it wasn't going to be the goddess, but the murderess who was probably going to end up in his bed? And *that* sure as hell wasn't going to make him sleep any better.

Miller picked up the fifth photo. It was a close-up of Mariah Robinson's face.

She was pretty in a sweet, girl-next-door kind of way. Her face was heart shaped, with broad cheekbones and a strong, almost pointed chin. Her mouth was generous and wide. Her smile revealed straight white teeth and made dimples appear in her cheeks. Her eyes were light colored—Miller couldn't tell from the black-and-white photo if they were blue or light brown. But they sparkled with some secret amusement, as if she were laughing at him.

Miller felt a swirl of anticipation deep in his gut. It was sexual energy combined with something else, something deeper and far more complicated. Something that made his pulse quicken. Something he couldn't identify.

Captain Blake smoothed one hand along the top of his nearly bald head as he shuffled through his copy of the file. "How long do you think it'll take till we can get a cover in place for an agent to portray potential husband material?" he asked.

"A week," Taylor answered. "Two at the most. In order to match the profiles of the previous victims, we'd need to find an agent who could pose either as a much older man or a man in poor health. We'd need to provide fictional background, complete with financial records and heavily padded bank accounts. You can bet Serena will run a credit check on anyone she's considering targeting. We'll need to prep the agent, set up protection and a surveillance team—"

Miller sat forward. "I could be ready to go down to Garden Isle tomorrow."

Taylor stared at him, unable to hide his expression of surprise. "*You?* You're not old enough."

"Husband number three was only twenty-nine years old," Daniel pointed out mildly. "And husband six was in his mid-thirties."

"Both were in extremely poor health, one in a wheelchair."

Miller took two copies of his file from his briefcase, handed one to Blake and tossed the other onto the table in front of Steven Taylor. "Meet Jonathan Mills," he said. "I'm thirty-nine years old. Recently in remission after a long struggle with Hodgkin's disease—that's a kind of cancer of the lymph system."

Taylor opened the file and quickly skimmed Miller's investigation summary. His eyes widened. "You actually intend to *marry* this woman…?"

"If I don't, she won't try to kill me."

"You're going to *be* her husband," Taylor said. "You're actually planning to *sleep* with her…?"

Even Daniel had a hint of curiosity in his dark brown eyes as he waited for Miller's answer.

Pat Blake shook his head. "Should I not be hearing this?"

"Don't worry, Captain, the marriage will be legal. She'll be my wife," Miller said. "And I'll make a point to practice safe sex." He smiled. "Of course, in *her* case, that means no knives in bed." He stood up, scooping the photos and files off the table, and looked at Blake. "Am I good to go?"

The older man nodded. "Let's do it."

Daniel and Steven Taylor got to their feet, and Miller turned to leave the room.

"One moment, if you don't mind, John," Blake said.

He waited until the younger agents had left his office, then stood up and closed the door behind them. "You look like crap."

Miller knew Blake hadn't missed the fact that his hands were shaking. "Too much coffee," he said. "I'm fine, but thanks for your concern."

Blake nodded, clearly not buying it for one second. "I know we haven't exactly been friends down through the years, John. I've always just figured I'll stay out of your way, let you do what you do best, and you'll continue to give me the highest success record in the Bureau. But if you've got some kind of problem, maybe there's something I can do to help."

Miller met his superior's eyes steadily. "I just want to get to work."

"Do you have anyone at all you can talk to, Miller?"

"Will that be all, sir?"

Blake sighed. "I'm not supposed to give you a warning, but after this one's over, I'm bringing you in for a full psychological evaluation. So go on, get out of here. And try to spend a least *some* of your time on that resort island with your eyes closed and your head on a pillow."

Miller *had* to protest. "Over the past eighteen months my efficiency has *increased*—"

"Yeah, because you work twenty-two hours each day." Blake sighed again. "Go to Georgia, John. Catch this killer. Get the job done and make the world safe again for rich, dirty old men. But be ready to be stuck under a shrink's microscope when you get back."

Blake turned toward his desk, and Miller knew the conversation was over. He let himself out, aware that his pulse was racing, the sound of blood rushing through his veins roaring in his ears. Psych evaluation. Christ, he didn't stand a chance. Somehow, over the next few weeks, he was going to have to teach himself to sleep again—or face the new nightmare of a psychological evaluation.

God, he needed another cup of coffee.

He was halfway down the hall that led to the lounge when he heard voices coming from one of the tiny windowless cubicles assigned to the less experienced agents. He heard what's-his-name's voice. Taylor. Steven Taylor's voice.

"He's a time bomb, about to explode. You know that as well as I do. You wouldn't *believe* the rumors that are circulating about John Miller. Talk is that he's on the verge of some kind of breakdown."

"Do you always listen to rumors?" It was Daniel, and there was a hint of amusement in his voice.

"Not usually, no. But the man looks *terrible*—"

Daniel's voice was gentle now. "He's a living legend, Steve. He's the best there is. He looks terrible because he's got insomnia. It gets worse when he's between investigations. But believe me, he'll be fine. Don't request a transfer—you'll be able to learn a lot from this guy. Trust me on this one."

"Humph." Taylor didn't sound convinced. "Did you see the way his hands shook? No way do I want to be under the command of some flaky insomniac James Bond has-been who's on the edge. No, I'm outta here. Haven't you heard that his partners have a way of dying on him?"

Miller stepped into the room. "If you've got a problem with me, Taylor," he said coldly, "come and tell me to my face."

A flush of embarrassment darkened Taylor's cheeks

as he gazed at him in surprise. His eyes lost their focus for a second or two, and Miller knew that he was replaying his words in his mind, recalling all the harsh things he'd said that Miller had no doubt overheard.

Time bomb. Flaky insomniac. James Bond has-been.

"Excuse me, sir," Taylor said, making a quick exit out of the room.

That was one agent *he* was never going to see again. Miller turned to Daniel Tonaka. "Mind stepping into my office with me?"

Daniel didn't look perturbed, but then again, Daniel never did.

Miller went out into the corridor, leading the way back to his office. He went inside, then turned and waited for Daniel to join him.

"What's up?" Daniel asked evenly.

Miller closed the door and immediately lit into him. "If I hear you discussing my personal life with another agent ever again, you will be transferred off my team so fast, you won't know what hit you."

He'd truly caught Daniel off guard, and a myriad of emotions flashed across the young man's face. But he quickly recovered. "I was unaware that you believed your inability to sleep was a secret around here."

"I know damn well that it's no secret," Miller said coolly. "But it's not your business to discuss."

Daniel nodded and even managed to smile. "Okay. I can respect that, John. And I apologize for offending you."

Miller opened his office door. "Just be ready to leave first thing in the morning."

"I will." Daniel paused and smiled again before he

went out the door. "I'm glad we had this little time to talk and straighten things out."

Miller didn't let himself smile until he'd closed his office door behind Daniel. *I'm glad we had this little time to talk...* Hell, other men would've wet themselves. *Taylor* sure as hell would've—it was just as well he wasn't going to be hanging around, getting in the way.

Miller tossed his briefcase onto a chair and the photos Taylor had taken onto his desk. The blurred picture of Serena Westford had been on top, but it slid off the pile, and Mariah Robinson's laughing eyes peeked out at him.

Tomorrow he was going to be in Garden Isle, Georgia, and he was "accidentally" going to bump into Mariah Robinson. For the first time in weeks, he felt wide-awake with the buzz of anticipation.

Chapter 2

There was a dog on the beach, frolicking in the surf in the predawn light.

There was a dog—and a man.

It wasn't such a rare occurrence for a dog and its master to be on the beach outside of Mariah's cottage. The stretch of sand was nearly seven miles long, starting down by the resort, and ending at the lighthouse on the northernmost tip of the island. Ambitious runners and power walkers often provided a steady stream of traffic going in both directions.

No, finding a dog and a man on the beach wasn't odd at all, except for the fact that it wasn't yet even five o'clock in the morning.

Mariah had risen early, hoping to get some photos of the deserted beach at sunrise.

There was still time—she could ask them to move

away, off farther down the beach. But the man was sitting in the sand, his back slumped in a posture of exhaustion, his head in his hands. And the dog was having one hell of a good time.

Mariah moved closer. The wind was coming in off the water, and neither dog nor man was aware of her presence. She settled herself on her stomach in the sand and propped her camera up on her elbows as she focused her lens on the dog.

It was a mutt and probably female. Mariah could see traces of collie in the animal, along with maybe a little spaniel and something odd—maybe dachshund. Her coat was long and shaggy—and right now almost entirely soaked. She had short legs and a barrel-shaped body, a long, pointed nose and two ears that flapped ungracefully around her head. She may not have been eligible to win any beauty contests, but Mariah found herself smiling at her expression of delight as she bounded in and out of the waves. She could swear the dog was full-out grinning.

Her master, on the other hand, was not.

He stood up slowly, painfully, as if every movement hurt. He moved as if he were a hundred years old, but he wasn't an old man. His crew-cut hair was dark without even a trace of gray, and the lines from the glimpse she saw of his face seemed more from pain than age.

As he straightened to his full height, Mariah saw that he was tall—taller even than she was by at least a few inches. He wore sweatpants and a windbreaker that seemed to fit him loosely, as if he'd recently lost weight or been ill.

Together, man and dog made a great picture, and Mariah snapped shot after shot.

The dog bounded happily up to the man.

"Hey, Princess. Hey, girl." His voice was carried on the wind directly to Mariah. "Time to go back."

His voice was low and resonant, rich and full.

Dog and master were silhouetted against the red-orange sky, making a striking picture. Mariah moved her camera up to snap another photo, and the dog turned toward her, ears up and alert. She launched herself in Mariah's direction, and the man turned, too.

"Stop," he commanded. He spoke softly, just one single word, but the dog pulled up. She backed off slightly, her entire backside wagging as she grinned at Mariah.

Mariah looked from the dog to the man.

The man was far better-looking—or at least he would be if he smiled.

His hair was dark and severely cut close to his scalp, almost as if it was growing in after he'd shaved his head. Despite the austerity of his crew cut, he was a strikingly handsome man. His features looked almost chiseled, the bone structure of his face more elegant than rugged. His eyebrows were thick and dark, and right now forming a rather intimidating scowl over eyes that she guessed were brown. His chin quite possibly was perfect, his lips generously full, but his nose was large and slightly crooked.

On closer scrutiny, Mariah realized that it was possible some people might not have found this man worthy of a second glance. Actually, he wasn't conventionally handsome—he'd certainly never grace the cover of a men's fashion magazine. But there was something about his looks that she found incredibly appealing.

Or maybe it wasn't his looks at all, Mariah thought with a smile, remembering how the young woman in the natural-food store on the mainland had spoken of cosmic reverberations and auras. Maybe as far as auras went, his was a solid ten.

As he stepped closer, she saw in the pale morning light that his face was lined with weariness and gray with fatigue. Still, despite that and his too-short hair, she found him to be remarkably attractive.

"Hi," Mariah said, sitting up and brushing the sand off the front of her T-shirt. His eyes followed the movement of her hand, and she became self-consciously aware of the fact that she'd only thrown a pair of shorts on underneath the T-shirt she'd worn to bed. She wasn't wearing a bra and she didn't have the body type that allowed for such wardrobe omissions. The only times she didn't bother to put on a bra were mornings like this, when she was certain she would be alone.

But she'd been wrong. Right now, she most definitely was not alone.

"I'm sorry," she said, trying to fold her arms across her chest in a casual manner. "I didn't mean to intrude."

Dear God, would you listen to her? She was *apologizing* for being on her own stretch of beach.

She didn't have to apologize for that. And she certainly shouldn't bother to apologize for her missing bra. Despite the man's earlier scowl, it was clear from the way that his gaze kept straying in the direction of her breasts that he, for one, was not in the least put out by her lack of underwear.

He pulled his gaze away from her long enough to glance up at the cottage. "Is this your place?"

Mariah nodded. "Yeah," she said. "I'm renting it for the season."

"Nice," he said, but his eyes were back on her, sweeping along the lengths of her bare legs, skimming again across her body and face. "I hope we didn't disturb you. The dog can get loud—she's still young."

"No, I woke up to catch the sunrise on film."

He glanced up at the sky. The sun was already above the horizon and climbing fast. "I'm sorry," he said. "We were in your way."

"It's all right."

He held out one hand, offering to help her up.

Taking his hand meant she'd have to unfold her arms. But there was no way she'd be able to get to her feet with her arms folded anyway.

What the heck, Mariah thought, reaching up to clasp his hand. With a face like his, this man had no doubt seen a vast array of female bodies, and probably wearing far less than a worn-out T-shirt. She was nothing new, no big deal.

He, on the other hand, was a very, *very* big deal. He pulled her up from the sand, and she found herself standing much too close to him. But when she moved to back away, he steadied her with his other hand, his fingers warm against her elbow.

He was tall, with shoulders that went on forever and a broad chest that tapered down to a narrow waist and slim hips and… Embarrassed, Mariah quickly brought her eyes back to his face.

His eyes were blue. They were electric, brilliant, neon blue. And they sparked with the heat of attraction. Dear God, he found *her* attractive, too.

"Is it just you?" the man asked, and Mariah gazed up at him stupidly, wondering *what* he was talking about.

"Renting the house," he added, and she understood.

"Yes," she said, gently pulling free and putting some distance between them. "I'm here by myself."

He nodded. God, whoever he was, he was *so* serious. She'd yet to see him smile.

"How about you?" she asked. "Are you vacationing with your family?"

He shook his head. "No, I'm here alone, too." He motioned vaguely down the beach. "I'm staying at the resort, at least temporarily. I was thinking about renting one of the houses up on this part of the beach. I'm getting tired of room service—I'd like to have my own kitchen."

"It's a trade-off," Mariah told him. "Renting a house is more private, but you lose the benefits of having a hotel maid. And if you're not careful about cleaning up after yourself in the kitchen… Well, the variety of insect life you can attract is immense. You can't leave *any*thing out. Not even a plate with crumbs on it. You have to keep all the food in the refrigerator—or in plastic containers. But as long as you don't mind doing that, it's great."

He nodded. "Maybe I'll stick with room service for a while longer."

Princess the dog inched forward and pressed her cold nose against the back of Mariah's knee. "Yikes!" Mariah exclaimed.

"Princess, back," the man said sharply.

"She was just playing," Mariah protested as the dog immediately obeyed. "It's okay—she just startled me. I don't mind. She's…an unusual mix."

There was a glint of amusement in his eyes. "You're unusually tactful. But it's okay. She's not a mix of anything. She's a pure mutt, and she knows it. There's no ego involved—for either one of us."

"She does what you say," Mariah said. Princess gazed up at her, tongue lolling from her mouth, eyes sharp, ears alert, tail thumping slightly even though she was sitting down. She seemed to understand every word of the conversation. "That's worth more than a pedigree."

"She was well trained," he told her. "I…inherited her from a friend a few years ago."

He glanced out over the ocean as if trying to hide the sudden sadness in his eyes. Or maybe she only imagined she saw such an emotion there—when he looked back at her, it was gone.

He held out his hand. "I'm Jonathan Mills."

His fingers were warm and large and made her own hand seem slender and practically petite. "I'm…" She hesitated for a moment, uncertain of which name to give him. "…Mariah Robinson," she decided. It wasn't as if she were telling a lie. It had become true. Over the past two months, she'd acted less and less like Marie Carver and more and more like Mariah Robinson. At least more like the Mariah Robinson she'd heard about from her grandmother. The Mariah her own childhood nickname had come from.

He was still holding her hand, but his gaze had dropped to her breasts again.

"Are you here for the week?" she asked.

He looked up, and for half a second, Mariah thought she saw a flash of embarrassment in his eyes—embarrassment that he'd been caught staring. But it, too, was quickly gone. This man was a master at hiding his feelings.

"I'm here until my hair grows back in," he told her.

Mariah gently pulled her fingers free from his grip. "Well, that's one way to handle a bad-hair day."

Jonathan Mills almost smiled. Almost, but not quite. He ran one hand across his short hair. "Actually, today's a rather good hair day, if you want to know the truth."

God, had she insulted him? "I'm sorry, I didn't mean that your hair looks bad…or anything…" Her voice trailed off.

He finally smiled. "It's okay. I know exactly what it looks like, and it looks much better than it did a few days ago."

He had a nice smile. It was only a small smile, barely playing about the corners of his elegantly shaped lips, but it was very nice just the same.

He looked down at the camera she was holding, its strap still encircling her arm. "Are you a professional photographer?" he asked.

Mariah shook her head. "No, no, I'm…not." God, what was her problem? It had been two decades since she was a seventh grader, so why was she suddenly acting like one? "It's a hobby."

Was it her imagination, or had Jonathan Mills just gone another shade paler?

"I've got a camera, too," he said, "though I've got to confess I'm not sure I can get it to work. I bought it a few years ago and don't use it much. Would you mind if I brought it over sometime? Maybe you could show me how it works."

Would she mind? "Of course not."

He looked down the beach in the direction of the resort. "I think I better go," he said.

He *was* more pale. And perspiration was beading

on his upper lip. He wiped it away with the back of his hand. The morning sun was hot, but it wasn't *that* hot.

"Are you all right?" she asked.

He pressed his temples with both hands. "I'm not sure. I'm feeling a little...faint."

He was a stranger. Mariah knew she shouldn't invite him into her house. But it couldn't hurt to bring him up so he could sit for a minute in the shade on her deck, could it?

"Why don't you come up to the house and sit in the shade?" she suggested. "I've got some iced tea in the fridge."

Jonathan nodded. "Thanks."

His entire face was slick with sweat as he followed Mariah up toward the cottage.

Even Princess was subdued, trailing after them quietly.

Mariah walked backward, watching him worriedly. "You're not, like, having a heart attack on me, are you?"

Whatever was happening, he was hurting. His lips twisted in a smilelike grimace. "My heart's fine."

Mariah could see that it took him some effort to speak, so she didn't ask any other questions. He staggered slightly, and she quickly moved to help him, unthinkingly supporting him by putting her arm around his back and his arm across her shoulders.

He was warm and he was solid and he was pressed against her side from her underarm all the way to her thighs. She may have reached for him unthinkingly, but now that she was in this rather intimate position, she could do nothing *but* think.

When was the last time she'd walked arm in arm with a man like this?

Never.

The thought flashed crazily through her mind as she misinterpreted her own silent question. She'd walked arm in arm with plenty of men—although not recently—but she'd never walked arm in arm with a man like this.

Jonathan Mills was different from all of the men she'd ever known. Including Trevor. Maybe especially Trevor.

"I'm really sorry about this," he murmured as they reached the stairs that led to her deck.

"Can you make it up here?" Mariah asked.

But he'd already started to lower himself down so that he was sitting on the third step. He shook his head. "Can you do me a favor?"

"I can try."

"Call my assistant at the resort. His name's Daniel Tonaka. Room 756. Will you ask him to come and please pick me up?"

"Of course."

Mariah took the steps up two at a time, leaving Princess sitting and worriedly watching her master.

It didn't take long to make the phone call. She woke Daniel Tonaka up, but he snapped instantly awake. She gave him directions, and he told her he was on his way. Mariah had to wonder. Did this happen often?

She poured a plastic tumbler of iced tea as she spoke on the phone, then carried it back to the deck. "It shouldn't take him much more than ten minutes to get over here from the resort...."

Jonathan Mills was no longer sitting on the stairs. He wasn't on the deck, and she would have seen him if he'd come into the house...

Down in the sandy yard, Princess barked sharply. Mariah went halfway down the stairs and then she saw Jonathan.

He was crumpled in the sand, out cold.

At first she thought he was dead, he was lying there so completely motionless. She set the glass of iced tea down on the stairs but knocked it over in her haste to get down to him as quickly as possible.

She found the pulse in his neck beating slowly and steadily and she breathed a sigh of relief. His skin was warm and the stubble from his chin felt rough against her fingers. When was the last time she'd touched a man's face? Surely not an entire five years, back before Trevor finally left? Still, she honestly couldn't remember.

"John," she said softly, trying to rouse him but not wanting to shout in his ear.

He groaned and stirred, but didn't open his eyes.

Mariah could feel the early morning sun already beating down on her head and her back. "John," she said again, louder this time, touching his shoulder. "Come on, wake up. We've got to get you out of the sun."

He was a large man, but Mariah was no lightweight herself, and she was able to hoist him up by taking hold under both arms. As she dragged him toward the shade, he roused slightly, trying to help her. He opened his eyes, but quickly shut them, wincing against the brightness of the sun.

"God, what happened?"

"I think you fainted," she told him.

There was a bit of shade at the side of the house, and he sank to the ground.

"Can you sit up?" she asked.

He shook his head. "Still dizzy."

He lay on his back, right there on the sandy ground. His eyes were closed, and he had one arm thrown across them as if for added protection from the brightness. There were bits of gravel and sand stuck to the side of his face, and Mariah gently brushed them off.

"John, I'm going to go get some cold towels," she told him. "Don't try to stand up, all right?"

"Yeah," he managed to say.

Mariah dashed back up the stairs and into the house. She grabbed two hand towels from the linen closet, stopping only to dampen one with cool water in the kitchen sink.

Jonathan hadn't moved when she reached him, but he did open his eyes again at the sound of her footsteps. "I'm really sorry about this," he said. His eyes were so blue.

Mariah sat down next to him, lifting him slightly so that his head was off the hardness of the ground and resting instead in her lap. She pressed the cool towel against his forehead and he closed his eyes. "I really hope whatever this is, it's not contagious."

Another flash of blue as he looked up at her. "It's not. I'm…not contagious, I promise. I haven't been sleeping that well and… I'm really sorry about this," he said again.

Someday their children would marvel at the story of the way they'd met….

Where had *that* thought come from? It had simply popped into Mariah's mind. Their *children?* What was *that* about? Still, she had to admit, this made one heck of a good story. They meet on the beach, and he turns green and passes out. It certainly was different, at any rate.

"I don't know what happened," he admitted. "I was sitting on the steps, and I was positive I was going to get sick to my stomach, so I stood up and..." He laughed, but it was painful-sounding, embarrassed. "I don't think I've ever fainted before."

He seemed to want to sit up, so Mariah helped him. She could tell with just one touch that he was a mass of tension, a giant bundle of stress. She could feel it in his body, in his shoulders and neck, even see it in the tightened muscles in his face. Gently, she massaged his shoulders and back, wishing she had the power to teach this man in one minute all that she'd learned in the past two months, all the relaxation techniques and stress-reduction exercises that had helped her.

"God, that feels good," he breathed.

"There's a licensed masseur at the resort," Mariah told him. "You should definitely schedule some time with him. You're *really* tense."

He was starting to relax, the tightness in his shoulders melting down to a more tolerable level. He sighed and she saw that his eyes were closed as he sat slumped forward, forehead resting in his hands.

"Don't fall asleep yet," Mariah leaned closer to whisper. "I think your friend just pulled up in front of the house."

Her lips were millimeters away from the softness of his ear, and on a whim, she closed the final gap, brushing her lips gently against him in the softest of kisses.

His eyes opened again, and he turned to stare at her, as if she'd taken a bite out of him instead.

Mariah felt her cheeks heat with a blush. Obviously, she'd finally lost her mind. It was the only explanation

she could come up with, the only reason she had for
kissing this stranger who'd fainted in her yard.

But his eyes seemed to soften as he saw her blush,
and with that softness came an almost haunting vulnerability.

That vulnerability was something she instinctively
knew that he usually kept hidden. He kept a lot hidden,
she knew that, too. There was quite a bit about this man
that she recognized, that seemed familiar.

"Wow, John, are you okay?"

Daniel Tonaka was a man of slightly shorter than
average height. But he was stronger than his lean build
suggested. He leaned over and easily helped Jonathan
to his feet.

Daniel looked at Mariah. "What happened?"

"I don't know." She shook her head, gracefully rising
and helping Daniel support John as they headed toward
his car. "He walked out here from the resort, along the
beach. We were talking, and then suddenly, wham-o.
He started to sweat and then he passed out."

"I just need some breakfast," John insisted as they
helped him into the passenger seat. "I'm all right."

"Yeah, man, you look about as all right as roadkill."

Mariah reclined the seat slightly, then leaned across
John to fasten his seat belt. Her breasts brushed his
chest, and when she glanced down at him, his eyes were
open again, and he was looking directly at her.

"Thank you," he said, giving her one of his almost
smiles.

Mariah's mouth was dry as she backed out of the car
and closed the door.

"Come on, Princess," Daniel said.

The dog jumped into the car, taking a surefooted stance on the back seat.

"Thank you very much, Miss…?" Daniel called to her. "I'm sorry, I've forgotten your name."

"Robinson," she told him. "Mariah Robinson."

Jonathan Mills lifted a hand in a weak wave as the car pulled away.

Mariah looked at her watch. It wasn't even 6:00 a.m. The day had barely just begun.

She saw them through the window of the resort health club.

She worked out for several hours early each morning—earlier than most other people used the resort facility. She was here only to tone and strengthen her body. She wasn't here to flash her spandex-clad reflection in the mirrors on the wall, to catch the attention of some healthy, weight-lifting, muscle-bound man.

No, the man she was looking for wasn't going to be found pumping iron.

A car pulled into the parking lot alongside the building—the only thing moving in the early-morning stillness. As she worked her triceps, she watched a young Asian man help another man out of that car and toward the wing that held the more expensive rooms. A dog trotted obediently behind them.

The older man was bent over, his shoulders stooped as if from fatigue or pain. His skin had a grayish cast. Yet there was still something about him that caught her eye.

She set down her weights and moved closer to the window, watching until they moved out of sight.

* * *

Mariah Robinson belonged to him.

The game had begun early this morning, and already he'd gotten much further than he'd hoped.

John Miller pulled to a stop in Mariah's driveway. He took a deep breath, both amused and disgusted by the sensation of anticipation that was flowing through him.

This woman was his way to get closer to a suspected killer. No more, no less.

He tried to tell himself that the anticipation he was feeling was from being under cover, from closing in on the Black Widow. And those flowers he had on the car seat next to him were all part of his plan to make friends with a woman who was close to his suspect.

Miller had ordered a dozen roses yesterday—a thank-you gift for helping him—before he'd even met Mariah Robinson, as she was currently calling herself. But as he'd gone into the florist's to pick them up this afternoon, he'd spotted a display of bright yellow flowers—great big, round flowers that brought huge, colorful splashes of brilliance into the room.

He'd known instantly that Mariah would prefer wild-looking flowers like that over hothouse roses. On a whim, he'd canceled the roses and bought a huge bouquet of the yellow flowers instead, mixed together with a bunch of daisies and something delicate and white called baby's breath.

He should've stomped down his impulse and bought the damned roses. The roses were part of his plan. The roses said an impersonal thanks. But the yellow flowers echoed the memory of Mariah's gentle hands touching his face, her strong, slender fingers massaging his shoulders, her lips brushing lightly against his ear.

And that was trouble.

The yellow flowers had nothing to do with catching Serena Westford and everything to do with the unmistakable heat of desire that had flooded him as he'd gazed into Mariah's soft brown eyes.

She was everything her picture had shown and more.

And now he was going to walk into her house with these stupid flowers and lie to her about who he was and why he was here. But the biggest lie of all would be in denying the attraction that had flared between them. Jonathan Mills was only to become Mariah's friend. It was John Miller who wanted to take this woman as his lover and lose himself in her quiet serenity for the entire rest of the year.

It was John Miller who'd found himself unable to tear his eyes away from the soft cotton of Mariah's T-shirt as it clung revealingly to her body out on the beach that morning. He'd caught himself staring more than once, and he could only hope that she hadn't noticed.

But he knew damn well that she had. He'd seen the slight pink of her blush on her cheeks.

Miller got out of the car and, carrying the flowers with him, went to Mariah's front door and rang the bell.

There was no answer.

He knew she was home—Daniel had been out on surveillance all day and had just called saying that Mariah was back home after an afternoon of running errands in town. Sure enough, her bike was leaning against the side of the house.

Miller went around toward the back, toward the beach, and nearly ran smack into Mariah.

She'd come directly from the ocean. Her hair was wet, her dark curls like a cap against her head. Her skin glistened from the water, and her tank-style bathing suit was plastered to her incredible body. The sun sparkled on a bead of water caught in her eyelashes as her eyes widened in surprise.

"John! Hi! What are *you* doing here?"

God, she was gorgeous. Every last inch of her was fantastic. But she wrapped her towel around her waist as if self-conscious of the way she looked in a bathing suit.

He held out the yellow flowers. "I wanted to thank you for helping me this morning."

She took the flowers, but barely looked at them. Her attention was fully on him, her gaze searching his face. "Are you all right? You didn't walk all the way out here, did you?"

"No, I drove."

"By yourself?" She looked over his shoulder at the car, parked in her drive.

"I'm feeling much better," he said. "It was just… I don't know, low blood sugar, I guess. I didn't have much dinner last night, and I didn't have anything to eat before I left the resort this morning. But I had some breakfast and even managed to catch a few hours of sleep after Daniel gave me a ride back to my room."

"Low blood sugar," she repeated her gaze never leaving his face.

She clearly didn't believe him. It was the perfect opening for him to begin to tell her Jonathan Mills's cover story. But the words—the lies—stuck in his throat, and for the first time in his life, he almost couldn't do it.

What was wrong with him? This was the part of being under cover that he always enjoyed—getting close to the major players in the game. He'd never thought of his cover story as lies before. It was, instead, the new truth. His cover became his new reality. He *was* Jonathan Mills.

But as he looked into Mariah's eyes, he couldn't push John Miller away. No doubt the fatigue and the stress of the past few years were taking their toll.

"Actually," he said, clearing his throat, "it was probably a combination of low blood sugar-and the fact that I've just finished a course of chemotherapy." He ran his fingers through his barely there hair as he watched realization and horror dawn in Mariah's eyes. He should have felt a burst of satisfaction, but all he felt was this damned twinge of guilt. He hardened himself. He was the robot, after all.

"Oh," she said.

"Cancer," he told her. "Hodgkin's. The doctors caught it early. I'm…I'm lucky, you know?"

She was looking down at the flowers now, but her gaze was unfocused. When she glanced back up at him, he could see that she had tears in her eyes. Tears of compassion, of sympathy. He knew he'd moved another step closer to his goal, but robot or not, he felt like a bastard.

"Would you be interested in that glass of iced tea I offered you this morning?" she asked, blinking back the tears and forcing a friendly smile.

Miller nodded. "Thanks."

Mariah led the way up the stairs to her deck, her hips swaying beneath her beach towel. Miller let himself look. Looking was all he was going to be able to do, God help him.

"These flowers are beautiful. I've never seen anything like them before." She gestured toward a round, umbrella shaded table, surrounded by cushioned chairs. "Why don't you sit down?"

"Thanks."

Mariah carried the flowers into the kitchen and set them down on the counter. Cancer. Jonathan Mills had cancer. He'd just finished a course of *chemotherapy*.

She gripped the edge of the counter, trying hard to keep her balance.

Talk about stress. Talk about pain. Talk about problems. Her own petty problems were laughable compared to having an illness that, left unchecked, was sure to kill him. And even with the treatment, there was still a pretty big chance that he wouldn't survive.

Cancer. God. And *he* was the one bringing *her* flowers.

Mariah took a moment to put them in water, gathering the strength she needed to go back out onto the deck and make small talk with a man who was probably going to die.

Taking a deep breath, she took two glasses from the cabinets and filled them with ice, then poured the tea. *Cancer.*

Somehow, she was able to smile by the time she carried the glasses back out to the deck.

But he wasn't fooled. "I freaked you out, didn't I?" John asked as she set the glass down in front of him. "I'm sorry."

Mariah sat down across from him, arranging her towel so that it covered most of her legs, grateful that he wasn't going to ignore the fact that he'd just told her he was so desperately ill. "Are you able to talk about it?" she asked.

He took a sip of his iced tea. "Sometimes it seems as if it's all I've talked about for the past year."

"If you don't want to, it's—"

"No, that's all right. I guess I…wanted you to know. I haven't always made a habit of doing nosedives into the sand at the drop of a hat." He took a deep breath and forced a smile. "So. I'll give you the *Reader's Digest* version. I was diagnosed with Hodgkin's disease, which is a form of cancer of the lymph nodes. Like I said, my doctors caught it early—I was stage one, which means the cancer hasn't metastasized. It hasn't spread. The survival rate is higher for patients with stage one Hodgkin's. So I took the treatments, did the chemo—which made me far sicker than the Hodgkin's ever did—and here I am, waiting for my hair to grow back in." He paused. "And to find out if I'm finally out of danger."

Mariah remembered the tension she'd felt in his shoulders. Was it any wonder this man was a walking bundle of nerves? He was waiting to find out if he was going to live or die. He looked exhausted, sitting there across from her, the lines in his face pronounced.

"No wonder you're not eating well. You're probably not sleeping very well, either," she said. "Are you?"

Something shifted in his eyes, and he looked out at the ocean, shimmering at the edge of the sand. He didn't answer right away, but she just waited, and he finally turned back to her. "No," he said. "I'm not."

"Is it that you can't fall asleep?" she asked. "Or after you fall asleep, do you wake up a few hours later and just lie there, thinking about everything, worrying…?"

"Both," he admitted.

"I used to do that," she told him. "Two hours after I fell asleep, I'd be wide-awake, lying in bed, suffocating underneath all these screaming anxieties…." She shook her head. "That's not a fun way to live."

"I have nightmares." Miller heard the words leave his mouth, and it was too late to bite them back. Jonathan Mills didn't have nightmares. The nightmares were John Miller's albatross. They belonged to Miller alone. He drank the last of his iced tea and stood up. "I really didn't mean to stay long. I know you probably have things to do. I just wanted to thank you for… everything."

Mariah stood up, too. "You know, I have a book on stress-reduction techniques that I could lend you, if you want."

A book. She could lend him. How perfect was that? He could drop by to return it some afternoon—while Serena Westford just happened to be visiting. What a coincidence. Serena meet Jonathan Mills. John, this is Serena…

"Thanks," Miller said. "I'd like that."

With the swish of her towel against her legs, she disappeared into the darkness of the house. The book must've been right in the living room because she came out almost immediately.

He took it from her, glancing quickly at the cover, which read *101 Innovative Ways to Relieve Stress*. "Thanks," he said again. "I'll bring it back in a few days."

"Why don't you keep it," she said. "I've gotten pretty good at most of the exercises in there. Besides, I can always pick up another copy."

Miller had to laugh as his perfect plan crumbled. "Don't you get it? I *want* to return it. It gives me an excuse to come back out here."

Mariah's soft brown eyes got even softer, and John was reminded of the way she'd looked at him this morning after she'd gently kissed his ear. "You don't need an excuse to come over," she told him quietly. "You're welcome here. Anytime."

Miller tried to force a smile as he thanked her. What was wrong with him? he wondered again as he walked around to his car. He should be feeling triumphant. She liked him—that couldn't have been more obvious. This was working out perfectly.

Feeling like an absolute bastard, he put the car in gear and drove away.

Chapter 3

Mariah was on the roof when she saw Serena's sports car pull up in front of the Foundations for Families building site.

"Hel-lo!" Her friend's bright English accent carried clearly up to her.

Mariah used the back of her hand to wipe the perspiration from her forehead. Tomorrow she was going to have to remember to bring a sweatband—the weather forecast had predicted more of this relentless heat. She was dirty and hot, with stinging salt and sunblock dripping into her eyes, and her back was starting to ache.

But she was surrounded by people who laughed and sang as they worked. Today she was driving nails alongside Thomas and Renee, the man and woman who would own this house, watching the pride they took in being able to help build the home that would shelter them and their two daughters—Jane Ann and Emma.

Foundations for Families started each day with a minute of silent meditation, of joining hands and closing their eyes, just taking a moment to touch base with the powers that be—God, or Mother Nature, or even Luke Skywalker's Force—it didn't matter which. Meals were something out of an old-fashioned barn raising with sandwiches and lemonade provided by volunteers. And each day, Thomas and Renee would call to Mariah and thank her by name—sometimes even enveloping her in an embrace as she left to go home.

Mariah couldn't remember ever being happier.

Down on the ground, Serena shaded her eyes to gaze up at her. "What time are you done here?"

Mariah rested her hammer against her work boot and unfastened her water bottle from her belt. She took a long swig before answering. "My shift ends at six," she said.

"Good. Then you can meet me at seven, at the resort," Serena decided. "We can eat at the grill out by the pool, then prowl the bars, husband hunting as you so aptly put it."

The resort. Where Jonathan Mills was staying. Except Mariah was almost certain he wasn't the type to hang out in a bar. Still, she was almost tempted to go over there. Almost.

She hooked her water bottle back onto her belt and hefted her hammer. "Sorry. Can't," she told her friend, glad she had an excuse. She wasn't the type to hang out in bars, either. They were noisy, crowded and filled with smoke and desperation. "I'm coming back out here tomorrow. I've got to be up early in the morning. Laronda scheduled a building blitz. We're gonna get this sucker watertight by sundown."

Serena looked at the rough plywood that framed the modestly sized house and skeptically lifted an elegant eyebrow. "You're kidding."

"Nope," Mariah said cheerfully. "Of course, we could always use more volunteers. I don't suppose you're interested...?"

"Not on your life." Serena snorted. "I did my share—in Africa fifteen years ago, with the peace corps."

The peace corps. Funny. Mariah knew Serena had spent nearly eighteen months with the peace corps—building roads and houses, working in a part of Africa where electricity hadn't found its way to this very day. They'd talked about it quite a bit, but Mariah *still* couldn't picture the elegant blonde actually getting her hands dirty digging latrines. Serena? No, she just couldn't imagine it. Still, why would the woman lie? And she spoke of her time in the corps with such authority.

"Sure I can't talk you into having some fun tonight?" Serena asked.

Mariah shook her head. "I'm having fun right now," she told her friend.

"You," Serena said, "are one seriously twisted woman." She called back over her shoulder as she headed toward her car, "Don't forget about my party Friday night."

"You know, Serena, I'm not really the party type..."

But Serena had already climbed behind the wheel, starting her car with a roar.

Mariah didn't want to go to any party. She'd been to several of Serena's affairs before and stood uncomfortably while Serena's chic resort friends talked about nothing of any substance. The weather. The stock market. The best place to rent jet skis.

Last time, she'd left early and vowed to make up an excuse if Serena ever invited her again. She'd have to think up something convincing...

But she wasn't going to think about it right now. She had a house to build. No worries. No problems.

Mariah got back to work.

Miller was running on empty.

He'd awakened before dawn, after only a few hours of rest, jarred out of sleep by an ominous dream. It wasn't his usual nightmare, but it was a dream filled with shadows and darkness, and he knew if he fell back to sleep, he'd soon find himself outside that damned warehouse.

So he'd made himself a cup of coffee, roused Princess and headed down the beach, toward Mariah's cottage.

The first glimmer of daybreak had been lighting the sky when he'd reached the part of the strand where he'd met Mariah two mornings ago. And as he'd watched, the light in her beach house went off, and she came outside, shouldering a backpack.

She climbed on her bicycle and rode away, down the road toward town, before he was even close enough to call out to her.

He stayed for a while, hoping she would return, but she hadn't. Later, he'd found her bike, locked to a rack by the public library.

Having to wait for her to come back was frustrating, but Miller had been on stakeouts that had literally lasted for months, and he knew how to curb his impatience. He'd set up camp under the shade of a brightly

colored beach umbrella, lathered himself with sunblock
and waited.

He'd spent the first part of the morning reading that
book Mariah had lent him. It was one of those touchy-
feely books that urged the reader to become one with
his or her emotions, and to vent—to talk or cry. Emotional release was necessary—according to the author,
a Dr. Gerrard Hollis from California, of course—before
the anxiety causing stress could be relieved.

Miller flipped through the chapters on breathing
exercises and self-hypnosis techniques, focusing instead on the section about reducing stress through sex.
There was nothing like regularly scheduled orgasmic
release—according to the esteemed Dr. Hollis, whoever
the hell he was—to counter the bad effects of stress on
the human nervous system.

Each of the exercises outlined in the book—and this
section went on for an entire detailed chapter—were
designed to be both physically and emotionally relaxing. They were also designed to be done either by a
couple, or by an individual. Women could make use of
certain "assistive" devices if they so desired, Dr. Hollis pointed out.

Miller had gotten a hell of a lot of mileage out of
thinking about Mariah performing those exercises, with
or without assistive devices.

But she still hadn't returned by lunchtime, and Miller
had gone back to the resort. He'd spent the afternoon
helping Daniel fine-tune the surveillance equipment the
younger man had planted in Serena Westford's rented
house. Yesterday, around noon, their suspect had gone
off island. Instead of following her, assuming that if she
was going over the causeway to the mainland she was

planning to stay for a while, Daniel had used the opportunity to hide miniature microphones in key spots in Serena's home.

Their surveillance system was up and running.

And now Miller was back outside Mariah's house, watching the sun set, wondering where she had gone, feeling slightly sick to his stomach from fatigue.

He heard the squeak of her bicycle before he saw her. As he watched, she turned up her driveway, getting off her bike and pushing it the last few feet up the hill. She put down the kickstand, but the sandy ground was too soft to hold it up, and she leaned it against the side of the house instead.

She slipped her arms out of her backpack and tossed it down near the foot of the stairs leading up to her deck. And then, kicking her feet free from a pair of almost ridiculously clunky work boots, she pulled her T-shirt over her head and headed directly toward the ocean.

As Miller watched, she dropped her shirt on the sand and crash-dived into the water. She didn't notice him until she was on her way back out. And then she saw Princess first.

Mariah's running shorts clung to her thighs, their waistband sagging down across her smooth stomach, the pull of the water turning them into hip huggers. The effect was incredibly sexy, but she quickly hiked her shorts up, pulling at the thin fabric in an attempt to keep it from sticking to her legs.

"John," she said, smiling at him. "Hi."

She was wearing some kind of athletic bra-type thing, the word "Champion," emblazoned across her full breasts. There was nothing she could do to keep *that* wet fabric from clinging, but she seemed more concerned with keeping her belly button properly concealed.

And Miller couldn't think of anything besides the exercise that Dr. Hollis called "Releasing Control." And the one the good doctor called "Pressure Cooker Release." And something particularly intriguing that was cutely labeled "Seabirds in Flight." It was a damned good thing *his* shorts weren't wet and clinging to *his* body.

"Hey." Somehow he managed to make his voice sound friendly—and as if he *wasn't* thinking about how incredible it would be to reenact that famous beach scene in *From Here to Eternity* with this woman right here and now. "Where've you been all day?"

"Were you looking for me?" She couldn't hide the pleasure in her voice or the spark of attraction in her eyes.

Miller felt that same twinge of something disquieting and he forced it away. So she liked him. Big deal. "I came by this morning," he told her.

The waves tugged again at her shorts, and she came all the way out of the water to stand self-consciously, dripping on the sand. She had no towel to cover herself this time, and she was obviously uncomfortable about that. But she leaned over to greet Princess, enthusiastically rubbing the dog's ears.

"I went over to the mainland," she told Miller, rinsing her hands in the ocean. "I volunteer for Foundations for Families, and I was working at a building site. We got the vinyl siding up today."

"Foundations for Families?"

She nodded, squeezing the water out of her ponytail with one hand. "It's an organization that builds quality homes for people with low incomes. The houses are affordable because of the low-interest mortgages Triple F arranges, and because volunteers actually build the houses alongside the future home owners."

Miller had heard of the group. "I thought you had to be a carpenter or an electrician or a professional roofer to volunteer."

She narrowed her eyes at him. "And how do you know I'm not one?"

Miller covered his sudden flare of alarm with a laugh. She wasn't challenging him or questioning him. She hadn't suddenly realized he knew all about her background through his FBI files. She was teasing. So he teased her back. "Obviously because I'm a sexist bastard who archaically thinks that only men can be carpenters or electricians or roofers. I apologize, *Miz* Robinson. I stand guilty as charged."

Mariah smiled. "Well, now that you've confessed, I can tell you that I'm *not* a carpenter. Although I *am* well on my way to being a professional roofer. I've helped do ten roofs since I got here a couple of months ago. I'm not afraid of heights, so I somehow always end up working there."

"How many days a week do you do this?"

"Three or four," she told him. "Sometimes more if there's a building blitz scheduled."

"A building *blitz?*"

"That's when we push really hard to get one phase of the project finished. Today we blitzed the siding. We've had weeklong blitzes when we start and finish an entire house inside and out." She glanced at him. "If you're interested, you could come along with me next time I go. I've got tomorrow off, but I'm working again the day after that."

"I'd like that," he said quietly. The uneasiness was back—this time not because he was deceiving her, but because his words rang with too much truth. He *would* like it. A lot.

Means to an end, he reminded himself. Mariah Robinson was merely the means to meeting—and catching—Serena Westford.

But Mariah smiled almost shyly into his eyes and he found himself comparing them to whiskey—smoky and light brown and intoxicatingly warming.

"Well, good. I leave early in the morning—the van picks me up at six. You could either meet me here or downtown in front of the library." She looked away from him and glanced up at the sky. The high, dappled clouds were streaked with the pink of the setting sun. "Look at how pretty that is," she breathed.

She was mostly turned away from him, and he was struck by the soft curve of her cheek. Her skin would feel so smooth beneath his fingers, beneath his lips. Her own lips were slightly parted as she gazed raptly out at the water, at the red-orange fingers of clouds extending nearly to the horizon, lit by the sun setting to the west, to their backs.

And then Miller followed her gaze and looked at the sky. The clouds were colored in every hue of pink and orange imaginable. It *was* beautiful. When was the last time he'd stopped to look at a sunset?

"My mother loved sunsets," he said, before he even realized he was speaking. God, what was he telling her? About his *mother...?*

But she'd turned to look at him, her eyes still so warm. "Past tense," she said. "Is she…?"

"She died when I was a kid," he told her, pretending that he had only said that because he was looking for that flare of compassion he knew was going to appear in her eyes. Serena Westford, he reminded himself. Mariah was a means to an end.

Jackpot. Her eyes softened as he knew they would. She was an easy target. He was used to manipulating hardened, suspicious criminals. Compared to them, Mariah Robinson was laughably easy to control. One mention of his poor dead mother—never mind that it was true—and her eyes damn near became filled with tears.

"I'm so sorry," she murmured. She actually reached for his hand and gently squeezed his fingers before she let him go.

"She always wanted to go to Key West," Miller said, watching her eyes. "She thought it was really great that the people on Key West celebrate every single sunset— that they stop and watch and just sit quietly for a few minutes every evening. God, I haven't thought about that in years."

Mariah gave him another gentle smile, and he knew he was lying to himself. He was doing it again. This was *his* background, *his* history, not Jonathan Mills's cover story. He was telling her about his mother because he wanted to tell her. He'd known Tony for nearly two decades, and the topic had never come up in their conversations. Not even once. He knew this girl, what? Two days? And he was telling her about his mother's craziest dream.

They'd planned to rent a car and drive all the way

from New Haven down to Key West. But then she'd gone and died.

Mariah was silent, just watching the sky as the last of the light slipped away. Who was controlling whom? Miller had to wonder.

"Do you have plans for this evening?" he asked.

She turned to scoop her T-shirt up off the sand. "A friend wanted me to go barhopping, but I turned her down. That's not exactly my idea of fun. Besides, I'm beat. I'm going to have a shower, a quick dinner, and then sit down with a good book with my feet up."

"I should go," Miller murmured. He definitely had to go. Serena Westford was probably that friend, and if she was out, she probably wasn't going to be dropping by tonight. He'd come back in the morning when the sun was up, when the soft dusk of early evening wasn't throwing seductive shadows across everything.

"Oh, I almost forgot," Mariah said. "I picked something up for you on the mainland this morning."

She hurried back up the beach toward the backpack she'd left at the bottom of the stairs. Miller followed more slowly. She'd picked something up for him?

"Wait a sec," she said, bounding up the stairs, carrying the heavy-looking backpack effortlessly. "I want to turn on the deck light."

Princess followed her up the stairs.

"Hey, what are you doing?" he heard Mariah say to Princess. "You can't go in there. My rental agreement distinctly says no dogs or cats. And I hate to break it to you, babe, but you're definitely a dog. I know you don't believe me...."

The light came on as Miller started up the stairs. It

was one of those yellow bug lights, easy on the eyes. It cast a golden, almost fairy-tale-like glow on the deck.

Mariah had her backpack on the table as she unzipped one of the compartments. He stopped halfway up the stairs, afraid to get too close, fighting the pull that drew him toward her. Means to an end, he reminded himself.

"There's a Native American craft shop on the mainland," she told him as she drew a heavy tool belt out and set it on the table. "I love going in there—they've got some really beautiful jewelry and some fabulous artwork. But when I went past this morning, I was thinking about you and I went in and bought you *this*." She pulled a bag out of her pack and something out of that bag.

It was round and crisscrossed with a delicate string of some kind, intricately woven as if it were a web. A feather was in the center, held in place by the string, and several other longer feathers hung down from the bottom of the circle.

Miller didn't know what the hell it was, but whatever it was, Mariah had bought it for *him*. She'd actually bought him a *gift*.

"Wow," he said. "Thanks."

She grinned at him. "You don't have a clue what this is, do you?"

"It's, um, something to hang on the wall?"

"It's something to hang on the wall by your bed," she told him. "It's a dream catcher. Certain Southwestern Native American tribes believed having one near while you slept would keep you from having nightmares." She held it out to him. "Who knows? Maybe they're right. Maybe if you hang it up, you'll be able to sleep."

Miller had to climb the last few steps to take the

dream catcher from her hands. He wasn't sure what to say. He couldn't remember the last time anyone had bought him anything. "Thank you," he managed. She had been thinking about him today. They'd only met twice, and she had been thinking about him….

That was good for the case, he tried to tell himself, but he knew the real truth. It had nothing to do with Serena Westford and everything to do with this sudden ache of desire he couldn't seem to ignore.

For the briefest, wildest moment, he actually considered following through on his urges to make his relationship with Mariah a sexual one. But even he couldn't do that. Even he wasn't enough of a son of a bitch to use her that way.

Still, when Miller opened his mouth to take his leave, he found himself saying something else entirely. "I haven't had dinner yet. Can I talk you into joining me? There's a fish place right down the road…?"

"I'm really not up to going out," Mariah told him. "But I've got a swordfish steak in the fridge that I was going to throw on the grill. I'd love it if you'd join me." She didn't give him time to respond. "I've *got* to take a shower," she said, pushing open the sliding door that led from the deck into the house. "I'll be quick—help yourself to a beer or a soda from the kitchen."

She was inside the house before he could come up with a good reason why he *shouldn't* stay for dinner. But there were plenty of reasons. Because eating here, in the seclusion of her cottage, was too intimate. Because he wasn't sure he'd be able to maintain this pretense of wanting to be only friends. Because the thought of her in the shower while he was out here waiting was far too provocative. Because he didn't trust himself to keep his distance.

But Miller didn't say anything.

Because, despite the fact he knew he was playing with fire, he wanted to stay here with Mariah Robinson more than he'd wanted anything in years.

"Car alarms," John said as he helped Mariah carry the last of the dishes back into the kitchen. "The company makes car alarms, and in the late eighties the business boomed. I took over as CEO when my father retired. I've been gone too long—I need to get back to work in a month or two."

Mariah leaned back against the sink. "How have the sales figures been since you've left?"

He shrugged. "Holding steady."

"Then you don't *need* to do anything," she told him. "Particularly not throw yourself back into the rat race before you're physically ready. Give yourself a break."

He smiled very slightly. "I still look pretty awful, huh?"

"Actually, you look much better." Over the past few days, his hair had grown in quite a bit more. Mariah figured he must be one of those men who needed a cut every two weeks or so because his hair grew so quickly. It was dark and thick and he now looked as if he'd intentionally gotten a crew cut rather than as if he'd been attacked by a mad barber with an electric razor.

His skin looked a whole lot less gray, too. He actually had some color, as if he'd been out in the sun for part of the day.

His eyes were a different story. Slightly bloodshot and bleary, he still looked as if he hadn't slept in weeks.

"Did you get a chance to look at that book I gave you?" she added.

"Yeah." He couldn't hide his smile. "It was…educational. Particularly the chapter about stress reduction through sex."

Mariah felt her cheeks heat with a blush. "Oh, God," she said. "I forgot all about that chapter. He *does* go into some detail, doesn't he? I hope you didn't think I was—"

"I didn't think anything," he interrupted her. "It's all right. I was just teasing."

She laughed giddily. "And I was just going to ask you into the living room to try out one of my favorite stress-relieving exercises, but now I'm not sure how you'll take that invitation."

"It wouldn't happen to be the exercise called "Pressure Cooker Release," by any chance?" he asked.

She knew exactly which one he was talking about, and she snorted, feeling her face turn an even brighter shade of red. "Not a chance." But maybe after she got to know him quite a bit better…

He smiled as if he was following the direction of her thoughts. Jonathan Mills had the *nicest* smile. He didn't use it very often, but when he did, it softened the harsh lines of his face and warmed the electric blue of his eyes.

She found herself smiling back at him almost foolishly.

He broke their gaze, glancing away from her as if he were afraid the heat that was building in both of their eyes had the potential to burn the house down.

Pressure cooker release indeed.

Mariah waited for a moment, but he didn't look back

at her. Instead, he poured himself another mug of decaf, adding just a touch of sugar, no milk.

The conversation had been heading in a dangerously flirtatious and sexually charged direction. John had started it, but then he'd just as definitely ended it. He'd stopped them cold instead of continuing on into an area peppered with lingering looks and hot sparks that could jolt to life a powerful lightning bolt between them.

Mariah didn't know whether to feel disappointed or relieved.

Jonathan Mills had proven himself to be the perfect dinner guest. He'd started the gas grill while she was in the shower and had even put together a salad from the fresh vegetables she'd had in the refrigerator.

He was clearly good at fending for himself in a kitchen. He had to be—he'd told her over dinner that he'd never been married. He'd told her quite a bit more about the successful business he'd inherited.

What she couldn't figure out was why no woman had managed yet to get her hooks into such an attractive and well-to-do man.

Not that Mariah was looking to get involved on any kind of permanent basis. She wasn't like Serena, eyeing every man who came her way for eligibility and holding a checklist of whatever characteristics she required in a husband. Money, Mariah thought. Serena wouldn't want a man if he didn't have plenty of money. John had that, but he also had cancer. Serena probably wouldn't be very interested in acquiring a man who was fighting a potentially terminal illness.

Nobody would.

Who would want to risk becoming involved with

a man who had Death, complete with black robe and sickle, hovering over him?

Mariah cleared her throat. "Well," she said, "if you're interested in giving it a try, the relaxation exercise I'm thinking about is one I found extremely effective and..."

He looked a little embarrassed. "I don't know. I've never been very good at that kind of thing. I mean, it's never worked for me in the past and—"

"What can it hurt to try?"

John met her eyes then. He laughed halfheartedly, sheepishly. "I really don't have much patience for doing things like lying on your back and closing your eyes and having someone tell you to imagine you're in some special place with a waterfall trickling and birds singing. I've never been to a place like that and I can't relate at all and—"

Mariah held out her hand. "Just try it."

He looked from her face to her hand and back, but didn't move. "I should just go."

She stepped closer and took his hand. "I promise it won't hurt," she said as she led him into the living room.

Miller knew he shouldn't be doing this. This kind of touchy-feely stuff could lead to actual touching and feeling. And as much as he wanted that, it wasn't on his agenda.

He was here to catch a killer, he reminded himself. Mariah was going to provide his introduction to that killer. Her role was to be that of a mutual friend. A *friend,* not a lover. A means to an end.

As Mariah passed a halogen lamp, she turned the switch, fading the light to an almost nonexistent glow. It was a typical rental beach house living room. Sturdy furniture with stain-resistant slipcovers. Low-pile, wall-to-wall carpeting. Generic pictures of lighthouses and seabirds on the walls. A rental TV and VCR all but chained to the floor. White walls and plain, easy-to-clean curtains.

But Mariah had been here for two months, and she'd added touches of her own personality to the room.

A wind chime near the sliding glass doors, moving slightly in the evening breeze. Books stacked on an end table — everything from romances to military nonfiction. A boom box and a pile of CDs on another end table. A crystal bird on a string in front of a window, sparkling even in the dim light. A batik-print throw across the couch. The bouquet of bright yellow flowers he'd brought her just a few mornings ago.

She released his hand. "Lie down."

"On the floor?" God, he hated this already. But he did it, lying on his back. "And close my eyes, right?"

"Mmm-hmm."

As he closed his eyes, he heard her sit on the couch, heard her sandals drop to the floor as she pulled her long legs up underneath her.

"Okay, are your eyes closed?"

Miller sighed. "Yeah."

"Okay, now I want you to picture yourself lying in a special place. In a field with flowers growing and birds flying all around and a waterfall in the distance..."

Miller opened his eyes. She was laughing at him.

"You should see the look on your face."

He sat up, rubbing his neck and shoulders with one hand. "I'm glad I entertained you. Of course, now my stress levels are so high I may never recover."

Mariah laughed. It was a husky, musical sound that warmed him.

"Lie down here on the couch," she said, moving out of his way and patting the cushions. "On your stomach this time. I'll rub your back while we do this, get those stress levels back down to a more normal level—which for you is probably off the scale, right?" She stopped, suddenly uncertain. "What I meant to say was, I'll rub your back if you *want*..."

Miller hesitated. Did he want...? God, yes. A back rub. Mariah's fingers on his neck and shoulders... He moved up onto the couch. Surely he was strong enough to keep it from going any further.

"Thanks," he said, resting his head on top of his folded arms.

"It'll be easier if you take your shirt off," she told him, "but you don't have to if you don't want to," she added quickly.

Miller turned to look up at her. "This is just a back rub, right?"

She nodded.

"You're doing me a favor. Why wouldn't I want to make it easier for you?"

Mariah was blunt. "Because people sometimes misinterpret removing clothes as a sign that something of a sexual nature is going to follow."

He had to smile. "Yeah, well, that's mostly true, isn't it?"

She sat down next to him, on the very edge of the couch. "If I was going to come on to you, I would be honest about it. I would tell you, 'Hey, John, I'm going to come on to you now, okay?' But that's not what I'm doing here. Really. We just met. And if *that* weren't enough, you have issues. *I* have issues."

"You have issues?" he asked. Did they have something to do with the reason why she'd traveled more than halfway across the country to live under an assumed name?

"Not like yours. But yeah. I do. Doesn't everyone?"

"I guess."

She was remarkably pretty, sitting there above him like that, her clean, shiny hair falling in curls and waves down to her shoulders.

She'd put on a pair of cutoff jeans and a tank top when she came out of the shower. She smelled like after-sun lotion, sweet and fresh.

Miller pulled his T-shirt over his head, rolling it into a ball and using it, along with his arms, as a pillow. As he shifted into position, he could feel Mariah's leg pressed against him. It felt much too good, but she didn't move away, and he was penned in by the back of the couch. He had nowhere to go.

But then she touched him, her fingers cool against the back of his neck, and he forgot about trying to move away from her. All he wanted was to move closer. He closed his eyes, gritting his teeth against the sweet sensation.

"This is supposed to make you relax, not tighten up," Mariah murmured.

"Sorry."

"Make a fist," she told him.

Miller opened his eyes, lifting his head to look back at her. "What?"

She gently pushed his head back down. "Are you right-or left-handed?"

"Right-handed."

"Make a fist with your right hand," she said. "Hold it tightly—don't let go."

"Am I allowed to ask why?"

"Yeah. Sure."

"Why?"

"Because I'm telling you to. You agreed to do this exercise, and it won't work unless you make a fist. So do it."

"I never agreed to do anything," he protested.

"You gave your unspoken consent when you lay down on this couch. Make a fist, Mills." She paused. "Or I'll stop rubbing your back."

Miller quickly made a fist. "Now what?"

"Now relax every other muscle in your body—but keep that fist tight. Start with your toes, then your feet. You've surely done that exercise where you relax every muscle, first in your legs and then your arms and then all the way up to your neck?"

"Yeah, but it doesn't work," he said flatly.

"Yes, it does. I'll talk you through it. Start with your feet. Flex them, flex your toes, then relax them. Do it a couple of times."

She ran her fingers through his hair, massaging the back of his head and even his temples. Christ, it felt heavenly.

"Okay, now do the same thing with your calves," she told him. "Tighten, then relax. You know, this is actually an exercise from a Lamaze childbirthing class. The mothers-to-be learn to keep the rest of their bodies relaxed while one muscle is tensed and working hard. Of course they can't practice with the actual muscle that's going to be contracting, so they contract something else, like a fist." Her voice was soft and as soothing as her hands. Despite himself, he felt his tension draining away. He actually felt himself start to relax. "Okay, tighten and relax the rest of your legs. Are you doing it? Are you loose?"

He felt her reach down with one hand and touch his legs, shaking them slightly.

"That's pretty good, John. You're doing great. Relax your hips and stomach…and your rear end. And don't forget to breathe—slow it down, take your time. But keep that fist tight."

Miller felt as if he were floating.

"Okay, now relax your shoulders and your arms. Relax your left hand—everything but that right fist. Keep holding that."

He could feel her touching him, her hands light against his back, caressing his shoulders and arms.

"Relax the muscles in your face," she told him softly. Her husky, musical voice seemed to come from a great distance. "Loosen your jaw. Let it drop open.

"Okay, now relax your right hand. Open it up as if you're setting everything free—all of your tension and stress. Just let it go."

Let it go.

Let it go.

Miller did as she commanded, and before he could stop himself, he sank into a deep, complete, dreamless sleep.

Chapter 4

Mariah woke up, heart pounding, sure she'd been dreaming.

But then she heard it again. A strangled, anguished cry from the living room. She nearly knocked over the lamp on her bedside table as she lunged for it, using both hands to flip the switch.

Four fifty-eight. It was 4:58 in the morning.

And that was Jonathan Mills making those noises out in her living room.

He'd fallen asleep on her couch. He'd lain there motionless, as thoroughly out cold as if he'd been hit over the head with a sledgehammer. Mariah had stayed up reading for as long as she could, but had finally given in to her own fatigue. She hadn't had the heart to wake him and send him home.

She'd put an old blanket under the patio table for

Princess to curl up on and covered John with a light sheet before she went to bed herself.

He cried out again, and she went out into the hall, turning on the light.

He was still asleep, still on the couch. He'd thrown off the sheet, shifting onto his back. Perspiration shone on his face and chest as he moved restlessly.

He was having a nightmare.

".John," Mariah knelt next to him. "John, wake up."

She touched him gently on the shoulder, but he didn't seem to feel her. His eyes opened, but he didn't even seem to see her. What he *did* see, she couldn't imagine—the look of sheer horror on his face was awful. And then he cried out, a not quite human sounding "No!" that ripped from his throat. And then the horror turned to rage. "No!" he shouted again. *"No!"*

He grabbed her by the upper arms, and Mariah felt a flash of real fear as his fingers bit harshly into her. For one terrifying moment, she was sure he was going to fling her across the room. Whoever it was he saw here in her place, he was intending to hurt and hurt badly. She tried to pull away, but he only tightened his grip, making her squeal with pain.

"Ow! John! God! Wake up! It's me, Mariah! Don't—" Recognition flared in his eyes. "Oh, *God!*"

He released her, and she fell back on the rug on her rear end and elbows. She pushed herself away from him, scooting back until she bumped into an easy chair.

She was breathing hard, and he was, too, as he sat, almost doubled over on the couch.

The shock in his eyes was unmistakable. "Mariah, I'm sorry," he rasped. "What the hell happened? I was… God, I was dreaming about—" He cut himself off abruptly. "Did I hurt you? God, I didn't mean to hurt you…."

Mariah rubbed her arms. Already she could see faint bruises where his fingers had pressed too hard in the soft underside of her upper arms. "You scared me," she admitted. "You were so *angry* and—"

"I'm sorry," he said again. "Oh, God." He stood up. "I better go. I'm so sorry…."

As Mariah watched, he turned to search for his T-shirt. He couldn't find it and he had to sit down on the couch again for a moment because he was shaking. He was actually physically shaking.

"You don't ever let yourself get good and angry," Mariah realized suddenly. "Do you?"

"Do you have a shirt I can borrow? Mine's gone."

"You don't, do you?" she persisted.

He could barely meet her eyes. "No. Getting angry doesn't solve anything."

"Yeah, but sometimes it makes you *feel* better." She crawled back toward him. "John, when was the last time you let yourself cry?"

He shook his head. "Mariah—"

"You don't cry, either, do you?" she said, sitting next to him on the couch. "You just live with all of your fear and anger and grief all bottled up inside. No wonder you have nightmares!"

Miller turned away from her, desperate to find his shirt, desperate to be out of there, away from the fear he'd seen in her eyes. God, he could have hurt her so badly.

But then she touched him. His hand, his shoulder, her fingers soft against the side of his face, and he realized there was no fear in her eyes anymore. There was only sweet concern.

Her face was clean of any makeup and her hair was mussed from sleep. She was wearing an oversize T-shirt that barely covered the tops of her thighs, exposing the full length of her statuesque legs. Her smooth, soft skin seemed to radiate heat.

He reached for her almost blindly, wanting only... what? Miller didn't know what he wanted. All he knew was that she was there, offering comfort that he couldn't keep himself from taking.

She seemed to melt into his arms, her face lifted toward his, and then he was kissing her.

Her lips were warm and soft and so incredibly sweet. He kissed her harder, drinking of her thirstily, unable to get enough.

Her body was so soft, her breasts brushing against his chest, and he pulled her closer. She fit against him so perfectly, the room seemed to spin around him. He wanted to touch her everywhere. He wanted to pull off her shirt and feel her smooth skin against his.

He pulled her back with him onto the couch and their legs intertwined. Not for the first time that night, Miller wished he'd worn shorts instead of jeans.

He shifted his weight and nestled between the softness of her thighs, nearly delirious with need as he kissed her harder, deeper.

This was one hell of a bad mistake.

She pushed herself tightly against him, and he pushed the thought away, refusing to think at all, losing himself in her kisses, in the softness of her breast cupped in his hand.

She was opening herself to him, so generously giving him everything he asked for, and more.

And he was going to use her to satisfy his sexual desires, then walk away from her without looking back the moment she introduced him to Serena Westford—her friend, his chief suspect.

He couldn't do this. How could he do this and look himself in the eye in the mirror while he shaved each morning?

But look where he was. Poised on the edge of total ecstasy. Inches away from paradise.

He pulled back, and she smiled up at him, hooking her legs around him, her hands slipping down to his buttocks and pressing him securely against her.

"John, don't stop," she whispered. "In case you haven't noticed, I *am* coming on to you now."

"I don't have any protection," he lied.

"I do," she told him. "In my bedroom." She reached between them, her fingers unfastening the top button of his jeans. "I can get it…."

Miller felt himself weaken. She wanted him. She couldn't be any more obvious about it.

He let her pull his head down toward hers for another kiss, let her stroke the solid length of his arousal through the denim of his jeans, all the while cursing his inability to keep this from going too far.

He was a lowlife. He was a snake. And after all was said and done, she would hate him forever.

Somehow, Miller found the strength to pull back from her, out of her arms, outside the reach of her hands. "I can't do this," he said, nearly choking on the words. He sat on the edge of the couch, turned away from her, running his shaking hands through his hair. "Mariah, I can't take advantage of you this way."

She touched his back gently, lightly. "You're not taking advantage of me," she said quietly. "I promise."

He turned to look at her. Big mistake. She looked incredible with her T-shirt pushed up and twisted around her waist. She was wearing high-cut white cotton panties that were far sexier than any satin or lace he'd ever seen. She wanted to make love to him. He could reach for her and have that T-shirt and those panties off of her in less than a second. He could be inside of her in the time it took to go into her bedroom and find her supply of condoms.

He had to look away before he could speak.

"It's not that I don't want to, because I do," he told her. "It's just…"

Miller could feel her moving, straightening her T-shirt, sitting up on the other end of the couch. "It's all right. You don't have to explain."

"I don't want to rush things," he said, wishing he could tell her the truth. But what *was* the truth? That he couldn't make love to her because he was intending to woo and marry a woman she considered one of her closest friends?

He had to stop thinking like John Miller and start thinking like Jonathan Mills. He had to *become* Jonathan Mills, and his reality—and the truth—would change, too. But he'd never had so much trouble taking on a different persona before.

"I'm not ready to do more than just be friends with you, Mariah. I just got out of the hospital, my latest test results aren't even in and…" He broke off, staring out the window at the dawn breaking on the horizon, Jonathan Mills all but forgotten. "It's morning."

As Mariah watched, John stood up, transfixed by the smear of color in the eastern sky.

"I slept until morning," he said, turning to look at her. He smiled—a slight lifting of one side of his mouth, but a smile just the same. "Whoa. How'd *that* happen?"

She smiled back at him. "I guess you're going to have to admit that my silly relaxation exercise worked."

He shook his head in wonder, just gazing at her. She could still see heat in his eyes and she knew he could see the same in hers.

He looked impossibly good with his shirt off and the top button of his jeans still unfastened. He was maybe just a little bit too skinny, but it was clear that before his illness he'd been in exceptionally good shape.

She could guess why he didn't want to become involved with her. He was just out of the hospital, he'd said. He didn't even know if he was going to live or die. And if he thought he was going to die…

Another man might have more of a live-for-today attitude. But John refused to take advantage of her. He was trying to keep her from being hurt, to keep her from becoming too involved in what could quite possibly be a dead-end relationship in a very literal sense.

But it was too late. She already was involved.

It was crazy—she should be pushing to keep her distance, not wanting to get closer to him. She didn't need to fall for some guy who was going to go and die. She should find his shirt for him, and help him out the door.

But he found his shirt on his own, on the floor next to the couch. He slipped it on. "I better go."

He didn't want to leave. She could see it in his eyes.

And when he leaned over to kiss her goodbye—not just once, but twice, then three times, each kiss longer than the last—she thought he just might change his mind.

But he didn't. He finally pulled away, backing toward the door.

"I'd love it if you came over for dinner again tonight," she told him, knowing that she was risking everything—*every*thing—with her invitation.

Something shifted in his eyes. "I'm not sure I can."

Mariah was picking up all kinds of mixed signals from him. First those lingering goodbye kisses, and now this evasiveness. It didn't make sense. Or maybe it made perfect sense. Mariah wasn't sure which—she'd never been this intimate with someone dealing with a catastrophic illness before.

"Call me," Mariah told him, adding softly, "if you want."

He looked back at her one more time before going out the door. "I want. I'm just not sure I should."

Serena went through the sliding glass doors, past the dining table and directly into the kitchen, raising her voice so that Mariah could hear from her vantage point on the deck. "Thank God you're home. I'm so thirsty, I was sure I was going to die if I had to wait until I got all the way to my place."

"Your place is not *that* much farther up the road." Mariah glanced up from the piles of black-and-white photographs she was sorting as Serena sat down across from her at the table on the deck, a tall glass of iced tea in hand.

"Three miles," Serena told her after taking a long sip. "I couldn't have made it even one-*tenth* of a mile.

Bless you for keeping this in the icebox, already chilled. I was parched." She leaned forward to pull one of the pictures out from the others, pointing with one long, perfectly manicured fingernail. "Is that me?"

Mariah looked closely. Ever since her initial meeting with Serena, she had tried to be careful not to offend her friend by taking her picture. Or rather, she had tried not to offend Serena by letting her *know* her picture was being taken. Mariah had actually managed to get several excellent photographs of the beautiful English-woman—taken, no less, with one of those cheap little disposable cameras. Serena was incredibly photogenic, and in color, even on inexpensive film, her inner vibrance was emphasized. Mariah was careful to keep those pictures hidden.

But yes, that was definitely Serena, caught in motion at the edge of a particularly nice shot of the resort beach, moments before a storm struck. "You must've walked into the shot," Mariah said.

Serena picked it up, looking at it more closely. "I'm a big blur—except for my face." She lifted her gaze to Mariah. "Do you have any copies of this?"

Mariah sifted through the pile that photo had been in. "No, I don't think so."

"How about the negative? You still have that, right?"

Mariah sighed. "I don't know. It might be down in the darkroom, but it might've been in the batch I just brought over to B&W Photo Lab for safekeeping."

"Safekeeping?" Serena's voice rose an octave in disbelief. "Forgive me for being insensitive, but, Mariah sweetheart, no one's going to want to steal your negatives. You know I love you madly, dearest, but it's not as if you're Ansel Adams."

Mariah laughed. "I bring them to B&W for storage. I don't have air-conditioning here, and the humidity and salt air are hell on film."

Serena slipped the photo in question into her purse. "You realize, of course, that I'm going to have to kill you now for stealing my soul," she said with a smile.

"Hey, you were the one who stuck your soul into my shot," Mariah protested. "Besides, I'll get the negative next time I'm over at B&W. You can have it, and your soul will be as good as new."

"Do you promise?"

"I promise. Although it occurs to me that you might want to get yourself a more American approach to having your picture taken. You're not living in Africa anymore."

"Thank God." Serena took another sip of her drink. "So. How are you?"

"Fine." Mariah glanced suspiciously at the other woman. "Why?"

"Just wondering."

"Don't I look fine?"

Serena rested her chin in the palm of her hand, studying Mariah with great scrutiny. "Actually, you don't look half as fine as I would have thought."

Mariah just waited.

"You're not going to tell me a thing, are you?" Serena asked. "You're going to make me ask, aren't you? You're going to make me pull every little last juicy detail out of you."

Mariah went back to work. "I don't know what you're talking about."

"I'm talking about the man."

"What man?"

"The one I saw leaving your house at five-thirty this morning. Tall, dark and probably handsome—although I'm not certain. I was too far away to see details."

Mariah was floored. "What on earth were *you* doing up at five-thirty in the morning?"

"I get up that early every morning and go over to use the resort health club," Serena told her.

"You're kidding. Five-thirty? *Every* morning?"

"Just about. This morning the tide was low, so I rode my bike along the beach. And as I went past your place, I distinctly saw a man emerging from your deck door. I'm assuming he wasn't the refrigerator repairman."

"No, he wasn't." Mariah didn't look up from her photos.

"Well...?"

"Well what?"

"This is the place in the conversation where you tell me who he is, where you met him, and any other fascinating facts such as whether he was any good in bed, and so on and so forth?"

Mariah felt herself blush. "Serena, we're just friends."

"A friend who happens to stay until dawn? How modern of you, Mariah."

"He came over for dinner and fell asleep on my couch. He's been ill recently." Mariah hesitated, wanting to tell Serena about Jonathan Mills, but not wanting to tell too much. "His name is John, and he's very nice. He's staying over at the resort."

"So he's rich," Serena surmised. "Medium rich or filthy rich?"

"I don't know—who cares?"

"*I* care. Take a guess."

Mariah sighed in exasperation. "Filthy rich, I think. He inherited a company that makes car alarms."

"You said he's been ill? Nothing serious, I hope."

Mariah sighed again. "Actually, it *is* serious. He's got cancer. He's just had a round of chemotherapy. I think the prognosis is good, but there's never any guarantees with something like this."

"What did you say his name was?"

"Jonathan Mills."

"It's probably smart to keep your distance. If you're not careful, you could end up a widow. Of course, in his case, that means you'd inherit his car alarm fortune, so it *could* be worse—"

"Serena!" Mariah stared at her friend. "Don't even *think* that. He's *not* going to die."

The blonde was unperturbed. "You just told me that he might." She stood up. "Look, I've got to run. Thanks for the tea. See you later tonight."

Mariah frowned. "Later...tonight?"

"My party. You've forgotten, haven't you? Lord, Mariah, you're hopeless without your date book."

"No, I'm *relaxed* without my date book. Oh, that reminds me—can I borrow your car this afternoon? Just for an hour?"

Serena looked at her watch. "I'm getting my hair done at half past two. If you want to drive me to the salon, you can use the car for about an hour then."

"Perfect. Except I'm not sure I can make it to the party—I'm tentatively scheduled to have dinner again with John." Except she wasn't. Not really. She'd asked, but he'd run away.

"Bring him. Call him, invite him to my party, and bring him along with you. I want to meet this *friend* of yours. No excuses," Serena said sternly as she disappeared down the deck steps.

Mariah gazed after her. Call him. Invite him to the party. Who knows? Maybe he'd actually agree to go.

He was the one. The gray-faced man from the resort. She'd recognized him right away.

The fact that he'd spent the night with that silly cow only served to make him even more perfect.

Tonight she would begin to cast her spell.

Tonight she would allow herself to start thinking about the dinner she would serve him.

Oh, it was still weeks away—maybe even months. But it was coming. She could taste it.

And tomorrow morning, she would go shopping for the perfect knife.

The message light on his telephone was blinking when Miller returned to his suite of rooms after lunch.

Daniel had the portable surveillance equipment set up in the living room. The system was up and running when Miller came in. Daniel was wearing headphones, listening intently, using his laptop computer to control the volume of the different microphones they'd distributed throughout Serena Westford's house. The DAT recorder was running—making a permanent record of every word spoken in the huge beach house.

"Lots of activity," Daniel reported, his eyes never leaving his computer screen. "Some kind of party is happening over at the spider's web tonight."

"I know." Miller picked up the phone and dialed the resort desk. "Jonathan Mills," he said. "Any messages?"

"A Mariah Robinson asked to leave voice mail. Shall I connect you to that now, sir?" the desk clerk asked.

"Yes. Please."

There was a whirr and a click, and then Mariah's voice came on the line.

"John. Hi. It's me, Mariah. Robinson. From, um, last night? God, I sound totally lame. Of course you know who I am. I just… I wanted to invite you to a party that a friend is having tonight—"

"Jackpot," Miller said.

Daniel glanced in his direction. "Party invitation?"

Miller nodded, holding up his hand. Mariah's message wasn't over yet.

"…going to start at around nine," her voice said, "and I was thinking that maybe we could have dinner together first—if you're free. If you want to." He heard her draw in a deep breath. "I'd really like to see you again. I guess that's kind of obvious, considering everything that happened this morning." She hesitated. "So, call me, all right?" She left her phone number, then the message ended.

Miller really wanted to see her again, too. *Really* wanted to see her again.

Daniel glanced at him one more time, and Miller realized he was standing there, staring at nothing, listening to nothing. He quickly hung up the phone.

"Everything all right?" Daniel asked.

"Yeah." He was well aware that Daniel had said not one word about the fact that Miller hadn't come back to the hotel last night until after dawn. The kid hadn't even lifted an eyebrow.

But now Daniel cleared his throat. "John, I don't mean to pry, but—"

"Then don't," Miller said shortly. "Not that it's any of your business, but nothing happened last night." But even as he said the words, Miller knew they were a lie. Something *had* happened last night. Mariah Robinson had touched him, and for nearly eight hours, his demons had been kept at bay.

Something very big had happened last night.

For the first time since forever, John Miller had slept.

Mariah was dressing up.

She couldn't remember the last time she'd worn anything besides shorts and a T-shirt or a bathing suit. She'd gone to Serena's other parties in casual clothes. But tonight, she'd pulled her full collection of dresses—all four of 'em—out of the back of her closet. Three of them were pretty standard Sunday-best, goin'-to-meeting-type affairs, with tiny, demure flowers and conservative necklines.

The fourth was black. It was a short-sleeved sheath cut fashionably above the knee, with a sweetheart neckline that would draw one's eyes—preferably Jonathan Mills's eyes—to her plentiful assets. Her full breasts were, depending on her mood, one of her best features or one of her worst. Tonight, she was going to think positively. Tonight they were an asset.

She briefly considered sheer black stockings, but rejected them in place of bare legs and a healthy coating of Cutter's—in consideration of the sultry evening heat.

Usually when she went out with a man, she wore flats, but Jonathan Mills was tall enough for her to wear heels. They might make her stand nose to nose with him, but she *wouldn't* tower over him.

Since the moment he'd called to tell her that he wasn't available for dinner but he'd love to go to the party with her, Mariah had been walking on air. She was ridiculously excited about seeing him again—she'd thought about almost nothing else all afternoon.

She couldn't remember the last time she'd felt this way. Even in college, when she was first dating Trevor, she hadn't felt this giddy.

Even the dark cloud of anxiety cast by John's potentially terminal illness didn't faze her tonight. They'd caught the cancer early, he'd told her. The survival rate for this type of cancer was high. He was going to live. Positive thinking.

Mariah felt another surge of anticipation as she slipped into her shoes and stepped back to look at herself in the mirror.

She looked…sexy. She looked…well proportioned. It was true that those proportions were extra large, but they had to be to fit her height. And in this case, she was using her body to her advantage. In this dress, with this neckline, she had cleavage with a capital *C*. All that without a WonderBra in sight.

The doorbell rang, and she smoothed the dress over her hips one last time, leaning closer to check her lipstick.

Ready or not, her date had come.

Praying that she wasn't coming on too strong, what with the attack of the monster cleavage and all, Mariah opened her front door.

"Hi," she said breathlessly.

John's eyes skimmed down her once, then twice, then more slowly, before coming back to rest on her face as he smiled. "Wow. You look…incredible."

She stepped back and opened the door wider to let him in.

"Incredibly tall," he added as he noted the heels that put them eye to eye.

Was that a compliment? Mariah took it as one. "Thank you," she said, leading the way into the kitchen. "I'm ready to go, but I wanted to show you something first."

He was dressed a whole lot more casually than she, in a faded pair of jeans, time-softened leather boat shoes and a sport jacket over a plain T-shirt.

"I think I might be underdressed," he said.

"Don't worry about it. Knowing Serena's friends, there'll be an equal mix of sequined gowns and tank tops over swimsuits." Mariah opened the door to the basement.

"Serena?" he asked.

"Westford," she told him, turning on the switch that lit the stairs going down. "She lives a little more than three miles north, just up the road."

"Is she one of the Boston Westfords? Funny, maybe I know one of her brothers."

Mariah shook her head, poised at the top of the stairs. "She hasn't talked about Boston. Or any brothers. When we met, she *did* give me a business card with a Hartford hotel, but I think that was only a temporary address. I think she lived in Paris for a few years." She started down, careful of the rough wooden steps in her heels. "Aren't you coming?"

"Into the basement? Is your darkroom down there?"

"My darkroom's down here," Mariah told him, "but that's not what I want to show you."

She turned on another light.

The ceiling was low, and both she and John had to duck to avoid pipes and beams. But it was a nice basement, as far as basements went. The concrete floor had been painted a light shade of gray and it had been carefully swept. Boxes were neatly stacked on utility shelves that lined most of the walls.

A washer and dryer stood in one corner, along with a table for folding laundry. Another corner had been walled off to make the darkroom.

But she led him to the open area of the basement, where an entire concrete-block wall and the floor beneath it had been cleared. Only one box sat nearby, in the middle of the room on top of a broken chair.

Mariah reached inside and pulled out one of the plates she'd bought dirt cheap at a tag sale that afternoon, when she'd borrowed Serena's car. It was undeniably one of the ugliest china patterns she'd ever seen in her life. She handed it to John.

He stared at it, perplexed.

"It occurred to me this morning that you probably never give yourself the opportunity to really vent," she explained.

"Vent."

"Yes." She took another plate from the box. "Like this." As hard as she could, she hurled the china plate against the wall. It smashed into a thousand pieces with a resounding and quite satisfying crash.

John laughed, but then stopped. "You're kidding, right?"

"No." She gestured to the plate in his hands. "Try it."

He hesitated. "Don't these belong to someone?"

"No. Look at it, John. Have you ever eaten off something that unappetizing? It's begging for you to break it and put it out of its misery."

He hefted it in his hand.

"Just do it. It feels…liberating." Mariah took another plate from the box and sent it smashing into the wall. "Oh, *yeah!*"

John turned suddenly and, throwing the plate like a Frisbee, shattered it against the wall.

Mariah handed him another one. "Good, huh?"

"Yeah."

She took another herself. "This one's for my father, who didn't even *ask* if I wanted to spend nearly seven years of my life working eighty-hour weeks, who didn't even *try* to quit smoking or lose weight after his doctor told him he was a walking heart attack waiting to happen, and who died before I could tell him that I loved him, the bastard." The plate exploded as it hit the wall.

John threw his, too, and reached into the box for another before she could hand him one.

"This one's the head of the bank officer who wouldn't approve the Johnsons' loan for a Foundations for Families house even when the deacons of their church offered to co-sign it, all on account of the fact that she's a recovering alcoholic and he's an ex-con, even though they both have good, steady jobs now, and they both volunteer all the time as sponsors for AA."

The two plates hit the wall almost simultaneously.

"We only have time for one more," Mariah said, breathing hard as she prepared to throw her last plate of the evening. "Who's this one for, John? You call it."

He shook his head. "I can't."

"Sure you can. It's easy."

"No." He glanced at the plate he was holding loosely in his hands. "It gets too complicated."

"Are you kidding? It simplifies things. You break a plate instead of someone's face."

"It's not always that easy." He gazed searchingly into her eyes as if trying to find the words to explain. But he gave up, shaking his head. Then he swore suddenly, sharply. "This one's for me." He threw the plate against the wall so hard that shards of ceramic shot back at them. He moved quickly, shielding her.

"Whoa!" Mariah said. She wasn't entirely sure what he meant by that, but he was catching on.

"I'm sorry. *God*—"

"No, that was *good*," she said. "That was *very good*."

He had a tiny piece of broken plate in his hair, and she stepped toward him to pull it free.

He smelled delicious, like faintly exotic cologne and coffee.

"We should get going," he murmured, but he didn't step back, and she didn't, either, even after the ceramic shard was gone.

As Mariah watched, his gaze flickered to her mouth and then back to her eyes. He shook his head very slightly. "I shouldn't kiss you."

"Why not?" He'd shaved, probably right before he'd come to pick her up, and his cheeks looked smooth and soft. Mariah couldn't resist touching his face, and when she did, he closed his eyes.

"Because I won't want to stop," he whispered.

She leaned forward and brushed his lips with hers. With her heels on, she didn't even need to stand on her toes. She kissed him again, as softly and gently as before, and he groaned, pulling her into his arms and covering her mouth with his.

Mariah closed her eyes as he kissed her hungrily, his tongue possessively claiming her mouth, his hands claiming her body with the same proprietary familiarity.

But just as suddenly as he'd given in to his need to kiss her, he pulled himself away, holding her at arm's length. "You're dangerous," he gasped, half laughing, half groaning. "What am I going to do with you?"

Mariah smiled.

"No," John said, backing even farther away. "Don't answer that."

"I didn't say anything," she protested.

"You didn't have to. That wicked smile said more than enough."

Mariah started back up the stairs. "What wicked smile? That was just a regular smile."

When she reached the top of the stairs, she realized he wasn't behind her.

"John?" she called.

From the basement, she heard the sound of a shattering plate.

"Did that help?" she asked with a smile, as he came up the stairs.

He shook his head. "No." His expression was so somber, his eyes so bleak, all laughter gone from his face. "Mariah, I'm...I'm really sorry."

"Why, because you want to take some time before becoming involved? Because you're trying to deal with a life-threatening illness? Because it's so damn unfair and you're mad as hell? Don't be sorry about that." She gazed at him. "We don't have to go to this party. We can stay here and break some more plates." She paused. "Or we could talk."

He tried to smile, but it didn't quite cancel out the sadness in his eyes. "No, let's do it," he said. "I'm ready to go." He took a deep breath. "As ready as I'll ever be."

Chapter 5

Serena Westford. She was small and blond and green-eyed with a waist Miller could probably span with his hands. Her fingernails were perfectly manicured, her hair arranged in a youthful style. She was trim and lithe, dressed in a tight black dress that hugged her slender curves and showed off her flat stomach and taut der-riere to their best advantage. She had sinewy muscles in her arms and legs that, along with that perfect body, told of countless hours on the Nautilus machine and the StairMaster.

She was beautiful, with a body that most men would die for.

But Miller knew more than most men.

And even if she wasn't his only suspect in a string of grisly murders, he *still* wouldn't have wanted to give her more than a cursory glance.

But she *was* his suspect, and even though he didn't want to look at anyone but Mariah, he smiled into Serena's cat green eyes. He'd come into this game intending to do more than smile at this woman. He was intending to marry her. Until death—or attempted murder— do us part.

Of course, his plan depended quite a bit on Serena's cooperation. And it was entirely possible that she wouldn't hone in on what Mariah was clearly marking as her territory with a hand nestled into the crook of his elbow. Serena was probably a killer, but Miller's experience had taught him that even killers had their codes. She may not hesitate to jam a stiletto into a lover's heart, but hitting on a girlfriend's man might not be acceptable behavior.

And that would leave Miller out in the cold, forced to bring in another agent to do what? To play the part of his even more terminally ill friend? A buddy he'd met in the oncology unit of the hospital?

God, if Serena wouldn't take his bait, the entire case could well be lost. Still, he found himself hoping…

But Serena smiled back at him and held his hand just a little too long as Mariah introduced them, and Miller knew that he was looking into the eyes of a woman who had no kind of code at all. If she was interested, and he thought that she was, she would do what she wanted, Mariah be damned.

"Look at us," the blond woman said, turning back to Mariah. "We're wearing almost exactly the same thing tonight. We're twins." She flashed a glance directly into Miller's eyes, just so that he knew she was well aware of the physical differences between the two women.

Miller forced himself to smile conspiratorially back

at Serena, knowing that Mariah was going to see the exchange, knowing that she was going to interpret it as friendliness. At first.

Later, when she'd had time to think about it, Mariah would realize that he'd been flirting with her friend right from the start.

"You wouldn't happen to be from the Boston area, would you?" he asked Serena. "I know a Harcourt West-ford from my Harvard days—his family came from...I think it might've been Belmont."

"No, as a matter of fact, I've never even been to Boston."

She was lying. She'd met, married and murdered victim number six in Hyannisport, out on Cape Cod. The victim's sister had told investigating officers that her brother and his new wife—she was using Alana as an alias back then—frequently went into Boston to attend performances of the BSO.

"Help yourself to something from the bar," Serena directed them. "And the caterer made the *best* crab puffs tonight—be sure you sample them."

As Serena moved off to greet other arriving guests, she glanced back at Miller and blew him a kiss that Mariah couldn't see.

"Are you okay?" Mariah's fingers gently squeezed his upper arm. "You look a little pale."

He met her eyes and forced a smile. "I'm fine."

"Why don't you sit down and I'll get us something to drink?"

"You don't have to do that." He didn't want her to go. He didn't want to have to use the opportunity to watch Serena, to smile at her when he caught her eye.

"I don't mind," Mariah told him. "What can I get you?"

"Just a soda."

"Be right back."

Miller couldn't stop himself from watching her walk away, knowing that by the time she came back, he'd be well on his way toward destroying the easy familiarity between them.

There were chairs along the edge of the deck, but he didn't sit down. If he sat down there, he wouldn't be able to see Serena Westford where she was standing on the other end of the wide deck, at the top of the stairs that led down to the beach.

He made his way to one of the more comfortable-looking lounge chairs instead. He'd have a clear view of Serena from there.

Serena was watching him. He could feel her glancing in his direction as he gingerly lowered himself into one of the chairs. From the corner of his eye, he saw her lean closer to the man she was talking to. The man turned to look over at the bar and nodded. As he walked away, Miller sensed more than saw Serena heading in his direction.

His cover flashed through his mind like words scrolling down a computer screen. He was Jonathan Mills. Harvard University, class of '80. M.B.A. from NYU in 1985. Car alarms. Hodgkin's. Chemotherapy. Never married. Facing his own mortality and the end of his family line.

Forget about Mariah. God knows she'd be better off without a man like him in the long run. He was "The Robot," for God's sake. What would a woman who was so incredibly warm and alive want with a man rumored to have no soul?

"Are you feeling all right?" Serena's cool English voice broke into his thoughts. He glanced over to find her settling onto the chair next to his. "Mariah was telling me how you've recently been ill."

There was an unmistakable glint of interest in her eyes.

Miller nodded. "Yeah, I have been." Across the deck he could see Mariah, a glass of something tall and cool in each hand, held in conversation by the same man who'd been talking to Serena earlier. She glanced at him, but he looked away before she could meet his eyes.

"How awful," Serena murmured.

"Mariah didn't tell me anything at all about *you,*" Miller countered, knowing that everything she was about to tell him about herself would be a lie.

In the past, this game of pretend had had the power to excite him, to invigorate him. She would lie to him, and he would lie to her, and the game would go on and on and on until one of them slipped up.

It wouldn't be him. It never was him.

But tonight he didn't want to play. He wanted to turn back the clock and spend the next one hundred years of his life reliving this morning's dawn, with Mariah in his arms, the taste of her kisses on his lips.

"I think our Mariah has something of a crush on you," Serena told him. "I don't think she was eager for you to meet me."

Meaning that it was an indisputable fact that the moment Miller met Serena, he would turn away from Mariah, and—in Serena's opinion—rightly so.

This woman's self-confidence and ego were both the size of the Taj Mahal.

Miller leaned closer to Serena, feeling like Peter in the Garden of Gethsemane. "I don't really know her—not very well. We just met a few days ago, and...I know we're here together tonight, but we're really just friends. She seems very nice, though."

Meaning, he hadn't made up his mind about anything.

"Tell me," Miller said, "what's a woman like you doing on Garden Isle all by yourself?"

Meaning Serena was definitely interesting and attractive to him with her petite, aerobicized body and her gleaming blond hair and killer smile.

Serena smiled.

The game had moved into the next round.

Mariah felt like a giantess. Standing next to Serena, she felt like a towering football linebacker despite the dress and heels. Maybe *because* of the dress and heels. She felt as if she'd dressed up like this in an attempt to fool everyone into thinking she was delicate and feminine, but had failed.

Miserably.

John and Serena were deep in a conversation about Acapulco. Mariah had never been to Acapulco. When had she had the time? Up until just a few months ago, she hadn't gone anywhere besides the office and to the occasional business meeting up in Lake Havasu City or Flagstaff.

Feeling dreadfully left out, but trying hard not to let it show, Mariah shifted her weight from one Amazon-sized leg to another and took a sip of her wine, wishing the alcohol would make her feel better, but knowing that drinking too much would only give her a headache in the morning.

This evening was *so* not what she'd hoped. Silly her. She'd never even considered the fact that Jonathan Mills would take one look at Serena and be smitten. But he was obviously infatuated with Mariah's friend. He'd watched the blond woman constantly, all evening long. The few times Mariah had been alone with him, he'd talked only about Serena. He'd asked Mariah questions about her. He'd commented on her hair, her house, her party, her shoes.

Her *tiny* shoes. Oh, he didn't say anything about size, but Serena's feet were small and feminine. Mariah hadn't worn shoes that size since third grade.

All those signals she'd thought she'd picked up from him were wrong. Those kisses. Had he kissed her first, or had she kissed him? She couldn't remember. It was entirely possible that she had made the first move this morning on the couch. She *knew* she'd made the first move down in the basement.

And each time she'd kissed him, he'd told her in plain English that he thought they should just be friends.

But did she listen? Nope, not her. But she was listening now. It was all that she could do—she had nothing worth adding to the conversation. Acapulco. Skiing in Aspen. John and Serena had so much in common. So much to talk about. Art museums they'd both been to in New York...

Serena seemed just as taken with John as he was with her. In spite of the fact that she herself had warned Mariah about becoming involved with a man who could very well die, Serena looked for all the world as if she was getting ready to reel John in.

Some friend.

Of course, Mariah had told Serena that she and John were just that—friends. Still, Mariah had the sense that even if she'd told her friend that she was already well on her way to falling in love with this man, Serena wouldn't have given a damn.

Neither John nor Serena looked up as Mariah excused herself quietly and went back to the bar.

The hard, cold fact was that Mariah didn't stand a chance with John if Serena decided that she wanted him for her own. And it sure seemed as if she wanted him.

Disgusted with all of them—herself included— Mariah set her empty glass down on the bar, shaking her head when the bartender asked if she wanted a refill. No, it was time to accept defeat and beat a retreat.

The bartender had a pen but no paper, so Mariah quickly wrote a note on a napkin. "I'm partied out, and I've got to be up early in the morning. I've gone ahead home—didn't want you to feel obligated to drive me. Enjoy the rest of party. Mariah."

She folded the napkin in half and asked the bartender to bring it to John in a minute or two.

Chin up, she silently commanded herself as she took off her shoes and went barefoot down the stairs that led to the beach. Jonathan Mills wasn't the man she'd thought he was anyway. He was just another member of the jet set, able to talk for hours at a time about nothing of any importance whatsoever. Frankly, she'd expected more of him. More depth. More soul. She'd thought she'd seen more when she'd looked into his eyes.

She'd thought she'd seen a lover, but she'd only seen the most casual of acquaintances.

She headed down the beach, toward home, determined not to look back.

"John." There was the briefest flare of surprise in Daniel Tonaka's eyes as he opened the door to his hotel room and saw Miller standing on the other side. "Is there a problem?"

Miller shook his head. What the hell was he doing here? "No. I…" He ran his hand through his too short hair. "I saw that your light was still on and…" And what? "I couldn't sleep," he admitted, then shrugged. "What else is new?"

What was new was his admitting it.

Daniel didn't comment, though. He just nodded, opening the door wider. "Come in."

The hotel suite was smaller than Miller's room, but decorated with the same style furniture, the same patterned curtains, the same color rug. Still, it seemed like another planet entirely, strange and alien. Miller stood awkwardly, uncertain whether to sit or stand or beat a quick exit before it was too late.

He remembered the way he used to go into Tony's room without even knocking, the way he'd simply help himself to a beer from Tony's refrigerator. He remembered the way they'd pick apart every word spoken in the course of the night's investigation, hashing it out, searching for the hidden meanings and subtle clues, trying to figure out from what had—or hadn't—been said, if their cover had been blown.

They'd done the same thing in high school, except back then the conversation had been about girls, about basketball, about the seemingly huge but in retrospect quite petty troubles they'd had with the two rival gangs that ruled the streets of their worn-out little town. They'd often been threatened and ordered to choose sides, but Tony had followed Miller's lead and remained neutral. They were Switzerland, for no one and against no one.

Switzerland. God, Miller hadn't thought about *that* in ages.

"Can I get you something to drink?" Daniel asked politely. "A beer?"

"Are you having one?"

Daniel shook his head. "I don't drink." He paused. "I thought you knew that."

Miller gazed at him. "I knew that when you were around me, you chose not to drink. I didn't want to assume that held for all the times you *weren't* with me."

"I don't drink," Daniel said again.

"I shouldn't have bothered you. It's late—"

"Be careful about coming on too strong with the suspect," Daniel warned him.

Miller blinked. "Excuse me?"

The kid's lips curved slightly in amusement. "I figured that's why you came over here, right? To ask my opinion about where you stand with Serena Westford?"

Miller didn't know why the hell he was here. He turned toward the door. "I'll let you get back to whatever you were doing."

"John," Daniel said, "sit down. Have a soda." He unlocked the little self-service refrigerator and crouched down to look inside. "How about something without any caffeine?"

Miller found himself sitting down on the edge of the flower-patterned couch as Daniel set a pair of lemon-lime sodas on the coffee table.

Daniel sat across from him and opened one of the cans of soda. "I listened in on most of your conversations," he said. "I think it went well—Serena kept talking about you even after you left. She was asking people if they knew you. She's definitely interested. But she kept referring to you as Mariah's friend, John, and it was more than just a way to identify you. I got the feeling that she's getting off on the idea of stealing you away from her friend."

Miller gazed at his partner. He'd never heard Daniel talk quite so much—and certainly not unless his opinion had been specifically solicited. "Yeah, I got that feeling, too," he finally said.

"What are you going to do about it?" Daniel asked.

"What do *you* think I should do?"

It was clear that Daniel had already given this a great deal of thought. "The obvious solution is for you to see the friend again. Play Serena's game. Hook her interest even further by making it seem as if you're not going to be an easy catch." The kid gazed down at the soda can in his hands as if seeing the bright-colored label for the first time. "But that doesn't take into consideration other things."

Other things. "Such as?"

Daniel looked up, squarely meeting Miller's gaze. "Such as the fact that you really like this other lady. Mariah. Marie. Whatever she wants to call herself."

Miller couldn't deny it. But he could steer the conversation in a slightly different direction. "Mariah invited me to go out to the Triple F building site tomorrow morning." Of course, that had been *before* he'd ignored her so completely at Serena's party.

Daniel nodded. "What are you going to do?"

"I don't know."

Miller had never hesitated over making this kind of a decision before. If he had a choice to do something that would further him in his case, by God, he'd do it. No questions, no doubt. But here he was wavering for fear of hurting someone's feelings.

It was absurd.

And yet when he closed his eyes, he could still see Mariah, hurt enough to leave the party without him, but kind enough to write a note telling him she was leaving. He could see her, head held high as she went down the stairs to the beach.

He'd left the party soon after and followed her to make sure she'd arrived home safely. He'd sat in his car on the street with his lights off and watched her move about her house through the slats in her blinds. He watched her disappear down the hall to her bedroom, unzipping the back of that incredible dress as she went.

She'd returned only a moment later, dressed in the same kind of oversize T-shirt that she'd worn to bed the night before. When she'd curled up on the couch with a book he'd driven away—afraid if he stayed much longer he'd act on the urge to get out of the car, knock on her door and apologize until she let him in.

And once she let him in, he knew damn well he'd end up in her bed. He'd apologize and she'd eventually accept. He'd touch her, and it wouldn't be long until they kissed. And once he kissed her, there'd be no turning back. The attraction between them was too hot, too volatile.

And then she would *really* be hurt—after he slept with her, then married her best friend.

So he'd make damn sure that he wouldn't sleep with her.

He'd show up in front of the library tomorrow at 6:00 a.m. He'd see her again—God, he wanted to see her again—but in public, where there'd be no danger of intimacies getting out of hand. Somehow he'd make her understand that their relationship was to be nothing more than a friendship, all the while making Serena believe otherwise. Then Serena could "steal" him from Mariah without Mariah getting hurt.

Miller stood up. "I'm going to do it. Figure I'll be out of the picture all day tomorrow."

Daniel rose to his feet, too. "I'll stay near Serena." Miller turned to leave, but Daniel's quiet voice stopped him. "You know, John, we could do this another way."

His cover was all set up. He was here, he was in place. And all of his reasons for not going ahead would be purely personal. He'd never pulled out of a case for personal reasons before and he sure as hell wasn't about to start now.

"I haven't come up with a better way—or a quicker way—to catch this killer," he flatly told his partner. "Let's do this right and lock her up before she hurts anyone else."

Chapter 6

Mariah saw him as soon as she rounded the corner.

Jonathan Mills was sitting on the steps to the library, shoulders hunched over, nursing a cup of coffee.

He couldn't have been waiting for her—not after last night. Not after he'd been visibly dazzled by Serena.

And yet she knew there was no one else he could have been waiting for. She was the only one on all of Garden Isle who regularly volunteered for Foundations for Families. Occasionally there would be a group of college students on vacation, but the Triple F van would pick them up over by the campground.

Mariah briefly considered just riding past. Not stopping. Flagging the van down near the drugstore or the post office. Leaving her bike…where? This bike rack in front of the library was the only one in town.

Maybe if she ignored him, he'd go away.

But Mariah knew that that, too, wasn't any kind of solution, so she nodded to him briefly as she braked to a stop.

He stood up as if every bone in his body ached, as if he, too, hadn't had an awful lot of sleep last night.

"I realized as I was getting ready to meet you here that I don't have a tool belt," he told her.

Her own belt was in her backpack, weighing it down, and she slid it off her shoulders and onto the sidewalk as she positioned her bike in the rack. She didn't know what to say. Was he actually serious? Did he really intend to spend the day with her?

Her cheeks still flushed with embarrassment when she thought about last night. And the night before. She'd actually thought he was as attracted to her as she was to him. She'd gone and thrown herself at him and...

She could think of nothing worse than spending the entire day with this man, yet she couldn't simply tell him to go home. She couldn't bring herself to do it. Yes, she'd resolved last night that she'd have nothing more to do with him. Yes, she'd come to the conclusion that he was far more shallow and self-absorbed than she'd previously thought. Still, she couldn't tell him to go away.

"I couldn't sleep again last night," he told her, "and I was lying there in bed, listening to the radio. I had it tuned in to that college station on the mainland, and they were playing this song—these two women singing with guitars, it was really nice. But it was the words that got to me. There I was, listening to the lyrics of this song, something about getting out of bed and getting a hammer and a nail or something like that, and I couldn't stop thinking about you. It was as if they wrote this song about you."

Mariah turned and really looked at him for the first time. He was dressed in jeans, sneakers and a T-shirt. He looked as if he'd climbed out of bed without a shower or a shave. His chin was rough with his morning beard, and he wore a baseball cap on his head, covering his hair. It was silly, actually. His hair was still too short to be rumpled from sleep.

But she knew the song he was talking about. It was a wonderful song, a thoughtful song, a not-at-all shallow song. "That was the Indigo Girls," she said.

"Was that who they were? It was good. I liked them. I never used to listen to music...you know, *before*."

Before he'd been diagnosed with cancer. Cancer—the reason she couldn't just tell him to go away. He could very well be living the last of his days right now. Who was she to tell him he couldn't spend his time doing exactly as he pleased?

"Mariah, I'm really sorry about last night. I didn't realize I was neglecting you, and then you were gone and—"

"I think my expectations were too high," she admitted. "You had no way of knowing."

"I really want to be your friend," he said quietly.

Mariah turned and looked at him. He'd told her point-blank that he wanted to be her friend before, too. Was it his fault that she hadn't listened? Was it his fault that her feelings already were much stronger than mere friendship?

"Please let me come with you today," he added.

Mariah could see the Triple F van approaching, and she shouldered her backpack.

"All right," she said, knowing that she was a sucker. *He* wanted to be friends. So she'd spend the day with him because *he* wanted to be friends, never mind the fact that every moment she was with him made her like him even more. Want him even more. As more than just a friend.

The really stupid thing was that she would have turned another man down. But for Jonathan Mills, with his sad smile, his startlingly heaven-blue eyes and his catastrophic illness, she was ready to cut a great deal of slack.

Even though she knew damn well she was going to live to regret it.

Miller was getting into the rhythm. Take a nail, tap it gently, then drive it in.

He'd never really had much of an opportunity to work with a hammer before. It fitted well in his hand, though. Almost as well as his gun did.

Mariah glanced over at him, wiping ineffectively at a river of sweat that streamed down her face despite the sweatband she wore. "Tired yet?"

"I'm fine."

When they'd first arrived, she'd set him up in a lawn chair in the shade, like some kind of invalid. Like the invalid he was *supposed* to be.

But he'd been unable to sit and watch. Even though it jeopardized his cover as a weak and ailing man, it hadn't been long before he'd begged an extra hammer and was working alongside Mariah.

They were inside the little house, putting plasterboard up, turning the framed-off and already electrically wired areas into real rooms. They'd completed the living room, with several more experienced members of the volunteer building crew cutting out the holes for the electrical outlets and the light switches. They'd worked their way down the hall and into the larger of two bedrooms. The place was starting to look like a home. Sure, the seams had to be taped, and the tape and the nail heads covered with spackle, then sanded before the rooms could be painted, but all of its promise gleamed through.

The owners of the house, a tall black man named Thomas and a slender, proud-looking woman named Renee, kept wandering through every time they took a break, holding hands like a pair of wide-eyed schoolchildren, going from room to room.

"Glory be," Thomas kept saying, tears in his eyes. He'd never owned his own home before, never thought he'd be able, he kept saying. He'd even stopped at one point to pull Miller into his arms, giving him a heartfelt hug of thanks.

Miller knew why Mariah liked this work. He'd caught her with a tear or two in her own eyes more than once. And when everyone on the work crew wasn't busy fighting back tears of joy, they were singing. They sang anything and everything from current pop tunes to spirituals as the radio's dial got moved back and forth, depending on who was in control at the moment. Miller even found himself joining in once or twice when the Beatles came on. He remembered the Beatles from when he was very young. To his surprise, he still knew almost all of the words to their songs.

But as the sun was rising in the sky, the little house was starting to heat up. Miller had long since pulled his shirt off. He wished to hell he'd worn shorts instead of these jeans. It had to be near ninety—and the mercury was climbing.

Mariah set down her hammer and took off her T-shirt. She was wearing another athletic bra—a sweatshirt-colored gray one this time. She used her shirt to mop her face and then hung it over her tool belt.

Miller tried not to watch her, but it was damned hard. He drove another nail into the wall, narrowly missing hitting his thumb.

In the other bedroom, someone turned the radio to a classical station.

"Mozart," Miller said, barely aware he'd spoken aloud. He looked up to find Mariah watching him. "His clarinet concerto," he continued, giving her a half smile. "My mother loved this piece. She swore that listening to Mozart would make you smarter."

"I've heard that, too," Mariah said. "The theory being that the complexity of the music somehow expands your ability to reason."

"Lemonade break," Renee said cheerfully, carrying two tall glasses into the room.

Mariah put down her hammer and took one of the plastic glasses as John took the other. He nodded his thanks to Renee, then sat down next to Mariah on the dusty plywood floor.

Mariah drained half her glass in one long drink. "God," she gasped, catching her breath, "what I *really* need is a hosing down. Can it get any hotter?"

"Yes."

Mariah laughed. "That was *not* the correct answer." She leaned her head back against the newly erected plasterboard and pressed the cool plastic against her neck as she closed her eyes.

Miller let himself stare. As long as her eyes were closed, he could take the opportunity to drink her in.

Her eyelashes were about a mile long. They rested, thick and dark, against her sun-kissed cheeks. She had a sprinkling of freckles on her nose. Freckles on her shoulders and across her chest, too.

He looked up to find her eyes had opened. She'd caught him doing all but drooling. Perfect.

But she didn't move away. She didn't reprimand him.

"Thomas and Renee can't wait to move in."

It took him a moment to realize what she was talking about.

"This is a really nice little house," Mariah continued. "It's a popular one—I've helped build at least seven just like it."

Miller nodded. "I lived in a house with a layout almost exactly like this when I was a kid."

Mariah pulled her knees up to her chest, her eyes sparking with interest. "Really?"

"Yeah, it's almost weird walking through here." He pointed down the hall. "That was my bedroom, next to the bathroom. This one was my mother's."

Mariah was watching him, waiting for him to tell her more. He knew that once again he'd already said too much, but her eyes were so warm. He didn't want her to stop looking at him that way.

Besides, he'd figured out a way to make it work—this odd blending of his background and the Jonathan Mills cover story. As Mills, he would have the same background as Miller, except when he was eleven, when his mother died, he hadn't gone into foster care. He—Mills—had gone to live with his fictional estranged father, the king of the car alarms. It would work.

"I can still remember how the kitchen smelled," he told Mariah. "Ginger and cinnamon. My mother loved to bake." He glanced up at the white plasterboard they'd just used to cover the wall opposite the closet, gesturing toward it. "She also loved books. That whole wall was covered with bookshelves and *filled* with books. Everything and anything—if it was any good, she read it." He smiled at Mariah. "She was kind of like you."

As he said the words, he realized how accurate they were. Physically, Mariah looked nothing like his mother. His mother had been average height and willow thin. But their smiles had the same welcoming glow, the same unconditional acceptance. When he was with Mariah, he felt accepted without question. It was something he hadn't felt in years.

"She worked as a secretary," he told Mariah. "Although she swore she was four times smarter than her boss. I remember, even though it was expensive, we kept the house heated well past seventy degrees all winter long. She would get so cold. I used to walk around in T-shirts and shorts, and she'd be wearing a sweater and scarf." He smiled, remembering. "And then there was the year she let me pick the color we were going to paint the living room. I must've been six, and I picked yellow. Bright yellow. She didn't try to talk me out of it. People's eyes would pop out of their heads when they came into the house."

"When did she die?" Mariah asked softly.

"A few days before I turned eleven."

"I'm sorry."

"Yeah, I was, too."

"You talk about your mother, but you've never said anything about your father," she said quietly.

Miller's real father had died in Vietnam. He was a medic who'd been killed evacuating a bombed Marine barracks, two weeks away from the end of his tour of duty.

He shrugged. "There's not much to say. He and my mother were divorced," he lied. "I went to live with him after she died." He shifted his weight, changing the subject. "We always talk about me. You've never really told me about yourself."

"My life has been remarkably dull."

"You mentioned your father dying of a heart attack," he pointed out. "And at dinner the other night, you told me you'd once been married, but you didn't go into any detail."

"His name was Trevor," she told him. "We were married right out of college. We parted due to irreconcilable differences in our work schedules, if you can believe *that*. He wanted kids and I couldn't schedule them in until late 1999. So he left."

Miller was quiet, just waiting for her to say more.

"He married again about six months after we split," she said. "I ran into him downtown about a year ago. He had two little kids with him. His new wife was in the hospital, having just delivered number three."

She was silent for a moment.

"I looked at Trevor and those kids and I tried to feel really bad—you know, that could have been my life. Those could have been my cute little kids. Trevor still could've been my husband…."

"But…" he prompted.

"But all I could feel was *relieved*. And I realized that I had married Trevor because I couldn't really think of a good reason *not* to marry him. I loved him, but I'm not sure I was ever really *in* love with him. I never felt as if I'd die if he didn't kiss me…."

She trailed off, and Miller found himself staring at her, memorizing her face as she in turn stared down at the empty glass in her hands.

"If I ever get involved with anyone again, it's going to be because I find someone I can't live without. I want to find the kind of passion that's overpowering," she told him. "I want to lose control."

Lose control. Overpowering passion.

The kind of passion that started wars and crumbled empires. The kind of passion that made it difficult even for a hardened expert like Miller to do his job. The kind of passion that made him want to break every rule and restriction he'd set for himself and pull this woman into his arms and cover her mouth with his own.

She was talking about the kind of passion that flared to life between them even when they did no more than sit and quietly talk. It was a one-of-a-kind thing, and Miller hated the fact that he couldn't take it further—push it to see where it would lead.

Mariah was quiet, lost in her own thoughts.

Miller tried not to watch her. Tried, and failed.

"Mariah!" One of the little girls—one of Thomas and Renee's young daughters—came skidding into the room. "Jane Ann climbed way, *way* up into the big ol' tree in the backyard and now she can't get down!" the girl wailed. "Papa says he's too big—the branches up that high won't hold him. And Mama's got no head for heights. And Janey's crying cause she can't hold on much longer!"

Mariah scrambled to her feet and ran.

Miller was right behind her.

A crowd had gathered beneath the shade of the monstrously large tree that dominated the quarter-acre plot. It was a perfect climbing tree, with broad, thick branches growing well within even a child's reach of the ground. But the branches became narrower as they went up the trunk. And up where Janey was sitting and howling like a police siren, way up near the top of the tree, the branches were positively delicate-looking.

Mariah moved quickly, navigating her way up through the branches effortlessly and efficiently. But she was no lightweight herself. Despite the fact that she'd told him she was good with heights, good at climbing, this was going to be tricky.

"Mariah!" Miller called. "We can call the fire department for help."

She only glanced down at him very briefly. "I think Jane Ann wants to come down right now, John," she told him. "I don't think she wants to wait for the fire truck to arrive."

He didn't know what to do—whether to climb up after her, or wait there on the ground, hoping that if she or the child slipped, he could somehow cushion their fall. He turned to the girl's father.

"Thomas, didn't I see some kind of tarp out front? Thick plastic—it was blue, I think—the kind of thing you'd use to cover a roof that's not quite watertight, in the event of rain?"

Thomas didn't understand.

"If we stretched it tight, it could break the girl's fall," he explained. "We could try to catch her if she slips."

Thomas gave a curt order and two teenaged boys ran quickly to get the tarp.

Miller looked up into the tree. Mariah was moving more slowly now, more carefully. He could hear the soothing rise and fall of her voice as she spoke to the little girl, but he couldn't make out the words. But the girl was finally quiet, so whatever Mariah was saying was working to calm her.

The boys came back with the tarp, and everyone but Miller took an end, pulling it taut, ready for disaster. Miller, instead, started up into the tree.

Mariah had climbed as far as she dared and she held out one hand to the little girl. Her other arm was securely wrapped around the rough trunk of the tree. Miller knew she was willing the child to move closer, just a little bit closer, so that she could grab hold of her.

Slowly, inch by inch, Jane Ann began to move.

There was an audible sigh of relief from the ground as Mariah pulled the child close to her and the girl locked her arms around Mariah's neck.

But the worst was not yet over. Mariah still had to get back down—this time with the added weight of an eight-year-old girl threatening her balance.

Mariah stepped down, one branch at a time, testing its strength before she put her full weight upon it.

And then it happened.

Miller saw the branch give before he heard the rifle-sharp snap. In nightmarish slow motion, he saw Mariah grab for the branch above her, holding them both with only one hand, one arm. He could see her muscles straining, see her feet searching for a foothold.

And then he saw her fingers slip.

"Mariah!" The cry ripped from his throat as she began to fall.

But somehow, miraculously, she didn't fall far. She jerked to a stop, still holding tightly to the little girl in her arms.

Her tool belt. Somehow the back of her belt had gotten hooked upon the stub of a branch—a branch sturdy enough to hold both of them. They hung from the tree, facing out, dangling like some kind of Christmas ornament.

Miller raced up the tree, the bark rough against his hands and sharp against his knees, even through his jeans.

As he drew closer, he could see that Mariah's elbow was bleeding. Her knees, too, looked scraped and the worse for wear. The belt was holding her not around the waist, but rather around the ribs. Still, she managed to smile at Miller. "That was fun," she whispered.

"Are you all right?" He saw them then—bruises on the insides of her upper arms. The tree hadn't done that to her—*he* had. That night that he'd fallen asleep on her couch. He'd grabbed her, thinking she was Domino. God, he could have killed her. The thought made him feel faint and he brought himself back to here and now. He'd have enough time to feel bad about Mariah's bruises *after* he got her down from this tree.

"I think I may have rearranged a rib," she told him. "I had the breath knocked out of me, too. Take Janey. Please? Jane Ann, this is John. He's going to take you down to your mommy and dad, okay?"

The little girl looked shell-shocked. Mariah gave her a kiss on the cheek and Miller lifted her out of Mariah's arms without a fuss. "Let me get you down from there," he said to Mariah.

"Take Janey down first," she told him, still in that odd, whispery voice. "I think you're going to need two hands for me."

Miller nodded, moving as quickly down the tree with the child as he dared. He looked back at Mariah, but she'd closed her eyes. Rearranged a rib. He knew she'd put it that way so as not to frighten Jane Ann. Her tool belt had slammed into her ribs with the full weight of her body against it. And it wouldn't take much for a broken rib to puncture a lung.

Miller felt a flash of fear as he glanced back up at Mariah. Had she simply closed her eyes or had she lost consciousness?

He practically threw Jane Ann into her father's waiting hands, then swiftly climbed back up to where Mariah was still hanging by her belt.

She opened her eyes as he approached, and he nearly fell out of the tree from relief.

"Ouch," she said. "Can I say ouch now?"

Miller nodded, looking hard into her eyes for any sign of shock. "Can you breathe? Are you having trouble breathing?"

She shook her head. "I'm still a little...squashed."

"Can we unfasten your belt?" he asked.

She shook her head. "I already thought of that, but the buckle seems to be in the back. And it's not easy to undo even in the best of circumstances."

They were going to have to do this the hard way.

Miller braced each foot on a separate branch, pressing his body up close to Mariah's. "Hold on to me," he ordered her. "I'm going to lift you up and get your belt free."

She hesitated.

"I'm a little sweaty," he apologized. "I'm sorry. There's not a lot I can do about that. Lock your legs around my waist."

"Maybe I should wait for the fire department."

"Put your legs around my waist," he said again. "Come on, Mariah. Just do it."

She did it.

Miller refused to think about anything but getting her down from there. Yes, she was soft, she was warm, and yes, she smelled delicious. Yes, she was everything he remembered from that night on her couch, but she was also in danger of falling and breaking her neck.

"Hold me tighter," he commanded as he tried to shift her up, one hand reaching behind her, searching for the stub of the branch that had hooked her tool belt and saved her and Janey's lives.

He found it. He found the wetness of blood, too— Mariah's blood—where the sharp edge of the branch had scratched and scraped and stabbed into her back. Her ragged intake of breath told him how much it hurt.

"Try to lift yourself up," he told her. "Help me get you free."

Her legs tightened around him as he pushed her up, every muscle straining. His head was pressed against the soft pillow of her breasts, but there was nothing he could do about that.

Finally, *finally,* with a strength he didn't even know he possessed, he got the tool belt free. His muscles tensed as he held Mariah's full weight. She clung to him now, more tightly than he'd ever dreamed she'd hold him.

"I'm not feeling very secure here," she told him.

"I've got you," he said. "I won't let go."

And he wouldn't. At least not until they reached the solidness of the ground.

He helped her find her footing, helped her down to

the larger, sturdier branches, but still she held on to his hand.

Her face was still mere inches from his, and her eyes were swimming with unshed tears.

"I think I have to cry," she told him.

"Can you wait just a few minutes more?" he asked. "Until we get you down onto the ground?"

She forced a wavery smile. "Yeah."

One branch at a time, they moved slowly down the tree. When they got to the bottom, Miller knew he was going to have to let her go.

Sure enough, Renee and Thomas were there, reaching out to help her, along with the entire rest of the site crew.

But she still didn't cry. She smiled at them. She made light of her scrapes and scratches. She pooh-poohed the angry-looking cut on her back. And when Jane Ann and the other little girl, Emma, leaped at her, nearly knocking her over, she hugged them back, hiding the fact that she was wincing.

Miller approached Laronda, the site coordinator. "I want to take Mariah over to the hospital," he told her quietly. "I think she might've broken a rib and she'll probably need stitches for that cut on her back. Can someone give us a lift, or do you want to give me the keys to the van?"

"I was going to have Bobby take her over, but if you're thinking about going, too..."

"I *am* going. Definitely."

Laronda nodded. "Show me your driver's license, Mr. Mills, and I'll let you take the van."

Miller took out his wallet and within moments had the keys to the van in his pocket. He briefly went inside to get his T-shirt. Pulling it over his head, he intercepted Mariah. He took her arm and led her toward the van.

She protested. "I want to wash up."

"You can wash up at the hospital."

Mariah nodded. "All right."

The fact that she didn't protest further was not a good sign. She *was* hurt worse than she was letting on.

Miller helped her up onto the hot vinyl of the bench seat in the front of the van, then went around and climbed behind the wheel. He started the engine and pulled onto the street, moving carefully over the potholes so as not to jar Mariah.

He glanced at her as he pulled up to the stop sign at the end of the street. She was sitting very still, with her eyes closed, arms wrapped around herself.

"You can cry now," Miller said softly. "No one's here but me."

She opened her eyes and looked at him and he put the van in park. It was crazy and he knew he shouldn't do it, but he held out his arms and she reached for him as she burst into tears.

"I thought that little girl was going to fall," Mariah sobbed as she clung to him. "I was sure that I'd killed her—and myself, too."

"Shhh," Miller whispered into her hair, holding her as close and as tightly as he dared. "It's all right. It's all right now."

What was he doing? This was sheer insanity. Holding her this way, giving her this kind of comfort… His body responded instantly to the sensation of her in his arms, his wanting all but overpowering his sense of right and wrong.

He couldn't kiss her. He *would not* kiss her.

"I'm sorry," she said, half laughing, half crying as she lifted her head to look up at him. "I'm getting your shirt all wet."

He wanted to kiss her. Her mouth was right there, inches away from him. Her lips would taste so soft and sweet....

Miller clenched his teeth instead. "Don't worry about my shirt."

A new flood of tears welled in her eyes, "I don't think I've ever been so afraid. But I didn't drop her. Even when all the air was knocked out of me, even when it felt like that branch went into my back like a knife, I didn't let go."

Miller smoothed her hair back from her face, knowing that he shouldn't touch her more than was necessary. Except, this felt very necessary. "You did great," he told her. "You were amazing."

"I was stupid not to wait for the fire department."

"You were brave—and lucky."

She nodded. "I *was* lucky, wasn't I? Oh, God, when I think about what might've happened..."

She held him tighter, and he felt his arms closing around her, too.

Think about what might've happened... He couldn't think about anything else—except maybe how much he wanted to kiss this woman.

It was not the right thing to do. He knew that, but he did it anyway.

She met his lips eagerly as if she, too, was as starved for his kisses as he was for hers.

God, it was heaven.

And it was hell, because he knew it had to end.

He forced himself to lift his head. He made himself pull back as he gazed into Mariah's whiskey-colored eyes.

"I need to get you to the hospital." His voice didn't come out more than a whisper.

She nodded, a flare of embarrassment in her eyes. "I'm sorry. I'm…doing it again, aren't I?"

"Doing what?"

She pulled away, moving back to her side of the bench seat. "Kissing you," she told him with her usual blunt honesty. "I seem to be unable to keep myself from kissing you." She wiped her face with her hands, pushing away her tears. "Come on. The hospital's not far from here. I drove José over a few weeks ago when he stepped on a nail."

Miller put the van into gear, uncertain of how to respond. He'd made another mistake by kissing her, yet she seemed to think it was *her* mistake.

He took a left out onto the main road, wishing not only that he'd been strong enough to keep from kissing her again, but that he was weak enough to be kissing her still.

John was waiting for Mariah as she came out of X ray.

He looked sweaty and hot, and with that unshaved stubble and covered with the grime of a full morning's worth of construction work, he looked dangerously sexy. He also looked as worried as hell.

"I'm okay," she told him. "Nothing's broken. Not even cracked. Just bruised."

He smiled then, one of his crooked half smiles. "Good." He looked up at the nurse who was wheeling Mariah's chair. "What's next?"

"She's got a cut on her back that's going to need a stitch or two," the nurse told him. "Unfortunately, she's going to have to wait for the doctor."

"May I sit with her?" John asked.

"Of course."

"I mean, if she wants me to," he added, glancing down at Mariah.

"Thanks," Mariah said, feeling strangely shy as she briefly met his eyes. "I'd like that."

The nurse brought them back into one of the emergency rooms. There were six beds in this one, each with a curtain on runners that could be pulled around to give them some privacy.

John helped Mariah up onto the bed. During her X ray, she'd taken off her athletic bra, and now she wore only a hospital gown over her shorts. It was tied loosely at her neck, and she could feel the coolness from the air conditioner blowing against her exposed back.

It was the front of the gown that made her self-conscious, though. The cotton was thin, and every time she moved, it seemed to cling provocatively to her breasts, outlining every detail, every curve. She pulled it up at her neck, wishing there was some way to ensure that it wouldn't fall off.

Her movement made the short sleeves of the gown ride up, and John reached for one of her arms, pushing the sleeve even farther up. He turned her arm over, exposing the bruises she had there. There were five of them—little oval finger-and-thumb-shaped bruises. She had a similar set on her other arm.

He looked into her eyes. "I'm so sorry about this."

"I know." She held his gaze. "What were you dreaming that night?"

He didn't look away, but he didn't speak for several long moments, as if he was deciding what to tell her. "Tony, my best friend, was…an officer of the law," he finally said. "He was executed by a drug runner's gang. Shot in the head."

"Oh, my God." Mariah couldn't believe what he was telling her. "Were the people who killed him caught?"

John nodded. "Yeah. They were caught. That doesn't keep me from dreaming about them, though. I see their faces and…" He broke off, turning away. "I shouldn't be telling you this. I must be insane."

"Did you know the men who did it?"

For a moment, she thought he wasn't going to answer.

"One of the guys working for the drug lord went to high school with Tony and me." He shifted his weight, looking away from her. "I keep wondering if his bullet killed Tony. I keep thinking I should've beaten the hell out of him—and put the fear of God in him—in high school, when I had the chance."

"That's where you got Princess," she guessed. "Tony was the friend that you inherited her from."

He nodded. "Yeah. She still misses him." He glanced back at her. "I do, too."

"So you dream about him dying. Were you there when it happened? God, you didn't see it, did you?"

He shook his head, his voice bitter. "No. I got there too late." He changed the subject. "Mariah, I'm sorry that I hurt you."

He was talking about the bruises on her arms, but for a moment, she could have sworn he was talking about the way he'd treated her at Serena's party.

"And I'm sorry about your friend." She paused. "You knew him—Tony—since high school?"

Miller pulled a chair closer to her bed and sat down. God, why had he told her about Tony? Tony hadn't been friends with high-class Jonathan Mills. At age sixteen, Tony had befriended John Miller, the new kid in school—the poor kid, the *foster* kid, the troublemaker. Tony had accidentally broken a window, and Miller willingly took the fall. It hadn't been hard to fool everyone—everyone expected that the troublemaker in foster care was the kid who'd broken the glass, anyway.

He'd been living with his current foster family long enough to know that he would be preached-at to death, but he wouldn't be hit. Tony, on the other hand, had a brute of a stepfather who didn't care enough even to keep his blows from marking the boy's face.

Miller had stepped forward, confessed to a crime he hadn't committed, and in return had won Tony's undying loyalty. Not that Miller had wanted it. Not at first. But eventually, Tony had pushed his way past Miller's hardened shell and the two boys became friends.

There was no way in hell he could tell Mariah any of this—foster families and stepfathers with iron fists didn't fit in with Jonathan Mills's world of yacht clubs and tennis lessons and stock dividends.

"How many stitches do you think I'm going to need?" Mariah asked, changing the subject after his silence had dragged on and on and on.

Miller shook his head. "I don't know."

Silence again. Miller could feel her watching him. "How are *you?*" she finally asked. "In all the excitement, I forgot that just a few days ago you were feeling ill enough to faint on the beach. And here you are, suddenly building a house and climbing up and down a tree…" She was still gazing at him, her eyes questioning now. Wondering. "Carrying Janey. Carrying me. If you're this strong now, how strong did you *used* to be?"

"I'm feeling pretty tired," he said, hoping she wouldn't notice that he hadn't answered her question. He prayed that she wouldn't think too long or too hard about the fact that he *had* moved up and down that tree with the balance and strength of a man who couldn't possibly have just completed a crippling round of chemotherapy. He knew one way to get her mind off this topic and fast. "Mariah, about before…in the van…?"

She blushed, but she met his gaze steadily. "John, I'm really sorry about that. I know—you just want to be friends. It's taking a while to sink in, but I'm finally starting to get it and—"

"I wanted to apologize to you."

"To me? But—"

"I kissed you," he told her. "You didn't kiss me until after I kissed you, and I shouldn't have, so I'm sorry."

She was gazing at him, wide-eyed. It was all he could do not to kiss her again. "It *wasn't* me."

Miller shook his head. "I couldn't resist."

"I don't get it," she said. "If you can't resist kissing me, and *I* can't resist kissing *you,* then why aren't we doing a whole heck of a lot more kissing?"

The doctor came in, saving Miller from even attempting to answer her. He stood up, grateful for the escape. "I'll wait outside."

"John."

He stopped and looked back at her.

"Forget I ever said that, okay? We're friends. That's enough—it's okay with me."

Miller nodded and went out the door. He just wished he could close his eyes and fall asleep and wake up in a place where simply being friends with Mariah Robinson was okay with him, too.

He was seeing her, too.

He was still seeing her. They were gone all day, and she realized he must have gone to that silly house-building.

She found it amusing, but nothing to worry about.

When it was time to make a choice, he would choose correctly. There was no doubt about it.

Chapter 7

Two stitches. Two tiny little stitches, and she had to stay out of the water and away from Foundations for Families for another unknown quantity of days.

It wouldn't be so bad if she knew precisely how long it was going to be before she could get back to her routine. Two days? Two weeks? Two *months?* Nobody would give her any definite answers, and meanwhile, her entire life was on hold.

All for two little stitches.

She was working hard to control her impatience. But Foundations for Families was counting on her. She'd already missed too many of her shifts. She needed to get back and…

Mariah did one of her breathing exercises. She sounded like Marie. This was not Mariah, with her no-worries, no-stress attitude. Mariah would take these imposed days off as a gift. A chance to lie on the beach and catch up on her reading. A chance to sleep late, to take the time to cook herself delicious, healthful dinners, to watch the sunset and see the stars come out at night.

The first few days actually had been fun. Jonathan Mills had dropped by once a day, bringing her things to eat and books to read, videotapes to watch and tacky little toys from the souvenir shop to amuse her. A goofy-looking duck made from seashells glued together. A Garden Isle coloring book and a thirty-six-pack of crayons. A booklet of Mad-Libs.

Funny things. Silly things. The kind of things one friend would give another.

John's visits were nothing but friendly. In fact, he seemed to take special care that they never touched— that they never got close enough even to brush against one another by accident.

Their conversations were safe, too. They talked about books and movies and newspaper headlines. They talked about Foundations for Families and the best place on the island to get an omelet.

Mariah wasn't certain when John's latest medical test results would be coming in, but she was more than ready for him to receive a clean bill of health. From things he'd said, little hints he'd dropped, she had to believe that he'd be getting word soon. Maybe then he'd let himself give in to the attraction she still saw simmering in his eyes whenever he thought she wasn't looking.

Of course, it was entirely possible that when he wasn't looking at her, he was looking at Serena with the exact same heat in his eyes. Serena didn't come to visit, not even once, and Mariah couldn't bring herself to call her. She suspected, though, by John's noticeable absence at dinnertime, that the two of them were together. She suspected, but she hoped it was only her too-vivid imagination, fueled by jealousy, rearing its ugly little head.

She tried to stomp it back into place, but it peered at her from dark corners. She tried to bring it out into the light. So what if John was seeing Serena? He'd made it clear to Mariah that he and she were no more than friends. She could be happy with his friendship. She could be content to keep their relationship on that level.

And her Aunt Susan was the pope.

The truth was always there—a tiny voice that never failed to remind her of how she'd felt when John had kissed her. The voice reminded her of the way she'd been so ready to give herself to him in every way imaginable. The voice was always there to point out just how much she wanted this man, even despite his rejection.

She was a fool, yet every time he came to her door, she let him in. She knew damn well that in her case, being friends *wasn't* better than nothing, but she couldn't get past his illness.

What if she shut him out, what if she turned him away, refused his friendship, and he died?

He was comfortable with her. She could see him visibly relax as they sat and talked. How could she deny him that?

She was a sucker, too kind for her own good, but at least she knew it.

As of this morning, it had been nearly a day and a half since John had last stopped in.

Afraid to overstep the bounds of friendship, Mariah hadn't even called. She'd picked up the phone more than once. She'd even dialed the resort. She'd gone as far as inquiring if Mr. Jonathan Mills was still staying there.

He was. But she didn't leave a message, fearful of her tendency to want too much where John was concerned.

She more than missed him. She worried about him. Was he feeling sick? Was he relapsing? Where the heck *was* he?

A dog was barking, down on the beach.

Mariah looked up from the book she was trying her best to concentrate on, hoping it was Princess. And John.

It was Princess all right, but John was nowhere in sight. The funny-looking little dog was dancing in and out of the water, barking at the seagulls. There was no one around her for quite some distance in either direction.

Mariah laid her book aside and went down onto the beach. She whistled and the little dog looked up, ears alert. "Princess!"

Princess seemed almost to grin as she trotted toward Mariah.

"Hey," Mariah said to her, "what are you doing out here all by yourself? Where's John? Where's your master?"

The dog, of course, didn't answer.

Mariah was under doctor's orders to take it easy, but a nice, slow walk down the beach...? Now, that couldn't hurt, could it?

"Come on, Princess," Mariah said. "Let's get you something to drink and let me grab some shoes and we'll go find John."

Returning his wandering dog was clearly a friendly gesture. It was neighborly—something even just a casual acquaintance would do.

It was also the best idea she'd had all day.

* * *

Serena Westford was waiting for him in the most elegant of the resort's lounges.

Miller went slowly inside, letting his eyes adjust. Even at this time of the morning, the room was barely lit. In small bits and pieces, light filtered in through the heavy curtains that covered the windows, giving the room an odd, almost smoky feel.

Serena sat in the corner, sipping a cup of coffee, her perfect legs gracefully crossed, her dress an angelic shade of white.

Miller felt a sense of dread as he approached her. They'd met for dinner two nights ago. He'd gone directly from Mariah's house to pick her up, and he'd been late. He hadn't wanted to leave.

He'd been far too comfortable at Mariah's, far too at home, and he'd cursed himself soundly even for going there in the first place. He'd visited her for several days running—well above and beyond the call of duty. The truth was, duty had nothing to do with his visits. They were for pure pleasure—his own pleasure as well as Mariah's.

Mariah. She'd been unable to hide the flare of happiness in her eyes whenever he arrived. It was addictive, and he'd found himself visiting her more often than he should.

He'd been careful to keep his distance since their kiss in the Triple F van. But the minimum distance he *should* have maintained was at least several miles wide. The truth was, he should have stayed at the resort.

But he couldn't do it. He couldn't stay away.

And two nights ago when he'd left to pick up Serena, it had been all that he could do not to pull Mariah into his arms and tell her everything. He wanted to tell her who he really was and *what* he really was. And he wanted to kiss her until they melted into one, kiss her until time itself stood still.

Instead he'd left to meet Serena. He'd spent yesterday afternoon with Serena, too, purposely staying away from Mariah's house. They'd shared another early dinner and he'd sat in the resort restaurant, and thought about Mariah while Serena told him about her fictional past, working for the peace corps in Africa. He'd been far less attentive than he should have been. After dinner, they had a drink out on the restaurant's veranda, and he found Serena gazing at him, waiting for him to respond to some question she'd asked.

He hadn't had a clue what they had just been talking about, and that scared him. He hadn't kept his mind on his job. He'd been standing there thinking about how badly he wished he was with Mariah.

The power Mariah had over him scared him to death, and at the time he did the only thing he could think of— he took Serena into his arms and he kissed her.

He'd kissed her hard, trying to banish the ghost of Mariah that seemed to hover permanently in his subconscious. He'd tried to call up some degree of passion, but even though Serena had pressed her sinewy, lithe body against him, even though she'd responded enthusiastically, Miller had been left feeling bitterly cold— and thinking once again of the fire Mariah could start within him with just one look.

He hadn't liked kissing Serena Westford, but she hadn't seemed to notice. As he approached her now, he hoped to God he wouldn't have to kiss her again.

But Serena only lifted her cheek for him to brush

with his lips, and as he sat down next to her, she poured him a cup of steaming coffee from a silver coffeepot.

"Good morning," she said. He knew the English accent was a fake, but unlike most Americans who slipped into unauthentic-sounding British accents, Serena clearly had listened quite carefully to tapes, almost as if she was learning an entirely new language. "Did you sleep well last night?"

"Like a child," he lied. In fact, he'd stared at the ceiling for hours...thinking of Mariah. And when he finally *had* fallen asleep, it was not his nightmare that had jerked him awake before dawn, but rather an all too realistic erotic dream. He and Mariah, tangled together on her couch, clothing melted away as she opened herself to him and...

He'd awakened, disoriented, reaching for her, aching with need. But, of course, she wasn't there.

Serena was gazing at him, her cat green eyes watching him closely. He managed a smile. It was time to move this game up to a new level. "I spoke to my doctor today," he told her, mentally bracing himself, knowing that upon receiving his "good news" Serena was going to kiss him again. "He had the results from my most recent blood test. So far, it looks as if I'm not going to die."

"Oh, John, that's such wonderful news," Serena said. Sure enough, she leaned forward to kiss him.

And sure enough, Miller wished he was kissing Mariah instead.

There was an ambulance waiting outside the resort. The moment Mariah saw it, her heart began to pound, and her mind flashed to the worst-case scenario. The paramedics had come because of John. He'd fallen ill again. He was dying. He was already dead.

She stopped herself cold. That was ridiculous. It was extremely unlikely. Thinking that way wasn't going to do her one bit of good. Still, she went quickly toward the front desk, holding tightly on to Princess's collar. Through the window, she could see the ambulance pulling away. "Excuse me, can you please tell me which room Jonathan Mills is in?"

The desk clerk was cheerfully apologetic. "I'm sorry, we can't give out room numbers. But we can ring a guest's room for you, if you like."

"Yes, please. Jonathan Mills."

The clerk handed her the telephone. It rang. And rang. And rang. No answer.

The fear was returning, lodging in her throat, when Princess pulled free.

"Hey!" Mariah tossed the phone back to the clerk with a quick thanks and ran after the dog. Just because John wasn't in his room, she told herself, didn't mean that he was inside that ambulance.

Princess slipped out the doors that led to the deck by the pool, and Mariah followed. She hurried down the steps and ran nearly smack into Jonathan Mills.

He caught her elbows to hold her steady. "Mariah?"

"John!" She threw her arms around his neck. "Thank God!" He felt so warm and solid and he smelled so good—like sunblock and coffee. He always smelled like coffee. Maybe if he stopped drinking so much coffee, she thought inanely, maybe then he'd be able to sleep.

He pulled her even closer, held her even tighter for just a fraction of a second. It was so brief, she wondered if she'd imagined it, but she knew she hadn't.

He'd held her like that before—almost desperately—all those mornings ago, on her couch. But instead of kissing her, the way he'd done that morning, he quickly moved back, away from her.

And that was when she saw Serena.

Looking cool and impossibly young and pure in a white sundress and hat, Serena moved to rest her hand possessively on John's arm. "Mariah," she said. "What a surprise."

Daniel, John's assistant—the slender young Asian man Mariah had met the day John had fainted on the beach—was also standing nearby. At a nod from John, he took Princess by the collar and led the dog away.

"We were…uh, we were just going to have lunch out here by the pool," John told Mariah. "Would you, um, care to join us?"

"Mariah's on some kind of macrobiotic diet," Serena told him. "There's nothing on the menu here that she could possibly want."

John and Serena. They were standing there, looking very much like a couple. Although the truth was that she was too short for him—they didn't look quite right together. Still, there they were. About to have lunch. Together.

Mariah could easily imagine them having spent the morning together. The morning—and maybe even longer. Maybe even the night before. When *had* she seen John last?

Mariah cleared her throat, gazing up into his eyes, knowing that he could clearly see her hurt, knowing she had no right to feel hurt, but unable to hide it. "I found Princess on the beach. Alone. I haven't seen you in a few days, so I was worried. I thought maybe you were sick or hurt or…and I can see right now that you're definitely not, so I guess I'll just…go."

She backed away.

"Did you hear the good news?" Serena asked as if she was totally unaware of the tension that seemed to leap and crackle between Mariah and John. "Jonathan got the first of his test results this morning. His doctor is almost certain the cancer's gone." She smiled up at John. "He's going to live to a ripe old age, aren't you, darling?"

This morning. He'd known this morning and he hadn't even bothered to call. "That's such good news," Mariah managed to say. She even managed a smile, despite the tears in her eyes. "John, I'm so glad for you."

True, she'd imagined him getting the news and coming to *her,* not Serena. Still, that didn't make the news any less wonderful. But now he was going to have lunch with Serena, and Serena had made it clear that their table was only for two.

"I better go," she said. She gazed into John's eyes for just a moment longer. "I'm *so* glad."

Miller couldn't believe it. Despite his careful talk of friendship, Mariah clearly had had expectations that were now dashed upon seeing him here like this with Serena. Yet her words were sincere and heartfelt. He'd hurt her, probably badly, yet she was honestly happy for him.

She looked out of place at the resort grill, dressed the way she was in cutoffs and a T-shirt. Her hair was wind-blown—her soft curls tumbling down to her shoulders. Her eyes were filled with tears—still she was smiling.

"So glad," she whispered again.

As Miller watched, she turned and walked away.

He wanted to follow her. He was dying to follow her.

But he couldn't. He couldn't even take a moment and feel like crap for hurting her this way because Serena was watching him. He had to smile and pretend that the expression he'd seen on Mariah's face wasn't making his heart ache.

His heart *was* aching.

A surprising turn of events for a man who wasn't sure he even had a heart just a few short weeks ago.

"Shall we have lunch?" Serena murmured.

Miller nodded and gave her another smile. Tonight he was planning to ask her to marry him, and sometime in the next few weeks, she would try to stick a knife into his heart.

Even if she succeeded, he suspected it would not be a new sensation.

"Hi, it's me. Is this a good time to talk?" Mariah asked.

There was a brief silence on the other end of the line, then Serena's cool voice answered, "If you're wondering if I'm alone, yes, I am. But I'm a little busy right now. I'll call you back."

The line went dead, and Mariah stared for a moment at the phone in her hand. Instead of hanging up, she pressed redial. But this time, Serena didn't answer. This time, her answering machine didn't even come on.

That was odd. Serena was nearly obsessive about getting her phone messages. Why she should leave the house without turning her machine on was a mystery.

But the phone rang before Mariah even started clearing her lunch dishes off the table. She picked it up. "Hello?"

It was Serena. "Sorry—I had to get *out* of there. I'm

calling from the pay phone in front of the Northbeach pizza parlor. My place is *crawling* with bugs. I've had an infestation of some kind of disgusting cockroaches. *Awful.* I'm going off island for the rest of the afternoon and evening. To Atlanta—I have some business to take care of. Can I get you anything from the real world?"

She didn't let Mariah answer. "God, I can still see those nasty little bugs when I close my eyes. There were so *many* of them. The exterminator came and said they had to spray some awful poison, and even then, they'd need to come back every few days or so to spray again. I told the rental office that I *wouldn't* be coming back. Not to *that* cottage."

"Will you be coming back?" Mariah asked, hardly daring to hope.

"Of course. I'll probably stay at the resort for a few days until I can find something less populated by the native insect life."

The resort. That would put Serena closer to John. How convenient.

Mariah took a deep breath. "Serena, I wanted to talk to you about John."

"Jonathan Mills?"

"Yes."

"He was *so* excited when he received those favorable test results," Serena told her. "Just like a little boy. Of course, one set of favorable tests doesn't necessarily mean he's in remission or whatever. He still could die."

"If you think that, then what are you doing with him?" Mariah asked. "You want a husband who's alive, don't you?"

Serena laughed. "A husband? Who said anything about a husband?" Her voice changed. "Has Jonathan mentioned anything to you about wanting to get married?"

"No."

"Well, see? We're just friends. You're his friend. Can't *I* be friends with Jonathan, too? Really, Mariah, it's nothing serious. The man hasn't done more than *kiss* me," Serena pointed out. "He's had plenty of opportunities to come home with me or take me back to his place, but he hasn't." She paused. "Yet."

John had kissed Serena. Mariah closed her eyes as she fought the wave of jealousy and hurt that threatened to consume her. "It might be nothing serious for you, but…" She knew John pretty well by now. "John's *always* serious. And he's fragile in a lot of ways. His cancer has made him vulnerable. And he has those awful nightmares."

"Are you trying to scare me away—or give me instructions on how to hold his hand and warm his milk for him at night when he has a bad dream?"

"These aren't bad dreams. These are violent nightmares. Hasn't he told you?"

"Maybe he's afraid he'll scare me away if he tells me all of his dark secrets," Serena said.

Or maybe when he was with Serena, he didn't spend any time talking.

"He should realize that I don't scare easily," Serena added. "What are the nightmares about? Being sick?"

"No," Mariah told her. "A friend of his was a police detective and he was killed in the line of duty. It haunts him."

"Isn't that interesting," Serena mused. "A police detective, you said?"

"Actually, John said his friend—Tony—was a cop.

Tony was killed on the orders of an organized-crime boss."

"Well, that certainly adds a new dimension to the game."

"Serena, if this is just a game to you—"

"Life is a game," Serena said. "You play it, and then you die. No matter what rules you play by, dying is the one given. Everyone dies sooner or later. Some, sooner. If the cancer doesn't kill Jonathan—who knows, maybe he'll be hit by a bus."

"That's a terrible thing to think!"

"Oh, please, Mariah," Serena said. "The Pollyanna act gets old after a while."

"Maybe when you leave today, you shouldn't come back."

Serena laughed. "Maybe I won't." She paused. "Was that really the most awful thing you could think of to say to me?"

Mariah gazed out over the ocean, curbing her impulse to say the words that were really on her lips. "No," she admitted. "But we're friends. I don't want to say anything that—"

"Did you get that negative back from the photo lab?" Serena interrupted.

"No, I haven't been off—"

"Now I've *got* to come back." Serena sounded annoyed. "Have it ready for me tomorrow, please. I'll come by to pick it up."

"Tomorrow? I'm sorry, I can't—"

The line was dead. Serena had hung up without even saying goodbye.

Chapter 8

A light was on in Mariah's cottage.

Miller stood on the beach, gazing up at the house, wishing he'd been able to sleep. He wished he hadn't given up and climbed out of bed. He wished he hadn't roused Princess and brought her out onto the beach. He wished he'd walked in the other direction.

Most of all, he wished he could erase the memory he had of Mariah's face as she turned away at lunch. But the hurt and disappointment in her eyes had been burned into his brain. There was no escaping it.

He shouldn't have come out here.

But something had pulled him in this direction. Something strong. Something he couldn't resist.

Nothing had gone right tonight. He'd planned to take Serena to dinner and ask her to marry him. But she'd called and left a message, canceling their date. She hadn't told him where she was going or when she'd be back—just that she had to go to the mainland to take care of business and that she'd be back soon.

His first thought was that she was on to him. Somehow, she'd made him. She knew he was FBI.

She was dangerously smart, and he had screwed up all over the place with this case, starting with his obsession with Mariah and continuing with his failure to stick to his cover story and play the part of the invalid at the Foundations for Families building site. He knew what chemotherapy did to a person, and it was highly unlikely that, had he had the treatments he was pretending to have had, he would've been able to rescue that eight-year-old from the tree, let alone Mariah.

Yeah, and then there was his telling Mariah about Tony. That was a real stroke of genius. He'd actually told Mariah that Tony was a *cop*. What had he been thinking?

He *wasn't* thinking. He was reacting. He was feeling. He was wanting. He was leading with a part of his anatomy that didn't have a very high IQ.

And that was how agents got themselves and their partners killed. And God help him, he may not give a damn about his own life, but he would not—*would not*—bury another partner.

He gazed out at the horizon, squinting to make out where the sky ended and the ocean began. A light haze obscured all but the brightest of the stars, and a steady breeze blew off the water, carrying with it a salty mist. It was almost cold.

He was exhausted, bone weary, yet he still couldn't sleep. He couldn't sleep because he was afraid to sleep. He was afraid to fall into his nightmare. Afraid to gaze down into Tony's sightless eyes. Afraid to hear Tony's voice, tight with fear. Afraid to face his own guilt.

Princess was halfway up the path that led to Mariah's, looking back at him with a quizzical expression on her fuzzy face. *Aren't you coming?*

"No," Miller said, softly but firmly. "Come back here, Princess. *Now*."

But the dog either couldn't hear him over the wind and the surf, or maybe she simply chose not to hear. She trotted steadily toward the shelter of Mariah's deck.

Miller went after her, breaking into a run, but she was too far ahead. As she started up the wooden steps of the deck, she barked sharply. Once. Twice.

Damn. That was all he needed—for Mariah to know he was here, skulking around outside her house, hoping for what? To get a glimpse of her? To talk to her? To kiss her? To fall back with her onto her bed? To lock her bedroom door and never come out?

All those things. *Dammit,* he wanted *all* those things.

"Princess, get your butt down here," he hissed, starting up the stairs after her.

The door slid open. "Hey, what are *you* doing here?" Mariah greeted his dog. Her voice was not so friendly when she turned and spotted him, frozen on his way up the stairs. "John?"

He climbed up the last few steps, silently cursing Princess, silently cursing himself. "Hi. Yeah, it's me. I'm sorry—I didn't mean to bother you, but the dog has a mind of her own."

Mariah looked incredible. She was wearing those same cutoffs she'd had on at lunchtime, the same clingy T-shirt. Her legs were long and tanned and looked as if they'd be deliciously smooth to touch. She'd pulled her hair up and off her neck, holding it in a messy bundle on top of her head with one of those giant bear-trap-type clips.

But she also looked tired—her normally sparkling eyes were shadowed. She looked wary and leery and not at all happy to see him.

As he watched, she took a breath, and the slight movement made her breasts strain against the cotton of her shirt. God, what he wouldn't have given to pull her into his arms.

She glanced back inside the house, twisting slightly to look at the clock on the wall. "It's after one. Couldn't you sleep?"

Miller shook his head. "No. I never can. Sleep, I mean. Except for that one time here…"

She was silent for several long moments, just gazing at him. He couldn't read her eyes, couldn't read her body language. He had absolutely no idea what she was thinking.

"It's cold tonight," she finally said. "Why don't you come inside?"

She turned and went in, not waiting for him to answer.

Miller knew he should take Princess and go. But he'd left everything he knew he should do behind a long time ago. And Princess was already curled up in the dry, protected corner of the deck. So instead, he followed Mariah into the house and closed the door tightly behind him.

It was outrageously bright in there after the darkness of the beach. Mariah had brought most of the lamps from other rooms over to the dining table near the sliding doors, and that part of the house seemed to glow.

He stepped past the lights and into the dimness of the living room.

"How's your back?" he asked awkwardly, wishing that she would ask him to leave. It would make everything so much easier if she just kicked him out.

"It's fine." She was standing in the middle of the room, arms folded across her chest, watching him.

"What are you doing...you know, up so late?"

"I couldn't sleep, either," she admitted. "I thought I'd put some of my pictures in albums. I've been trying to organize them." She gestured back toward the dining-room table. Photos of all shapes and colors were spread across its surface, along with albums of all sizes.

Music was playing softly in the background. It wasn't soft music; it was just turned down low, as if she'd adjusted the volume when she heard Princess out on the deck. A slide guitar wailed over a heavy country backbeat. Vocalists in tight harmony came in—singing about a girl with a tattoo in the shape of Texas. Miller had to smile.

"You know, I always pictured you as being so serene, with your stress-reduction exercises and your crystals," he told her. "I guess I always imagined that when you were alone you'd listen to New Age music—not kick-ass country."

She smiled very slightly. "Oh, please. I thought you knew me better than that. New Age music puts me to sleep."

"Maybe we should both try listening to it, then."

Mariah turned away from him and sat on the end of the couch, her legs underneath her, tailor-style. It was dim in the living room, with all the lights moved into the dining area. She looked mysterious sitting there, shadows falling across her face. "Tell me about the test results."

Miller stepped away from the table and farther into the darkness of the living room. He sat down in the rocking chair opposite her and cleared his throat before he told her a lie. Another lie. There had been so many, yet at the same time, he'd told her more about himself than he'd ever told anyone. All those memories of his mother.

"There's not much to tell. My blood tests show vast improvements. If it keeps going like this, I'm going to be considered in remission. If the cancer doesn't recur in five years, I'm going to be considered cured."

He sounded bitter. He *was* bitter. He knew so much about Hodgkin's disease and about the so-called survival rate because his mother had been one of the ones who hadn't survived. She'd been in remission. She'd even been pronounced cured. And still, she'd relapsed and the second time around, the cancer had won. She'd died.

"Five *years...?*" Mariah leaned forward. "John, you've got to stop worrying about it. You can't not sleep for five years." She sighed. "Have you considered going into therapy?"

He wanted to sit next to her on the couch. God, he wanted her so badly he could barely speak.

Why was he here? What was he doing here? There was nothing—absolutely nothing—good that could possibly come of this. Nothing but a few brief moments of comfort, a temporary respite from the hell his life had become. Mariah could give him that. But what about her? What about all that he'd be taking away from her in return?

"I know you don't think so, but I'm okay about the Hodgkin's. It's not even real to me." Miller stood up swiftly, aware that he was saying the wrong thing again. What was he telling her now? Damn right the cancer wasn't real to him, because it *wasn't* real. But it *was* real to Jonathan Mills.

Except he *wasn't* Jonathan Mills. He was John Miller. John Miller was the one who couldn't sleep, the one with the terrible nightmares. He was the one with all the guilt, all the suffocating blame. He was the one who had come here tonight, seeking her out.

Mariah stood, too, looking at him, her eyes wide. "John, are you all right?"

He shook his head. "No. I have to…" What? What did he have to do? Run away. God, he never thought he'd ever run away from anything. But here he was, forced to run from the one person who maybe could save him, given the chance.

But he couldn't give her—or himself—any kind of a chance.

She was moving toward him slowly, the way someone would approach a frightened animal. "John, when was the last time you slept?"

He shook his head. "I don't know." But that was another lie and he was tired of lying to her. He knew damn well when he'd last slept. "It was here," he said. "That time I was here."

Her eyes widened. "That was over a week ago!"

"I've had some naps since then, but…" He shook his head.

"But you wake up with that nightmare, and then you can't—or won't—go back to sleep, right? My God, you're shaking!"

He was. He jammed his shaking hands into the front pockets of his jeans and turned toward the door. "I have to go."

Mariah blocked his path. "Let me call Daniel to come and get you."

"No, I'm fine."

"You are so *not* fine. Look, just sit down. On the couch."

Miller didn't move.

"Please? John?"

He sat.

She sat down next to him. All he could think about was how badly he'd wanted to sit next to her. Well, now here he was.

"Talk to me," she said quietly. "Tell me about Tony. Why do you blame yourself for his death? What really happened, John?"

Miller turned to look at her, and with a flash of clarity that nearly pushed him down onto the floor, he knew why he wanted to be here, why he wanted to be with Mariah so desperately.

Why do you blame yourself for his death?

He did. He blamed himself. And yet he knew that Mariah would forgive him. He knew that without a doubt. Mariah would tell him that even if it *was* his fault that Tony had died, even if he *had* been to blame, even if there was something he could have done to save his partner and best friend, she would *still* forgive him.

He should have gotten out of the van sooner. He should have known there would be a snafu with the backup. He should have anticipated the fact that the choppers wouldn't arrive. His list of recriminations went on and on, but regardless of its length and content, the bottom line was the same.

He'd failed.

But Mariah, with her gentle smile and warm eyes, would forgive him for failing. She would forgive him his mistakes, forgive him for being human.

God help him, he wanted that forgiveness. He wanted to hear her say it. And he knew with that same flash of clarity, brighter than all the lights gathered around the dining-room table, that he had to get out of here, and soon, or he'd break down in tears, crying like a baby. Crying for Tony, and crying for himself—for everything that he'd lost that awful night two years ago. Crying because the one time it had really mattered, the one time his reputation of never failing, of not accepting the word "impossible," of being "The Robot" with his superhuman ability to get the job done—the one time that would have really made a difference, reality had stepped in and Tony had died.

He knew he had to get out of there, but Mariah reached out and took his hand, and he couldn't move.

"I couldn't save him," he told her, his voice hoarse.

She touched his face. "But you tried, didn't you? You *were* there."

Miller had to close his eyes to keep his tears from escaping. "I didn't see it. But I heard them kill him. God, I heard him die!" He turned away as more than two years of pain and grief and rage erupted in an emotional cataclysm. His tears burned his face and his lungs ached for air and his body shook as he broke down and wept. "I was too late. I got there too late."

Miller felt Mariah's arms around him and he tried to pull away, tried to stop his tears, tried to shut himself off and push everything he felt back down inside him. He might've succeeded had she not held on to him so tightly.

"What if you'd gotten there earlier?" she asked, her voice as soothing as the gentleness of her hands in his hair. "How could you have stopped them from killing him? What would you have done?"

He knew the answer—and he knew that she knew it, too.

"You probably would've been killed, as well, wouldn't you?" she asked quietly.

"Yes." Not probably. Definitely. He would've died. It was only because he'd arrived after most of Domino's men had emptied their bullets into Tony's head that he'd managed to take them all out without being killed himself. If he'd shown up any sooner, he would've been lying on that concrete floor, just as dead as Tony.

"John, you've got to forgive yourself for not dying with your friend."

That was why he'd come here, wasn't it? For absolution. For the relief of his soul. But he wanted relief for his body, too. He wanted it so badly he was afraid he'd give in to the temptation. God, it wouldn't take much to push him over the edge.

He tried to pull free from her hands, well aware that her touch was giving him far more than comfort. Her touch was lighting him on fire, reminding him of the sweet oblivion that awaited him if only he gave in. He had to get out of here.

But she wouldn't let him go. "It's all right," she murmured, her hands in his hair, on his face, soothing his shoulders and back. "Let it out, John. Let it go. It's okay to feel angry and hurt. It's okay to grieve. If you don't, it'll poison you. Just let it all go."

Miller couldn't stop himself. Mariah held him even more tightly as he clung to her desperately. Please, God, don't let her kiss him. If she did, he'd be lost.

He closed his eyes as she began talking to him soothingly, softly, walking him through that same relaxation exercise she'd helped him with last week. And once again, like last week, his exhaustion crashed down upon him.

He was barely conscious as she pulled him back onto the couch with her, her arms tightly around him, his back pressed against her front.

"Forgive yourself," she murmured. "I'm sure Tony does."

Mariah couldn't sleep.

The couch wasn't meant to hold two people lying down—especially not two people her and John's size. But she wasn't uncomfortable. In fact, she liked the sensation of John's body pressed against hers, their legs intimately intertwined.

She liked it too much.

She listened to the steady, quiet rhythm of his breathing and cursed herself for being a fool.

At least she hadn't had sex with him. Although, that was really only because he hadn't asked. If he'd wanted to, she probably wouldn't have been able to turn him down.

God, what had happened to her since that first morning she'd set eyes on this man? Where on earth had Jonathan Mills gotten the power to transform her so totally into some kind of doormat?

He stirred slightly, and she took the opportunity to pull her arm out from underneath him.

It was the cancer thing. The idea that this man had faced—and was still facing—the very real possibility of his imminent death did her in. His plight reduced her to a quivering mass of emotions and reactions.

It had to be that. Because she'd fallen in love before without losing her sense of self, her strength and…

Fallen in love.

She looked down at John's face. He looked impossibly young, improbably innocent, his lips slightly parted in sleep.

She was in love with him.

Mariah knew in that instant that her doormat days were done. She was in love, and yet she was more unhappy than she'd ever been in her entire life. She hadn't felt this bad even while she was going through her divorce from Trevor.

She couldn't do this to herself anymore.

She wasn't crazy. And yet here she was, holding John while he slept when she knew for a fact that he'd been sharing more than meals with Serena. From now on, he was going to have to go to Serena for the comfort he needed to get him through the blackest hours of the night.

Mariah peeled herself away from him, climbing off the couch. He stirred again, but he didn't wake up as she stood there, looking down at him.

She should have felt better. Pushing him away from her like that should have been empowering.

But without his body next to hers, warming her, all Mariah felt was cold.

* * *

She came back to the hotel quite late. She'd closed the bar down, drinking and dancing.

Her dress smelled of smoke and sweat, and she peeled it off, letting it fall in a heap on the soft, expensive carpeting. She wouldn't take it with her when she left in the morning.

She was going to have to go back. She needed that negative. Except the stupid cow hadn't sounded as if she was going to go out of her way to get it back from...

Where was it she kept her negatives? B&W Photo Lab. Just over on the mainland from Garden Isle. It would be easy enough to find, easy enough to walk in there and get hold of her entire collection of negatives.

She caught sight of herself in the mirror and stopped for a moment to admire her body, her face.

She'd had plastic surgery to remove all but one of her scars. One she kept—a little one, just along the line of her left eyebrow.

The first one had done that to her. The first one had given her all her scars—at least all the scars that her father before him hadn't given her.

She closed her eyes, remembering the thrill she had felt when the policeman had come to her door, waking her in the middle of the night to tell her that the first one was dead. A car accident. He'd drunk himself into a stupor, and instead of coming home and beating her to a pulp, he'd driven his car into a tree.

The undertaker's wife, mistaking her round-the-clock vigilance at his coffin for grief, cut her a lock of his hair to remember him by.

But it hadn't been grief keeping her there—it had been fear. Fear that unless she watched him, unless she made damn sure he stayed right there in that wooden box until they nailed it shut, he might somehow escape. He might jump up and run away and come back to haunt her.

She'd nearly thrown the hair into the toilet, but on second thought, she'd kept it, wrapped in cellophane, at the bottom of her jewelry box.

The insurance money, along with a stash she'd found in a suitcase in the garage, had been enough to get her to St. Thomas. She'd picked herself a new name, afraid that whoever owned the money that had been in that suitcase would come looking for her.

That was when she'd met the second one.

He was rich and old and nearly as mean as the first one. Except the abuse *he* dished out wasn't physical. And when a piece of chicken caught in his throat during dinner, she had stood by and watched him choke.

She didn't call for help. She just watched—watched the look in his eyes as he knew she would do nothing to save him, watched as he realized he was, indeed, going to die. She'd liked it—liked the power, liked the feeling of control.

The third one she'd married with the intention of killing.

It had been laughably easy. She was so much smarter than all of them.

Smarter than Jonathan Mills, who wasn't really named Jonathan Mills.

She knew that sooner or later the police would try to trap her. She'd been watching for them. She'd been ready. And when she'd found their clumsily hidden microphones all over her house, she knew that Jonathan Mills had been sent to stop her.

Instead, she'd escaped.

She climbed between the crisp hotel sheets, feeling a flare of regret.

She would have liked pushing her knife blade into Jonathan Mills's heart.

Chapter 9

Miller opened his eyes to the sound of the telephone ringing.

It was daylight. Bright, gleaming morning. The sun had been up for at least an hour and he simply lay for a moment on the couch, staring up at the light playing across the ceiling, hazily wondering why that should seem such an amazing thing.

"Yes." He heard a soft voice from the other room. "Yes, he's here. I'll see if he's awake."

Then he heard the sound of footsteps coming into the living room, and he sat up, automatically raking his hair back with one hand, pushing it from his forehead. Except the hair his fingers connected with was shockingly short, and he remembered instantly both where he was and who he was supposed to be.

Dear God, he'd slept all night again. This time, without even a trace of his nightmare.

"Phone's for you," Mariah said quietly, handing him a cordless telephone.

She didn't meet his gaze. She hardly looked at him at all.

Miller quickly played back the previous evening in his mind. God knows he had plenty to be embarrassed about, what with breaking down and crying the way he'd done. But he couldn't recall a single thing Mariah had done that should make her so uncomfortable.

She hadn't even kissed him.

God help him—he'd somehow managed to spend all that time here last night without ever kissing Mariah. Although he had a very definite memory of falling asleep cradled in the softness of her arms.

He brought the telephone to his ear, still watching Mariah as she opened the sliders to let in the fresh morning air. Last night's coolness remained, but it wouldn't for long, not in the heat from the sun. She stayed for a moment, just looking out at the ocean, her fatigue evident in the way she stood, in the set of her shoulders.

He might have slept well last night, but she clearly hadn't.

"Yeah?" Miller said into the phone.

"John, it's Daniel. I'm sorry to have to call you there, but Serena appears to have gone for good."

Miller didn't move a muscle. He just sat and watched Mariah watch the ocean. "Based on...?"

"Based on the fact that yesterday she notified her rental agent that she was terminating her lease agreement. Her place is empty, John. All her things are cleared out. I went over there early this morning. All the surveillance microphones are still in place—it doesn't look as if she touched any of them, but that doesn't mean anything. I've got to believe she found 'em, got spooked and ran."

Miller swore sharply. Mariah glanced back at him, but quickly looked away. "Call Pat Blake," he told Daniel. "Advise him of the situation and then get back to me."

He should've proposed marriage to Serena yesterday at lunch, when he'd had the chance. But he'd hesitated, and now she was gone. And in his experience, when a suspect fled, that suspect was gone for good.

The case was over—at least this stage of it was—with the suspect still at large. But other than that first sharp flash of annoyance, all Miller felt was relief. Because, for the first time in his life, he had found something that he wanted even more than he wanted to solve this case.

He'd found Mariah.

He pushed the button to disconnect the phone, then set it on the end table. He stood up stiffly, stretching out his legs and back. "Mind if I use your bathroom?"

Mariah turned to face him. "No, of course I don't," she said stiffly, politely. "But afterward, I think you should leave."

He froze mid-stretch. Leave?

He'd found Mariah—who wanted him to leave.

She turned swiftly, disappearing into the kitchen.

It was too damned ironic. For the first time since he'd met her, Miller finally felt free. True, the case wasn't officially over. He couldn't tell her who he was or what he'd been up to—not yet anyway. But he could pull her into his arms and kiss her without knowing for damn sure that she was going to end up hurt.

Miller didn't believe in happily ever after. He had no misconceptions regarding his ability to make Mariah happy in the long run. He knew damn well that kind of future wasn't in his cards. But he was sure that he could make her smile in the short term. He was *very* sure of that.

He went into the bathroom, relieved himself, then washed up. As he splashed cold water on his face, he caught sight of himself in the mirror. Despite the sleep he'd gotten, he still looked tired. For the first time in years, he found himself longing to crawl back into bed. For the first time in years, sleep beckoned invitingly instead of looming over him dangerously, like some snarling, vicious beast.

With Serena out of the picture, he had nothing to do, nowhere to go—at least not until Daniel contacted Pat Blake. Knowing Blake, he'd call a meeting, maybe even come down here himself to inspect the scene of the disaster firsthand. But that wouldn't be for hours, maybe even days.

Mariah wanted him to leave, but Miller wanted to stay. And for the first time, he *could* stay.

He took a deep breath before he opened the bathroom door. Mariah was in the kitchen. He could hear the sound of water running.

"I gave Princess some water," she told him without even looking up as he paused in the doorway.

"Thanks," he said. He hesitated, suddenly oddly embarrassed, a picture of the way he'd wept last night flashing into his head. "And thanks…for last night, too. I feel…" He smiled crookedly. "I feel *okay*."

Mariah turned to face him then. "You slept for a long time."

He nodded. "First time in over two years I've slept through the sunrise."

"You never let yourself grieve for him before, did you?" she asked quietly, talking about Tony.

Miller squinted slightly as he looked out the window at the brightness of the day. "No."

"It wasn't your fault that he died."

He shook his head very slightly. "No. No, it wasn't." He laughed very softly. "I know it wasn't. Logically. Rationally. I guess I just don't quite *believe* it wasn't." He paused, gazing at her, feeling that familiar ache of longing. He wanted to pull her into his arms, but she was sending out all kinds of signals warning him to keep his distance. "Maybe you could help me work on that."

"Gee, I'm sorry, but I can't." She took a deep breath. "I don't want to be your therapist anymore, John," she said bluntly. "What you're dealing with isn't going to be solved by breaking plates or silly little relaxation exercises. You need to find someone professional who can really help you. And I..." Her voice broke. "I need you to stay away from me. I can't pretend to be your friend anymore. Maybe that's petty of me, because I know you really need me as a friend, but I can't do this anymore. I respect myself too much to play this crazy game with you. Do you want me or don't you? Every time I think that you do, you back away. And just when I'm convinced that you don't, you look at me like...like... *that*. Don't look at me like that, dammit, because I'm not going to play anymore. I want you to leave."

He stepped toward her. "Mariah—"

Mariah lifted her chin, folding her arms across her chest, holding her ground despite the tears that filled her eyes. "The door's in the other direction."

John stopped moving toward her, but he didn't retreat, either. He just gazed at her. In spite of his long, quiet sleep, he still looked weary, his chiseled features in high relief. His chin was covered with dark stubble, making him look doubly dangerous. But it was the bright blue of his eyes that caught her and held her in place. Beneath the heat of desire that nearly always simmered there, his eyes were filled with apology and darkened with a haunting vulnerability.

"Whatever you do, don't think that I don't want you," he whispered. "Because I do. I've wanted you right from the start—and every minute from then till now."

She couldn't believe what she was hearing. She laughed, but it came out sounding more like a sob. "Then why have you been kissing Serena?"

He didn't seem surprised that she knew—and he didn't try to deny it. "I can't... I can't explain that."

"Try."

John just shook his head.

He was blocking the only way out of the room, but Mariah couldn't stand to be there a moment longer. She tried to push past him, but he caught her arm, his fingers locking around her wrist. "Mariah, wait—"

"Let *go* of me!"

Miller let go. No way was he going to risk hurting her again. Seeing those bruises on her arms had made him sick to his stomach. "I kissed her because I hoped it would make me stop wanting *you*." That was only part of the truth, but he hoped it would be enough.

She turned to look back at him, her eyes filled with anger, her lips tight with disgust. "You are so full of—"

Miller kissed her. He knew it wasn't playing fair, but he didn't give a damn. He knew kissing her would melt her anger and ignite her passion, leaving the arguments and harsh words far behind. He knew he was good at word games, but Mariah had told him point-blank that she didn't want to play games anymore.

This kiss would eliminate everything but the most basic of truths—that he wanted her and she wanted him.

And yes, she still wanted him.

He tasted it in the fire of her kiss, in the heat of her melting embrace. He kissed her harder, sweeping his tongue deeply into her mouth, and she met him with a fierceness that took his breath away. She pulled him closer, her hands gliding up his back, her fingers on his neck, in his hair, even as his own hands explored the softness of her body, cupping the fullness of her breasts.

"Make love to me, Mariah," he whispered, kissing her again. Her response was clear from the strength of her answering kiss.

She pulled back slightly, and he could see molten desire in her eyes. "If I do, I'm going to regret this, aren't I?" she said huskily.

"No," he said. "This is going to be too good to regret."

Her smile was tinged with sadness. "I just made up my mind to stay away from you, and now you go and totally mess me up. I mean, God! Give me one good reason why I shouldn't kick you out right here and now."

He couldn't. There was no reason, other than he wanted to stay, and she wanted him to stay, too. He leaned forward to kiss her again, but she stopped him with a finger against his lips.

"I don't know, maybe I haven't made this totally clear, but I'm emotionally involved here. Taking you into my bedroom and getting naked with you is going to be more than just great sex to me. It's going to be making love. Love, John—do you understand what I'm trying to say to you?" Mariah took a deep breath and let it all out in a rush. "In plain English, I'm in love with you. So if you're going to get all freaked out and scared about that, maybe you should just run away now—*before* you tear my heart out."

Miller couldn't move. He couldn't speak. He couldn't breathe. Mariah was in love with...*him?*

He gazed down into her eyes, unable to look away, feeling an odd tightness in his chest. "That sounds like a good reason for me to stay," he whispered.

He wanted to be loved. God, how he wanted that. He was shaken by how badly he wanted that, wanted more than just lust, more than physical gratification. He wanted to be cared for, to be cherished. In the past, he'd run away from such emotions, but as he looked into Mariah's eyes, he only wanted to move closer. He wanted her to love him. He wanted *her.* And somehow she knew. He could see in her eyes that she knew.

Still, it wasn't quite enough.

"I need you to promise me something," she told him.

"Mariah, I can't promise much—"

"I'm not looking for any major commitment or anything like that," she countered. "Just..." She had to start again. "Don't sleep with Serena, okay?"

That was easy. "I won't," he said. "I promise."

That was all she needed. Taking his hand, she led him to her bedroom.

The morning sun shone through green curtains, giving the room a greenish tint. The ocean breeze made the curtains move, and the light seemed to shift and dance across the ceiling. It was like being underwater. Or maybe up in heaven.

Mariah's bed was in the center of the small room, the headboard pushed against the wall. It was rumpled, unmade, the white sheets exposed beneath a green spread. Miller knew that Mariah had spent much of the night in here, unable to rest while he'd been fast asleep on the couch.

Mariah kissed him, and he knew his second assessment was right. This was definitely heaven.

She kissed him slowly, deeply, shifting her body against his in a way that made him groan. He knew from the burst of heat in her eyes that she liked the involuntary sound of his desire.

Her hands slid up underneath his T-shirt, traveling slowly up his back, and Miller closed his eyes.

This was too good, too intense, and too damn slow. But if she wanted it like this, dammit, he was going to curb his raging impulses and make love to her slowly.

He knew without a shadow of a doubt that he'd go to superhuman degrees to give her anything she wanted, anything at all.

She tugged at his T-shirt and he helped her pull it up and over his head. But when he reached for her shirt, she stopped him.

"Have you noticed that when it comes to sex, guys don't like to get naked first?" she said, kissing his shoulders, his neck, his chest. Her fingers moved down to the waistband of his jeans, lightly brushing against his stomach as she unfastened the top button. "It's a dominance thing," she added, smiling up at him as she slowly unzipped his pants, "a power thing. It makes sense, doesn't it? The person still dressed has a certain amount of power over the person who's naked."

"Are you, um, into that?" Miller asked.

She pushed him back onto the bed, pulling his jeans down his thighs. "And then there's the female thing," she continued as if she hadn't heard his question. "Women tend to be afraid to take the lead for fear of coming on too strong. Socially, we're taught to lie back—let the man take off our clothes. Let him set the pace. Let him choose the time and place and position. Let him do the work. Hence the passive phrase 'to be made love *to*.' I much prefer 'making love *with*.'" She tossed his jeans onto the floor. "*That's* what I'm into."

He reached for her, pressing her back on the bed with the force of his kiss. But then he moved away, suddenly remembering. "Your back—is it all right?"

"It's fine." She pulled him toward her for another kiss, molding herself against him.

The sensation of the smoothness of her legs intertwined with his nearly overwhelmed him. He pulled her T-shirt up, over her head, and this time she didn't protest.

He gazed down at her and she smiled back at him, just letting him look. She was impossibly sexy, lying there like that. Her bra was white, covering her full breasts with some kind of stretchy lace material that allowed him tantalizing glimpses of dark pink nipples. He covered her breasts first with his hands, then with his mouth, suckling her through the lace of the bra, tugging on the desire-hardened tips with his lips, with his tongue.

She moaned, opening herself to him, cradling his swollen sex against the heat between her legs.

Miller reached for the button on her shorts, and she let him unfasten them and pull them down her legs. They soon joined his jeans on the floor.

Mariah closed her eyes. For all her liberated talk, she was lying there, letting him undress her. And cringing because she was nearly naked—and afraid he wouldn't like her because she didn't have the body of a Barbie doll.

She felt John's hands skimming her body. She knew he was looking at her.

"God, you're incredible," he breathed.

About to protest, she opened her eyes, but then she saw the fire in his gaze, the sheer admiration on his face. He was serious. He honestly liked what he saw.

He wasn't one of those men who went for boyishly figured women like Serena. He wasn't like Trevor, who had been forever trying to get her to go on a diet, to lose weight, to shrink herself down to his height.

No, John clearly liked *women*. Real women. And maybe especially women who were six feet tall, and generously—and appropriately—proportioned for their height.

As Mariah watched John's face, her shoulders were no longer too broad. Her thighs weren't too big, her legs too thickly muscled. Her hips weren't too wide, or her breasts too full.

Mariah sat up and unfastened the front clasp of her bra—for the first time in her life voluntarily exposing herself to the eyes of a man without hiding in the cover of the darkness of night.

The look in John's eyes was well worth the risk. He smiled, a short, hot smile that nearly scalded her, as he pulled her up toward him.

The sensation of the hard muscles of his chest pressed against her bare breasts and his rock-solid arousal against the softness of her stomach was dizzying as she knelt with him, there on her bed. His kiss made her sway, and she clung to him as he slipped one hand beneath the lace of her panties, his exploring fingers touching her lightly, intimately.

She reached between them, too, finding him hard and sleek and hot.

He groaned. "Mariah..."

She opened her eyes to find herself gazing directly into his. The connection was just as physical as his touch.

"You said you had protection," he said.

At just the same moment, she asked, "Will you put on a condom?"

They both laughed.

"I'll get one," Mariah said, pulling free from his grasp.

She rummaged through her bedside-table drawer, searching for the packet of condoms that her aunt had given her, complete with a note telling her to have a *very* good vacation. Mariah had rolled her eyes and tossed the box into her suitcase, hardly expecting to find call to use it. As she found the box, way down at the bottom of the drawer, John came to stand behind her, pressing himself intimately against her, covering her breasts with his hands and kissing her neck. It felt delicious—a hard promise of things to come.

And Mariah knew that she didn't want to wait a moment longer. He'd taken off his briefs and now he slipped her panties down her legs, as well, as she turned to face him.

They were both naked, but she was more so—because she'd told him that she loved him.

This should have been strange—standing here like this, just looking at this beautiful, naked man, letting him look at her. But it wasn't strange at all, despite the fact that it had been years since she'd been with a man this way. She'd been attracted to John from the first moment she'd laid eyes on him. She'd liked him from the first time they'd talked. And somewhere between then and now, she'd fallen deeply in love with him, too. And it was that love she felt that kept this from being strange, that instead made this moment perfect.

She knew he didn't love her—she didn't try to kid herself about that. But he liked her. She knew he really liked her. And on many levels, she preferred that steady, milder emotion to the short, hot, quick-burning flash of infatuation that many people mistook for love.

She pressed one of the condom packets into his hand. "Put this on," she told him. "Then lie down and close your eyes."

John laughed softly. "What are we doing? Pressure Cooker Release? Seabirds in Flight?"

Mariah gently pushed him onto the bed, unable to hide her smile. "You'll see." She was going to make this an experience he'd never forget. "I'll be right back."

She pulled on her robe and went quickly into the living room. She unplugged her boom box from the wall, found the CD she wanted, then carried both back into the bedroom.

John was on the bed, as she'd asked. He was gorgeous—all dark hair and sleek, hard muscles beneath his tanned skin. Lying there against the white sheets, he looked impossibly healthy. How could this physically perfect man have been in a hospital fighting for his life just a few weeks ago?

He was up on one elbow, watching her as she set the CD player on her dresser and plugged it in.

Miller's blood was burning with anticipation. He'd barely been able to get the condom on, he was so aroused. And now Mariah was putting a CD into her portable player, her brightly colored silk robe hanging open, revealing tantalizing glimpses of her incredible body.

When he'd first seen her picture, he'd thought of her as a goddess. He'd had no idea how completely right he had been.

With a swirl of turquoise silk, she turned to face him. "One more thing," she said, giving him a smile that put dimples of mischief and amusement in her cheeks. A small square that looked something like a speaker sat on the bedside table. She touched it, adjusted it, and the sound of flowing water filled the room. "A waterfall," she said. She smiled at him again as she let her robe flutter to the ground. "Close your eyes."

Miller didn't want to. He wanted to look at her—he'd never tire of looking at her.

She moved back to the CD player and turned it on, too, adjusting the volume.

It wasn't music that came on. Miller listened closely, trying to identify the sounds that were playing over the high-quality speakers.

Birds.

They were birdcalls. Sweetly melodic chirping and tweeting.

Mariah sat next to him on the bed, leaning forward to kiss him. "Close your eyes," she said again.

Miller closed them.

He felt her straddle him, felt her kiss him again, her stomach pressed against his erection, the tight beads of her nipples brushing erotically against his chest. He was on fire, but he wanted to please her, so he did what she asked. He stayed on his back and kept his eyes closed. But he couldn't keep from touching her, his hands sweeping down the softness of her skin. He filled his palms with her breasts, loving the sound of her breath catching in her throat.

And then she moved her hips, covering him with her soft heat, and he couldn't help himself. He pressed himself up, wanting more, needing to feel himself inside her. Now. *Now.*

She kissed him again and he groaned. "Mariah, please…"

She shifted her hips again, granting him access, and with one velvet-smooth thrust, he was ensheathed by her.

He held on to her hips, pressing himself more tightly inside her, praying that she wouldn't move even the slightest bit, sure that if she did, he would lose control. Too soon. It was too soon.

But she didn't move. She kissed him instead, her lips gentle against his mouth, his cheek, his chin and jaw, his ear.

"You are now in a very special place," Mariah said softly, laughter in her voice, her breath warm against his ear, "with birds singing and a waterfall trickling…."

Miller opened his eyes to find her smiling down at him, amusement dancing in her whiskey-colored eyes.

"The next time someone tells you to close your eyes and picture yourself in your special place," she continued, "you'll have no problem imagining yourself *right* here. And I mean right here." She moved her hips for emphasis.

Miller had to laugh. And then he had to kiss her. As he claimed her mouth, she began to move slowly on top of him. Each stroke was sheer heaven as she took her sweet time.

She was driving him mad, and she knew it, too. He could tell from the little smile she gave him as she sat up above him.

He reached for her, pulling her down against him, drawing her breasts toward his hungry mouth, pulling hard on her desire-swollen nipples.

She moved faster then, harder, and he moved with her, filling her again and again as she cried out her pleasure. Time seemed to stop as his entire world shrank completely down to this one woman who was touching him, loving him. Nothing else existed, nothing else mattered. He filled himself with her, all his senses working overtime as he watched his own ecstasy mirrored on her face, as he heard her cries and murmurs of pleasure, as her softness and warmth surrounded him completely.

He felt the shuddering thrill of her climax and he buried his face in the softness of her breasts as he, too, went up and over the edge. The rush of his release engulfed him, rocketing him to a dizzying height.

Mariah collapsed upon him as slowly, very slowly, the roar subsided, leaving him warm and relaxed and peacefully calm.

He became aware of Mariah's soft hair against his face. He became aware of the way her breath caught slightly as she sighed contentedly. He became aware of birds singing and the sound of water splashing enticingly down a steep hill.

A special place. Yes. This was a *very* special place.

Mariah turned her head and brushed her lips against his neck. She didn't say the words, but she didn't have to. He knew that she loved him.

This was what it was like to make love with someone who really cared. It was incredible—being loved so completely, on so many levels. It made the rather ordinary act of sex seem a miracle. It heightened all his senses and made his heart seem ten times as big. It took his breath away and filled his lungs with sheer joy and laughter. It made him want to smile—all the time.

Miller wondered if Mariah felt the wonder of this miracle. He wondered if she knew, if she felt it, too.

He didn't say the words, either. He didn't know how.

But he knew without a doubt that he loved her.

She left the photo lab carrying the box of negatives.

The nice man had seen no problem in letting her take them to her friend.

Once inside her car, she lifted the lid and looked inside. One by one, she held the strips of film up to the windshield, using the sunlight to illuminate them. She went through about twenty of the plastic-encased strips before she gave up.

She was going to have to burn the entire box.

She looked down into the box and saw there was a paper folder—the kind that drugstores use to enclose color prints. She pulled it out, almost on a whim. There were no photos inside, but there were several smaller strips of negatives.

She held one to the light and...

Quickly, she pulled out another and another.

These were other photographs of *her*. Somehow that bitch had taken more pictures of *her!*

Her rage was laced with fear. If there were negatives, then somewhere there were photographs.

She was going to have to go back.

She took a deep breath, calming herself. It didn't matter. She was smarter than they were. She could get the photos. She *would* get the photos. She would destroy the evidence and punish the bitch who had brought her this trouble.

Her calm soon turned to anticipation. She *was* smarter than they were. She could do all that, and more.

She put the lid back on the box and threw her car into gear. She had lots to do. *Lots* to do.

Chapter 10

Mariah focused the lens of her camera on John. "Smile," she said.

He laughed as he glanced over at her. "You're taking a picture of me doing the dishes?"

She snapped several photos in rapid succession before looking up from the camera to smile at him. "No, I'm just taking pictures of you. The doing-the-dishes part isn't important. You know, I really wish I'd developed those pictures of you I took that day we first met."

He lifted an eyebrow as he drained the soapy water from the sink and dried his hands on a dish towel. "What? You mean you took pictures of me when I was lying with my face in the sand?"

She had to laugh. "No. I took pictures when I first saw you—when you were out on the beach with Princess. I wonder what I did with that roll of film. It's probably around here somewhere. But I wish I had those pictures to show you for comparison. It's amazing—you look so different now. You look so relaxed and…happy."

"That's because I got lucky this morning." John pulled her close and kissed her below the ear. "And I happen to know that the esteemed Dr. Gerrard Hollis recommends that particular activity we took part in as his number one means of relieving stress. So, yeah, I'm extremely relaxed."

"I'm not sure Dr. Hollis put it in quite those words," Mariah said, laughing in dismay. "Getting lucky."

He kissed her again, on the mouth this time, so sweetly she felt herself start to melt. "I got lucky all right," he said, searching her eyes. "I don't think I've ever felt this lucky in my entire life. I really hit the jackpot when I met you, Mariah."

Mariah's throat felt tight as she gazed back at him. What was he telling her? There was a softness, a gentleness in his eyes that, were she feeling foolhardy enough, she might interpret as love. But she didn't want to interpret it. She didn't want to hope or wish or even *think* about it.

The telephone rang, and she pulled away from him, grateful for the interruption.

It was the doctor's office, finally returning yesterday's call. The doctor seemed to think she could resume normal activities—provided she didn't push herself too hard.

Miller poured himself another cup of coffee as he watched Mariah talk on the phone. He wished he could take *her* picture. Dressed the way she was in only her silk robe, her hair still rumpled from the time they'd spent in bed, she looked incredible—as warm and welcoming and as satisfying as the breakfast they'd made together and shared out on the deck in the soft morning sunlight.

Normally, he resented anyone's intrusion into his morning routine. The morning was his private time. But as he gazed at Mariah, he knew he would enjoy having all of this on a regular basis—breakfast, watching her across the table, even doing the dishes. It was relaxed and easygoing. It felt right. Even the silences were comfortable.

He could easily imagine seeing Mariah's beautiful face first thing every morning, feeling her luscious body next to his every night. He could imagine coming home each evening and losing himself, *submerging* himself in her sweet warmth and love.

That was a dangerous way to be thinking. Mariah had done and said nothing to let him believe she was interested in anything more than a vacation romance. And before they could progress to anything beyond a casual love affair, they both had to come clean and confess as to why they were using false names.

Miller smiled wryly. It was only a matter of time before this investigation was declared defunct. But what was the best way to tell a lover that she didn't know his real name? When was the best time? Right after making love? Or maybe over a quiet dinner? *By the way, darling, you don't really know who I am....*

And he wasn't the only one working under an a.k.a. Mariah, too, had something of her own to share during show-and-tell. Marie Carver. Former CEO of Carver Software out in Phoenix, Arizona.

He'd checked the files. The company was doing fine. There'd been no reports of embezzlement—and no rea-

sons for it either. Marie—Mariah—had inherited her
father's share of the company when he had died and
under her hand it had thrived. Even though she was
no longer CEO, she still owned a large percentage of
the business—which, if it was sold right here and now
would easily put fifteen million dollars into her personal bank account. No, Mariah had no reason to turn
to embezzlement. And according to the IRS, both her
personal and business taxes had all been paid both ac-
curately and on time.

So what was she doing, living under an alias, all
these thousands of miles away from her home?

Miller had tried to find out during breakfast. Asking leading questions, giving her a clear opening to tell
him the truth. But she'd sidestepped all his questions
about her business, and somehow they'd ended up talking about Princess instead.

As she hung up the phone, he tried again.

"Mariah is such a pretty name," he told her, leaning
back against the counter as he sipped his coffee. "What
made your parents name you that?"

"Actually…"

Here it came. She was going to tell him the truth.

"Actually, my parents didn't name me Mariah," she
said. "My grandmother did." She took his mug from
his hands and set it down on the counter, then slid her
arms around his waist.

Miller closed his eyes as she held him tightly, as his
body leapt in response to her sweet softness.

"Mariah was *her* grandmother's name," she told
him between dizzyingly delicious kisses. "My great-
great-grandmother. She was born not far from here, in
Georgia, before the Civil War. According to my grand-

mother, by the time Mariah was twelve, she was an active member of the Underground Railroad. That's partly why I came to Garden Isle. To see where she lived. I've always been fascinated by the stories Grandma told about her."

Miller was wearing only his jeans, and her silk-covered breasts felt incredibly smooth against his bare chest—but not as sinfully good as her skin would feel. Her belt was already loose and it opened easily as he parted the front of her robe and slipped his hands against the softness of her skin, pulling her against him.

She pulled his mouth down to hers and Miller lost himself in her kiss.

He felt her fingers on the button of his jeans and experienced a wave of euphoria. Was this great, or was this great? She wanted him again. Her own attraction to him was clearly as insatiable and intense as his was for her. Mutual overpowering lust.

True, undying love.

That thought came from out of nowhere, and Miller shook it away, unwilling to think about the way he'd felt as he'd held Mariah in his arms after making love.

But it was the way he still felt. It hadn't faded. It hadn't disappeared.

He kissed her harder, wanting only to feel the intense physical pleasure she gave him. It was overpowering, unlike anything he'd ever felt—desire of a caliber he'd never really thought existed. He'd heard people talk about the sensation of being hit by a truck, of being blinded to everything but need, but he'd always thought they were weak. They were weak, and he was strong, except here he was, unable to see anything but Mariah, unable even to catch his breath from the weight of the desire that bore down upon him like a runaway train.

He thought his need for this woman would be abated by making love to her, but that had only served to make him want her more. He'd had a taste of her heaven, and he was shamelessly addicted now.

He lifted her right onto the counter, and she willingly opened her legs to him as he kept on kissing her, his mouth trailing down her neck toward her luscious breasts, one hand working to free himself from his pants and...

Mariah pulled back. "John! We need to get a condom."

What the hell was he doing? He had been mere seconds away from thrusting deeply inside of her with absolutely no protection—without one single *thought* of protection. God help him, this woman drove all sane thoughts clear out of his head.

Mariah looked at the expression on John's face and started to laugh despite the adrenaline that passion had kicked into her system. He looked thoroughly, adorably stunned. "I don't want you to stop," she told him. "I just want you to get a condom." She slid down off the counter, pressing herself against him, loving the sensation of his arousal hard against her stomach. She kissed him quickly. "I'll get one. You wait here."

Mariah's heart was still pounding as she ran down the hall to her bedroom. Her bedside-table drawer was still open, the box of condoms on the top. She grabbed one and the phone rang.

Damn! The cordless phone was there in her bedroom, so she quickly picked it up, praying it wouldn't be one of the ladies from the Garden Isle Historical Society, wanting to talk on and on for fifteen or twenty minutes about the latest event at the library. "Hello?"

"I'm sorry to bother you again, Ms. Robinson, but is John still there?"

It was Daniel with the Asian-sounding last name—the dark-haired young man who was John's personal assistant.

"Um, yes, he is, actually." Mariah carried the phone into the kitchen. "Just a moment, please." She covered the mouthpiece with her hand as she held out the phone to John. "It's for you. It's Daniel."

He fastened his pants before he took the phone—as if Daniel would somehow be able to tell that he was standing there nearly naked and mere moments from sexual fulfillment.

"Yeah," John said into the phone. "What's up?" He met Mariah's eyes briefly and smiled. Even with his jeans zipped, it was still very obvious—at least to the two of them—exactly what was up.

Mariah hadn't bothered fastening her robe, and John's smile faded and his eyes turned even a deeper shade of blue as he looked at her. Another woman might've found the intensity of his expression frightening. But Mariah loved it. She loved the way he seemed to burn for her. She stepped toward him, and he reached inside the thin silk to touch her.

"When?" he said into the phone. He glanced at the clock on the stove and swore softly. "That soon?" Another pause. "Yeah, all right. I'll be there."

He ended the connection with a push of a button, and Mariah took the phone from him, pressing the condom packet into his hand.

He swore again. "Mariah, I'm sorry, I have to go."

"Daniel can wait five minutes, can't he?" She unbuttoned his pants.

"Mariah—"

She pulled down his zipper. "*Three* minutes...?"

He groaned as she touched him, then crushed his mouth to hers. Before she could even blink, she found herself back up on the counter. She heard the tear of the wrapper, felt him pull back for just a second, and then she felt him fill her with a hard, fast thrust that took her breath away.

He groaned, too, still kissing her as he drove himself into her again and again, setting a wild, delirious, feverish pace. It was raw, almost savage sex, and Mariah dug her fingernails into his back, urging him on, wanting more, even more.

It was breathtakingly exhilarating. She had never been made love to like this before. She'd never had a man go so totally out of control over her before. It was more exciting than she'd ever dreamed. He was touching her everywhere, kissing her, caressing her in ways that filled her with fire, and she exploded almost instantly with pleasure, crying out his name.

He followed her lead, and she felt the power of his release as it rocketed through him, shaking him, pushing her even higher to a place of even more pleasure.

He held her tightly, his face buried in her neck as they both struggled to catch their breaths.

"I know you have to go now," Mariah said, when she finally could speak. "But is there any chance I can bribe you with the promise of dinner so that you'll come back later and do that again?"

He lifted his head and laughed. "The hell with dinner. I think we've discovered an entirely new use for the kitchen." His smile softened. "You know, I can go for days without a meal, but I don't think I can go for more than a few hours without making love to you."

John gently touched the side of her face, tracing her lips lightly with his thumb, as if he could see from her eyes how much she melted inside when he said things like that. And why shouldn't he see? She wasn't trying to hide anything from him. She'd told him she loved him. It wasn't a secret.

And for one heart-stopping moment, Mariah seemed almost sure that he was going to tell her that her feelings were mutual, that he loved her, too.

But he only said, "I'll be back by seven at the latest."

Still gazing into her eyes, John leaned forward and kissed her gently on the lips, then pulled her forward and helped her down from the counter. He kissed her again before disappearing for a moment into the bathroom as she straightened her robe and tied her belt. When he came back down the hall, he was pulling on his T-shirt.

"I've got to hurry now," John said, stopping to kiss her on the mouth—a quick brushing of the lips that turned into a much longer, lingering kiss. He groaned softly, forcing himself to pull away from her. "I'll see you later, okay?"

"Seven o'clock," Mariah said.

As he moved toward the sliding doors, past the dining-room table, he suddenly stopped short. "My God!"

"What?"

John picked up one of the pictures that were spread out on the table. It was a color photo she'd taken of Serena with that cheap, disposable camera. "Where did you get this?"

"I took it—I think it was a few weeks ago. Why?"

There was an intensity in his gaze that she'd never seen before. It made the blue of his eyes seem hard and flinty. He swore sharply, almost excitedly, adding, "This is good. This is *very* good. Do you have any other pictures of her?"

Mariah gazed at him, her heart sinking like lead into the pit of her stomach. Why should John care if she had photographs of Serena? Unless he was still… No, she refused to think that way.

"Yes," she said, moving toward the table and turning on several of the lights that were still positioned around that part of the room. "I managed to take four or five of them without her noticing. She's amazingly photogenic. Still, she doesn't like to have her picture taken. It's kind of strange."

"Yeah, I know," he said. He looked down at the seemingly haphazard piles of pictures as if he wanted to search through them but was afraid to mess up her organizational system. "Where are the others? Do you still have them?"

Unless he was still infatuated with Serena… This time she couldn't prevent the thought from coming through.

"They're here somewhere," Mariah said, quickly flipping through one of the piles, again cutting off that errant thought. He didn't want Serena. He wanted *her.* He'd told her that—she knew it was true. How could he have made love to her the way he just had if it wasn't true? "Probably close to where you found the first one." She unearthed three more pictures of Serena.

One photo caught the blond Englishwoman in nearly perfect profile. The three others were either three-quarter or full face.

"May I have these?" John asked.

Mariah laughed. "You're kidding."

He suddenly seemed to realize the inappropriateness of his request. Just a short time ago—mere *minutes* ago—he'd been making love to Mariah, yet now he wanted her to give him pictures of the woman he'd last dated. Dated—and at the very least, kissed. Mariah didn't want to think about the possibility that John had made love to Serena, but it was far too easy to imagine the two of them together.

John shook his head. "It's not what you think."

"It's not? Then please, tell me. What exactly *is* it? I'd like to know. Why do you want these pictures?" She was willing to give him the benefit of the doubt. Maybe he *did* have some genuine reason for wanting those pictures.

But John shook his head. "Look, I'm sorry. Never mind, all right?" He put the pictures back on top of the pile she'd found them in. "It's just…I was going to send one to a friend of mine up in New York. I think the two of them would really hit it off—she's just his type and…"

He was lying through his teeth. He was standing there and telling her some lame *lie* as if he actually thought she would accept it. But she didn't buy it, and he knew it.

He swore softly. "I can't tell you why I really need them, Mariah, but I promise you, my wanting those pictures doesn't have anything to do with you and me."

"I really don't want you to take them," Mariah said.

"I'm sorry. Serena didn't know I took them, and...I don't want you to have them."

"That's all right." He nodded. "That's okay. I understand. Just...trust me, please?"

Mariah folded her arms. "You're going to be late," she said. "You better go."

But he hesitated. "I'm going to tell you everything really soon, all right?"

She tried to smile. "I'm not certain just what happened here, but sure. Whatever you want to tell me, whenever you want to tell it to me, would be nice."

"I will." John gazed at her steadily, real consternation in his eyes. "I'll tell you soon." But then he squinted out the door, up at the hazy blueness of the sky. "Damn, I don't have any sunblock with me," he said, and when he turned to look back at her, she could see a hint of that same dishonesty in his eyes. "I'm going to fry without it. Do you have anything number fifteen or higher that I could use?"

Mariah knew that if she left the room, he was going to pocket those pictures of Serena. He was going to *steal* them, even though she'd told him point-blank that she didn't want him to have them. Trust me, he'd said. Trust me.

She cleared her throat. "Yeah, it's in the bedroom— in my beach bag. I'll get it." She turned away. What could she do? Short of accusing him of theft or denying him the use of her sunblock? *Please let me be wrong.*

Miller watched Mariah walk down the hall and into her bedroom.

Quickly, he took two pictures of Serena—the profile and the best of the full-face shots—and slipped them into the back pocket of his jeans. He hated the fact he had to do it this way—to take them without Mariah's permission—but these photos would be invaluable in tracking down Serena Westford. With a photo of this quality on an APB sent to all law enforcement agencies, the FBI would actually have a chance of finding her again before she altered her appearance. It was a slim chance, but a chance just the same.

And it wasn't going to be long until this part of the case was deemed over and done with, and he'd be able to tell Mariah everything. Surely if she knew the truth, she wouldn't deny him access to the photos.

She returned with the sunblock, and he quickly spread it across his nose and cheekbones.

He kissed her again, one last time, trying to tell her with his kiss the way she made him feel. Despite the wariness in her eyes, she kissed him warmly, sweetly.

"I'll see you later," he said. He slipped out the door and onto the porch where Princess was napping in the shade. "Come on," he said to the dog. "We've gotta run. We're already late."

He set off down the beach at an easy jog, Princess loping beside him. His legs felt weak, his body still buzzing from the pleasure he'd allowed himself to partake of only moments before.

On impulse, he turned to look back at the cottage. Mariah was standing on the deck, watching him. He waved, lifting an arm, and she waved back.

Picking up his speed, he smiled. Yes indeed, he was going to be late to this meeting with Pat Blake. When Daniel had called the second time, Blake's plane had already landed at the little airport on the mainland. His car would be pulling into the resort driveway in a matter of moments, and Miller would arrive a good five minutes after him—unshowered, unshaved and smelling distinctly like Mariah. Sweet, sexy Mariah. What a reason to be late….

Blake would nearly swallow his teeth at the sight of him—Miller couldn't remember ever attending a meeting such as this one in anything other than a dark suit and tie. But all would be forgiven the moment he produced these photographs.

Miller hoped Mariah would be as quick to forgive when he told her the truth. God, he wanted to tell her the truth soon. And maybe then she'd tell him why she was here on Garden Isle using a fake name.

So Mariah was just a nickname. What did your parents call you? That's what he should have asked. He should've pushed the conversation in that direction, but he'd been waylaid by her kisses. He'd been overcome by the promise of ecstasy. All rational thought had simply ceased to exist.

Damn, she drove him out of his mind.

He turned to look back once more at Mariah's house, but this time she was gone.

Mariah watched in the dim darkroom light as the photos she took just that morning slowly developed. She was feeling that familiar gnawing of worry and upset that she'd worked so hard to eradicate over the past few months.

Stress was making her shoulders tight and she rolled them, silently chanting her mantra: No worries. No problem.

But she was lying to herself. She *was* worried. There *was* a problem.

She was in love with a man who'd not only lied, but had stolen from her.

As she rinsed the chemicals from the paper, Jonathan Mills smiled directly up at her from the photo, his eyes warm and flashing with amusement. Mariah looked more closely at his eyes, trying to see if maybe his dishonesty had been captured through the camera's lens. She wanted to know if he'd been lying right from the start. But all she could see was warmth and life.

The pictures she'd taken in her kitchen were sharply in contrast to the shots she'd taken on the beach the day they'd met. Mariah had found that roll of film and developed it first. Those pictures now hung, drying. John's gaunt silhouette against the backdrop of a lightening sky. His profile—a face etched with pain. He looked cold and distant. But he didn't look deceptive.

She wasn't exactly sure what she was looking for—perhaps a shiftiness in the eyes. Or a glint of malice. In reality, it was probably the case that the most deceptive people gave away nothing at all. Her stomach started to hurt and she rolled her shoulders again. *No worries.*

Mariah carefully hung the more recent pictures of John next to the ones from the first roll of film. Someone glancing at them all would find it hard to believe this smiling man was the same person as in the others.

Mariah looked again into John's laughing eyes. This was the man who'd come to her for comfort as he'd finally allowed himself to grieve for his friend's death. This was the man who had made love to her so passionately. This was the man who had told her he wanted *her,* not Serena. She found it hard to believe that this was the same man who lied to her, who had actually *stolen* from her.

Mariah hadn't allowed herself to look through her piles of photos after he'd first left. And she'd hated herself for mistrusting him when she'd finally given in to the temptation. But she'd been right to mistrust him. Two pictures were missing. John had taken two of the photos of Serena even after Mariah had specifically said she didn't want him to have them.

The phone rang, and Mariah picked up the cordless extension she'd brought downstairs with her, half hoping it was John and half hoping it was not. "Hello?"

"Hey, girl, how's your back?" It was Laronda, the site coordinator from Foundations for Families.

"It doesn't hurt at all anymore," Mariah told her. "And I just got the all clear from the doctor this morning. I'm allowed to go back to work."

"God is truly watching over me," Laronda exclaimed melodramatically. "I'm in desperate need of roofers. Tropical storm Otto is heading on almost a direct path to the Washburtons' house. It wasn't supposed to rain—at least not hard—until the end of the week, and we gambled and took advantage of a local electrician who had some time off. We had the electrical work done before the roof was finished. But now the weather bureau is saying oops they made a big mistake. We're gonna get high winds *and* flooding rain. We need to get that baby sealed up tight before old Otto makes some bad voodoo by mixing water with those wires. Can you help? We're doing a blitz—round the clock from now until we're done. I'll take you for as long a shift as you can give me."

As usual, Mariah wasn't wearing a watch. "What time is it?"

"Nearly noon. Just say yes and I can have the van

pick you up in fifteen minutes. Door-to-door service today."

"I'll be ready. But, Laronda—"

"Bless you, girl!"

"I have to be home by seven."

"We'll get you there."

Mariah took one last look at her pictures of John before she turned off the light and went up the basement stairs. She'd be back by seven, all right. And then she was going to get some answers.

Chapter 11

Mariah's sliding glass door was open, the screen un-locked.

"Mariah?" Miller called.

No one answered. Nothing moved.

Miller stepped into the house and closed the screen door behind him.

Without Mariah to brighten the place up with her laughter and life, the room seemed almost shabby. Miller moved quietly to the dining-room table, intending to slip the two photographs he'd borrowed and had copied back into the pile. She'd never even know they were gone.

In theory, it worked, but in theory, Mariah hadn't checked up on him. In reality, she had. The other pictures of Serena had been separated out from the stack. She knew he'd taken two of them. He set the two in question down on the table with the others.

It didn't really matter. He'd had every intention of telling her the truth—and he could now. During his short meeting with Pat Blake, this portion of the case had been officially closed. Hanging around here and waiting for Serena to return had been deemed a waste of time and finances. Even at this moment, Daniel was back at the resort, packing up the equipment.

Miller had been helping him, determined to get the work done and his report filed in time to meet Mariah for dinner at seven. But something Daniel had said during the meeting had started him thinking. Daniel had pointed out that in the past, Serena had always been so careful about having her picture taken. Was it possible that she knew about these pictures?

Miller knew it damn well was possible that she was on to him. She could have found the bugs in her house and correctly identified Miller as FBI. And if that was the case, she might've purposely left these pictures behind as part of some kind of weird game she was playing.

But what exactly was that game?

Had she left intending to alter her appearance so thoroughly that leaving photos behind didn't even matter? Was this possibly some kind of arrogant challenge?

Or had she truly slipped up? Had she found the microphones in her house and run scared? And after she calmed down enough, would she realize that because Mariah was a photographer it was more than likely she had pictures of Serena, taken either intentionally or unintentionally? And if that was the case, would Serena come back? And if she did come back, would Mariah then be in danger?

That thought had made Miller break out in a cold

sweat, and he'd called Mariah, but she didn't pick up the phone. Thinking she might be on the beach enjoying the early-afternoon sunshine, Miller had left Daniel to deal with the equipment as he took the car and drove out to Mariah's cottage as quickly as he could.

"Mariah?" he said again, moving into the kitchen.

A jar of peanut butter was out and open on the kitchen counter. She'd told him the first time they'd met that leaving food out in the kitchen was an invitation to disaster. Ants or enormous American cockroaches would come in almost immediately and they were nearly impossible to get rid of.

A plate with bread crumbs sat nearby—as if she'd made herself a sandwich there, then taken it with her as she'd left.

Left to go where? Her bike was leaning up against the side of the house. He'd seen it when he'd arrived. There was no sign of her in the yard or out on the beach.

Wherever she'd gone, she'd left in a hurry.

Miller made a complete circuit of the house. There were signs in the bathroom that Mariah had taken a quick shower—a wet towel had been tossed onto the floor along with the robe she'd been wearing this morning. A tube of toothpaste was open and left out on the sink. In her bedroom, the bed was unmade, the sheets still rumpled from their lovemaking.

Miller sat down on the edge of the bed, letting himself lie back among the sheets. He closed his eyes, breathing in the sweet scent of Mariah's perfume. Where had she gone in such a blessed hurry?

Even with his eyes closed, he could picture the house and all its telltale signs of a hasty exit. He was known for his ability to take the clues he'd been given and hypothesize the most likely scenario. Only this time, he didn't much care for the scenario he'd almost instantly come up with.

He had one Mariah Robinson living under an assumed name, telling him specifically that he could not have those pictures of Serena. He had Mariah go through the photos after he'd left, pulling out the shots of Serena and discovering that he had, in fact, taken two of those pictures with him. He had Mariah quickly take a shower, quickly make a sandwich and then leave the house in such a hurry that she didn't even lock the back door.

Going where? To meet Serena? To warn her that Miller had those pictures?

Miller could place Mariah—or Marie Carver, her real name—in Phoenix, Arizona, three years ago, during the time Serena had been there, too, preparing to off husband number five. The possibility that the two women had met at that time opened the door to all kinds of nasty questions, such as: Had Mariah/Marie come here to Garden Isle to act as some kind of accomplice or assistant? Was Mariah/Marie some kind of Black Widow killer-in-training?

Miller sat up. Dammit! He'd obviously been working for the FBI for too long. How could he possibly think such things about Mariah? Sweet, gentle Mariah...

He hadn't checked the basement because it was dark, but now he went down there anyway, hoping to find something that would tell him where Mariah had gone.

He'd never been inside her darkroom, and he turned on the light as he pushed open the door. It was a small room, with built-in counters lining the walls. It had a sink and shelves for chemicals and other supplies—even a small refrigerator for storing film. Different kinds of equipment were set up on the counters, including something big that looked like an enlarger.

Miller knew with just one glance that this room—combined with the beachfront property and the incredible view of the ocean—was the reason Mariah had rented this particular cottage. Dozens of places were more lavishly furnished or nicely decorated, but Mariah cared more about having a place with a darkroom.

There were photos hanging from some kind of clothesline assembly, curling slightly around the edges as they dried. Miller looked closer. The pictures were of him.

They were black-and-white photographs, but they still managed to capture the beauty of the sunrise. He and Princess were just silhouettes in many of them, but in several, Mariah had used her zoom lens, and he could clearly see his face, etched with relentless fatigue. The pictures echoed his pain.

But there, right in the middle of these pictures of his bleakly grim face, was a close-up. It was one of the pictures Mariah had taken just that morning. He was smiling at her, smiling into the camera.

Miller stared at the picture. It was him. He knew it was him. He remembered her taking the picture. He remembered smiling. But he'd never seen himself looking quite like that before. His eyes were reflecting the morning light coming in through the window and they seemed to sparkle with warmth and life. His smile was wide and sincere.

He looked nothing like a man who had been dubbed "The Robot."

And he wasn't, Miller realized. When he was with

Mariah, he *wasn't* a robot. He was a real, live, flesh-and-blood man, capable of feeling—and releasing—deep emotions.

He closed his eyes, remembering the way she had held him as he'd given in and cried for Tony for the first time in two years. He remembered the strength of the emotion he'd felt as he'd held her in his arms after making love.

That man, that flesh-and-blood man would never have entertained such doubts about Mariah. It was only "The Robot" who could think that way—mistrusting everyone.

God, he wanted Mariah to come back. He wanted her to transform him once again into that real man. He despised himself for being this way, for having all these doubts about her.

With one last look back at Mariah's photographs, Miller turned off the darkroom light and went upstairs. As he locked the back door, he heard the crunch of tires in the gravel driveway and turned to look out the front window, hoping it was Mariah.

It wasn't.

It was *Serena's* car pulling into the driveway. It was Serena. My God, she'd come back. Miller's heart nearly stopped. Then it kicked back in, beating double time with a vengeance.

As he watched, she parked next to his car and got out. She didn't seem perturbed by the fact that his car was there—she knew he and Mariah were friends. And Miller knew from the time he'd spent with her that Serena had complete confidence in her sexual allure. Miller had no doubt that Serena didn't view Maria as any kind of a rival.

He moved to the front door, intending to step outside when Serena rang the bell. But she didn't ring, she just opened the screen and came in.

"Mariah's not here," he told her. "I stopped by to see how she was doing. The back door was unlocked, and—"

Serena kissed him. It was a kiss meant to curl his hair, to thoroughly numb him, to drop him—dizzy with passion and desire—to his knees.

Instead, Miller had to fight to hide his revulsion. She'd caught him off guard, that much was true. He kept close track of her hands, suddenly keenly aware that this woman might very well have killed at least seven times by forcing a knife blade into her husbands' hearts. It was true that he was not her husband, but it was possible she knew he was FBI. Although if she *did* know that, this was one hell of a dangerous game she was playing by returning to Garden Isle.

"Did you miss me?" she murmured.

"Absolutely," he lied.

As quickly as she'd started kissing him, she broke away, making a quick circuit around the room, stopping to look at the photos on the dining-room table. She picked up one of the pictures of herself.

"Oh, good," she said. "Mariah must've set these aside to give to me. I'd asked her about them last week. She's a remarkable photographer, isn't she? I mean, for an amateur."

"Yeah," he said. "She's pretty good."

"For an amateur," Serena repeated.

As Miller watched, she slipped all four of the pictures into her purse.

"So where did our little Mariah—or should I say *big*

Mariah—go off to?" Serena mused. "Her tool belt's not by the door. I'll wager she's off trying to save the world, one family at a time."

Miller couldn't believe it. For all his highly touted skills as one of the FBI's top agents, he hadn't thought to check and see if Mariah's tool belt was missing. Sure enough. Her belt and her backpack were both gone.

"I've never been down this hall past the loo," Serena said, disappearing down the hallway that led to Mariah's bedroom. "What's down here? Her bedroom probably."

Miller followed her. "Serena, don't go back there."

"Why not?"

"Because you're invading Mariah's privacy."

"She left the door unlocked, didn't she?" Serena said almost gaily, sitting down on Mariah's unmade bed, surveying the small bedroom. "I don't know why she lives in a little dumpy place like this. She has plenty of money, you know."

Miller stood in the doorway. "We should leave."

He would've had to be a fool not to catch the meaning of the glint in her eyes. She was coming on to him. She was attempting to seduce him right there in Mariah's room, on Mariah's bed.

"I suppose we could go to your place." Serena leaned back on both elbows as she gazed up at him. "But I confess I like it here. Think of the excitement from knowing that Mariah could come home any moment and find us here together."

God, the thought made him sick, but he couldn't deny that this was what he'd wanted for so long. He'd wanted an opportunity to be in a position where it would seem natural for him to propose marriage to this woman.

But he hadn't wanted to do it like this.

Not here in this room where he'd discovered such pleasures with Mariah.

But he couldn't take Serena back to his room at the resort where Daniel was packing up crates of electronic equipment. They'd brought the gear into the resort in inconspicuous suitcases, but there had been no need to leave with it that way, so most of it was clearly labeled with its destination, Quantico—FBI headquarters—in big black, official-looking letters.

"Why don't we take a walk on the beach?" Miller suggested.

"In these shoes?" Serena reached for his hand, tugging him down so that he was sitting next to her on the bed.

Mariah's bed.

It took everything Miller had in him not to stand up, not to pull away. Apprehending Serena was his job. Catching a killer was never fun. He didn't have to like it, he just had to do it.

He tried to convince himself that he wasn't betraying Mariah as he let Serena push him back onto the bed. He tried not to think about what Mariah would assume if she came home to find him here with Serena, entangled in an embrace in the very bed in which he'd made love to Mariah just mere hours earlier.

This wasn't real. He felt distant, removed both physically and emotionally from this woman who was kissing him so passionately. That distance worried him—surely she'd be able to tell that she left him feeling cold. Surely she'd realize that he wanted to kiss her about as much as he wanted to kiss Daniel. Less.

He'd made one hell of a mistake in assuming that Serena had gone for good. He'd messed things up royally. He'd made love to Mariah this morning, and this afternoon he was going to propose marriage to Serena.

Serena ground herself against him, and, suddenly giddy, Miller knew the truth. He didn't want to do this. But what was he supposed to do? Was he supposed to tell both Daniel Tonaka and Patrick Blake that he was taking himself off the case? How could he do that after coming this far? The setup had worked after all—he had the suspect exactly where he wanted her.

Or maybe she had *him* right where she wanted him.

Daniel was sure to understand and forgive him. But Blake wouldn't. Not after getting to this point. Blake would send him in for that psych evaluation, assuming that Miller had finally snapped. The unit shrink was sure to find him crazy—crazy in love with Mariah.

Miller was just about to push Serena off him when she spoke.

"Please," she said, kissing his face and his neck as she sat straddling him, her head bent over him, her golden hair finding its way into his mouth. "Please, John. I know that you want me, darling, but please, can't we wait to do this until after we're married?"

Miller was astonished. He nearly laughed aloud. *She* was on top of him. She was the seductress, yet her words sounded as if she were an innocent being seduced. She was overpowering, yet she was presenting him with the illusion of being the powerful one. The approach must've worked well for her in the past. He'd never once—in any of their conversations—mentioned marriage, yet she spoke of it as if they'd been discussing it for weeks.

He spit her hair out of his mouth.

"Please, darling," Serena whispered. "We can fly to Las Vegas—be married by tonight."

It was too easy. He couldn't turn her down. He'd been after her for too long.

Still, he hesitated. Mariah would be devastated.

Yet to turn Serena down meant that when the photos of her next victim—and there was sure to be a next victim—crossed Miller's desk, he would know he could have prevented that death. And the next one, and the next one. He would know that he could have stopped her. And he wouldn't be able to bear that. He wouldn't be able to handle having failed. He *could* stop her, right now, right here.

"I'll charter a flight," Miller said to Serena.

He didn't want to do it, but he didn't have a choice.

Chapter 12

Mariah could hear the phone ringing and she took the stairs up to the deck two at a time.

Maybe it was John. Maybe he was finally calling to tell her why he'd left a message canceling last night's dinner plans.

His insomnia was contagious. She'd spent most of last night tossing and turning—sometimes feeling hurt, sometimes concerned, sometimes terrified that she'd been played for a fool.

She scooped up the phone, praying she'd reached it before the answering machine kicked on. "Hello?" she said breathlessly.

"Oh, good. You *are* there." It was Serena. "Can you come over and see my new place?"

Mariah cursed silently. "Now's not a really good time because I've—"

"I've rented that house right up the hill from you," Serena told her.

"The big one?"

"I suppose compared to *your* place, it might be considered big—"

"Serena, that house is a palace. You've wanted to live there since you first came to the island. How on earth did you manage to arrange to move in there?"

Serena lowered her voice. "Oh, I've only got it for a short time. There was a week-and-a-half block in between renters. It's expensive, but considering that this is my honeymoon—"

"Your *what?*"

"I flew out to Vegas last night and got married," Serena said with a silvery laugh. "It was rather unexpected."

Married. Serena was married. Who did she know well enough to marry? Not Jonathan Mills? Dear God, had she gone and married John? Mariah felt a flash of disbelieving heat followed quickly by a blast of cold fear. "Who's the lucky man?" she managed to ask, somehow sounding casually nonchalant.

Serena just laughed again. "That's my surprise. I want you to come over and meet him."

Serena's new husband couldn't possibly be John. He wouldn't do that to her. Mariah refused to believe that he was capable of such a thing. He'd told her he wanted *her,* not Serena. He'd promised her he wouldn't sleep with Serena. Of course, she hadn't made him promise that he wouldn't *marry* Serena….

"Serena, just tell me who he is."

"If you ride your bike, it'll take you even less than

three minutes to get up here," Serena said, laughter bubbling in her voice. "See you in a few."

Mariah stared at the telephone receiver, listening to the buzz of the disconnected line. With a curse, she hung up the phone.

She was going to have to go up there.

Not to please Serena, who clearly wanted to show off the house, but to put her own mind at ease.

She'd go up there, see for herself that the man Serena had married wasn't John. She'd see for herself that he was probably some older man with the ability to write million-dollar checks without blinking.

This was good, Mariah told herself as she tied the laces of her sneakers and went out to where her bike was leaning against the side of her house. With Serena safely married, Mariah wouldn't have to worry about the blonde actively competing for John's time and attention.

Provided, of course, he came back from wherever he'd gone. And provided he came equipped with a good explanation as to why he'd stolen those photographs.

"What are you looking at?"

Miller turned to see Serena standing in the door to the elegantly high-ceilinged formal dining room. "Just...checking out the view from the windows."

She pointed through the treetops. "Look. There's the roof of Mariah's little cottage."

Miller nodded. He knew. That's what he'd been looking at.

He hadn't planned on living quite so close to Mariah. But Serena had rented this monstrously huge example of modern architecture on the morning before they were married and had insisted they return here for their "honeymoon."

He'd intended for them to stay in Nevada. He'd planned to call Mariah from a pay phone in one of the casinos to tell her that he was sorry, but he'd been pulled out of town on business—he wouldn't be back for a few weeks. He'd hoped Mariah would never have to find out about his charade of a marriage to Serena.

But...Serena hated Vegas.

And when he'd offered to take her on a honeymoon anywhere, *any*where in the world, she chose Garden Isle. She was adamant about returning there, and although Miller had put up a good fight, he'd eventually had to give in for fear she'd become suspicious.

That, of course, was assuming she wasn't suspicious of him in the first place.

"I love this room," Serena said, circling the banquet-sized table. "We ought to throw a dinner party."

"Sounds good to me."

She stepped closer to him and slipped her arms around his waist, embracing him from behind. "Or maybe we should just have our own *private* dinner party."

He tried to sound sincere. "That sounds even better." Miller gently pulled free from her arms. "Look, Serena, I called my doctor this morning," he told her. "He said it could be a few months before I'm...back to normal." He cleared his throat tactfully. "You know..."

He'd told her last night—their wedding night—that he was still suffering from the side effects of the chemotherapy he'd recently undergone. He'd informed her that one of those side effects was impotence. He'd told her it was a temporary condition, and he'd apologized for not telling her sooner.

She'd offered to see what she could do to arouse him, but he'd quickly made up some story about how he'd been advised not even to try since trying and failing could cycle into a more permanent psychological problem.

She hadn't been too upset.

They'd spent the night watching old movies on one of those classic-movie cable channels. Miller had stayed awake even when Serena had dozed off. He didn't much like the idea of waking up with a cold blade of steel in his chest. Or not waking up at all.

He'd slept some on the plane back east, knowing that Daniel was awake and watching out for him.

"I've decided what I want for a wedding gift," Serena told him.

"You have?" This time, he encircled her in his arms, brushing his lips against her forehead. Her perfume was too strong, too floral, too cloying. He forced himself to smile down at her.

"Yes," she said. "This house. It's on the market, you know."

This was good. This was very good. According to her pattern, she would ask him for a check or a transfer of funds into her private account. She would tell him that part of the gift would be the thrill of making the purchase herself from the money he had given her.

"I'll call the broker first thing tomorrow," Miller said.

She pulled back slightly. "You know what I would really love?"

"Something more than this house?"

She laughed. "No. But I'd like to negotiate this deal myself. I'd love to be able to write a check for a substantial deposit from my own account."

Miller kissed her again, as condescendingly as possible. "If that would make you happy, I'll simply transfer enough money into your checking account."

She kissed him again.

"Oh, my God!"

There was a clatter in the doorway, and Miller looked up from Serena's lips and found himself gazing directly into Mariah's horrified eyes.

Her bike helmet spun on the hardwood floor where she'd dropped it.

"Oh, hello," Serena said. "Funny, I didn't hear the bell."

"There was note on the door saying to come in," Mariah said, her eyes never leaving Miller's. Somehow she managed to sound completely calm.

"Isn't this the most exciting surprise ever?" Serena enthused, taking Miller's hand and pulling him toward Mariah. "Introducing Mr. and Mrs. Jonathan Mills. Can you believe it?"

"No." Mariah shook her head. "No, I can't, actually." She laughed, and as Miller watched, the sheer hurt in her eyes turned to scorn. "Or, God—maybe I can. Maybe the sad thing is that I *can* believe it. Excuse me, I have to go."

She scooped her helmet up off the floor and headed for the stairs.

Serena followed her. "Mariah, don't you want to see the house?"

"No," Mariah said, her voice echoing in the three-story entryway. "No, Serena, I don't want to see your house. I'm very happy for you. Just be aware of the fact that your husband doesn't think twice about breaking his promises, and you'll be fine."

"What is *that* supposed to mean?" Serena asked plaintively.

Miller opened the sliders that led to the small deck outside the dining room. There were stairs that led down and connected to the master bedroom's deck, and more stairs that went to the ground. He quickly went down them, intercepting Mariah just as she reached her bicycle.

"I don't have anything to say to you," she said tightly.

He held the handlebars of her bicycle to keep her from moving. "Yeah, well, I have something to say to you."

She threw her helmet onto the ground in anger. "Oh, yeah? Like what? What could you possibly have to say to me?"

"Mariah, I can't tell you what this is all about, but please, just trust me, okay? You *have* to trust me—"

She tried to jerk her bike away from him. "I don't have to do *any*thing—and the last thing I'm ever going to do again is *trust* you. You son of a bitch!"

Miller held tightly to her bike, talking fast and low. "Mariah, listen to me. Go away. Leave the island. Go to New York, or I don't know, back to Phoenix—it doesn't matter where you go. Just stay away from here for a week or two—"

She interrupted him with a terse phrase that instructed him to do the anatomically impossible as she wrenched her bike away from him. But she paused, looking back at him, heartbreaking hurt in her eyes. "To think I actually wasted my love on you," she whispered.

Miller watched her ride away, clenching his teeth to keep from calling out after her.

He turned back to the house, catching a flutter of movement out of the corner of his eye. Gazing up at the dining-room deck, he had to wonder. Had Serena been up there, watching them? And if so, what exactly had she seen?

This was going to be fun. More fun than she'd imagined.

There was something between them. Something strong. From the level of her upset, it seemed pretty obvious that he'd done It to her. Silly cow. Didn't she know men were pigs?

She deserved to die—to melt along with all of those stupid pictures she shot, day after day.

And he... She was going to make him watch before she separated his ugly soul from his even uglier body.

Yes, this *was* going to be fun.

Mariah stood in the basement, smashing dishes against the wall.

Maybe this would help. Each plate she threw was an outlet for her anger and hurt. Each plate she threw was accompanied by a bloodcurdling scream of rage.

Her voice was hoarse and her throwing arm was sore, but she kept at it, hoping, *praying* that eventually this raw wound where her heart used to be would begin to scab over.

She'd fallen off her bike on her way down the hill and scraped one elbow and both knees. But she hadn't cried. She *refused* to cry.

She cleaned up her scrapes in the bathroom, then took her suitcases down from the bedroom closet. She packed most of her clothes before she found herself here, breaking plates.

John had broken his promise.

Clearly, when he'd made it, that promise had meant nothing to him. *She* had meant nothing to him. He'd no doubt made love to her—no, not made love, had sex. It had been nothing more than sex, with the intention of never seeing her again. He'd probably already made his wedding plans with Serena.

Another piece of china hit the wall, shattering into a thousand pieces, just the way her heart had been broken.

And Mariah couldn't hold back her tears any longer. She crumpled onto the basement floor and cried.

"Can you hear me?" Miller said into the flower vase, making an adjustment to the miniature receiver he wore in his right ear.

"Roger," Daniel said from his position about a quarter mile to the south of the house. "Let's check those babies in the dining room once more before we move on into the bedroom."

Miller went into the elegant dining room where he'd planted a number of nearly invisible microphones underneath the huge table, along the sideboard, on several of the chairs and on the edges of one or two picture frames.

He stood in the center of the room. "Do you have me?"

"Loud and clear," came Daniel's reply. "Hang on a sec. Just let me fine tune this puppy... Got it."

The surveillance device in Daniel's car had been designed to look like nothing more than an intricate and expensive car stereo system. It was incredibly complicated to program—Miller was glad Daniel was the one doing it. He preferred the straightforward equipment that came inside the tinted glass of a surveillance van.

He wouldn't be able to wear his in-ear receiver tonight. Not as long as there was a possibility that Serena might find it.

"You know, I'm going to be fine here tonight. You could do this surveillance in comfort from the resort. She's not going to try anything until my bank transfers that money into her account," Miller told his partner.

"Yeah, I know," Daniel said. "I'd just feel better being close—at least for now. There's something in the air that's making my hair stand on end."

"Storm's coming," Miller said, moving to look out the window at the ocean.

A bank of dark clouds was gathering on the horizon. The late-afternoon sun was still shining, but the air was heavy with humidity and hard to breathe.

"Yeah, maybe that's it," Daniel said. "Whatever the case, I'll be out here, mainlining coffee and listening to every word you say. So don't say or do anything you don't want me to hear."

That wasn't going to be a problem. Miller found himself gazing down at the roof of Mariah's house. Was she in there right now, tearing all her pictures of him into tiny shreds? Was she in her bedroom, packing up her clothes and her CDs and her funny little speaker that made such realistic-sounding water noises? *Imagine yourself in a special place...*

"Any sign of Mrs. Mills?" Daniel asked.

Miller snapped himself back to the present, listening hard for any signs of movement in the house. When Serena had announced that she was taking a walk on the beach, he'd begged off. He claimed fatigue, but in fact wanted to use the opportunity to plant and test the surveillance system. He'd managed to get quite a number of the nearly invisible mikes placed while she was there in the house, but it was much easier doing it this way. He looked at his watch. Serena had left fifteen minutes ago. It was entirely possible that she was on her way back.

"I, um, haven't exactly been keeping track," he admitted.

There was a long silence from Daniel's end of the line. "John, I need you here one hundred percent," he finally said. "If you can't do that—"

Miller cleared his throat. "Look, Daniel, *I* need you to run over to Mariah's and encourage her to leave the island. Can you do that for me?"

"I'm a step ahead of you," Daniel told him. "I tapped into the phone lines and I've been monitoring her outgoing calls. It occurred to me that she might be in a position to jeopardize your cover if she decided to share with Serena the fact that you and she spent the night together on the eve of your wedding." He paused. "I may be assuming too much here, but I know that you like this lady an awful lot. That and your lateness to the meeting with Blake clued me in to the fact that you and she—"

"What's your point?"

"The fact is, she *is* leaving. I heard her call for a taxi for this evening. For seven o'clock. She asked for a cab with plenty of trunk room. She told the dispatcher she had quite a bit of luggage."

"Thank God." Miller closed his eyes in relief. Mariah was leaving the island. He could stop worrying about her safety. He knew it was highly unlikely that Serena would hurt anyone other than her targeted victim. Still, he would breathe easier with Mariah off the island.

He would stop worrying about her, but he wouldn't stop thinking about her—and wondering if the truth would be enough to make up for the heartbreak.

Chapter 13

Lightning forked across the sky, thunder boomed and the power flickered and went out.

Mariah swore like a sailor, bumping her shins on her suitcases as she felt her way into the kitchen where she knew there was a candle over near the toaster.

The matches were a little bit harder to locate, and with the candle held tightly in one hand, she felt along the counter with the other. She found the book of matches on the windowsill and lit the candle.

It had been burned down pretty far. Mariah estimated she had only about an hour or two of wax left at most. After that, it was going to be very, very dark in here.

But the kitchen clock was stopped at 5:37. With luck, her cab would arrive before the candle burned completely down.

She took the softly glowing light back downstairs

into her darkroom. That was the last of the rooms she had left to pack. Her clothes were all ready to go, and she was going to leave what was left of her food behind for the cleaning lady.

She gazed around the darkroom at all of her photographic supplies—at the pictures of John, long since dried.

Tears filled her eyes, and she shook her head in disgust. She'd thought she'd already cried herself dry. She had, she tried to convince herself. These tears were just leftovers—kind of like an earthquake's aftershocks.

She'd cried, she'd gotten it out of her system and she was okay now. So she'd made a bad call. She'd guessed wrong, misjudged someone. Life was going to go on.

She could hear the rain pelting against the roof. Mariah thought about the Washburtons' house. She thought about the way she'd worked on that roof all yesterday afternoon, along with nearly two dozen other volunteers. They'd all worked in perfect cooperation, their common goal to get the job done and done well.

If she left Garden Isle, she wouldn't be able to see the completion of that house. She wouldn't go to the housewarming, wouldn't watch Frank and Loretta Washburton's eyes fill with joy and pride as they welcomed friends and Triple F workers into their home.

If she left, she would be leaving behind the friends she made, the work team she'd come to know so well. Laronda. There couldn't possibly be another site coordinator as cool as Laronda.

If she left Garden Isle, if she let herself be pushed out, chased away from her great-great-grandmother's childhood home, she'd never forgive herself.

Why should *she* be the one who was forced to leave?

If Jonathan Mills was uncomfortable living two doors away from her, let *him* be the one to move.

Hell, she had the rent on this cottage paid through to the end of the month.

Thunder boomed, and she knew she was only kidding herself. What was she going to do? March up to John and Serena's house, interrupt their honeymoon and demand that they leave?

No, she couldn't do that, but she could just stay here, quietly keeping to herself-and feeling like crap every time John or Serena's car drove past, praying that she wouldn't run into them in the supermarket, dreading seeing them together on the beach, knowing that she still wanted him.

She still wanted him.

Jonathan Mills was a son of a bitch. The fact that he was confused, that he was tormented by painful nightmares, that he was stressed out from the strain of dealing with a potentially terminal illness—none of that gave him the right to make love to her one night and then marry Serena the next.

Yet she still ached for his touch.

She was a fool.

With a sigh, Mariah began packing up her darkroom equipment by candlelight, deciding what she had to take and what could be left behind.

Yes, she could refuse to leave the island. But as much as she hated the thought of slinking away, beaten down and defeated, she wasn't into self-torture.

She tossed the photos of Jonathan Mills into the trash can. Those could definitely be left behind.

* * *

"Wow, this is fancy." Miller stepped into the candlelit dining room.

Serena had cooked a gourmet meal and set one end of the heavy wooden table with elegant china place settings, a myriad of wineglasses and what looked to be the entire silverware drawer. There were salad forks, shrimp cocktail forks, dinner forks, dessert forks.

Miller had to wonder—was she actually planning to serve dessert tonight, or did she have something a little more macabre up her sleeve?

Actually, she wasn't wearing any sleeves. The dress she wore was black and sleeveless, timelessly chic, complete with an innocent-looking string of pearls around her neck.

"Fortunately, we have a gas stove," she told him as she opened a decanter of wine and poured them each a glass. "Or we'd be sending out to McDonald's for double cheeseburgers." She smiled at him. "And *that* wouldn't have done at all. I wanted this meal to be…special."

Special. The Black Widow's M.O.—*her* M.O.—was to serve her husband an elegant gourmet meal, drug him so that he couldn't fight back, then stab him in the heart shortly after the main course.

His nerves were strung much too tightly. Miller was as certain as he could possibly be that, just as he'd reassured Daniel that afternoon, Serena wasn't going to try to kill him tonight. It was too soon. She would wait until she had his money in hand—to do otherwise would be outside of her pattern, outside of her rules. And serial killers of this type rarely strayed from their set of rules.

"You should have told me we were going to have a

formal meal," Miller said for Daniel's benefit. "I would have dressed for dinner."

Serena handed him one of the two wineglasses. "Let's have a toast, shall we?"

Right then and there, Miller knew he'd been dead wrong. She'd poured him a glass of red wine, but it smelled much too sweet and the liquid in the glass was much too thick. Opium. She was trying to drug him by putting opium in the wine. Right now. Tonight. Without having received a penny from him, she was preparing to kill him.

"I don't feel very much like red wine tonight," he said, setting the glass down on the dinner table.

Serena smiled at him. "Let's not be cute," she said. When she put her own glass down, he realized she was holding a gun. The rules were all changing, and changing fast.

"Is that a gun?" he said.

She laughed. "Yes, it's a gun," she told him. She raised her voice slightly. "Did you hear that, Daniel? Or, oh my. Maybe you're not listening. Maybe you're not *able* to listen. Maybe someone smarter than you *and* your partner waited until the call of nature pulled you out of that car you've been sitting in. Maybe someone much smarter sweetened that coffee you've been drinking to stay alert all night long—sweetened it with more than sugar. Maybe you're leaning against the steering wheel right now, drooling, about to slide into a narcotic coma. Eventually you'll just stop breathing, poor thing. What a shame to die so young…."

Miller took a step toward her and she lifted the gun, aiming directly for his head. "Sit down at the table," she ordered. "And keep your hands where I can see them."

He slowly sat down. Sitting down was good. It put his hands that much closer to the gun he had hidden in his boot.

"Hands on the table," she warned.

If she would only get close enough, if she would stop aiming directly at his head, he might have a chance to go for his gun. But she was carefully keeping her distance. Her aim seemed sure, her hands steady. Outside the windows, lightning flashed and thunder roared, but she seem oblivious, almost inhuman in her concentration.

But she may have finally met her match because there was no way in hell he was going to let Daniel die. No *way.*

"Drink the wine," she ordered him.

"No."

"Funny, I don't believe I phrased that as a yes or no question."

"I'm not drinking it."

She closed one eye as she aimed her gun and fired.

The slap of the bullet going into his arm nearly knocked Miller out of the chair. She *shot* him. He didn't let his disbelief get in his way as he went with the force of the bullet, pushing back his chair and landing on the floor, hoping to get a chance to grab that gun from his boot. But the chance never came as Serena moved around the table, aiming her gun at his head. He swore sharply as pain from his wounded arm rocketed through him.

"Get up." From somewhere, she'd procured a pair of regulation handcuffs. "Sit down. Put your hands behind you."

Miller sat back in another chair, aware of blood

streaming down his left arm, aware of the teeth-clenching pain, aware of Serena's gun aimed, once again, directly at his head. He no longer had any doubts that she would use it. And once one of those bullets smashed into his brain, he'd be of absolutely no help to Daniel or anyone else.

Mariah. He closed his eyes briefly, praying that she was safe. She was due to be picked up at seven by a taxi that would take her off the island. He wasn't certain what time it was, but he knew it was close to seven. Please, God, let her be long gone....

He felt Serena cuff one of his wrists, felt her weave the metal through the heavy wooden back of the chair and then cuff his other wrist.

And then he felt her tug slightly at the hair growing at the nape of his neck. She was cutting a lock—probably as some kind of sick keepsake. A souvenir. She probably had an entire collection of hair, and once he found it, it was going to be the evidence he needed to tie her to *all* of the murders.

"I'm not going to let you keep that," he told her.

She just laughed. "Are you sure you don't want that wine?" she asked. "It works as a painkiller, you know." She sat on the table, her gun in her lap, but too far away for him even to consider going for her.

"I can't drink it by myself," he told her, willing her to get closer, to try to force-feed him that wine.

But she laughed again. "You don't really think I'm going to let you spit it in my face, do you?" she scolded him. "This is a designer dress. No, I think we'll do this another way."

She set the gun down on the table as she lifted one of the domed plate warmers. Instead of a roasted chicken, there was only a syringe lying there beside the parsley garnish.

"Morphine," she told him. "It'll make your arm feel all better in, oh, about five minutes." She moved behind him, and he felt the cold steel barrel of her gun pressed tightly against the base of his head. "If you as much as move," she warned, "I'll shoot you."

He felt her tug at his shirt, felt the sharp stab of the needle into his back. Dammit, he hadn't had a very good look at that syringe. He had no idea how much she'd given him. He suspected it would be enough to paralyze, but not enough to kill. She would want the pleasure of skewering him with her sharp little knife.

"You'll have to forgive me for not disinfecting the area of injection," she told him. "But I think that stray germs are the least of your problems."

Miller watched her walk around to the other side of the table. Backlit by the stormy sky, she looked entirely in her element.

Five minutes, she said. In five minutes, he'd be stupid and drooling, just like all her other husbands had been. Or maybe he wouldn't be. Maybe he could hold on, fight the dizzying effects of the drug. Maybe he could make her believe he was weak and vulnerable. Maybe then she'd get close enough. Maybe she would let down her guard and he could overpower her….

"Oh, by the way, I have a little surprise for you," she said. "I want to tell you about it before the morphine starts working. It won't be as much fun to tell you if you don't really understand what's happening." She paused. "Are you listening?"

"I'm listening."

Serena smiled. "I put a bomb in Mariah's basement.

All those pesky photographs that she had—I got her negatives out of storage and realized she'd been lying to me. She'd taken quite a number of pictures of me without my knowing it. I put the negatives next to some extremely flammable chemicals in her darkroom. This way, they all go up in flames—photos, negatives…and photographer, too."

Miller felt the cold fingers of death clutching at his heart. Mariah… "No."

"Don't worry, darling, the morphine I've given you will ease the sting." Serena looked at her watch. "The timer's set for six-thirty. That's in another six minutes. From where you're sitting, you'll have an excellent view of the fire. Of course, by then you probably won't care."

"Serena! God!" Miller's voice sounded harsh to his own ears. "Mariah doesn't know anything, I swear to you. Don't bring her into this."

"Too late."

"No, it's not. Call her. Call her and tell her to get out of the house. All you really want is to destroy those photos. You don't need to kill her!"

"My, my, my. You *do* care, don't you? You should have thought of that *before* you came after me. *Before* you listened in on me and stalked me like some kind of wild animal."

Her fingers tightened on the trigger of the gun and Miller nearly stopped breathing. Please, God, don't let her kill him now. Not yet. Not while there was still a chance that he could talk her into saving Mariah.

Her face was taut with anger. "Did you really think you could outsmart me? Did you really think I wouldn't notice that my house was *infested* with hidden microphones—just like the ones you hid here!"

"Mariah had nothing to do with that. Call her. Tell her to get out of there. Serena, she was your *friend*."

Something shifted in Serena's face. "Four minutes," she said. "And I can't call her. The phone lines went down when the power went off." She smiled. "Come on, John. I want to hear you scream."

Miller could feel a vein throbbing in his neck. It was an odd sensation, countered by a feeling of floating, of drowsiness, of numbness. God help him, the drug was kicking in.

God, this was his worst nightmare happening all over again. Except this time, it wasn't Tony in a warehouse he wasn't going to be able to save. This time, it was Mariah, in a cottage where a killer had planted a bomb. This time he wouldn't hear her die. Instead, he'd see the flames that were devouring her. He'd see them over the tops of the trees.

Rage blinded him, and he used it to fight the unbalancing effect of the drug as he strained at his handcuffs, praying Serena would step just a little bit closer....

That was funny. Mariah couldn't remember putting that box down here, next to her supply of chemicals. The box had B&W Photo Lab's familiar logo on the side, and she pulled it off the shelf and opened it, holding the candle up to illuminate what was inside.

Negatives. The box was filled with dozens of plastic sleeves that held her negatives. That was weird. She'd been storing these over at the photo lab on the mainland. How on earth had they found their way back here? Who could have put the box on this lower shelf, where in the darkness she probably wouldn't have noticed it even with the power working and the overhead light turned on and...

She held the candle up again and looked deeper into the darkness of the bottom shelf. What the heck...?

She looked closer, then started backing away.

Whatever was in there, it looked a *hell* of a lot like a bomb. Not that she'd ever seen a bomb before—not up close and personal like this. But it looked like the bombs she'd seen in movies—some kind of sticks of explosive tied together, hooked into an alarm clock that was ticking quietly....

Mariah grabbed her candle and ran. She ran up the basement stairs, through the living room and out into the pouring rain. The candle went out the moment she burst through her front door, and she threw it down onto the lawn. She grabbed her bike from the side of the house and jumped on it, pedaling furiously down the driveway, taking a left to head toward town, toward the police station, toward somebody, *any*body who might have some sort of idea why there was a *bomb* in her basement.

The rain soaked her almost instantly, and the wind ripped at her hair and tore at her clothes. She had to squint hard, to squeeze her eyes nearly shut to see through the driving rain, but still she pedaled standing up, muscles straining.

Somebody wanted to kill her. Somebody wanted to *kill* her.

She hadn't gone more than a tenth of a mile before she saw car headlights up ahead. They weren't coming toward her, but rather, they were motionless, the light pointing crazily into the heavy underbrush that grew along the side of the road. As she drew closer, Mariah could see that the car had skidded off the road and slammed into a tree.

There was no way she was going to stop. Someone had planted a *bomb* in her basement. Someone wanted her dead, and she wasn't going to stop until she reached the safety of the police station downtown.

She would have gone past with a silent apology and a promise to herself to tell the police about the accident right away when she recognized the car. It was *Daniel's* car. And God, that was Daniel, still in the front seat, slumped over the steering wheel.

Cursing, she braked to a stop and dropped her bike along the side of the road. She cursed louder still at the sting of the branches that whipped against her legs in the wind. She moved as quickly as she could through the sodden underbrush, and bracing herself for the worst, she jerked open the driver's-side door of the car.

It looked as if the air bag had been inflated, and Daniel had somehow deflated it again. But he was resting his head against the steering wheel as if he had some kind of injury. Or as if he were drunk.

The radio was on—some kind of a talk show or a dramatized broadcast—a man and a woman were talking. And what looked to be close to half a dozen large thermoses of coffee littered the floor, along with an empty doughnut shop bag.

Mariah felt Daniel's neck for a pulse. It seemed uncommonly slow. But there was no sign of blood, no sign of any kind of injury. She touched the side of his face. "Daniel?" God, he *was* drunk. She smacked him lightly, then a little bit harder. "Daniel, wake up!"

He roused slightly. "Mariah!" he said. "Gotta warn you! A bomb!"

Mariah pulled back, aghast. "What did you say?"

"FBI," he mumbled. "Me an' John. Tracking a killer. Gonna blow up Mariah."

"Who's FBI?" Mariah was shocked. "*You're* FBI? You and…" John?

"Gotta save John, too." Daniel was fighting to stay awake, but it was clearly a losing battle.

"What's wrong with you?" Mariah shook him, feeling a flare of disbelief, of unreality. This couldn't be real, it couldn't be happening. "Are you drunk? What are you saying to me?"

"Somethin' in the coffee," Daniel breathed. "Gotta get help, gotta save John."

"Where is John?" Mariah asked, suddenly terribly, horribly afraid. Daniel's eyes were closed and she shook him again. "*Dammit, where's John?*"

But he didn't answer.

Something in the coffee. Someone had put something in his coffee—and a bomb in her basement.

Soaked to the skin and sobbing with frustration, Mariah used all her strength to push Daniel over into the passenger seat. She climbed in behind the steering wheel and tried to start the car. *Get help.* Unable to drive from the effects of whatever the hell had been put in his coffee, Daniel had crashed his car as he'd tried to go get help. Or maybe not to get help. Maybe to warn her. Maybe he was coming to warn her about the bomb.

Although how would he have known?

She turned the key in the ignition and the engine almost turned over. Almost. She tried again, but this time it only wheezed and died.

She tried again, but there was only silence. Silence,

and those infernal radio talk show hosts talking and talking and talking and...

"Less than a minute now," the woman's voice was saying. "Thirty seconds and Mariah and her stupid photographs will be nothing more than a smudge of smoke in the sky."

"I'm going to kill you," the man's voice said. His speech was slightly slurred, slightly slow, slightly shaking with rage, but the voice was unmistakable. It was John. "I'm going to break free from this chair, and I'm going to kill you."

And the woman's voice was Serena's.

Mariah couldn't breathe.

"Twenty seconds," Serena said. "Shall we count down together?"

"No!" John said. "No!" It was a howl of rage and pain nearly identical to the cry Mariah had heard the night he'd had a nightmare when he'd slept on her couch.

"Ten," Serena said. "Nine, eight, seven, six, five, four, three, two, one—"

The explosion rocked the car as flaming bits of shingles and wood rained down around them, extinguished almost instantly by the deluge. Mariah looked back up the road. Where her cottage had been was roaring flames—the fire too big and too hot to be put out by the rain.

"Oh, my God," she breathed.

Over the radio, she could hear John, his voice little more than a keening cry. "No," he said over and over again. "No!"

"Oh, please," Serena scoffed. "I know the morphine tends to make one overly emotional, but show a little backbone, won't you? I would've expected more from someone sent to catch *me*."

Mariah's heart was in her throat. John thought she was dead.

"I'm not dead," she said aloud, but, of course, he couldn't hear her.

"Mariah…" he whispered. "Oh, God, Mariah…"

"You really expect me to believe you cared that much about that great, huge *cow* of a woman?"

"You *bitch*," Mariah exclaimed. "I am *not* a cow!"

"You can stop the act," Serena continued. "I know what you're trying to do. You're trying to make me think that you're thoroughly anesthetized—totally helpless. You want me to come close enough so that you can try for me. What are you planning to do with your arms bound behind your back, John? Snap my neck with your legs?"

"Mariah…" he breathed. "No…"

John's arms were somehow tied. Serena had somehow managed to overpower him and tie him up. She'd given him morphine, too. That's what was making John's speech sound so slurred. Maybe Serena had put something similar in Daniel's coffee.

"I think I'll wait another few minutes or so before I get too close," Serena said. "I don't care to have my neck snapped today."

John took a deep, shuddering breath, then spoke softly, quietly. "Just do it, Serena," he said. "Just get out your stiletto and get it over with. Because I'm already dead. You killed me when you killed Mariah."

"No!" It was Mariah who cried out this time. "Oh, God, no!"

Whatever she was going to do, she had to do it fast. She tried to start the car again to no avail. She tried to rouse Daniel, but he was as unresponsive as the car's engine.

FBI, he'd said. He and John were FBI.

And FBI agents carried guns....

Mariah searched through Daniel's pockets and through his clothes. It wasn't until she pushed him over and patted around his waist that she found what she was looking for. A gun, in some kind of holster at the small of his back.

"I'm really sorry, but I think I need this," Mariah said to the unconscious man, as with shaking hands, she pulled his shirt free from his pants and drew out the gun. It was small and deadly looking, and warm to the touch from Daniel's body heat.

She pushed open the car door and stepped out into the driving rain, pushing the gun into the back pocket of her shorts, praying that it had some kind of safety attachment that would keep her from shooting herself in the butt by mistake.

She picked up her bike and pointed it back up the hill—away from town and the police. Her muscles strained as she started up the slight incline. She started to gather some real speed as she went past the still flaming ruins of her cottage.

The neighboring house that lay between hers and Serena's was silent and empty, and the last of her hopes for getting help sank. There was no one home there. There was no way anyone could be home and not be out on the porch, or at least at the windows, watching the inferno next door.

Still, Mariah kept pedaling up the hill. She didn't understand *half* of what was going on, but she knew one thing for damn sure. Serena wasn't going to kill John. Not if *she* had anything to say about it.

Chapter 14

"I never quit," Tony said sternly. "I confess I did a stupid thing, I got myself into a situation that there was no getting out of, but I spit at Domino as his boys were squeezing the triggers of their guns to blow me away."

Miller's mouth was dry, his stomach queasy and his head felt as if it were floating a good twelve inches above his body. "Mariah's dead," he said. "She killed Mariah."

"No talking," Serena said sharply. "No more talking!"

Tony moved closer, lowering his voice. "You know, she's having some kind of ritualistic meal, getting into some kind of sicko trance while she's getting ready to skewer you, pal. And look at you. You've got your head on the table in a puddle of drool."

"I don't care," Miller told him.

It was amazing, actually. He had a bullet in his left arm, but it didn't hurt. He couldn't feel it. He couldn't feel anything. Nothing hurt. Nothing mattered. He honestly didn't care.

"I can't believe it," Tony said. "This bitch killed Mariah, and you're going to let her get away with it? You're going to just quit? I don't know what happened in the past two years, baby, but you're not the John Miller *I* used to know."

"I loved her," Miller said.

"Yeah, right, maybe." Tony didn't sound convinced.

"I told you to shut up!" Serena snapped.

"I did," Miller insisted. "I loved her more than anything."

"Not more than you love yourself," Tony pointed out. "If you did, you wouldn't quit. But you're scared because you know it's going to hurt you more than you can bear to wake up tomorrow morning and still be alive while Mariah's not. You *want* this bitch to shish-kebab you because Mariah's dead, because you couldn't save her, and because you can't deal with that."

"Damn right I can't deal with that! God, every day for the rest of my life?"

Serena clapped her hands together and the noise seemed to thunder around him. "I'm warning you!"

Miller lifted his head, working hard to focus his eyes. "Go to hell," he snarled.

"Attaboy," Tony murmured. "Get mad. Fight back."

Mariah was dead. Mariah was dead. Christ, Mariah was *dead*.

The pain of reality came stabbing through all of the layers of drug-induced numbness and apathy. Sweet, beautiful Mariah was gone forever, and Miller knew that Tony was right. As easy as it would be to quit, he couldn't do it. He couldn't just put his head down on the table and die.

Not without making Serena pay.

So instead, he put his head down on the table and waited for Serena to come closer.

With his eyes opened and focused, Tony was gone. He was on his own here, without even his dreams and hallucinations to back him up. He tried to formulate a plan, tried to make his brain turn back into a brain again, rather than the soggy basket of wet laundry it had become.

She would come close, and he would use every bit of strength he had left in his jellolike muscles, and he would…do something.

No, no! He had to come up with something specific. He had to figure out the details. He was always so good with details, good with alternate plans. He was good at making plans for every variable, every difference in every detail.

But for now, he'd have to skip the little details. For now, he'd focus on an overall plan. His mind was too foggy for anything but the big picture. It was hard enough to concentrate on how exactly to get from where he was sitting right now to being the one in control of the gun.

Gun.

There was something about a gun that he should remember….

He had a gun. He could…shoot her with the gun that was still inside his boot! Yeah. That was a great idea.

Except his hands were cuffed behind his back and he couldn't reach his gun.

Miller fought a wave of dizzying fatigue by calling to mind Mariah's beautiful face, her gorgeous smile. He focused on the dimples that appeared in her cheeks, the flash of laughter that danced in her eyes. That was gone, all gone, forever gone. Serena had stolen Mariah from him. Serena had taken all his hopes and his dreams when she'd so casually snuffed out Mariah's life.

He used the pain to bring himself back from the edge, to push back the fog that threatened to overpower him.

Think. He had to *think*.

He had to figure out what he had to work with, his strengths as they were—not an easy task since he was finding it harder and harder to remember his name.

His legs.

His legs were free. They weren't tied.

He could kick the dining table over on top of her. Crush her. Or, like she herself had suggested, he could put her in a leghold and snap her neck.

He had the chair. He could throw himself forward, chair and all, and use the chair he was cuffed to as a weapon.

And the morphine. He could take that which weakened him the most and use it to his advantage. He could break his legs from the force of the blow he intended to deliver, and he wouldn't feel any pain.

Miller forced his eyes open. He could see Serena sitting way down at the other end of the table, eating her elegant dinner. She was halfway through the main course, and he knew that when the main course was through, she would take out her razor-sharp little knife.

And then she would come closer.

If he was lucky, he *would* break her neck. He'd take her out for good.

And if he was really lucky, she'd take him out with her and he wouldn't have to wake up tomorrow and know that Mariah was dead.

The house was dark and quiet.

Mariah stood in the pouring rain, straining to listen for something, *any*thing at all.

All she heard was the rain.

She'd rushed over here as fast as she could ride on her bike, but now that she was here, she wasn't quite sure what to do.

Ring the bell? Knock on the door as she pushed it open, calling, "Yoo-hoo, Serena, did you just try to blow me into a million little bits by planting a bomb in the basement of my house, and are you about to murder your husband and my lover—who, in fact, seems to be some kind of federal agent?"

Stealthily, she tested the doorknob. The door was unlocked. She turned the knob slowly and just as slowly pushed the door open.

It was as dark inside as it was out.

Darker.

Mariah silently closed the door behind her and stood for a moment, letting her ears adjust to the now muted sound of the rain on the roof, hoping her eyes would adjust to the eerie, smothering darkness, as well.

She became aware of a new sound—the sound of water dripping from her clothes and onto the Mexican-tiled floor. And as she took a step farther into the entryway, her sneakers squished. Moving as quietly as she could, she stepped out of them.

Her eyes *were* starting to adjust to the dark. She could see a dim light coming from somewhere upstairs. She looked around for a place to hide her sneakers, but gave up as she realized she might be able to hide them, but there was no way she could hide the puddle of water she'd brought inside with her. She might as well leave them by the door and pray she found Serena before Serena realized she had uninvited company.

Mariah heard a voice speaking sharply, echoing from an upstairs room. It was Serena. She couldn't make out what the woman was saying, but she sure as heck didn't sound happy.

Mariah went up the stairs as quickly and quietly as she could, reaching into her back pocket and wriggling free Daniel's deadly little gun.

Dear God, she had no idea *what* she was going to do. She pictured herself leaping through the doorway, gun raised and held in both hands, like one of the cops on *NYPD Blue,* shouting for Serena to freeze.

And then what? What was she going to do if Serena had her own gun? Was she going to shoot Serena?

Now *there* was an unlikely scenario. Mariah had never fired a gun before, let alone fired one at a living, breathing human being.

As she drew closer to the top of the stairs, she saw that there was candlelight coming from the dining room—the room where all her dreams had come crashing down around her just this morning. It was the same room where she had found Serena and her new husband—Jonathan Mills.

She crept toward the door, careful to stay out of the light, pressing herself against the wall, gun raised. She held her breath and closed her eyes briefly, waiting for the trembling in her knees to stop, hoping that she would hear John's voice, praying that he was still alive.

The next move was hers. It was totally up to her. She could stand here for another two minutes, or she could get ready and—

"My gun is aimed at Jonathan's head." Serena's voice was crisp and clear, echoing in the silence. "I know you're out there, and if you don't step into the light with your hands held high, I'm going to kill him right now."

The next move wasn't Mariah's after all. Dear God, Serena must have heard her coming up the stairs.

"Do it now!" the older woman said sharply, "or I swear, I'll kill him."

Mariah stuffed the gun back into her back pocket and stepped into the light, hands held up over her head.

"You?" Serena laughed. Sure enough, she held a gun trained with steady confidence directly at John's head. "Well, well, look who's come to rescue you, John. It's Mariah, back from the dead."

"Run!" John shouted. "Mariah, run!"

Mariah couldn't move. It was as if she'd stepped into some scene from a horrific nightmare, and she couldn't move an inch.

John was sitting behind the long dining table, his hands behind his back. His left arm was soaked with blood. It looked as if it was all he could do to hold his head up. And Serena was standing across the room, perfectly dressed as usual in an elegant black sheath dress, with pearls and a gun as accessories.

It was unreal. Mariah didn't understand. What the hell was going on? Why was the FBI after Serena? What had she done? Why would she want to kill John and drug Daniel? Why would she put a bomb in Mariah's basement? It didn't make any sense.

But Serena held the gun calmly, confidently, as if she was accustomed to it. Clearly, she wouldn't hesitate to shoot—obviously she'd shot John once tonight already. She swung the gun toward Mariah.

"No!" Miller was drowning. The shock of seeing Mariah whole and alive had transformed rapidly from near euphoric joy to screaming fear. She was alive—but she wouldn't be for long if she didn't get the hell out of here.

"Well, isn't *this* different," Serena said. "You *are* a fool, aren't you? He married *me,* and yet here you are, rushing to his rescue, empty-handed. You know, he was only using you to get closer to me. Did you know that Jonathan Mills isn't even his real name? God, Mariah, I'm sure absolutely nothing he's told you is true."

Mariah took one step and then another and another toward Miller. "John, are you all right?" She was soaking wet, shivering slightly as she knelt next to him, as she touched his blood-soaked sleeve. He could smell her perfume, and reality shifted. For one incredible moment, he was back in her bed, making love to her and… He shook his head, trying to bring his focus back to here and now.

"Gun in my boot," he whispered, praying that she would understand, knowing that he had to act, and act fast. As much as Serena was loath to kill him with a gun, she'd have no problem using a bullet to kill Mariah.

"Of course, Mariah was playing her own game," Serena continued. "Mariah Robinson isn't her real name either. I wonder, John. Did you consider her a suspect because of that?"

Miller looked directly into Mariah's eyes. "Gun," he started to whisper again.

She cut him off. "I know. I'm really mad at you," she added, reaching behind him to touch his hand. Except wait—those weren't her fingers that touched him. It was something cold and...

It was amazing, but somehow she'd managed to get the gun out of his boot without his noticing. Without Serena noticing. Miller's hands were numb, but he took the safety off, preparing the gun to fire.

Still, this gun wasn't going to do him a whole hell of a lot of good as long as he was holding it behind his back. He was a good shot—at least he was when he wasn't pumped full of narcotics—but trick shooting had never been his forte.

"Take it back," he told Mariah.

She shook her head. "I can't."

Serena's gun was still pointed loosely at Mariah, yet now she brought her hand up higher, taking better aim. "What are telling her?" she asked him sharply, then said to Mariah, "Move away from him."

"Take it," Miller said. *"Now!"*

Mariah didn't want that gun. She knew damn well there was no way she could aim it at Serena and pull the trigger.

But John dropped it into her hand as he used both of his legs and kicked the enormous table onto its side. A shot rang out as he tipped his chair over in front of her, and Mariah realized Serena was shooting at them. She lifted the gun, closed her eyes and squeezed the trigger.

The recoil knocked the gun out of her hands and she screamed.

Miller tried to shield Mariah as the shot she fired

went wild. He could feel the dry wood of the old chair he was cuffed to splintering, and he pulled himself free of it.

His wounded arm should have hurt like hell as he contorted to slip his cuffed hands past his legs and around to the front of him, but he didn't feel even a twinge, thanks to the morphine Serena had given him. Weakness as strength. He was superhuman now. Nothing could hurt him, nothing could stop him—not even Serena's bullets.

He felt the force of one plow into his leg as he covered Mariah with his body, as he reached for the gun she had fired and dropped. He felt another bullet strike him as he took aim, and he saw Serena's eyes as she realized that only a direct hit to his head would take him down.

He fired.

And Serena fell instead, her gun falling from her hand.

In the sudden silence, he could hear the sound of sirens.

It was the sound of fire trucks, rushing to extinguish the blaze that once had been Mariah's cottage.

But they didn't stop down the street. They came all the way up the hill, all the way into the driveway. He heard the door burst open, heard the pounding sound of heavy footsteps on the stairs.

He leaned back, resting against the toppled-over table as Mariah tried to stop his bleeding.

Backup had arrived. Somehow Daniel had managed to call for backup, and they had arrived.

"I'm going to close my eyes now," he told Mariah.

"Don't," she said, tears in her own eyes. "Please, John, don't quit on me. Stay with me—"

He touched her cheek. It was wet with tears. "Don't cry. I never meant to make you cry. I'm so sorry," he murmured. "So sorry..." I love you, he wanted to say, but his lips didn't seem to be able to move.

"We need that stretcher up here stat!" he heard someone shout as the world went black.

Chapter 15

It was thirty-six hours, seventeen minutes and nine seconds before John opened his eyes.

Mariah knew, because she'd been counting every second. The nurses had brought in a cot for her, and she'd slept fitfully, not convinced that she would be roused if John woke up.

But he hadn't.

He had an IV dripping steadily into his right arm. He was hooked up to machines that monitored his heart rate and his breathing. Doctors came and went, seemingly satisfied with his progress despite the fact that he slept on and on and on.

Daniel came to before John did, and he sat quietly for a while, next to Mariah. He told her about Serena, about all her other husbands, about the years John had spent tracking her down. He told her how, after Mariah had left him in the car, he'd roused himself and crawled out into the rain. He'd forced himself to keep awake, keep moving, and eventually, he'd flagged down a passing car. The driver had taken him to the Garden Isle police station, where a team of local cops had donned their bulletproof vests and driven like bats out of hell to John and Mariah's rescue.

Except by the time they'd arrived at Serena's place, John and Mariah had pretty much managed to rescue themselves.

He told her that Serena was in custody, expected to recover from her gunshot wound. He added that her real name was Janice Reed and that they'd found her keepsake collection of hair, which tied her to nearly a dozen murders.

Daniel managed to answer only some of Mariah's questions. He said she'd have to wait for John to answer the others. Before John woke up, Daniel had been discharged from the hospital and he'd returned to the resort to finish packing their equipment.

And still Mariah sat next to John's bed.

Then, finally, he stirred and opened his eyes.

He just looked at her, and she just looked at him, fighting back the tears that immediately sprang to her eyes.

"You're not dead," he said when he finally spoke, and she realized that there were tears in his eyes, too. "I'm not really sure what I dreamed and what was real, but I'm glad as hell that you're not dead."

His mouth was dry, and she helped him by lifting the cup of water the nurses had left for him. She aimed the bendable straw so he could pull it into his mouth and take a long sip.

"My real name is Marie Carver," she told him without hesitation, "although my nickname has always been Mariah. I've spent the past few months on Garden Isle using the name Mariah Robinson because I read in a book that going on vacation and leaving your name behind was a good way to reduce stress."

He smiled very slightly as she put the cup back on the table next to the bed. "It's also a good way to make the local law enforcement officials very suspicious."

"I never even thought of that." She paused. "You didn't really think I was…a killer?"

"We pretty much knew it was Serena right from the start."

"I can't believe you married someone you suspected of being a serial killer! Is that part of your job description as an FBI agent?"

He laughed, then winced, holding tightly to his side where one of Serena's bullets had cracked a rib. "No. No, that was above and beyond the call of duty."

Mariah was quiet for a moment. She almost didn't ask, but she had to know. "How could you…sleep with her, knowing that she'd killed all her other husbands?"

He took her hand, interlacing their fingers. "I didn't sleep with her—I didn't want to sleep with her. Besides, I promised you that I wouldn't, remember? I told her I was impotent—that my condition was a side effect of my chemotherapy."

Mariah gazed into his eyes. Chemotherapy. Cancer. "You never really had cancer," she realized aloud. "That was all just part of your cover."

He nodded. "That's right. I'm sorry—"

"Sorry?" She laughed, leaning forward to kiss him hard on the mouth. "Are you kidding? That's *such* good news! It makes all this hell we've just been through worth it. You're not going to die!"

Her reaction was pure Mariah. She was focusing on the good, not the bad. Miller felt his heart flip-flop in his chest. God, he loved her.

He caught her chin, pulling her mouth down to his for another kiss. This kiss was more lingering, and when she pulled away, her eyes looked so serious, so solemn.

"I don't even know your real name," she told him.

"It's John Miller."

"I don't know anything about you—who you are, where you're from—"

"Yes, you do," he told her. "You know more about me than anyone in the world. I told you more than I've ever told Daniel. More than Tony ever knew."

"Tony was real?" she asked.

"Yeah."

She looked down at their hands, their fingers still intertwined. "Serena said you were only using me to get close to her."

"If you really believe that, what are you doing here, sitting next to my bed?"

She looked up at him then. "I don't know," she confessed. "I honestly don't know. I just…I had to know you were all right before I…left."

Before she left. God, he didn't want her to leave. But if she *was* going to leave, he wanted her to know the truth.

Miller took a deep breath. "I did meet you to get close to Serena," he told her. "Yes, that's true. But I kept coming back—I couldn't stay away—because I fell in love with you."

Her eyes were so wide, so beautiful.

"I love you, Mariah," he told her quietly. "I have almost from the very first day we met. I made a lot of mistakes in this case—even though I tried my damnedest to keep away from you, I couldn't. And when Serena left the island, I was so sure she had gone for good. And then after we made love, and she came back..." He exhaled noisily. "I made some very wrong choices. I knew that marrying her would hurt you, but I couldn't stand the thought of letting her get away, and I nearly got you killed because of that."

He took a deep breath, afraid that what he was about to say was going to drive her away for good. "You see, that's who I am," he continued. "I'm a man who can't stand to fail. I have a record of arrests that's unrivaled in the bureau. I have a reputation for always catching the bad guys, for never letting them get away. I'm supposed to be some kind of superhero—the toughest and meanest in the field. I have a nickname—the other agents call me 'The Robot,' because nothing matters to me outside of my job. They think I have no heart and no soul, and maybe they're right, because the truth is I have no life outside of the work I do. I have no family and no friends—"

"Daniel is your friend."

Miller nodded. "Yeah. I don't get it, but yeah. He's my friend."

"I'm your friend, too."

Miller had to swallow. He had to take another deep breath before he could say, "That's all I can really ask. That you be my friend."

She was very quiet, just watching him.

"I had this crazy dream," he told her, "that morning we made love. I was thinking, this could be my life. I thought, maybe I could feel this good every single day. This woman could love me, and I could become this peaceful, relaxed, happy man. I could be so much more than I've ever been before—than I'd ever thought I'd be. And I could picture us, forty years from now, still making love, still holding hands, still laughing together. I really liked that picture."

Mariah's heart was in her throat as he looked away from her, as he was silent for several long moments. As she watched, he swallowed hard, and when he looked back up at her, his eyes were luminous with unshed tears.

"But I'm not that man. I'm 'The Robot.' And I don't blame you if you can't love me—if you don't want to love me. I'm hard, and I'm driven, and my job matters too damn much to me. I wouldn't wish myself on anyone—maybe especially not on you." He took another deep breath and forced a smile as he squeezed her hand. "So, go on. Get out of here. You've seen for yourself that I'm okay. You can leave."

Mariah couldn't move, couldn't speak.

"It's okay," he said. "I'm okay. I'm just…I'm glad I had the chance to love you. To, you know, know that I could actually feel this way and…"

One of his tears escaped, rolling down his cheek and splashing onto Mariah's hand. He swore, turning away and tightly closing his eyes. But that only served to make more of his tears fall.

"John," Mariah said quietly, gently touching his face. "Robots don't cry." She leaned forward and kissed him and when she pulled back, she whispered, "What would Jonathan Mills think if I told him that I made a mistake, too? What would he say if I told him that really, all this time, I've been in love with a man named John Miller?"

He could feel all his emotions cross his face. Disbelief. Amazement. Confusion. Jubilation. She loved him. She *loved* him!

He made a sound that was something like a laugh as he fought to keep his eyes from filling with tears again. And then he didn't fight anymore. Hell, with Mariah, he didn't need to fight it. He wanted her to know, wanted her to see the way she made him feel.

"He would wish you the best of luck," he told her, "and he would warn you that with me, you're probably going to need it."

Mariah touched his cheek, touched the tear he knew was shimmering there. "And what do *you* think about that?"

"I think that if you still have the urge to change your name, you should consider changing it to Miller."

He'd caught her off guard. "Are you asking me to *marry* you?"

"Yes," he said. "Yes, I am."

This time, the tears that fell were Mariah's. "Yes," she whispered, "I'd love to change my name." She leaned forward and kissed him.

It was the sweetest kiss Miller had ever known.

* * * * *

USA TODAY bestselling author **Barb Han** lives in north Texas with her very own hero-worthy husband, three beautiful children, a spunky golden retriever/standard poodle mix and too many books in her to-read pile. In her downtime, she plays video games and spends much of her time on or around a basketball court. She loves interacting with readers and is grateful for their support. You can reach her at barbhan.com.

Books by Barb Han

Harlequin Intrigue

An O'Connor Family Mystery

Texas Kidnapping
Texas Target

Rushing Creek Crime Spree

What She Did
What She Knew
What She Saw

Crisis: Cattle Barge

Kidnapped at Christmas
Murder and Mistletoe
Bulletproof Christmas

Cattlemen Crime Club

One Tough Texan
Texas-Sized Trouble
Texas Witness
Texas Showdown

Visit the Author Profile page at Harlequin.com for more titles.

TEXAS
PREY

Barb Han

To Allison Lyons for the opportunity to learn so much with every book. To Jill Marsal for unfailing wisdom and support. To Brandon, Jacob and Tori for inspiration and kindness (I love you!). To John for finding true love.

This story is as much about friendship as it is about love. To Emily Martinez, Lisa Watson, Caroline York, and Raymon and Amanda Bacchus for yours!

Chapter 1

Rebecca Hughes held her chin up and kept alert as she thrust her shopping cart through the thick, oppressive North Texas heat. She blinked against the relentless sun, a light so intense her eyes hurt.

The van parked next to her car in the grocery store lot pricked her neck hairs. Blacked-out windows blocked her view of the driver's side or anything else that might be lurking, waiting, ready. A warning bell wailed inside her head as she neared her sedan.

Today marked the fifteenth anniversary of that horrible day when both she and her younger brother were abducted, and it always put her on edge. The two had been isolated in separate sheds. When an opportunity had presented itself to run, Rebecca had escaped, thinking she could bring back help. Instead, she got lost in the woods and never saw her baby brother again.

Steering her cart toward the center of the aisle, she made sure no one could surprise her by jumping from between two cars. Tension squeezed her shoulder blades taut as memories assaulted her. Those thirty-six hours of torture before she escaped without her little brother, the horror and Shane's disappearance would haunt her for the rest of her life.

Shuddering at the memory, she tightened her grip on the handle and pushed forward. The early Friday-morning crowd was out. Most people were just beginning to run errands at the same time her workday ended. Her overnight shift at the radio station kept her sane after years of being afraid to be home alone in the dark.

She and Shane had been twelve and seven respectively when she'd sneaked out to play that stupid game with her friends. They'd been told to stay inside while the annual Renaissance Festival was in town, in full swing. Parents were busy, distracted. Strangers in costumes were everywhere. People came from nearly every state, descending on Mason Ridge in RVs and trailers and filling camp sites. And Shane was supposed to be asleep when she'd slipped out her bedroom window to meet up with her friends, not following her.

But none of that mattered. She should've realized sooner that the little stinker was trailing behind, his favorite blanket in tow. Shane had been her responsibility. And she'd let him down in the worst possible way.

The unfairness of his disappearance and her survival still hit with the force of a physical blow. His screams still haunted her. An imprint left by the horrible man who'd been dubbed the Mason Ridge Abductor was the reason she still watched every stranger warily.

When no one else had disappeared and all leads had

been exhausted, law enforcement had written the case off as a transient passing through town. Logic said the man was long gone. Point being, he couldn't hurt her anymore. And yet, every time she got spooked he was the first person who popped into her thoughts. That monster had caused her to lose more than her sense of security. He'd shattered her world and taken away her ability to trust. Her parents had divorced and become overbearing; friends looked at her strangely, as if she'd become an outcast; and she'd eventually pushed away the one person she'd truly loved—Brody Fields.

The van's brake lights created a bright red glow, snapping her focus to the present. Panic pressed heavy on her arms. Maybe she could circle around the next aisle and get back to the store before being seen.

There were a million wackos out there waiting to hurt unaware women, surprise being key to their attacks. Rebecca was fully present. She tightened her grip on the cart handle a third time, turned around and stalked toward her car. No one got to make her feel weak and afraid again.

Reaching inside her purse as she neared her vehicle, she gripped her Taser gun. Anyone trying to mess with her would get a big surprise and a few thousand volts of electricity. She wouldn't go down without a fight. Not again. She was no longer a shy twelve-year-old who could be overpowered in the dark.

With every forward step, the tension in Rebecca's body tightened. Her gaze was trained on the van.

She heard footsteps coming toward her from behind. Turning in time to catch a glimpse of a man rushing toward her, she spun around to face him. He was less than three feet away, moving closer. He wore a sweatshirt with the hood covering his hair and half of his face. Sunglasses hid his eyes. Before she could react, he slammed into her, knocking her off balance. She landed flat on the ground.

This time, she knew it was him—*had* to be him. She'd recognize that apple-tobacco smell anywhere. The scent had been burned into her senses fifteen years ago.

With the Taser already in hand, she struggled to untangle her purse strap from her arm. She shook free from his grasp, but not without upsetting the contents of her purse.

"You sick bastard. What did you do to my brother?" Aiming the blunt end of the Taser directly at his midsection, she fired.

The man fell to his knees, groaning, as she scrambled to her feet.

"What are you talking about, lady? You're crazy," he bit out through grunts and clenched teeth, convulsing on the ground.

Shaking off the fear gripping her, she snatched her handbag and ran to her car. She cursed, realizing some of the purse contents were on the ground. No way could she risk going back for them. Not with him there.

She hopped into the driver's seat, then closed and locked the door. Her fingers trembled, causing her to drop the keys. Scooping them off the floorboard, she tried to force a sense of calm over her.

Fumbling to get the key in the ignition, her logical mind battled with reality. That had to be *him*, right?

This wasn't like before when she'd mistaken one of the garbagemen for her abductor. Or the time she'd been certain he was posing as a cable guy. Anyone who'd come close and roughly matched her abductor's description had given her nightmares.

The sheriff had been convinced that no one from Mason Ridge was capable of doing such a horrific act. He'd said it had to be the work of a trucker or someone else passing through because of the festival. The FBI hadn't been so sure. They'd produced a list of potential suspects that had pitted neighbors and small-shop owners against one another. Personal vendettas had people coming forward.

As the investigation unfolded, there was no shortage of accused. And a town's innocence had been lost forever.

Determined investigators had traced freight cars and truckers that had passed through Mason Ridge the night both her and Shane had been abducted. In the days following, they'd scoured known teen hangouts, drained a lake and even set off dynamite in the rock quarry. But they'd come up empty.

They'd been reaching, just as she was now.

Guilt hit at the thought she could be overreacting. She'd never actually seen the face of the man who'd abducted them all those years ago. Had she just nailed a stranger with her Taser?

A quick glance in the side mirror said it didn't matter. This guy wasn't there to help with her groceries. The hooded man on the ground inched toward her, a menacing curve to his exposed lips, his body twitching.

She turned the ignition again with a silent prayer.

Bingo.

The engine cranked and she shifted into Reverse. Her tires struggled to gain traction as she floored the pedal. Fear, doubt and anger flooded her.

She checked the rearview again as she pulled onto the street. When she could be certain he wasn't following her, she'd pull over and call 911.

A few seconds later, she turned right onto the road and then made another at the red light, zipping into traffic at the busy intersection. A horn blared.

Adrenaline and fear caused her hands to shake and her stomach to squeeze. Tears stung the backs of her eyes. A couple more turns, mixing lefts and rights, and she pulled into a pharmacy parking lot. She reached for her purse, remembering that half the contents had spilled out in the parking lot. Had any of her personal information fallen out? On the concrete? Right next to him?

But it couldn't be *him*, could it?

Why would he come back after all these years?

The festival? The radio show? Every year she mentioned her brother near the anniversary of his disappearance and got threatening letters at the station. The sheriff's office followed up with the same result as previous years, no enthusiasm, no leads.

Rebecca couldn't write it off so easily, had never been able to. She scoured social media for any signs of Shane. Last month alone, she must've sent a dozen messages to people who matched Shane's description. Although she still hadn't given up, her results weren't any better than the sheriff's. But her resolve was.

Maybe it was her own guilt that kept her searching. Or, a deep-seated need to give their mother closure.

Rebecca rummaged through her bag, desperate to locate her cell, and found nothing. It must've fallen out of her purse. The sheriff's office was nearby. She'd have to drive to the station to file a complaint against her attacker. She cursed. No way could she get there in time for them to take her information and then catch him. He'd be long gone, most likely already was. She fisted her hand and thumped the steering wheel.

If her on-air mention of Shane hadn't rattled any chains, the media might have. Every year before the festival the local paper ran some kind of article referencing Shane's disappearance. This year being the fifteenth anniversary had brought out the wolves. A reporter had been waiting in the parking lot at work two weeks ago, trying to score an interview. He'd said he wanted a family member's perspective. She'd refused and then gone to the sheriff to ask for protection. Again, they did nothing to stop the intrusion, saying no laws had been violated.

Even Charles Alcorn, the town's wealthiest resident, had reached out to her. He'd helped with the search years ago and said he'd like to offer assistance again. What could he do that hadn't already been done?

This time, the sheriff's office couldn't ignore her. They would have to do something. The attack was concrete and too close for comfort. The man had shown up out of nowhere. She'd been so focused on getting away that she hadn't thought to see if he'd retreated to a car. A make and model, a license plate, would give the sheriff something to go on.

Her best chance at seeing him behind bars, overdue justice for her brother, had just slipped away. *If* that was him, a little voice inside her head reminded.

Did he have her cell phone? A cold chill ran down her back.

Wait a minute. Couldn't the sheriff track him using GPS?

Anger balled inside her as she drove the couple of

blocks to the sheriff's office. What if they didn't believe her?

She hadn't physically been there in years, and yet she could still recall the look of pity on Sheriff Randall Brine's face the last time she'd visited. His gaze had fixed on her for a couple seconds, contemplating her. Then, he'd said, "Have you thought about getting away for a little while? Maybe take a long vacation?"

"I'm fine," she'd said, but they both knew she was lying.

"I know," he'd said too quickly. "I was just thinking how nice it'd be to walk through the surf. Eat fresh seafood for a change." Deep circles cradled his dark blue eyes and he looked wrung out. She'd written it off as guilt, thinking she was probably the last person he wanted to see. Was she a reminder of his biggest failure? Then again, it seemed no one wanted to see her around. "We've done everything we can. I wish I had better news. I'll let you know if we get any new information."

"But—"

His tired stare had pinned her before he picked up his folder and refocused on what he'd been reading before she'd interrupted him.

Rebecca had wanted to stomp her feet and make a scene to force him to listen to her. In her heart, she knew he was right. And she couldn't depend on the sheriff to investigate every time something went bump in the night or a complete stranger reminded her of him.

Somehow, life had to go on.

Heaven knew her parents, overwrought with grief, had stopped talking to each other and to their friends. Instead of real conversation, there'd been organized searches, candlelight vigils and endless nights spent scouring fields.

When search teams thinned and then disappeared altogether, there'd been nothing left but despair. They'd divorced a year following Shane's disappearance. Her dad had eventually remarried and had two more children, both boys. And her mother never forgave him for it. She'd limited visitation, saying she was afraid Rebecca would feel awkward.

After, both parents had focused too much attention on Rebecca, which had smothered her. There'd been two and a half years of endless counseling and medication until she'd finally stood up to them. No more, she'd said, wanting to be normal again, to feel ordinary. And even though she'd returned to a normal life after that, nothing was ever normal again.

Although the monster hadn't returned, he'd left panic, loneliness and the very real sense that nothing would ever be okay again.

Since then, she'd had a hard time letting anyone get close to her, especially men. The one person who'd pushed past her walls in high school, Brody, had scared her more than her past. He'd been there that night. He'd stepped forward and said she was meeting him to give him back a shirt he had to have for camp so she wouldn't have to betray her friends. Her mother had never forgiven him. He'd been the one person Rebecca could depend on, who hadn't treated her differently, and he deserved so much more than she could give. Even as a teenager she'd known Brody deserved more.

Separating herself from him in high school had been the right thing to do, she reminded herself. Because every time she'd closed her eyes at night, fear that the monster would return consumed her. Every dark room she'd stood in front of had made her heart pound painfully against her chest. Every strange sound had caused her pulse to race.

And time hadn't made it better.

She often wondered if things would have turned out differently if she'd broken the pact and told authorities the real reason they'd been out.

Probably not. She was just second-guessing herself again. None of the kids had been involved.

Once Shane had been discovered following her, they'd broken up the game and gone home. Nothing would've changed.

Rebecca refocused as she pulled into a parking spot at the sheriff's office. By the time she walked up the steps to the glass doors, she'd regained some of her composure.

The deputy at the front desk acknowledged her with a nod. She didn't recognize him and figured that was good. He might not know her, either.

"How can I help you?"

"I need to speak to the sheriff."

"Sorry. He's not in. I'm Deputy Adams." The middle-aged man offered a handshake. "Can I help you?"

"I need to report an assault. I believe it could be connected to a case he worked a few years ago." She introduced herself as she shook his hand.

The way his forehead bunched after he pulled her up in the database made her figure he was assessing her mental state. Her name must've been flagged. He asked a few routine-sounding questions, punched the information into the keyboard and then folded his hands and smiled. A sympathetic look crossed his features.

"I'll make sure the report is filed and on the sheriff's desk as soon as he arrives."

Deputy Adams might be well intentioned, but he wasn't exactly helpful. His response was similar as she reported her missing phone.

Not ready to accept defeat, she thanked him, squared her shoulders and headed into the hot summer sun.

Local law enforcement was no use, and she'd known that on some level. They'd let the man slip through their fingers all those years ago and hadn't found him since. What would be different now?

She thought about the fact that her little brother would be twenty-two years old now. That he'd be returning home from college this summer, probably fresh from an athletic scholarship. Even at seven, he'd been obsessed with sports. Maybe he still was. A part of her still refused to believe he was gone.

Rebecca let out a frustrated hiss. *I'm so sorry, Shane.*

What else could she do? She had to think. Wait a minute. What about her cell? If her attacker had picked it up, could she track him somehow? Her phone might be the key. She could go home and search the internet to find out how to locate it and possibly find him. And then do what? Confront him? Alone? Even in her desperate state she knew that would be a dangerous move.

Could she take Alcorn up on his offer to help?

And say what?

Would he believe her when the sheriff's office wouldn't?

She needed help. Someone she could trust.

Brody? He was back from the military.

Even though she hadn't seen him in years, he might help.

If she closed her eyes, she could remember his face

perfectly. His honest, clear blue eyes and sandy-blond hair with dark streaks on a far-too-serious-for-his-age face punctuated a strong, squared jaw. By fifteen, he was already six foot one. She couldn't help but wonder how he'd look now that he was grown. The military had most likely filled out his muscles.

When she'd returned to school after a year of being homeschooled, kids she'd known all her life had diverted their gazes from her in the hallway when she walked past. Conversations turned to whispers. Teachers gave her extra time to complete assignments and spoke to her slowly, as if she couldn't hear all of a sudden. Even back then, the pain pierced through the numbness and hurt. She'd felt shunned. As the years passed, she realized no one knew what to say and she appreciated them for trying. She got used to being an outsider. Her tight-knit group of friends had split up. She'd figured they were afraid to be connected with her or just plain afraid of her.

Not Brody. He'd stopped by her house every day after the incident even though her mother refused to allow him inside, especially after he'd stepped forward. It had been easier to take the blame than to admit why they'd really been out that night—to play Mission Quest. They'd had good reasons to lie, too. First of all, they weren't supposed to be playing that online game, let alone sneaking out to meet up with strangers to capture their friends' bases. And then there was the sheriff. He'd been looking for any excuse to bust their best friend Ryan's older brother, Justin, the guy who'd let them into the game in the first place. If they didn't cover for him, the sheriff would go after Justin like an angry pit bull. It would be his third strike and a one-way trip to a real jail. No more acting-out-against-an-abusive-father juvenile stuff. He'd be shipped off for good if their dad didn't beat Justin to death first.

Justin had cleaned up his act. And he deserved a second chance. Besides, it was no surprise that he'd taken a wrong turn in the first place with a father as cruel as his. The real miracle had been that Ryan hadn't followed in his older brother's footsteps.

Even though it would have meant turning on their friends, Brody had visited Rebecca in the middle of the night to tell her that she didn't have to keep the pact. Ryan would understand.

But Justin didn't have anything to do with Shane's disappearance. And there was no reason to screw up another family.

Shaking off the memories, Rebecca slipped into the driver's seat and started the engine. She put the car in Reverse and tapped the gas a little too hard.

An object flew forward underneath her feet. She hit the brake, bent forward and picked it up. Her cell. It must've fallen out when she was rushing into her car earlier.

A mix of relief and exasperation flooded her as the thought of tracking her assailant via her phone disintegrated.

It was too early to give up hope of finding him this time.

She couldn't do it alone. Brody had bought the old Wakefield Ranch. Rumor said he'd become a warrior overseas. Would he help? Could she reach out to him after all these years? How hard would it be to get his phone number and find out?

Rebecca pulled into another parking spot and

thumbed through her contacts. Her finger hovered over Ryan's number. They hadn't spoken in years, but she figured it wouldn't hurt to reach out to him. She sent a text message to him, unsure this was his number anymore. It didn't matter. It was worth a try. He still owed her one for helping to protect his brother.

The text came thirty seconds later with Brody's information.

Seeing it, needing to reach out to him, made this horror so much more real. And her heart pitched when she thought about facing him again.

Brody Fields leaned against his truck. The call from Rebecca Hughes had dredged up old feelings best left buried. He'd almost ended the call without finding out what she'd wanted. Except he couldn't do that to her. It was Rebecca. The sound of her voice had stirred up all kinds of memories. Most of them were good.

He'd known her since they were kids, but they'd been teenagers when he'd fallen for her. There was so much more than her physical beauty that had drawn him in. She'd been the only female Brody had ever trusted and allowed inside his armor after his mother had betrayed the family, stolen money from the town and then disappeared.

The mental connection he'd shared with Rebecca had been beyond any closeness he'd experienced. Looking back, maybe it was the loner in him that could relate to her isolation.

When she'd pushed him away and said she'd never loved him, it had hurt worse than any physical blow. Soon after, she'd left for college, and then eventually moved to Chicago. He'd been the most surprised to learn that she'd moved back to Mason Ridge.

For a split second, he'd hoped she'd called for old times' sake. Then, he remembered what day it was—the anniversary of Shane's disappearance—and he knew better.

The conversation had been short. She'd told him what had happened and requested to meet face-to-face at The Dirty Bean Coffee Shop. He'd agreed, ending their exchange. The place was on his way home. Driving to the meeting point had taken ten minutes.

The pale blue sedan parking next to his truck had to be hers.

Knowing she was about to step out of her car and he was about to see her again hit him hard. How many times had he secretly wished he'd run into her in the past few months? Where'd that come from?

Hearing that her abductor had returned hadn't done good things to Brody's blood pressure. He wouldn't refuse her plea for help. And a little piece of him hoped he'd figure out if her case and the memories were the reasons she'd rejected him all those years ago. He'd been a boy back then. Helpless. *A lot's changed.*

He'd grown up. Survived his mother's betrayal of his family and the town. Served his country. Gone on to become a leader of an elite-forces team. Spent time with a lot of interesting women. To be honest, not all of them were interesting, but they were smokin' hot.

He crossed his arms over his chest and tucked his hands under his armpits.

The first thing he noticed as Rebecca exited her vehicle was her jean-clad long legs and red boots. His body instantly reacted to seeing the woman she'd become. There were enough curves on her lean figure to make her look like a real woman. She still had the same chestnut-brown hair that fell well past her shoulders in waves. She'd be close enough for him to look into her light brown eyes soon. Were they still the color of honey?

Why did seeing Rebecca reduce him to being that heartsick seventeen-year-old brat again?

Brody ignored the squeeze in his chest. Fond memories aside, he didn't do that particular brand of emotion anymore.

That she moved cautiously, surveying the area, reminded him why she was there. It wasn't to talk about old feelings.

"It's good to see you." She took a tentative step closer to him.

Yep. Same beautiful eyes. Same diamond-shaped face. Brody hadn't expected her voice to sound this grown-up. Or so damn sexy. He didn't want to think about her in a sexual way. She'd been all sweetness and innocence to him at seventeen. And this wasn't a date. He glanced around the parking lot to make sure no one had followed her.

"Wish the circumstances were better. I'm glad you called." The conversation needed to stay on track. So, why did he feel another physical blow when he saw disappointment flash in her eyes? "Tell me why you think I can help."

"He's after me. Neither the sheriff nor the FBI caught him before. I'm scared. You're the only one I can talk to who knows what really happened that night." Her eyes flashed toward him nervously. "I've heard about the things you did overseas. I know you've done some security consulting on the side since you came back. I'd like to hire you to protect me while I sort all this out."

"I don't need your money. I'll help." He didn't have to think long about his answer. Brody had experience tracking down the enemy, and this case had always eaten at him. Guilt?

"I'd still like to pay you something. In fact, I'd rather do it that way. I'm not a charity case." She stared at him, all signs of vulnerability gone from her almond-shaped eyes.

He stared back. "Fine. We'll figure something out."

"Thank you."

He hadn't expected her to look so relieved. "You want to grab a cup of coffee while you fill me in?"

She nodded.

Brody followed Rebecca to the counter, where they placed their orders. She reached in her purse to pay for hers. He caught her arm. Big mistake. An electric volt shot through his hand, vibrated up his arm and warmed places that he didn't realize were still iced over.

There'd be no use denying he felt a sizzle of attraction being near Rebecca again. It was more than a mild spark. She'd grown into a beautiful woman. But if he didn't watch himself, she could put a knife through his chest with just a few words. And Brody had no intention of handing over that power again to anyone.

When their coffees were ready, she located a table in the corner. Brody followed, forcing his gaze away from her backside, ignoring how well the jeans fit her curves.

She took the opposite seat, her gaze diverting to someone behind him. Brody turned in time to see a fairly tall man sit a little too close for comfort. Then again, these coffee shops sure knew how to pack a hundred people into two-foot-square spaces. Brody had had to squeeze between the stacked tables to fit into the tight spot.

"Can you start right now?" Shoulders bunched, jaw set, she looked ready to jump if someone shouted an order over the hum of conversation. Tension practically radiated off her.

"Yes. I'll need to arrange care for my horses. I can make a call to cover that base. If I'm going to be able to help, you'll have to tell me everything." His voice was gruffer than he expected, borderline harsh. Between his need to be her comfort and inappropriate sexual thoughts, being near her wasn't exactly bringing out the best in him.

She glanced from side to side, told him what had happened that morning with more details this time, and then focused those honey browns on him. Tears welled in her eyes. "After all this time, he's after me, Brody. Why? It doesn't make any sense. Where's he been all these years?"

"That's a good question. One I intend to answer."

"And what about my brother? Is there any chance he could still be alive?" Her voice hitched on the last word.

"We'll find out." Brody gripped his cup so he wouldn't reach out to comfort her. "You've already been to the sheriff or you wouldn't be calling me."

She lowered her gaze. "Yes."

"What did he say?" The way she kept one eye on the door had Brody thinking he needed to ask her to switch seats so he'd have a better view. As it was, he didn't like his back facing the door.

"That I should be careful and to call if I see or hear anything suspicious."

"Did you tell them that's why you were there in the first place?" Frustration ate at him. He needed to control it in order to focus on the mission. Why would the man who'd abducted her and her brother all those years ago come back? To finish the job with her? She'd never been the intended target. When she'd witnessed a man grab her brother and run, she'd chased him into the woods. He had to know she hadn't seen or remembered enough of him to help the law track him down or he'd already be in jail. "It's been fifteen years. Why now? Where's he been?"

"Wish I knew." Her gaze ping-ponged from the front door to the exit. Fear pulsed from her. "Then again, the papers always dredge up the past."

"That wouldn't suddenly bring him out. They run stories every year." Brody tapped his finger on the table. "I've thought about this a lot over the years."

"Did we do the right thing back then? I mean, we were just kids protecting our friend by keeping that secret. What if that cost Shane his… What if someone saw something?"

"They would've come forward on their own if they had. Unless you think Justin was somehow involved?"

"No. It wasn't him. This guy was too tall. Plus, I remember that smell. No one in Ryan's house smelled like apple tobacco, least of all Justin." The admission brought a frown to her lips.

"The sheriff wrote the case off as a transient passing through town before and found nothing. It's time to change things up. We need to look at this through a new lens. Our guy could be connected to Mason Ridge in some way. This is where it all started and this is where it ends." Brody had every intention of following through on that promise.

And if that meant breaking the pact and digging up the past, so be it.

Chapter 2

Rebecca's shoulders slumped forward. "It's no use. We've been over this a million times and we never get anywhere. I've scoured the internet for years trying to find Shane. The case is closed. It was most likely a random mugging this morning. Even the deputy thinks I'm crazy."

"Except that we both know you're not." Brody resisted the urge to take her hand in his, noticing how small hers was in comparison, how much more delicate her skin looked.

"The sheriff told me years ago the trail had gone cold. I just didn't want to accept the truth. They're probably right. Shane's...long gone." Her almond-shaped eyes held so much pain.

"I know why your parents didn't leave the area after they divorced. They never gave up hope of finding him, especially your mother," Brody said, leaning forward. Everyone in town had held out the same hope Shane would be found. Hope that had fizzled and died as the weeks ticked by. "And neither did you."

"Seemed like a good enough reason to stay in the beginning."

"There's no reason to give up now."

"Do you know how slim the chances of solving a cold case are? I do." When she looked up, he saw more than hurt in her eyes. He saw fear. He already noted that she'd positioned herself in the corner with her back against the wall, insuring she could see all the possible entry points. And didn't that move take a page out of his own book?

"Except the case isn't cold anymore. He struck again. We know he's in the area."

"Do you have any idea how that new deputy looked at me when I reported the crime and he pulled me up in the system? No one believes me." Tears welled in her eyes, threatening to fall.

"I do." Brody meant those two words.

"He could be anywhere by now."

"And so could you. But you're not. You're here. And so is he." Brody needed the conversation to switch tracks. Give her a chance to settle down. It was understandable that her emotions were on a roller coaster. Her need to find her brother battled with the fear she never would. "What about after college? You disappeared. I heard that you swore you'd never set foot in Mason Ridge again. What happened?"

"I did. I moved to Chicago and got a job at a radio station. I came home three years ago because of my mom's health. She took a turn."

"I didn't know." Again he suppressed the urge to reach across the table and comfort Rebecca, dismissing it as an old habit that didn't want to die.

"I had no way to reach you while you were overseas. Doubt I could've found the right words, anyway."

Brody understood the sentiment. How many times had he thought about looking her up on social media over the years but hadn't? Dozens? Hundreds? "Is it her heart again?"

Rebecca nodded. The sadness in her eyes punctuated what had to be another difficult time for the Hughes family.

"What'd the doctor say?"

"That she isn't doing well. They're doing everything they can, but she's refusing to try a new medication that will help her. Says she's afraid of being allergic to it, which is just an excuse." She shrugged. "I always stop by and see her after I get groceries on Fridays. I couldn't go today, after what happened this morning. I called to let her know and prayed that she didn't pick up on anything in my voice. She shouldn't see me like this. It'll just make her worry even more."

"I'm truly sorry about your mom." And so many more things he wasn't quite ready to put into words. His own mother had freely walked away from his family after getting folks to hand over their hard-earned money under the guise of making an investment in Mason Ridge's future. She had no idea what it was like to stick around.

"Thank you." The earnestness in her expression ripped at his insides. "I can't help but feel that trying to reopen Shane's case is hopeless. The task force took all the facts into account fifteen years ago when they investigated his disappearance. All the leads from the case are freezing cold by now. My brother is still missing, probably dead. We're right where we started, except now this jerk's back as some twisted anniversary present to me." Tears streamed down her cheeks.

Brody reached across the table and thumbed them away, ignoring the sensations zinging through his hand from making contact with her skin and the warning bells sounding off inside his head.

She glanced at him and then cast her gaze intently on the table, drawing circles with her index finger. "It's all my fault. If I hadn't told him to sit down and wait for me by the willow tree so I could finish the mission he'd still be alive today."

"Don't do that to yourself. None of this is your fault."

Her shoulders slumped forward. "What else can we do?"

Yeah, her stress indicator was the same. And Brody wanted to make it better.

"I'll figure out a way to get a copy of the file so I can review the list of suspects again. I have a friend in Records and she owes me a favor. Fresh eyes can be a big help and might give us more clues." Brody rubbed the stubble on his chin.

"With the festival going on this guy could blend in again, couldn't he?"

"Yeah. We have to look at everything differently this time. He might be someone local who hides behind the festival. Maybe he knew that was the first place law enforcement would look."

"You're right. He could be a normal person, a banker or store clerk." A spark lit behind her eyes, and under different circumstances it'd be sexy as hell.

"It's likely. He could be married and involved in a church or youth group. He might be a bus driver or substitute teacher. It's very well possible he could work with kids or in a job where he has access to families. We have to consider everyone. Those are great places to start."

"I just focused on what the sheriff had said before, him being transient. None of these options occurred to me." She shuddered.

Brody sipped his coffee. "It's not a bad thing that you don't think like a criminal."

"If we need help, Charles Alcorn offered," she said.

"A man in his position would be a good resource to have on our side." Brody leaned forward. "So this is how it's going to go. I follow you. Everywhere. You got a date, I'm right behind you." The thought of sitting outside her house while another man was inside doing God knows what with her sat in his stomach like bad steak. And yet, they were both grown adults. It shouldn't bother him. Wasn't as if he'd been chaste, either.

"I'm not dating."

Brody suppressed the flicker of happiness those words gave him. He had no right to care.

"And I don't want to stop you from doing…whatever," she added quickly.

Why did the way she said that knife him?

"Don't worry about my personal life. I'm here to do a job. That's all I care about right now." Why was that more of a reminder for him than for her?

Working with her was going to be more difficult than he'd originally thought. And not because errant sexual thoughts crossed his mind every time he got close enough to smell her shampoo. It was citrus and flowery.

Being with her brought up their painful past, but they'd shared a lot of good memories, too. Like their first kiss. They'd skipped the Friday afternoon pep rally junior year and headed down to the lake in the old Mustang he'd bought and fixed up using money from his after-school job at his dad's garage.

As they sat on the hood of his car parked in front of Mason Ridge Lake, she'd leaned her head on his shoulder. And then decimated his defenses when she looked up at him with those honey browns. His heart had squeezed in the same way it did earlier today when he saw her again. She still had that same citrus and flowery scent and it made his pulse race just as it had before. He remembered the warmth of her body against his side, her soft lips as they slightly parted.

Brody had leaned in slowly and her lips gently brushed against his; her tongue flickered across his mouth.

Afterward, they'd just sat there, silent, before he'd pulled her into a hug.

The kiss had lasted only a few seconds but was burned into his memory. How many times had he thought about those sweet lips when he was an ocean away with his face in the dirt? How many times since? *Too many.*

Brody glanced at his watch. "I'll connect with my friend and see what I can find out about that file."

"Okay." She leaned forward, rubbing her eyes, suppressing a yawn. "What else?"

"You used to look for Shane everywhere. My guess is that you haven't stopped. Am I right?"

"Yes. I scan social media on my days off."

"Any hits?"

She shrugged. "Not real ones. I've been hit on plenty, though."

"Men can be such jerks."

"Women are far worse. You'd be shocked at the messages I get from someone calling herself Adriana." Rebecca rolled her eyes.

"I have a few like those, too," he said in an attempt to lighten the tension.

"I'm sure you've been exposed to worse, having been in a war zone."

"I've seen my fair share of everything, here and abroad," he said. "You ever follow up on any of those real messages?"

"A handful. Why?" She paused and her eyes grew wide. "You don't think one of them could be stalking me?"

"Not sure. I was thinking it might be a good place to start."

She brought her hand up and squeezed the bottom of her neck on the left side, subconsciously trying to ease the tension in her shoulders. Her face muscles bunched. Signs her stress levels were climbing.

"Has anything else out of the ordinary happened to you recently? He had to know your schedule to know where you'd be this morning. I don't believe the grocery store was a random encounter."

"Now that you mention it, I've been hearing noises in the evenings before I leave for work. I thought it was the neighbor's cat at first. Now, I'm wondering if it could've been him."

"We'll check the perimeter of your house. The recent rain might have left us with evidence."

There'd been one of those open-up-the-sky-and-let-the-rain-pour-down-in-buckets storms North Texas was known for the other night. She scooted her chair back and slung her purse strap over her shoulder.

"There was also that unusually persistent reporter last week. I think his name is Peter Sheffield. I got off a few minutes early, so I was alone in the parking lot. He nearly gave me a heart attack waiting at my car after my shift at the radio station. Do you think he could be involved?"

"From here on out, I want you to suspect every sound, every person." Brody's gaze narrowed.

"So, what you're saying is…act like I always do."

He didn't like the sound of those words. "This guy might've been trying to scare you into an interview."

"That's crazy. People actually do that?"

Brody tapped his knuckles on the table. "I remember him now. He used to hang out with Justin, didn't he? Then he dropped out of Texas State U to join the military."

"That's right. He did. Are you saying you think he might be involved?"

"We need to look at everyone who was out that night playing the game. And especially Justin's friends."

Rebecca nearly choked on her sip of coffee. "I hadn't thought about it being someone so young. The apple tobacco. I just figured it had to be someone older."

"Maybe it is. But we're not taking anything for granted this time." He took the last swig of coffee, tilted the cup and glanced at the bottom, then fixed his gaze on her. "You ready to do this?"

She nodded, stood, walked past him and headed straight to the door.

"I'll follow you home in my truck." He threw away

their empty cups, checking to make sure no one in the place seemed interested in either one of them. No one did.

Outside, the midday sun shone bright. Rebecca hesitated before spinning around to face him. He expected to be confronted with the same fear in her eyes, but she popped up on her tiptoes and brushed a kiss to his lips. "I'm not sure what I would do without you. Thank you, Brody."

The way his name rolled off her tongue brought back all kinds of memories he didn't need to be thinking about right now. "I haven't done anything yet."

"Yes, you have. An hour ago I was afraid of my own shadow."

"And now?"

"I'm relieved you're here. You look good, Brody."

The warmth her words spread through his chest almost made him wonder if going to her place was a good idea. He was a grown man, now. And he had desires to match.

"You do, too. Better than good." Brody took her hand in his, ignoring how right it felt, and walked her to her vehicle.

Once she was safely inside, he hopped in his truck and followed Rebecca home. Her house, a two-bedroom bungalow, was fifteen minutes from the coffee shop. He parked behind her car as he surveyed the quiet residential street. Since the attack had happened hours ago, the monster could be anywhere. No red flags, yet.

"How long have you lived here?" he asked, once they'd both exited their vehicles, examining the front windows for any signs of forced entry.

"I rented it three years ago when I moved back." Her hand shook as she tried to unlock the door.

"I can do that for you." He looped his arm around her waist as she turned to face him. Touching Rebecca came a little too naturally, so he pulled back rather than allow himself to get sucked into the comfort.

"Guess I'm still a little shaken up." She smiled weakly as she handed over the key ring. Her fingers brushed against his flat palm, causing a sizzle to spread through his hand.

"You're doing great, honey." He closed his fist around the key, then stepped beside her before unlocking and opening the door. A high-pitched note held steady until she hit numbers on the keypad, four beeps followed by silence. The state-of-the-art security system was no surprise, given her past.

This place was all Rebecca. Soft, earthy feminine colors. Furniture he could see himself comfortable on—especially with her nearby. Her place was exactly as he'd imagined it would be, which had him thinking about the strong mental connection they'd shared. Still shared?

That was a long time ago. People change. He'd changed.

Walking around the living room, he ran his hand underneath lamp shades, tables and other flat surfaces.

The coffee-colored cabinets in the kitchen were his taste, too. He checked them and then swept his hand along the white marble countertops, stopping at the sink. There was a nice-sized window looking onto the backyard. The best thing about this part of North Texas was having trees. Her yard was a decent size, so someone could easily hide and watch her while she worked in the kitchen. Especially if she stood at the sink. His first thought was to install blinds.

Brody started making a mental to-do list as he moved through the house. He'd run to the nearest big-box store and pick up supplies later. He could make the changes himself.

She had a decent alarm.

"Do you live here by yourself?"

"Yeah." She bit back a yawn. Dark circles cradled her brown-as-honey eyes.

"You should try to rest. I'm not going anywhere. I'll wake you if I get any new information."

"I'm okay." She moved to the kitchen. "Besides, my nerves are too fried to sleep. I can't force down another cup of coffee. Want some herbal tea?"

"No, thanks." He still needed to check the master bedroom and he couldn't stall any longer. He shuffled his boots down the hall. The thought of being in the exact place she brought other men didn't sit well. There'd been no framed pictures of her with another guy so far. Brody didn't want to admit how happy that made him.

Hoping his luck would continue, he breached her bedroom. He'd open the nightstand drawer last, in case there were condoms. It wasn't his business what she did anymore, or with whom, but he couldn't help feeling territorial about his first love. The thought of her in bed with another man would rank right up there as one of his worst mental pictures. And he really didn't want to see any leftover men's clothing or shavers in the bathroom, either. Which was exactly the reason he'd put off checking her master bedroom.

As he walked the perimeter of the room, nothing stood out.

"Everything okay in here?" The sound of her voice coming from the doorway coupled with the visual of her bed didn't do good things to him.

"Doesn't look like you slept here last night."

"I work deep nights at the radio station."

"Right. Of course." Why did that ease his tense shoulders?

She stopped, almost as if she was hesitating to cross the threshold. Did she sense the heat filling the short distance between them? All he had to do was reach out and he could pull her close to him, protect her.

Brody mentally shook off the thought and moved on. "What time did you go to work last night?"

"I go in at ten o'clock. The show airs from midnight to six. We always wrap afterward."

"Any new employees in the last couple of months?"

"No. Not much ever really changes in this town." Her smile warmed his heart, threatening to put another crack in his carefully constructed armor. He took a couple of steps toward the door.

"The body needs sleep in order to perform. Why don't you close your eyes and rest while I check out the grounds?"

She looked up at him with big, fearful brown eyes. "You're not leaving, are you?"

"No. You're stuck with me. Like I said, I'm not going anywhere without you until we figure this whole thing out." He shouldn't notice how good he felt when her face muscles relaxed into a smile. "I need to make some calls, though, and you might as well get some shut-eye."

"What if he…" She didn't finish, but Brody knew exactly what she was going to say.

"I doubt he'll show up while I'm here. Think about it. This creep snatched little kids before and then surprised you this morning, which sounds like someone who's afraid of confrontation. I doubt he has the gall to try something with me around."

She nodded and her shoulders lowered.

"You have an extra key?"

"Sure." She disappeared down the hall, returning a moment later with a spare held out on the flat of her palm. She relayed her alarm code.

Taking it caused his finger to brush her creamy skin again. The frisson of heat produced by contact pulsed straight from his finger, to his arm and through his chest. In the back of his mind, he was still thinking about the feel of her lips against his at the coffee shop, the taste of coffee that lingered.

Physical contact was a bad idea. If he couldn't find and keep his objectivity in this case, the moral thing to do would be to help her find someone who could.

"You need me, just shout," he said, resigned. He needed to get in touch with the sheriff's office, too. See if Brine would offer information about the case.

"Okay." She paused. "Any chance you could stay inside until I get out of the shower?"

"I'll be in the living room," he said, hearing the huskiness in his own voice. The last thing he needed was the naked image of her in his thoughts.

He almost laughed out loud. They'd been together in high school. Not in the biblical sense, but they'd been a couple. Twelfth grade was a long time ago. Feelings changed. Their current attraction was most likely residual. She was beautiful. No doubt about that. And she was exactly the kind of woman he'd ask out if they'd met today and could forget about the past. But all the extra chemistry he felt had to be left over from before. That was the only reasonable explanation. Because Brody hadn't felt like this toward any woman since her. And he'd been in several relationships over the years. Yet, something had always stopped him from taking the next step. Marriage was a huge commitment, he'd reasoned. There'd been no need to rush into a big decision like that.

"I saw a laptop in the living room. Mind if I use it?" he asked.

"Not at all. Go right ahead," she said.

"What's the password?"

"Capital *N-V-M-B-R*. Then the number fifteen."

Brody turned without giving away his reaction. November fifteenth was his birthday.

Rebecca checked the clock. She'd showered, hoping the warm water would relax her strung-too-tight muscles, before the tossing-and-turning routine began. She flipped onto her right side and placed a clean sock over her eyes to block out the light.

Rolling back to her left, she repositioned the sock. No luck.

The sun was firmly set in the eastern sky. She'd closed her black-out curtains. This was normally the time she'd be asleep, but the way her mind was spinning no way could she rest. All she could think about was the possibility of Shane being alive. Even she knew the chances were slim. And yet, odds didn't matter in her heart, where she still held hope.

She'd need more than a piece of material to block out her thoughts. Time was the enemy. A killer was after her. Thoughts of being locked in that shed brought the terrifying sensation of her abduction back. And everything that had happened after...

When she'd returned, the town had been in chaos. Volunteers were assigned to a search team. Hundreds of people fanned out over the fields surrounding Mason Ridge Lake. Others opened car trunks and abandoned structures. People carried guns and set up neighborhood patrols. Even the wealthiest man, Mr. Alcorn, had thrown considerable resources into the effort.

Later, searchers joined hands as they walked in a line through the fields near Mason High School.

Two FBI agents had taken up residence in the Hughes's front room. A half dozen crop dusters and military planes had circled the sky, searching. The 4-H club had sent riders out on horseback.

Local law enforcement had encouraged people to keep their porch lights on at night and be ready to report any activity that might be suspicious. The Texas State Police had set up a half dozen roadblocks. Railroad cars, motel rooms and the bus station were searched—as was every house in the city.

Shane's comb had been shipped off to the FBI lab near Washington for analysis. As had his favorite toys—trucks, LEGO and his handheld game system.

Rebecca had suddenly found herself under twenty-four-hour watch. Dr. Walsh, her pediatrician, had checked her for signs of sexual assault.

When a week of fruitless searching had passed, authorities had alerted residents to look out for scavengers, believing that Shane's body might have been tossed into a field or nearby farm. They'd been told to keep an eye out for large gatherings of buzzards and crows and were advised not to touch a body if one was found.

It wasn't long after that the FBI ran out of steam. Reporters had been a different story. They'd followed her parents for months, relentless.

Normally, Rebecca forced those thoughts out of her mind, unable to think about them. Having Brody in the next room brought way more comfort than it should. She told herself no one would care about her more than him, and that's why his presence gave her such a sense of well-being. Nothing about her current situation should cause her to let her guard down. The last time she'd gone against her better judgment, she'd ended up in a shed out in the woods. And her brother...

She couldn't even go there. Couldn't sleep, either. She tossed the covers and pushed off the mattress. She threw on a pair of shorts and a T-shirt, pulled her still-damp hair into a ponytail and met Brody in the living room.

He glanced up from the laptop, a look of determination creasing his forehead, and offered a quick smile. "Can't sleep?"

"No. This time of year is always...challenging. So, dealing with all this other stuff has my system out of whack." She threw her arms up, exasperated.

Brody studied her. His clear blue eyes seemed to see right through her. "I've said it before, but we will figure this out. I already reached out to Ryan and he's following up with the others, trying to see if we can figure out a good time for everyone to meet." He patted a spot on the sofa right next to him. He looked good. Damn good. He'd filled out his six-foot-two frame nicely. He was all muscle and strength and athletic grace. His blond hair was cut tight with curls at the collar. He wore a simple shirt and jeans.

Rebecca took a seat next to him, ignoring how her stomach free-fell the minute she got close. "Have you heard anything from your contact?"

"Yes. She emailed as much as she could. The suspect list is long." He had a pen and notepad out, scribbling notes as he flipped through a file on-screen. "I'd also like to take a look at your social-media account."

"Sure." She waited for him to click on the icon before giving him the password. "Nice pen."

He glanced at it and nodded. "A present from the old man."

"How is your father?"

"He's getting older, but he'd never admit it." Brody half smiled, still maintaining focus. "I've been thinking of moving him onto the ranch. Hate the thought of him being alone. But he's stubborn."

"Sounds like someone else I know." She laughed. "I doubt he'll give up his own place without a fight. He's a good man. I always liked him."

Brody nodded, but his expression turned serious again as he studied the screen.

"Find anything useful?"

"Hold on." He clicked through her chat messages, studying the accompanying faces. He stopped at one, considered it for a long moment and then clicked on the image, which opened the guy's home page. "There's something about this one. Randy Harper."

"If Shane was still…alive, I'd imagine him to look just like this. I mean, he and I look related, don't we?" Her cell, on the coffee table, buzzed. She picked it up and checked the screen. It was her father. She hit Ignore and tucked it half under her leg.

Brody had seen who the caller was. She steadied herself for the inevitable questions about why she was refusing to take her father's calls. The cell vibrated under her leg, indicating he'd left a voice mail. She didn't want to get into it with Brody right now, didn't want to think about her father's new life while she still hunted down what had truly happened to his old one.

She glanced up, catching Brody's stare. He didn't immediately speak. Then he said, "The others resemble you, too, but there's something special about Randy."

"I had the same feeling."

"How long ago did you find him?" he asked.

"Six months or so."

"He doesn't live far."

"Nope. But he didn't respond to my message. I've been doubling my efforts with him and a few others lately."

"The city of Brighton is located two counties east of here. I used to know a girl who lived out there while we were in high school...." His voice trailed off at the end, as if he suddenly realized who he was talking to.

Sure, a twinge of jealousy nipped at her. More than that, if she was being totally honest. But she had no right to own the feeling. Shoving it aside, she smiled. It was weak, at best, but Brody took the peace offering, returning the gesture.

He scrolled down the page. "He hasn't posted anything in months. He either hasn't been online or he's abandoned his page altogether."

"We can rule him out as a phony, then. He can't be a crackpot trying to rattle me if he doesn't even realize

I've tried to contact him. Plus, he's too old to be Shane. Look at the birthdate."

"You're probably right, but if it was him, then he might not really know when he was born. I've read about cases of abducted kids being told lies about when and where they were born to make it more difficult for them to dig around in the past."

"Wouldn't he need an actual birth certificate to enroll in school? My stepmother had to produce that, shot records, and a current electric bill for my half brothers," Rebecca said. She didn't want to feel the spark of hope that Shane might actually still be alive. She wanted her brother to be somewhere safe—had dreamed it, hoped it and prayed it. But she didn't want to create false expectations based on a social-media page.

"A birth certificate can be made. For a price. The rest would fall into place from there. Maybe we can find some of Randy's friends. Dig around a little in his background. Pay him a visit." Brody scribbled down a few names. "I don't want to invite them into your social network, so we'll have to reach out another way."

He scanned through photo after photo on the home pages of the people connected to Randy. A good fifteen minutes had passed when Brody made a satisfied grunt. "Look here. At this pic. And this one. Then, this one. See what's in the background?" He displayed the pictures in a larger window to view one at a time. Three friends had tagged Randy at a local restaurant called Mervin's Eats.

"When was the last picture posted?" Rebecca asked as another flicker of excitement fizzed through her.

"Three months ago." Brody glanced at the clock on the bottom right-hand corner of the screen. "Too early to go and check out the place now. Looks like we just figured out where we're eating tonight, though." He pulled up another screen, his fingers working the keyboard, and pulled up the address to Mervin's Eats in Bayville, Texas. He copied down the address in his notebook.

This was the first promising lead she'd had in fifteen years. It was hard to contain the enthusiasm swelling inside her. "For so many years, everyone's said he's gone. What if they were wrong?"

"I have plans to track down every possibility. That means we're going to run into dead ends." His honest blue eyes had darkened with concern.

"Believe me, I know better than anyone about disappointment." He was trying not to get her hopes up in case he had to dash them, and she appreciated him for it. "I've handled it before and I will again. It just feels nice to have a little hope for a change."

His nod and smile said he understood. "We need to keep working other trails, too. If we can figure out why or how our guy was connected to Mason Ridge before, maybe we can figure out what he's doing here now."

"I can't stand waiting around. I'd like to go out looking for him."

"Okay. Give me a chance to study these notes so I have a better idea where to start searching. See if I can find some connection either to this town or to your family."

She shivered as an icy chill ran down her back. That thought was unnerving. Could someone close to them have orchestrated Shane's disappearance? She hadn't considered it before.

Brody's gaze trained on her. "Have you eaten anything today?"

"Not yet. Stomach's been churning all morning. My brain, too. I was thinking about the fact the places where he took my brother and me weren't secure. It couldn't have taken him more than a half hour to get us both there, so they were close by. He had to know the area, which, now that I think about it, would rule out a random person passing through town. I told the sheriff all this before, but there's another thing I can't stop thinking about. He didn't want me. He wanted my brother. I got in the way when I followed them and the guy was distressed about it."

"Makes me think it might've been his first time to kidnap someone," Brody said quietly.

"Not the work of someone used to slipping into a strange town to snatch a kid."

"What else did the sheriff say?" Brody asked, his interest piqued.

"That he probably improvised, saw a couple of abandoned buildings and hid us there. But why? Wouldn't he want to get out of town as quickly as possible?"

"And the response to that?"

"Nothing to me. I did hear someone from the FBI tell my parents later that the guy most likely hadn't pre-planned the kidnapping."

If she could go back and trade places with her brother, she wouldn't hesitate. How many times had she wished she'd been the one to disappear, to die?

There was a slim chance that Shane was still alive, she reminded herself. The odds weren't good, Rebecca knew that, but she also knew better than to focus her energy on the negative.

That bastard had made a mistake once. She was living proof. All she needed was another misstep. With

Brody's eyes on this case, maybe he would figure it out and bring the monster to justice. Rebecca would do whatever it took to help. "If only I remembered more…"

Brody's arm around her shoulder, his fingers lifting her chin, stemmed the emotion threatening to unravel her.

"I hate that you're going through this again. I'm sorry it happened to you in the first place. Believe me, I'll do everything I can to find that jerk."

A mix of emotion played inside her. Fear. Anxiety. Sadness.

Hope?

"Let's get something to eat and we'll hit Woodrain Park. He's probably smart enough to pick a new place, but we have to cover it, anyway." His words wrapped around her like a warm blanket. She leaned over until their foreheads touched.

"I won't let him hurt you again." He said other sweet words—words that made her want to yield to his strength.

And yet, getting too close to Brody wasn't a good idea. No one could quiet the monster's voice in the back of her head for long. He would return. He always returned. And she'd slip into her armor, blocking out the world.

"I'll fix something to eat." She rose and walked toward the kitchen, stopping in front of the sink.

Brody followed. The gun tucked into the waistband of his jeans was a stark reminder of the dangers they faced. He rummaged around the fridge, tossing up an apple. "Not much here to work with."

"I left my groceries scattered across the lot."

He nodded and then searched the pantry, pulling out

almond butter, bread and cinnamon grahams. "These'll work."

She nodded.

He moved to the sink with the supplies, glanced up and froze. His gaze fixed on something out the window.

Cursing, he palmed his weapon and adjusted his position, stepping away from the window. "Get down. Now."

Rebecca dropped to her knees as panic roared through her, making her limbs feel heavy. "What is it? What's going on?"

"Someone's out there watching."

Brody crawled past her with the agility and speed of a lion zeroed in on his prey. "Lock the door behind me. Wait right here until I get back."

"No," she pleaded, trying to stop her body from shaking. She opened the drawer and gripped a knife. "Take me with you. I don't want to be here alone."

Chapter 3

"Stay close." Brody didn't like the cold chill pricking the hair on his arms. He didn't like how easily a stranger could watch Rebecca while she was in the house. And he sure as hell didn't like the fact that the man who'd tormented her and changed her life forever was most likely back.

Brody crouched low as he cleared the back door.

The figure, tall and thick-built enough to be a man, darted into the trees.

"Go inside, lock the door and set the alarm."

She didn't respond, but he heard her backtrack as he broke into a full run. No way could she keep up, and he didn't want to risk them being separated in the trees, leaving her exposed and vulnerable.

The unforgiving dirt and shrub stabbed his feet as he bolted across the yard. Brody regretted kicking his boots off and getting too comfortable. The male form disappeared to the left as Brody hopped the chain-link fence and breached the tree line.

Forging through the mesquites, maples and oaks, Brody winced as he stepped on scattered broken limbs. He pushed the pain out of his mind, maintaining full focus on his target. He could hear crunching ahead of him, although he couldn't judge the distance or the gap between them. At this point, the noise could come from an animal he'd spooked. Based on the weight, it would have to be one big animal. Even so, it was still possible. There was no telling for sure until he got eyes on whatever it was.

A dark thought hit. Brody was being drawn deeper into the trees; the underbrush was thickening, and Rebecca was alone at the house. Brody couldn't take the chance he'd been lured away.

Besides, the rustle of leaves was growing more distant, indicating the guy was too far ahead to catch.

Circling back, the pain of bare feet pounding against hard soil made running a challenge.

He didn't know how long he'd been going, but it took a good fifteen minutes to jog back to the bungalow. His feet had been cut and he was leaving a trickle of blood across the lawn on Rebecca's quarter-acre lot.

She must've been glued to the kitchen window, because as soon as he stepped onto the back porch, the door swung open and she rushed into his arms.

"Hey, hey." He took a step back as the full force of her impact hit him.

"I'm sorry." She buried her face in his chest.

Brody should put a little space between them. He

should take a step back and not be her comfort. He should keep a safe distance.

Should.

But couldn't.

Not with the way she felt in his arms. Not with the way her body molded to fit his. Not with her scent, citrus and flowery, filling his senses.

A tree branch crunched. Brody scanned the yard, didn't see anything.

Outside, they were exposed.

He guided them inside the house, then closed and locked the door behind them.

"It's okay," he soothed.

"I know," she said quickly, and he knew it was wishful thinking on her part.

He heard her muffled sniffles and suspected she wasn't stepping away from him because she didn't want him to see her cry.

Before he could debate the sanity of his actions, his arms encircled her waist, hauling her closer to him.

Flush against his chest, he could feel her rapid heartbeat. The whole scenario might be erotic if she wasn't shaking so damn hard.

"Should we call the sheriff?" Maybe they'd believe her this time with Brody there to corroborate her story. Rebecca took a step away from him, and then stared out the window.

"And say what? I saw a guy in the tree line? He didn't break any laws being out there," Brody said, a frustrated edge to his tone.

"He knows where I live. God only knows how long he's been out there spying on me." A chill raced down her spine at the thought of him watching her through her windows. She wasn't safe even in daylight now.

Brody took a step toward her and put his hand on her shoulder.

She turned to face him, ignoring the shivers his touch brought. Determination set his jaw, and the cloud forming behind his eyes said he wasn't sure she would like what he had to say.

"I don't know if I can protect you here. We most likely scared him off and he may not return, but it's a risk I'm not willing to take with you."

Those words sent an entirely different shiver down her body, a cold, icy blast that said everything she knew was about to be taken away from her again.

"Meaning what?"

"I need to take you someplace safe."

This bungalow might not be much, but it was her home. The thought of allowing that twisted jerk to force her out of her house churned in her stomach. He'd taken away so much already—from her, from her family. Part of her wanted to dig in her heels and argue because anything else felt as if she was sacrificing her power all over again. Except the logical part of her brain overrode emotion.

Brody had military experience. She'd hired him to keep her safe. Not listening to his advice would be more than stupid—it could be deadly.

His gaze stayed trained on her as she mentally debated her options. Options? What a joke that was.

So, she wouldn't be stupid. Of course, she'd go where she could be safe.

"I'll do whatever you need me to." The words tasted sour. Putting herself in Brody's hands wasn't the issue.

Relief relaxed the taut muscles in his face. "Good. Then, pack a bag and let's get out of here."

"Can we search for him? Go after him for a change? Maybe even put him on the run?"

"If that's what you want." His blue eyes darkened, the storm rising.

"I know what you're thinking. Yes, looking for him could be dangerous. I understand that and I need you to know I'm scared. But I'm also determined. He doesn't get to take away my power again. Sitting around, waiting for him to strike makes me feel helpless."

"I'll have your back. He has to get through me to touch you. And, darlin', that isn't happening on my watch."

Rebecca had sensed as much when they'd dated in high school. She'd gotten so used to being alone, to the isolation that came with being "damaged" and different. She'd quickly figured out where the term *kid gloves* came from. The sentiment might've been wrapped in compassion, but that didn't change the message to a child.

Well, she was no longer a child. And that psychopath didn't get to make her afraid anymore. Sure, she'd had a moment before in the kitchen. There'd be more, too. And she refused to apologize for her moments of weakness.

Being afraid was a good thing. It would make her cautious. It would keep her from making a stupid mistake that he could capitalize on. It would drive her to find him and possibly her brother, if Shane was still alive. Besides, being fearless had put her in this situation. She'd had no business sneaking out that night.

Mason Ridge might've been the Texas equivalent of Mayberry, but complacency meant being vulnerable.

"I just need a minute." She moved to the bedroom and opened a suitcase, thinking about the few items she couldn't live without. A sad note played in her heart. She had a few articles of clothing that had a special meaning, but that was about it. Shane's Spider-Man watch, his favorite possession on the earth, was inside her drawer. She retrieved it and pressed it to her chest.

She missed him.

Still missed him.

Everything good about childhood disappeared that hot night in late June. It was as though her mother and father had died along with the memory of Shane. Rebecca had no recollections of spring-break trips or campouts. Her parents had become obsessed with keeping her alive and in sight. Sleepovers stopped. There were no more séances or s'mores over a campfire, like there had been when Shane was alive.

It was as though all the color had been stripped out of life. No more blue skies or green grass. No more laughter. She'd been so distraught with grief at the time she didn't notice that while other kids gathered outside at the park for ball, she'd engaged in therapy with one of her many doctors.

She'd existed, had been treated like fine china, put on a display shelf and only handled with the utmost care. She'd spent most of her time in her room because being downstairs with her parents while they fought that first year had been even more depressing. Books had given her an escape and kept her somewhat sane, somewhat connected to the world playing out in front of her, all around her and, yet, so far out of reach.

When her parents had divorced, the rest of her fragile world shattered.

The truth was that Rebecca couldn't connect with anyone after losing Shane. Deep down, she didn't blame her father for wanting to start a new life. He'd tried to include her, make her feel part of his new world. But that would've been a slap in the face to her mother. And Rebecca already felt as though her mother had suffered enough.

She placed the watch gently inside her bag, then opened the next drawer and pulled out a few pairs of jeans, undergarments, and a variety of shirts, shoving them inside.

Rebecca stomped to her closet and jerked a few sundresses off their hangers. After rolling them up, she stuffed them inside the bag, fighting the emotions threatening to overwhelm her.

Toiletries from the bathroom were next on her mental checklist. She moved into the en suite and grabbed her makeup bag.

A wave of nausea rolled through her. His voice. The apple-tobacco smell. Her brain had blocked everything else out. She couldn't remember what he looked like other than a nebulous description.

Not even her psychiatrist had been able to hypnotize that out of her. She wished like hell she would've been able to give the sheriff and the FBI more to go on. She was the only one who'd had a glimpse of him, the one who'd lived, and she couldn't pick him out of a lineup if her life depended on it.

And, now, it would seem that it did.

Rebecca didn't realize she was shaking, until Brody's steady arms wrapped around her, stabilizing her.

"I was just thinking that I could've stopped all this if I'd just remembered."

"It's not your fault." His warm breath rippled down the back of her neck.

"I know, but—"

"It's not your fault."

Hadn't she heard those four words strung together a thousand times via counselors, teachers, her parents? "It just feels like if I'd been able to describe him—"

"Honey, there were grown men trained to track predators like him who couldn't get the job done. Him getting away wasn't the fault of a twelve-year-old girl."

On some level, she knew Brody was right. And, yet, guilt fisted her heart, anyway. He was being kind, so she'd spare him her true feelings. She tucked them away and forced a smile, ducking out of his hold.

"Good point." She moved to the bed, closed the suitcase and zipped it. "I've been thinking a lot about the old group. Think Ryan got ahold of them? All of us were out there that night. Maybe someone saw something they didn't realize could be important."

"I've been thinking the same thing. Ryan's working on getting everyone together. Dawson's not far. Dylan moved a town over, so he won't be hard to track down. We'll have to ask around for James. I don't know what happened to him after I left for the military. What about the girls? You talk to any of them?"

"Other than exchanging Christmas cards with Lisa and Samantha? No. Janet still lives here but I can't remember the last time we spoke and I don't think she was out that night. Melanie moved to Houston and never comes back."

"At least you have a few addresses. That's more than

I have to go on. Maybe the others will know once we get the ball rolling." He paused. "I don't remember seeing Melanie that night, either, or James for that matter but we should try to reach them, anyway."

Brody walked over and gripped the handle to her suitcase. "I can take you home with me, or we can go to a hotel. The choice is yours."

"We should be good at a hotel." A neutral place might keep her thoughts away from how much Brody had grown into a man she could respect. She led the way through the house, stopping in the living room to grab her laptop. "Not sure when I'll be back, so I better take this."

"I'm going to want to dig deeper into a few of the responses you received to your social-media messages."

"I almost forgot about the letters."

"You still have those?" Anger flashed in his blue eyes.

"Turned most over to the sheriff, but some new ones have turned up recently." She moved to the laundry room, where she'd been keeping the stack of mail.

More anger flashed in Brody's expression as she handed them over.

"There must be fifty letters here."

"This time of year always brings out the crazy in people." Arming the alarm, Rebecca had the feeling that once she walked outside she'd never be the same.

She locked the door behind them, hoping she could remember something else about that day…anything that might make the nightmare stop.

Chapter 4

Brody shouldn't want to show Rebecca his ranch, shouldn't want her to be proud of him. Hell, he'd already had her in his arms twice and he couldn't deny just how much it felt as if she belonged there, especially with the way her warm body molded to his. She'd asked to go to a hotel instead and his chest had deflated a little. The facts still remained the same. She'd rejected him and stomped on his heart before and she'd do it again. She wasn't cruel, just scared and confused. And it was all too easy for Brody to slip into his old role of being her shoulder to cry on, her friend. She'd confused those feelings for something else when they were young and she was doing it now. That was the only reason she'd go down that path again. How stupid was he not to figure it out before? Then again, Rebecca Hughes was his kryptonite. He reminded himself of the real reason she was there in the first place. She'd asked for his help.

All he was doing was helping Rebecca get her life back.

He owed her that.

Or maybe he owed it to himself. If he got her squared away, he could put the past behind him and move on. He could stop thinking about those hauntingly beautiful eyes, the fear he saw behind them, the frustration he felt when he couldn't take it away.

"Got a different idea of where we can hang out the next few days instead of a hotel."

"Oh, yeah. Where are we headed?"

"How do you feel about camping?" He stole a glance at her as he pulled out of the drive, needing to see the look on her face. She might've been born in the country, but Rebecca Hughes didn't sleep outside.

Based on the look she shot him, his attempt at humor had only made things worse.

"Is that your idea of a joke?" She tapped his arm.

"Yes. It is." Something needed to break the tension. Get the conversation on a lighter track. It looked as if her muscles were strung so tight she might snap.

"Well, it's not funny." Her face screwed up. And she finally smiled, too.

"Sorry about the joke. But your reaction made me laugh. And I needed that."

"Okay, funny man. Where are we really going?" There was something special about the curve to her lips, the way her eyes flashed toward him looking so alive. The few times he'd broken through to her in high school were some of his happiest moments. And how sad did that make him sound? Then again, after his mother had ripped off the town and disappeared, life had become dark and complicated for him and his father.

"How do you feel about a serious change in plans? Hanging out in a cabin in Texoma for a few days until we sort all this out instead of a hotel? No roughing it. The place will have all the modern luxuries."

She was shaking her head from the second she heard "Texoma."

"It's too far. By the time we drive out there and back, we'll lose four hours. No way." Her body had started shaking again, all hint of playfulness gone from her expression. He wondered if she even realized she was doing it.

"You sure you don't want to get away? I mean *really* get away?"

"I can't. I don't want to be that far from my mother. I need to call work, too. In fact, I should do that right now." She made a quick call and then dropped her phone in her purse. "I could always stay with my mother."

"That's not a good idea. Unless you want to tell her what's going on."

"No. You're right. It's bad enough that I skipped our visit this morning. That won't work. I'd rather keep her out of this as much as possible."

"I figured that's what you'd say."

"She needs me here. Can we get another place? Something closer?"

Brody stopped at the four-way stop sign at the end of her block. "My ranch is the perfect place."

"You bought the old Wakefield place, didn't you?"

"It's less than twenty minutes from here and it'll make it easier for me to check on the horses. If you really don't want to go there, my dad's house is another option."

"It would be nice to see him again. I'd like to stay at your place, though, if we can't stay at a hotel."

"It might be best if we don't leave a credit-card trail." He turned the steering wheel right. Pride he had no right to feel tugged at his heart. He needed to remember to keep a safe distance from the emotion. Nothing good could happen from touching a fire twice. "Let's swing by and get you settled before heading out to search for this guy."

"That's a better plan."

"Can I ask a question, though?"

"Okay." Her tone was tentative.

"Why didn't you take your father's call earlier? You two still at odds?"

"I'm not sure 'at odds' is the best way to describe our relationship. We don't really have one."

"Why is that, if you don't mind me asking?"

"It's complicated."

"I know." He kept his gaze on the road ahead. "I realize why you kept your distance before…how screwed up your mom was. I'm sure you felt conflicted. Love him and it betrays her. I get it. But, why now? Your mom's sick. You're doing all this alone and you don't have to."

"She's not his problem anymore."

"He said that?"

"No. Not in so many words. But he walked out. Divorced us."

"Her. He divorced *her*. There's a big difference."

"Same thing."

"Is it?" He shrugged. "I see Dylan with Maribel and

just because he's not together with her mom doesn't mean he loves that little girl any less."

"Dylan has a daughter?" She couldn't contain her shock.

"Long story, but yeah. He's a great dad, too."

"He's the last person I'd expect to have a family. Especially after what happened to him with his own parents. Didn't we vote him most likely to become a career criminal?"

"What can I say? The guy cleaned up his act. He'd do anything for Maribel. He's a changed man."

Brody's phone vibrated again, another text. "Can you check that for me?"

Rebecca picked it up from the seat and checked the screen, staring for a long moment.

"It's from Ryan. He spoke to Lisa and she said one of her cousins was in Woodrain Park when a strange-looking guy ran past. He fit the basic description of our guy." Her voice cracked on the last few words.

Brody gripped the steering wheel so tight his knuckles went white. He ground his back teeth. "Looks like we have a place to start our search."

"Something's been bothering me about this whole scenario." Brody finally broke the silence. "You asked the question before and it's the same one that's been on my mind. Why now? What's so significant about today?"

"I keep racking my brain, too. I always go back to the fact that it's the fifteenth anniversary."

"Yeah, but what's so important about this one? Why not the fifth, or the tenth?"

Good question. "Could it be the extra newspaper coverage we're getting this year?"

"It's possible. They run stories every year, right?"

"Uh-huh."

"Makes me think there was some kind of trigger that we haven't figured out yet."

"That makes sense. But what? I haven't done anything differently. I've been here working, taking care of my mother. My routine hasn't changed." Her life sounded depressing when she spoke about it out loud. It was true, though. Her entire world had been about existing and nothing more for more years than she could remember. Maybe didn't want to, either.

"You moved back a few years ago, so that's not it." He tapped the steering wheel with his thumb. "Any new friends?"

"I don't have time." She glanced down at her feet when she said it. Was that true? Or had she simply not made time?

"What about those letters? Anything stand out?"

"No. I get the same stuff every year," she said on a sigh.

"Any new employees at work?"

"We have a summer intern who started last month."

"Male or female?" His tone deepened a fraction, but she noticed it. He was onto something.

"Male. What are you getting at?"

"Who is it?" Brody's gaze stayed fixed on the road ahead.

"Alex Sweeny. Why?"

"How tall is he?"

"Six feet, I guess." Surely Brody wasn't saying what she thought. That Alex was somehow involved. She was already shaking her head. "He's way too young to be the guy we're looking for. Plus, he's related to the sheriff."

"You're right. We have to explore every possibility, though. And one of those prospects is that this guy could be involved somehow or wanting you to relive the past." His jaw clenched and released. His tension level matched hers.

"You mean like a copycat?" Rebecca didn't want to consider the possibility. If this was some twisted person trying to remind her of that horrible summer, then her chances of figuring out what had happened to her brother were nil.

And if not?

Then she had to face the horrible truth that any whack job could send her spiraling back to that dark place by imitating the crime. "What about the apple tobacco? The officers and FBI were careful about not letting that leak into the press exactly for this reason. How would he know about that?"

Rebecca kept on alert for two things. One was the scent of apple tobacco. The other was Shane's birthmark. He had a birthmark that looked like Oklahoma on top of his right foot.

Brody's face set with concentration for a long period. "With Sweeny being related to the sheriff he could get inside information of your case."

"I hadn't even thought of that. He would know about the threatening letters. The reporter. It was all common knowledge around the radio station."

"Why?"

"My boss wanted everyone on the lookout. He figured the best way to protect me and keep his other employees safe was to keep everyone informed." But could

Sweeny, a young kid, pull off an attack at the grocery store without her realizing who he was? "I still think the kid is innocent."

"And he might be. But until we figure this thing out, we follow through on every possible lead." Brody turned into Woodrain Park's lot.

Rebecca hadn't been back to that place, to those woods…ever. Icy chills raced up her arms. She crossed them to stave off goose bumps.

As if a door had been opened, emotions flooded, crashing into her.

The shed.

The desperation.

She stopped for a moment to stem the tears pouring down her cheeks. "I can't remember much of what happened in the shed. I must've blocked it out or something."

Brody had pulled over and parked. His hand covered hers, which did little to stop the shaking. "He can't hurt you anymore."

"What if I can't do it? Can't go back in there?" She motioned toward the wooded path.

"Then we'll look somewhere else. The chance he'd return is slim."

His words, his touch, breathed life into her. And a bit of courage. Besides, she couldn't avoid those woods forever. Maybe going, facing that horrible place, might help her remember something else. "You're right. He's most likely long gone by now. And even if he's not I have to do this. It might help. I keep thinking about how my brother's disappearance is my fault." A sob racked her. "I wish he would've stayed home that night instead of sneaking out to follow me. Wish I hadn't gone out that night and then none of this would've happened."

"I remember how close you two were. How you stood up for him when that bully threatened to beat Shane up after school."

"And you showed up at the rock quarry to make sure the bully never pulled that on younger kids again," she said.

Brody shrugged.

"Sorry about the black eye he gave you."

"That healed. I'm not so sure my pride ever recovered," he said with a smile that could melt Glacier Bay.

She leaned into him, into his comfort. She rarely ever spoke about the past, let alone laughed at some of the memories. Being with Brody was slowly bringing her back to life. He seemed to understand her need to keep everyone at a safe distance. He did the same. Maybe it was that she knew he'd been a loner most of his life and she could relate—she'd felt the same every day since that summer night when her life inexplicably changed. The only happy thought she'd held on to through college was Brody. He'd been her safe landing.

Regret filled her as he sat there quietly reassuring her, and for a split second she wished she could go back and make things right. Would she have pushed him away if she'd known no other man's touch would make her feel the way his did?

"You don't have to do this." Brody's voice, warm and understanding, pulled her back to the present. "We can go. Let the others look here. Ryan's on his way as we speak and he's bringing Dylan."

"I want to." How did she explain that while she realized facing these woods, that shed again, would be the most difficult thing in her life, it was also the only way to begin healing? All these years, she'd been going through the motions of her day, numb. Being with Brody, remembering that it was possible to feel things again, made her want to keep going. Do more than just exist.

"I don't want to go, believe me. Everything inside me is telling me to run the other way. But I'm afraid I'll feel even worse if I don't. What if I could have saved him and didn't because I was scared to go back? I can't live with that."

"I understand." And the hitch in his voice said he meant those words. He got out of the truck and then opened the passenger door. "It's not still there, you know. The shed."

"What happened?"

He rolled his shoulders in a shrug. "Me."

"You came out here?"

"It was after you left for college. I'd signed up for the service. Didn't want to ship out with unfinished business here."

She understood he wouldn't see another answer to his emotions. Brody had been quick to anger before and ready to fight the world. Except when it came to her and his family. He'd been tender and kind, which had made pushing him away all that much more painful.

The military looked to have done good things for him. He seemed to have grown into his own skin, was more at peace with himself and the world. Except when it came to her. There, he seemed as confused as she felt.

"I couldn't stand this place for what it had done to you. The fact that it was still standing six years later made me furious. I had to make sure another soul would never be taken to that place again. So, I tore it apart with my own hands to make sure."

"Thank you." She could totally see Brody doing something like that to protect her, to protect others. Maybe even out of frustration that the guy got away with it. His angry streak never would have been aimed at her or any other innocent person. But a bad guy, someone who was downright mean to others, should watch out.

She'd noticed it before, but there was a sense of purpose to Brody's stride now. Less anger, more determination. He was quiet calm, but, just like the surface of the ocean, danger lurked below. She had no doubt that if Brody met the man who'd hurt her today, he'd unleash hell. Just like he'd done all those years ago when faced with a bully. This time, Brody would win.

He took her hand as he guided her toward the pathway in the woods.

His cell buzzed. He checked the screen. "It's Dylan."

"Let's hope for good news."

Brody tipped his chin. "Tell me you found something we can work with."

He said "uh-huh" a few times into the phone, but Rebecca could tell from his tone there was nothing new to go on.

"We're at the park. We just got here." He went quiet. "Then you're not far from us." Another pause. "Yeah. That's exactly where we're headed. I know, man. I hear you."

She knew immediately that they were surprised she'd want to go back there. She couldn't say she was shocked at their reactions. No one in her right mind would do it. Maybe if she followed the killer's trail, she'd find something. It was a long shot but she had to try for Shane. She'd been a kid before, helpless, but she wasn't anymore.

She'd thought about this a million times. If she'd screamed for help instead of following and confronting the kidnapper, would things have turned out differently? Or what if she'd left some sort of trail so that others could find them?

A knot formed in her chest, tightening like a coil with each forward step.

It wasn't hard to tune out the rest of Brody's conversation. Rebecca was half-afraid of what Dylan thought about her after the way she'd left things with Brody, and she was afraid she'd overhear him warning Brody to stay away from her or something.

The only thing keeping her feet moving at this point was Brody's hand on her lower back, guiding each forward step, reassuring her.

"Dylan and Ryan are near Mason Ridge Lake. Said they'd head this way."

She needed to focus her attention on something besides the horror inside her escalating the farther they walked. "How are they?"

"Dylan and Ryan? They're good. I already told you about Dylan's little girl."

"You said he was bringing her up alone. What happened?" She needed to distract herself. Her pulse was rising and she needed to think about something else besides what lay ahead.

"He met someone on leave and fell pretty hard. Guess he was missing home and she reminded him of it. The relationship didn't last long, which is a long story, but he got Maribel out of it."

"What about the mother?"

"She was really sick when she finally told Dylan he had a child. He got to see her one last time before…"

"That's so sad. He didn't know?"

"No. She didn't tell him. Said she was afraid of what his reaction would be."

"He always said parenting was the cruelest thing people could do to children. She must've known."

"He didn't keep his feelings a secret. You should see him now. Maribel came to live with him when she was two. He had a rough year adjusting, but you wouldn't know it to see them together now."

It was hard to think of Dylan being tender with a toddler. If Brody had been tough back in the day, then Dylan had been an outlaw. Throw them both together and they'd be deadly.

Seeing Brody now, thinking about children, made Rebecca wish she'd handled things differently. The deep-seated sense of trust they'd shared was gone. She could see unease in his eyes. He was still as protective as he'd always been—some things would never change.

There were new scars on his body that weren't there before. He might've filled out in good ways, all muscle and strength, but he'd been hurt, too. Her heart squeezed thinking about the pain he must've endured. Rebecca knew full well external scars hurt far less than internal ones.

She'd lied to him and pushed him away. The only other time she'd been untruthful was for their friends.

Small towns were known for being bad places to hide secrets. Yet, they'd had to protect their friends. A cold chill raced up her spine, gripping her heart. A mistake?

The uneasy feeling intensified. Her feet felt heavier, legs weaker. A ball tightened in her chest.

Brody stopped. "You sure you want to keep going? You've been too quiet, which used to mean you were overthinking something. Now, I have no idea if it still means that. But I can tell that whatever's going on is spiking your blood pressure."

A branch snapped.

She turned around and gasped. "Oh. God. No!"

Brody instinctively reacted, dropping down low and pulling her down with him, a second too late to miss the large metal object from cracking his skull.

Chapter 5

Brody fought against the darkness trying to invade his body. The blunt-force blow to his head scrambled his brains. He instinctively felt around for a knot. Didn't take long to find one the size of an egg.

There was blood on his hand when he brought it back down. Lots of blood. He felt around in his pocket for his cell. It must've fallen out when the blow knocked him off balance.

Dizzy, vision blurred, he scrambled to stop a tall man from dragging Rebecca into the thicket. She fought like a wildcat, kicking and screaming, but she was outmatched in height, weight and strength.

Brody grabbed dirt, stumps, anything that would help him gain purchase as he crawled on his belly toward the attacker. He reached out in time to catch the guy's ankle and latched on to his pants.

The last thing he remembered was being dragged several feet before the darkness clawing at him won.

Now, he forced his eyes open, unsure how long he'd been out.

Dylan was there, consoling Rebecca, who looked shaken to the core.

She caught Brody's gaze and locked on, immediately moving toward him. "Thank God, you're awake."

Brody tried to speak, but his mouth didn't immediately move. He took a few slow breaths and reset.

"What happened?" he managed to get out. Brody didn't even want to think about what would've happened to Rebecca if the others hadn't shown.

"He was here." One look at Rebecca's dilated pupils, her wide, fearful eyes, and Brody figured she'd retreated to that space deep inside her that no one could reach. He'd seen it a few times in high school and nothing good ever came of it. The most notable time was when she'd broken up with him.

"Did you guys get him?"

She shook her head. Damn if her disappointment and fear wasn't a sucker punch to his gut. Not to mention the way her hands shook when Dylan gave her a bottle of water.

"When did you guys get here?" Brody was still fuzzy. He remembered having a conversation with Ryan a little while ago.

"We were nearby. Called the sheriff as soon as we got here. They're searching the woods for him as we speak. We'd be out there, too, but—"

"Thank you for sticking around." His gaze immediately shifted to Rebecca.

"No problem, bro. She fought like a banshee. It's the only reason she's still here and not God knows where."

Dylan helped Brody sit up and handed him a bottle of water. "Did you get a good look at the guy?"

"He's tall and thin, but quick. She got the best view. He nailed me before I had a chance to react. He knows these woods." Brody glanced around, trying to get his bearings.

"Think you can help her work with a sketch artist?" Dylan asked.

"Yeah. I can try. Like I said, he practically cracked my skull in two when he surprised me, so mostly he looked like a tall, skinny blur." Brody made a move to get up but sat right back down when his head felt like someone had split it open with an ax. "Any idea what he used on me?"

"We're lucky it wasn't a gun."

Brody glanced at Rebecca, who stood there stiff, looking like she might jump out of her skin if someone said boo to her.

"Get her out of here."

She whirled around on him. Determination set her jaw. "No. I'm not leaving. Not without you."

"Ryan can take you to the ranch and stay with you there." He checked his head and came back with more blood on his hand. "I'm not getting up anytime soon."

She stood there, brown eyes piercing through him. "I'm not going anywhere."

"How long was I out?" Brody's gaze shifted from Rebecca to Dylan.

Dylan cleared his throat before he spoke. "Not long. I'd say we arrived within a few seconds of you blacking out."

Rebecca might be there, standing close, but a wall had gone up around her. Her muscles were stiff, her jaw tight, and her arms were crossed over her chest. Everything about her body language had changed. "I'm not leaving with you still here."

"She should be fine. We're all here," Ryan said as he walked over. "EMTs are close."

About that time Brody heard sticks crunching in the brush behind him, growing louder. "You guys can't stay here. This is the closest anyone's been to him. I'm fine and he can't be far. Go, get him. I'll pick up the search when I'm cleared."

Ryan's expression said he'd carry Brody to the hospital himself if he had to. Dylan was just as unmoving.

"Let the paramedics get here and take a look at you first. Then, we can go together," Ryan said.

Brody blew out a breath, closed his eyes and leaned back. They were saying that they didn't want him doing anything stupid, like not getting proper medical attention. "Fine. But I'm going out there." He motioned toward the thicket. Nausea gripped him as blood trickled down his nose. He didn't want to admit how close he was to passing out again. It was in that moment his drill sergeant's words chose to wind through his thoughts. The first rule of being a good soldier was to take care of injuries.

The next time Brody woke, he was in the back of an ambulance.

He blacked out again, then woke to the news he was in the hospital being treated for lacerations and a possible concussion. "How long was I out this time?"

"A half hour?" The muscles in Rebecca's face tensed and he could see her pulse thumping at her neck. She was stressed. As shaken as she was, and emotionally closed off, she'd refused to leave Brody's side. He didn't want to acknowledge what that did to his heart.

"What's going on? Is everyone okay?" he asked.

She thanked the nurse and then waited for the older woman to leave the room and close the door behind her. "No. You're seriously hurt. And it's my fault."

He put his hand up before she could get too worked up. "Hold on a minute. This has nothing to do with you."

"Yes. It does. I brought you into this mess and now look." When she turned to him a tear spilled down her cheek. Something quick and explosive hit his chest when she made eye contact.

"Sweetheart, none of this is on you. If anything, I should've been more careful in the woods. I should've realized he would know that area like the back of his hand. Plus, we got a look at him this time. The sheriff has a better description to work with. And that's a good thing, right?"

She nodded as a few more tears escaped. She quickly wiped them away.

"Look at me. I'm here because I made a mistake. I underestimated the situation. I won't do that twice. And, I'm going to be okay. Believe it or not, I have a pretty hard head."

At least that last comment got a smile out of her.

The haunted look in her eyes had returned, though. Brody had no idea how to break through that. He'd tried and failed before. Didn't figure much had changed since then. Even so, it was good to see her again. Better than he wanted to admit.

And that was most likely because he'd missed home, too. Being far off in a desert, away from everything familiar, had a way of playing tricks on a man's mind and making him weak. Brody reasoned that was why he still had residual feelings for Rebecca. She was "known," and it had nothing to do with the curve of her hips into those long legs. Or her laugh, which sounded like music to his ears. He had missed her quick mind, her will to live even under extreme circumstances. She'd felt like home to him years ago. Those feelings resurfaced and that's why his heart hurt being close to her.

"Where are Dylan and Ryan?"

"They stayed with the sheriff to help search the thicket." She folded her arms. "Think I should call Alcorn? He might be able to get more resources out there."

"I want this guy caught, too, but that might not sit well with Ryan," Brody said.

"Right. I almost forgot how much they don't like each other." She rubbed her arms. "Besides, the guy is probably long gone by now."

"Dylan said something about a sketch artist."

"One is being sent over now." She glanced at her watch. "In fact, he should be here any minute."

Rebecca didn't want to admit how great it felt to see Brody sitting up, awake, sipping water. Or how much she wished she could get closer to him, touch him again. But she wouldn't, for her sake as much as his. And especially because his compassion was evident in his words and actions, but that was all he felt for her. He'd been clear.

A knock on the door made her heart leap. Resentment hit fast and hard that an unexpected noise had that effect on her again, just like before, just like she'd sworn would never happen again.

Well, the bastard wasn't going to get away with it this time.

"Come in," she said, popping to her feet, needing to walk off her nerves.

An older gentleman with a sketch pad tucked under his arm walked in, accompanied by a deputy.

Brody was already up, sitting on the edge of the bed, which agitated the machines he was hooked up to. They beeped loudly.

The older nurse rushed in.

"Mr. Fields, you need rest."

"Do whatever you need to me while I'm here, but as soon as this meeting is over, I'm walking out that door." He looked at Rebecca when he said, "Did you see my cell? I lost it back there."

She produced it and he took it from her, heat pulsing from where their fingers met.

"I wouldn't advise that. The doctor wants you to stay overnight for observation," the nurse warned.

"With all due respect, we're in the middle of an investigation and I don't have that kind of time."

She glared at him as she fiddled with dials, her gaze bouncing from him to the machine to Rebecca.

The deputy introduced both himself and the artist while Rebecca pulled extra chairs next to the bed. Brody made a move to help, but she motioned for him to stay put.

When the artist put the finishing touches on his sketch and showed it to her, dread wrapped around her shoulders. The finished product was still too vague. "That's not going to help. He's great at keeping his face hidden."

"It's a start," Deputy Holder said, and she could tell

he was reaching. At least he wasn't looking at her as if she had six foreheads, half curious, half afraid, and expecting her face to explode. "We'll circulate this. See if we can't stir the pot a little."

At least the sheriff's office took her seriously now. She thanked the men and closed the door behind them.

The nurse turned toward Brody. "Any chance I can get you to change your mind and stick around a little while?"

"No." He shot an apologetic look. "I know you're doing your job, but I have to do mine."

The nurse gave an understanding nod before saying she'd be back and then leaving.

"I didn't get a good look at him." Rebecca sat on the edge of the bed, facing him without looking at him.

"This will help. The sheriff's office will start getting more leads than they can handle."

"It feels...hopeless." She threw her hands up in the air.

"One thing I learned on missions was to stay focused on a positive outcome no matter how bad things look. A thousand things can go wrong when you're out there, but thinking about them doesn't do any good. Positive thinking has more power to create change than I ever realized. If others knew how strong their minds were, people's lives would be very different."

"What did you focus on? What was home for you?"

He shifted his position, breaking eye contact. "I had a lot of things to come back to. Buying the ranch for one. My dad for another. Texas, my home."

A little piece of her heart wished he'd said her. But why would he? Not after the way she'd hurt him.

"Those are great things to keep you grounded." Rebecca had very little to keep her centered. She had her mother, whom she loved. What else did she have besides work and a couple of friends? Sadly, not much. Even her bungalow was a rental.

Her father was remarried with two boys, her half brothers, whom she'd never really been able to connect with no matter how much they'd tried. They weren't bad kids, but they weren't Shane, either. She could see the selfishness in those feelings now, but her teenage self had been less aware. And maybe it was her dad's new life that she never felt she fit into after he left.

Had Rebecca really made an effort?

Or had she expected him to go the extra distance to make her feel comfortable. He hadn't, so they'd drifted apart for a few years until she stopped visiting altogether.

There'd been so many people poking around in her head, and all she'd wanted to do was be left alone and seem as normal as possible. Except she wasn't. She was damaged goods.

Had it been too easy to keep everyone at a safe distance?

And now? What had changed?

Rebecca had taken over as her mother's caregiver, helping coordinate doctor appointments and medicines, and that had taken her mind off her own problems. A little part of her had been relieved not to be the focus for a change.

If she were being honest, she'd admit that being near Brody awakened pieces of her she'd ignored for so long.

"Did you bring the laptop?" Brody asked, breaking through her heavy thoughts.

"Yeah. I drove your truck."

"You thought to bring it to the hospital?" He glanced up, and what looked like pride was on his face.

Her heart fluttered. "I knew you wouldn't want to wait for someone to pick us up, so I drove. They wouldn't let me ride in the ambulance, anyway. I'll run down and get the laptop."

"That'll give us something to do while we wait for my release papers." He smiled.

She would never get used to the flush of warmth rolling through her at seeing him look so pleased with her. Maybe it was the way she'd left things all those years ago, the hurt in his eyes she remembered to this day, but she wanted Brody to be happy because of something she did.

It took all of ten minutes for her to retrieve the laptop and return. She set it on the bed, where Brody immediately opened the file.

"We recognize a face, get a name and maybe we get lucky with an address." Brody pulled up the list of suspects.

"There are so many familiar names. Do you remember who that is?" She pointed to the top name.

"Wasn't he our bus driver in middle school?"

"Yes." Her shoulders sank forward. "It makes me so sad to look at these names and think they might be such horrible people."

"We've known them most of our lives."

"If it's someone local, then they've hidden it for this long. There's no way they'd let this kind of secret out now."

"Don't be discouraged. No one's had this much information to go on before. We have a general description."

"It's still pretty vague," she pointed out.

"Once we narrow the list by height, we'll rule out a substantial amount of suspects. We know it can't be our bus driver. Mr. Alba was our height in middle school." His joke was meant to lighten her somber mood.

It helped. "True. Do you know how many men there are in Texas over six feet tall?"

"Yeah. We grow everything bigger in Texas." Brody laughed, and her tension eased. "Still, knowing this guy is six foot two will be a huge help."

"What if they were right all along? What if he was just passing through town all those years ago?"

"That's possible. Then we look outside of Texas."

"And what if this isn't him? What if it's some whack job imitating him?" She knew she was letting her fears get the best of her, but there were so many questions.

"Could be. But then we have to consider both sides of the coin."

"Okay, say we get a name. He'll surely go into hiding now. Not only did he slip out of my sight fifteen years ago, but he's done so twice today. No way will he stick around after this. How will we ever find him now?" Bile rose from her stomach, burning her throat. She wrung her hands and paced.

"I thought about all those things, too. We might keep looking and not find anything to go on. We might dig until we've dug to China and come up empty-handed. But it won't be for nothing. You'll know something. You'll know that you've given this your best shot. And that will help you put this to rest when the time comes." He held steady to her gaze. "First things first. We search these files while we give my pain a chance to ease and make sure I'm not going to pass out when I walk.

Then, we head out and investigate. We don't stop until we find answers."

"And what if none of it helps?"

"It will."

She didn't respond, couldn't respond. She only wished she had his faith as she walked another ten steps to the window and back.

"Hey, come here."

She stopped, but her heart kept racing.

Brody patted the bed. "Let's look through this together. Maybe something else will stick out that the investigators missed before. You were closest to the scene and sometimes visuals help stimulate memories."

"Okay. You're right. Maybe we'll find something, and if we don't I'll figure out a way to live with it."

Rebecca's cell buzzed. She took the call, thanked the caller and then fixed her gaze on Brody.

"It's the nurse at the care facility. My mom needs me. I have to go."

Chapter 6

"Then let's go." Brody stood. His knee gave and he almost fell. He caught himself by grabbing hold of the chair.

"This is not a good idea. You should stay here until you're better. I'll go check on my mother and pick you up in a little while." She palmed the keys and slid her purse strap over her shoulder, giving the universal sign of a woman ready to go.

"Absolutely not, Rebecca. I will not leave you alone. You can drive, but I'm going with you." He'd regained his balance and looked steady on his feet. Steady and stubborn.

"The doctor hasn't released you yet, remember?"

"I'm not waiting around for someone to tell me to stay in bed for the next three days and rest. Besides, I'm better at assessing my injuries than anyone else. I know what my body can and can't handle."

She didn't want to think about why he knew how much punishment his body could take. Did it have to do with the three-inch scar running down his left arm?

He closed the laptop. "Besides, I can study the folder and make a few calls on the way to see your mother. That's the most efficient use of our time, anyway."

She stood there staring him down for a long moment. He was in a weakened state and she wanted, no, needed him to get better.

And yet he had that determined set to his broad shoulders and prominent chin. His sturdy jawline anchored his steady gaze, which was fixed on the door.

When Brody Fields made up his mind about something, he followed through. Period. He could be as obstinate as a bull terrier and, injuries or not, just as lethal. No way was he listening to her.

The nurse shuffled into the room.

"Bring whatever paperwork you need to keep the lawyers off your back, but do it fast. You have about a minute before I walk out that door." He inclined his head toward the only exit in the room.

The nurse yelled out for someone and Rebecca assumed it was the floor supervisor.

"Forty-five seconds."

The woman blew out a frustrated breath. She stared him down before calling out the name again.

"Thirty."

A disgusted grunt came. "Fine. If you're determined to hurt yourself, I have no legal grounds to stop you. I'll get your paperwork. Stay right here."

"No, thanks. Time's up." Brody leaned forward. Everything about his body language said he was about to walk out that door.

"Will you stop by the nurse's station to sign a release form?"

Brody clenched the muscles in his jaw, nodded.

"Follow me."

Signing out took all of ten minutes. Brody didn't want to give the nurse a heart attack, so he cooperated while she printed form after form and asked for his signature a dozen or more times.

Billing had decided to pay him a visit before he left, too. He'd given his credit card and signed for that, as well.

Once inside his truck, he checked in with Ryan. His friend had no news to report, which was expected since there hadn't been any texts or phone calls.

Dawson, another childhood friend, was tending to Brody's horses, so he gave him a ring, too. Last week Brody had gotten an injured stallion who might be ending his racing career. Lone Star Park kept him in horses that needed rehab. He also took in neglected animals. A dozen mares had been rescued days before dying from starvation because of an irresponsible breeder last month and they were doing nicely. He'd witnessed first-hand what humans could do to each other in war and at home. Seeing what they could do to animals hit him in a whole new place of frustration. Brody needed to check on his horses at some point this evening. There should be plenty of time to visit Mrs. Hughes and follow up on the restaurant lead they'd uncovered earlier.

"If it's not too late when we finish with your mother, I'd like to go to Mervin's tonight. See what we can find there, which might be nothing," he quickly warned.

"Okay. I don't think we should go alone, though."

Good point. He wasn't up to par in his weakened physical state. He was one more surprise attack away from being chained to a hospital bed with an IV that had something besides coffee in it. "I'll see which of the guys can go with us."

"I heard you invite them to Mother's," she said.

"Figured we could talk while you visit. I'm not going inside her room, considering I'm pretty much the last person she'll want to see. I was never her favorite person."

"That was a long time ago."

"Some things don't change."

She broke into a smile. "True. But she'll tolerate pretty much anything if it means I'll spend more time there."

Brody shouldn't say what he was about to say, but he couldn't help himself. "You have the same shy smile you did in high school."

And the same eyes, serious and intelligent.

"Do I? Here I thought I'd grown up so much. Guess not."

"Not so fast. There's nothing wrong with looking like you're still in high school. Some women might even consider that a compliment." He laughed. "I'd like to see more of that thing curving your face, though."

"Oh, Brody. It's been so long since I…" The smile faded too quickly. So did the sparkle in her eye.

"Go ahead. Finish your sentence," he urged.

"It'll make me seem even sadder than I already am, especially to you."

"It won't. Come on. Tell me. Please."

She compressed her lips.

"I said 'please.'"

"Okay, fine. Have it your way. It's been so long since I had anything to really smile about."

He shook his head. "That's a damn shame. A woman as intelligent and kind as you, as beautiful as you, should have everything she wants. Love. Laughter. Children."

Rebecca shrugged.

"Don't tell me you never think about having a family someday." He couldn't hide his shock.

"Have it your way. I won't tell you, then." No hint of a smile on her face now.

"Seriously?" Didn't every little girl dream of having a fairy-tale wedding, a big house and kids? Brody didn't have siblings, so he couldn't speak from personal experience on what little girls dreamed of, but they'd been portrayed that way his whole life. "You never think about it?"

"Not really. Not since I was a little girl and unafraid of the big bad wolf. Now that I know wicked things happen to children and what that does to a parent, I can't think about going down that road as the mother. I've seen what it did to mine."

"I get that." He could see anguish fill her. If she didn't fight, it would swallow her whole.

"It's not so bad, you know." She tapped her finger on the steering wheel. "I'm used to being alone."

Those five words haunted him more than he wanted to admit. Was it because he was the same? Had she hit a personal note?

He mentally shook it off. This was not the best time for a conversation about having children, not when emotions from the past were being dredged up. Besides, the incident in the woods had sent Rebecca into an emotional tailspin. He'd seen that lost look on her face once. Right before she'd broken his heart. No matter how close they were, now or then, she'd never be able to meet him all the way. Whoa. Why was he thinking about the two of them in a present-day relationship?

It didn't matter. He still didn't have answers to her case. He was considering all the options and yet the simplest explanation, the one the Feds kept coming back to, was that the guy wasn't connected to Mason Ridge. If he had been, then Brody's job of finding the jerk would've been easier. The faster he could bring this monster to justice, the better. If only he could help bring peace to her family. The man responsible for Shane's disappearance needed to pay.

Brody had every intention of burying the bastard.

Time had come to get back to the basics in this case. He opened the laptop and then the file, studying it again as she drove toward Apple Orchard Care Facility, where her mother lived. The suspect list seemed never-ending. If he searched long enough, there had to be a connection somewhere. He'd been looking for an association to the town or the family. Maybe he needed to look harder for a link within their group of friends. Maybe Justin's friends.

"It's okay, you know," Rebecca finally said. "I'm not going to fall apart like my mother."

No. Rebecca was a survivor. Even after all these years, she kept her chin up, kept searching. "I know."

She stopped at a red light. "Why did you call the guys? I mean I know what you said, but there's more to it, isn't there?"

"I'm interested to see if anyone remembers anything."

"It was a long time ago, Brody. I doubt anyone besides me even thinks about it anymore."

The light changed and she pressed the gas.

There's where she was wrong. How could Brody forget? How could anyone forget who was there that night or in that town? He already knew Ryan had thought about it, as did Dylan and Dawson. That night was etched into everyone's memories.

Brody had called a secret meeting after Shane had disappeared. Rebecca couldn't be there, of course. But everyone else had shown. Parents had strictly forbidden kids to leave the house, so Samantha, Lisa and Melanie had arranged to be together, watched by Samantha's older brother. Every available adult was out on a search team, scouring fields and abandoned buildings. No one wanted to leave their children unattended after the incident. Brody's father had allowed him to join the search, so he hadn't needed an excuse to be out. Brody and the guys had sneaked inside Samantha's first-floor bedroom window, risking everything to meet.

None of their friends had admitted to seeing anything. Afraid of being busted, everyone had scattered. But had they been lying? Surely they'd seen something. Maybe if they talked it through again, as adults, a detail would pop.

Brody figured the real reason Rebecca couldn't let this go was because she'd yelled at Shane when the game broke up, humiliating him, so he ran to get away from her. The weight she carried was so much more than letting him down because she'd always watched over her little brother. At first, she'd told him to sit by a tree and wait. He didn't listen. She'd embarrassed him in front of her friends, telling him he had no business following her. Teary eyed, he'd broken into a full run, little athlete that he'd been. Even then, he'd been fast as a whip. And she'd completely underestimated him. By the time she'd apologized to everyone for her little brother ruining their mission, he was gone.

The bullet that was Shane had already disappeared out of view. Rebecca had told Brody that she wasn't worried about losing sight of her brother. He'd head home. Where else would he go?

A noise had spooked the rest of the group. The game had been a bad idea that night. There were too many people out after dark because of the festival. Afraid of getting busted, they'd scattered in different directions.

Brody had offered to help find Shane. Rebecca had said she'd be fine. A few minutes later, alone, she'd heard a muffled cry.

The rest was history.

And Brody felt responsibility, too. What if he'd insisted on helping her search? Would he have made a difference? Surely, the kidnapper wouldn't have been able to subdue three kids. Even at twelve, Brody had been substantial. He might have been the tipping point they'd needed. How many times had he asked himself that question?

It still didn't matter. Brody hadn't gone. Shane had been kidnapped. History couldn't be revised.

At twelve, Rebecca had been a tower of strength.

Even now, she dug her heels in and went full force chasing a lead rather than roll over. She threw herself into the investigation even if it meant shutting out everything else around her. But then, she'd been good at that before, too.

With her mother gravely ill, Brody wondered who

Rebecca would have left after her mom was gone. Her father? They weren't close anymore. Was that part of why she'd clung to the idea that Shane could be alive? Fear of being alone?

Where did that leave Rebecca?

Brody wanted to be there for her, to see her through this now in a way he couldn't before. He hated the thought that she felt alone again, fighting for the life of someone in her family. She didn't need advice or someone to tell her what was best for her. He'd be there if she needed him, if she let him.

Watching her pain nearly killed him, but he knew the only way to put the past behind her was for him to be strong and, better yet, bring justice.

"Did you call your father back?"

"I've been with you every minute."

"I thought maybe you'd returned his call at the hospital when I was out."

"No. Not yet. I will, though." Her voice was unsteady, as if she was still trying to decide.

"When?"

"Soon."

"Why not now?"

"Can I ask you a question?" Rebecca's voice was far less frail and afraid than it had been earlier. He sensed that she was gaining her strength. She might've been shell-shocked, but she wasn't broken. Not even the Mason Ridge Abductor could take that away from her.

Too many places inside him needed Rebecca to be okay.

"Yeah. Sure."

"What happened with your mother? I mean, I've heard the rumors about her convincing the town to invest in a lakefront resort and then disappearing with the money. That true?"

"Yes."

"Does it still bother you?"

"No." Brody had hoped this one time that she couldn't read his mind. They'd shared a mental connection in high school that had him wondering if dating her had been a good idea. He wasn't sure he wanted someone to understand the pain he was in. He was a kid, and he'd been feeling sorry for himself.

"Are you in contact with her?"

"No."

"Why not?"

"Other than the fact that she hasn't tried to get in contact with me once since she left? I don't have anything to say to her."

"That all? You can be honest with me, Brody. I won't tell anyone. Not like I have a bunch of people to tell, anyway…" Her words trailed off at the end and he could tell she tried to come off as unaffected by the truth in those words. "It's more than that, isn't it? You value family."

Did he? He'd spent his teen years bitter about his mother's actions, his father's lack thereof. "I value loyalty more."

"That, too. But you never talk about her. I mean, you must feel something. Like with my dad, I was angry with him for starting another family. Especially since this one felt so…unfinished."

"Have you forgiven him? Moved on?"

"I guess not. But I am trying."

"Really? How so? By not answering his calls?" He

glanced at her in time to see regret darken her features. Damn. He didn't expect her reaction to hit him so hard.

"I deserve that." Chin up, she seemed ready for another punch.

"That wasn't fair of me—"

"Yes, it was. I'm the one who brought up the subject. I shouldn't dish it out if I can't take it, right?"

"I still didn't mean it."

"Don't worry. I get it. You're doing the same thing I do. Push those feelings down so deep that no one can touch them. They're buried. They can't hurt you. But, lately, I've been wondering if that's the right thing to do."

"Meaning you want to call your father." Was she right? Brody had done his level best to forget the feelings existed.

"For one. I mean, part of me wants to talk to him. The rest thinks it's too late to start our relationship now."

"He wouldn't try to get in touch if he didn't want to spend time with you. My situation's different. My mom took off and that was it. I never heard from her again. No birthday cards. No surprise high school graduation visit. She hasn't tried to get in touch once. And it's bad enough she stole from the town, but look what she did to my father. He never stopped waiting for her to come back, never got over her. She had to know how much he loved her, I loved her. And not one word in more years than I can count. Not exactly a person worth tracking down." Anger had those last words biting out. He never talked about his mother, not to anyone. He'd convinced himself that he no longer cared about her or the way she'd treated his father. Was that true? The venom he felt surging through him said otherwise. Was it good to dredge up the past?

"You're right. You're completely right. Our situations are totally different. But our way of dealing with them is pretty much the same." She hesitated. "I'm glad you talked about it. You never used to."

"Like I said, wasn't much to say before."

"And now?"

"Talking to you is different. We have history." It was more than that, but no way would he allow himself to dwell on that emotion. He didn't need to know how deep his feelings ran for Rebecca. The bottom line was that she'd shut him out just as his mother had. And Brody was nothing like his father. Brody wouldn't sit around licking his wounds, waiting for a woman who could so easily walk away from him to return.

He shoved those thoughts aside as Rebecca pulled into a parking spot and cut the engine. "I'll stick around out here and keep digging in these files while you go inside."

She lightly touched his hand, and even that little bit of contact sent sparks flying. Another reminder it was a bad idea to get too close to her this time around. Sparks ignited flames. Unchecked, flames developed into full-blown fires. A raging fire destroyed everything in its path. Just like his mother had. And his father had simply stood in its way and gotten burned.

But Rebecca's situation with her father couldn't be more different. "It's okay to love your father, you know."

"I do now. But by the time I realized it, his calls had slowed and it just seemed easier to leave things alone. Sleeping dog and all that. Now I'm thinking maybe I just took the coward's way out."

"You? Not a chance." Brody shook his head. He brushed against her right cheek with the backs of the fingers on his left hand. "You're one of the strongest people I've ever known."

She smiled, warming him, warning him that getting too close to fire would engulf him just like it had his father. Brody wasn't objective when it came to Rebecca. And that was dangerous.

"I'm sorry about your family, Brody." Her look was all compassion and sympathy, creating an intimacy between them he didn't want to acknowledge, and it stirred something in his chest he had no desire to think about.

"I guess there's no chance I can convince you to come inside with me."

The others hadn't arrived yet. Brody texted them to say that he had. A second later, he got a message that the guys would be running late. Dylan had to swing by and check on Maribel who wasn't feeling well. "I doubt your mother wants to see me."

"You might be surprised." She unbuckled her seat belt and reached for the handle. "Why not see for your self."

"Hold on a sec." Hopping out of the truck, his knee giving in the process, he steadied himself and rounded the front end, determined to open the door for her. Part of him wanted to be there for Rebecca, to hold her hand through it all, but the other part—the logical one—said going inside with her was a bad idea since he didn't want to upset her mother with his presence. Then again, the thought of Rebecca going anywhere alone didn't sit well, either.

Rebecca held out her hand.

Brody took it, ignoring how well hers fit.

"I know you're supposed to meet the guys out here, but will you go in for a minute?" she asked.

If she hadn't asked, he sure as hell wouldn't have volunteered. She had. Against his better judgment, he nodded.

She smiled and that annoying part of his heart stirred again. Sure didn't take much to get that going. *Way to be strong, Fields*.

But he was expert at swallowing his true feelings. Rebecca was no exception. Pretending he hadn't just told himself a big fat lie, he held out his arm for her.

The next touch, her hand to his forearm, was so light it barely registered. The electricity it sent up his arm was another story altogether. Frissons swirled up his arm, lighting a path straight to his chest. And he suppressed the thought that no other woman had that effect on him, chalking it up to unrequited love. Because if her feelings had run a fraction of his, then she wouldn't have been able to walk away all those years ago, would she? Unlike his father, Brody had no intention of being the fool twice. Between her and his mother, he was beginning to feel destined to associate with women who had no problem walking away from him. Wouldn't Freud have a field day with that one?

The facility was small and well kept. Purple and pink flowers lined the path to the front door of the two-story brick building. A large pot of flowers flanked each side of the oak door and white rocking chairs lined the oversize porch.

"You're sure this is a good idea? Me going inside?" Rebecca's mother had made her feelings toward Brody clear years ago, saying he wasn't good enough for her daughter. The fact that his mother later stole from the town hadn't improved his standing with Mrs. Hughes, even though he'd had nothing to do with it. Still, he didn't imagine her feelings had changed.

"I want you there."

"With her condition, I don't want to make things worse."

"It won't. She's changed a lot. For so many years she was afraid something else would happen to me. She didn't want me to leave the house for fear I wouldn't walk back in the door. Her feelings toward you back then had little to do with you and so much to do with everything else she was dealing with." Rebecca paused, stopping a few steps in front of the door. "Besides, she asks about you."

Well, didn't that last comment stop him in his tracks? "Me?"

The shy smile returned. "Yep. I know she wasn't nice to you back then, but if you could forgive her. I know it would mean the world to her."

"Already done. I don't have kids of my own, but I can only imagine what that's like after seeing Dylan with Maribel. Hell, I'd give my life for that little girl and she's not even mine. I understand where your mom is coming from."

Rebecca didn't immediately start walking again. Instead, she turned to Brody. The equivalent of a thunderstorm brewed behind her eyes. "I think she held on for so many years to the hope my brother would come back alive. Now, she's suffering. Her body wants to go, but she can't. I think it's because she never found closure. A little piece of her half expects him to come walking through the door at any moment."

"Because they never found out what happened to him?"

She nodded. "Mom's just this shell of a person, hanging on. And I know it sounds awful, but I just wish she could find peace. I wish she could let go. She's so tired. Her mind is going. Sometimes she talks about him like he's still here. Yet, she hangs on."

The reason Rebecca wanted Brody with her made a little more sense now. Based on the anguish on her face, she was barely holding on, too. If she needed him to be strong for her, to get through this, he could do that. For her. For him. As a tribute to their past.

Without thinking much about it, he hauled her against his chest. She buried her face as he dipped his head and whispered in her ear. "It's okay. I'm here. Nothing else bad is going to happen."

She gave in to the moment, softening her body against his. And Brody couldn't help but notice for the second time how well they fit. This close, he could feel her heartbeat increasing and the smell of her shampoo, that same mix of citrus and flowers, engulfed his senses.

There was nothing more or less that he could do then except cup her cheeks in his hands and guide her lips to his. Kissing her felt like home. Light at first, deepened when she opened her mouth for him and slid her tongue inside. Her fingers tunneled into his hair as the urgency of the kiss amplified.

Brody's logical mind said she was seeking temporary shelter in a storm. As soon as this blew over, they'd be right back where they started.

With great effort, he pulled back first. "We'd better head down the hall. Since the guys are running late,

I might just tell them to meet us at the restaurant in a little while."

Too quickly, her composure returned, her body stiffened. "You're right. I'm sorry."

"Don't apologize. I probably enjoyed that more than you did."

"I doubt it. And that's not where we need to be right now."

Didn't that confuse him till the cows came home? It had to be a strain to hold so much weight on her shoulders. "You know we're going to figure this out, right? You don't have to do this alone. I'm here. The guys are helping. Law enforcement's involved. He's not going to get away with this."

"I have to find him before he gets to me again, Brody."

A foreboding feeling tugged at him. "I know."

Chapter 7

Rebecca clasped her hand around Brody's as they turned toward her mother's wing. Warmth spread through her from the contact and she didn't fight it. Instead, she relaxed into it, letting it drift through her, calming her, grateful to have Brody's support even if that's where the connection between them had to end—at friendship.

As they rounded the corner to her mother's hallway, she saw a couple hovering. A man she immediately recognized as the reporter who'd hassled her at her car stood behind them, looking down. Was that jerk trying to hide?

Rebecca squeezed Brody's hand.

He glanced at her, must've seen the shock on her face and tucked her behind him.

The couple looked at Rebecca in unison, their faces

pale and desperate. Their gazes were intent as the woman rushed toward Rebecca.

"Ms. Hughes?" The panicked look on the woman's face said everything Rebecca needed to know as to why the lady was there. The expression was unmistakable, hope mixed with anxiety and fear. Gaunt eyes. Sallow skin.

"You want to get out of here?" Brody asked her quietly, his large frame blocking her view.

"Yes." She turned back toward the hallway they'd come from.

"Please, don't go." The woman's voice was full of terror. "It's our son. He's been missing since last year and we were hoping you could help. We're from Sunnyvale."

Hearing those words nearly ripped Rebecca's heart out again. Whatever had happened, Rebecca feared she wouldn't be able to help. She'd tried with her brother's case and look how well that had turned out. "I'm so sorry. I wish there was something I could do."

The woman's brows knit in confusion. "Peter Sheffield called and told us what happened." Brody took several steps forward, making progress toward her mother's door, using his body as a shield. He squeezed Rebecca's hand and she realized he was bringing her closer to her mother's room. She understood his message. Once she got close enough, she could duck inside and lock the door. Later, she'd have a conversation with security about how the reporter brought a couple into what was supposed to be a secure facility.

"It'll just take a minute of your time," the man Rebecca assumed was the father said. He had that same look—dark circles under his eyes, desperation written across his features.

Rebecca glanced at the reporter. Sheffield was tall and sinewy. He had the beady eyes of a rat. Why was he here? What kind of game was he playing?

"I'm sorry that Mr. Sheffield said I could help in some way. I'm afraid he's wrong." Rebecca had made a fatal mistake in making eye contact with the desperate mother. No way could Rebecca slip away now. Those eyes would torment her for the rest of her life if she didn't face the woman.

"He was seven. Just like your brother," the mother quickly added.

Brody's body stiffened as he folded his arms across his chest.

She touched his arm, moved around him, and whispered, "It's okay."

His brow went up when she passed him. He didn't make a move to stop her.

Meeting with a mother who was facing her worst nightmare head-on sent a jolt, like a shotgun blast, through Rebecca's chest. If there was anything she could say or do to ease this woman's pain, Rebecca would. "What do you think I can do to help?"

Sheffield pulled a small device from his pocket, no doubt ready to record everything he heard.

Rebecca shot a look toward Brody. He immediately bumped into Sheffield, mumbling an apology, knocking the recording device out of his hand. "Oops. Didn't mean to do that. Let me help you pick it up."

"No. I got it," Sheffield said, irritated.

Brody scooped up the device and took the battery out. He handed the small piece of metal over to Sheffield with a look that dared him to complain.

The woman's gaze flashed from Rebecca to Brody.

"I'm so sorry to bother you. It's just we heard about your situation and we thought you might be able to help us."

"I'd like to, but I'm not sure what I can do. I have my hands full caring for my mother right now and my brother's case is fifteen years old." She was careful not to reveal too much, or talk about what she was really working on.

"You're the only one who knows what we're going through." The mother who was in her mid-to-late thirties wrung her hands together. Her light brown eyes were red rimmed and dull, the sense of helplessness and despair written all over the dark circles underneath. She was small framed and looked as if she hadn't eaten in days. With her long brown hair and big eyes, she would be considered attractive under normal circumstances.

Her husband looked to be just under six feet with a runner's build, light hair with blue eyes. He had that same haunted look on his face, the one so familiar to Rebecca. He stood off to the side, looking hopeless and helpless. Everything about his body language said he needed to bring his child home.

Rebecca tried to speak, to find some words of encouragement for the desperate couple, but none came.

"Why don't you tell us your son's name?" Brody interjected.

"Jason." The woman took a step forward and her knees buckled. Before she hit the floor, Brody was on one side of her, her husband on the other. She looked up at him and a tender look passed between them. The gesture tugged at Rebecca's heart.

The love and concern on the couple's faces, their tenderness toward each other, outlined just how much love they shared. Had Rebecca's parents ever felt that way toward each other?

They'd grown up in a small town, had been high school sweethearts and married after he graduated college, as everyone had expected. They had history, had tried to be there for each other. But Rebecca wondered if they'd ever had *real* love like this. Her father had it now. She'd seen it with his second wife. A piece of her had been sad and it made her feel even more out of place at his house, like Christmas wrapping paper left over from the year before. Useful, but not exactly what he wanted anymore.

"Take her into my mom's room. I'll get a nurse," Rebecca said to Brody, grateful her voice had returned. There had to be something she could do to help this sweet couple.

Sheffield tried to follow, but Rebecca held her hand out. "Absolutely not. Not you."

The two men carried the woman, stopping to gently lower her into the chair near Rebecca's mother, who had propped herself up when they entered the room, her gaze traveling over the faces.

Rebecca touched her mother's arm. "I'll explain in a minute and then we'll talk about why you called."

The woman apologized several times before Rebecca could reassure her that it was all right. Her mother looked no worse than usual and Rebecca wondered if the call was a stunt for attention.

Mother responded with a blank look.

If Mother hadn't had the nurse call, then it had to have been Sheffield.

Brody disappeared to escort the reporter out of the building.

"Sometimes, I just walk into a room and it's like all the air gets sucked out and the world tilts. I get dizzy. I'm so sorry," the woman repeated.

Rebecca sat across from the woman on the edge of her mother's bed, listening.

A nurse hurried in and examined the woman. "Everything looks fine. A doctor will be in to check on you in a minute."

"No," the woman said, waving away the nurse, "I'll be okay. I just need a second to catch my breath and a glass of water."

Brody walked in, a confused look on his face.

"I'm sorry. Where are my manners? I'm Kevin Glenn, and this is my wife, Chelsea." He shook Brody's extended hand and then Rebecca's. "Our son disappeared last year. We spoke to law enforcement, FBI, and they haven't been able to find him."

"We know exactly how you feel," Rebecca's mother said, her chin out and determination in her gaze. "And we know exactly what you're going through. Come. Sit." She patted the bed near her, looking stronger than she had in months. "This is a lot to have thrown at you at once. Believe me, I understand."

Rebecca scooted down so that Kevin could sit next to her mother.

"Mrs. Hughes, I'm so sorry for your loss," he said, choking back a tear.

"Thank you," her mother replied. "What happened to us tore our family apart. I made a lot of mistakes. There comes a time when you have to focus on what you have left." Mother glanced from Brody to Rebecca. "And hope it's not too late."

Rebecca smiled at her mother.

Kevin's shoulders rocked as he swiped away tears. "I apologize for barging in like this. It's just when we heard about what happened to you this morning, we wondered if the kidnappings could be related. Sheffield had reached out to us to write an anniversary story on our son's disappearance. We haven't been speaking to the media, but then he said he thought our story might be related to yours somehow and that got our attention. Then he told us you had some kind of an accident in the woods. We've been waiting here ever since."

"We did and we reported it to the sheriff's office," Rebecca said, while holding her mother's gaze.

"You were with Sheriff Brine in the woods?" Mother gasped and brought her hand up to cover her heart.

"It was one of his deputies, but yes."

"What were you doing...*there*?"

"It's a long story, Mother. I don't want you to worry about me. I'm completely fine." Rebecca tried to smooth it over, but her mother's wild eyes said words weren't helping.

"You shouldn't have been there, Rebecca. You should let the sheriff's office do its job."

"They haven't done it so far."

"There's nothing else you can do. You have to let it go." Fear and panic raised her voice several octaves. All her mother's protective instincts seemed to flare at once. A spark lit her eyes as she sat up as straight as she could manage.

Rebecca moved to the side of her mother's bed, not wanting to rile her. Too much agitation wouldn't be good for her heart. "No. I can't. And not just because I want to find out what happened to Shane. The man is back and he's trying to hurt me. I can't allow it. And if

I can find out what happened before…then I owe it to you and me to do so now."

"Don't do it for me. You don't owe me anything, dear. It's not safe for you out there. I'll talk to the doctor about making space for you here." This was the most life Rebecca had seen from her mother in years. A piece of Rebecca wanted a reaction from her mother just to know that she was still alive in there. Usually, she stayed in bed day after day, watching TV and sleeping. Her daily exercise routine consisted of six trips to the bathroom.

"I understand why you'd panic. I didn't mention it to upset you." Rebecca held her mother's hand. The iciness was gone now. Hot, angry blood ran through her veins.

"Rebecca, be reasonable. You can't go out there while he's around. What if he comes after you again? I can't do anything from this bed. I can't protect you from here."

Her mother's blood pressure was increasing to unhealthy levels. "I hear what you're saying, but I have protection."

Her mother's gaze shifted from Rebecca to Brody and back. "No one can save you against a monster like that."

"The best thing you can do to help me is calm down." Her mother's eyes were wild now and her breaths came out in short bursts. Her gaze darted around the room, landing on the Glenns and then Brody. "Not even you will be able to stop him. No one could before."

Brody took a knee beside her bed, lowering himself to eye level. "Nothing will happen to your daughter as long as there's air in my lungs."

Tense, Rebecca readied herself for the fight that was sure to come.

"The best thing you can do for your daughter is trust her, trust me." He took hold of her mother's hand and held on to it.

Instead of responding with anger, she blew out a breath. Her shoulders slumped forward and, for the first time, she looked almost relieved. "I know you're right. My girl is smart. She's a lot tougher than I ever was."

"No one blames you for your reaction. Hell, I'd be the same way," Brody continued, his voice a calm port in the sea of tension that had been surrounding them. "And no one should have to go through what you did."

Her mother eased back onto her pillow, keeping a tight grip on Brody's hand. "I was worried about her. That's the reason I called. I'm glad she has you, Brody."

"We have a chance to find him. To know about…" Brody didn't immediately finish his sentence. "That's why Rebecca and I went to the woods. And, yes, we were attacked, but she fought that creep off until help arrived."

"You were close to him?" Her mother's eyes were now wide blue orbs.

"Yes, Mother," Rebecca said. "I had to be. He won't be out there much longer. The sheriff can't ignore me anymore. He'll get him this time. And if he doesn't, we will."

The excitement looked to be taking a toll on her mother. Her gaunt features paled as she suppressed a cough. She had the disposition of a deployed airbag.

"You should rest. Keep up your strength." Rebecca might not be able to bring her brother back, but she could help find the man who had taken Shane from them. She didn't have the heart to think *Shane's killer*. The small sprig of hope that had refused to die inside her had prevented her from doing so. Hope that the young man she'd located on social media would turn out to be Shane. Hope that she hadn't wasted more than half of her life searching for a brother she would never find.

Had she funneled all her energy into finding him in order to avoid acknowledging his death?

Kevin made a move to stand. Her mother caught his arm with her free hand. "Stay."

"We don't want to intrude. Your daughter's right. You should rest," he said. "We were foolish to show up like this. Sheffield said you could help. I'm really sorry. Your family has been through enough already."

"Will you keep me company for a while?" Her mother's voice, frail and tired, trailed off at the end of her question.

Kevin nodded as she closed her eyes.

"You don't have to," Rebecca whispered just out of her mother's earshot.

"We don't mind. It's just the two of us now. If it's okay with you, we'd like to stay here. I know it's going to sound weird, but it's nice, for a change, to be with people who understand. Who don't look at us like we're about to freak out or break."

"Believe me, I do get that." Rebecca reached out and patted Chelsea's hand.

Mother smiled softly. "It's nice to have company."

Brody's cell buzzed. He excused himself and disappeared into the hall.

When he returned, the look on his face said the others had arrived.

"We'll check in on you guys later," Rebecca said.

As she walked toward the door, Chelsea touched her

arm. "Good luck with your search. Will you let us know if you find anything?"

"Absolutely." Rebecca was grateful they were with her mother. The slight rattle to her breathing made her fear her mother didn't have much time.

"When you came back into Mother's room earlier, you looked confused. What happened?" Rebecca asked.

She didn't miss a trick. Or did she just read Brody that well? Probably both. He'd work toward being less transparent next time.

"I went out to see to if our friend found the front door all right. He was too easy to escort out."

"So he got frustrated and left."

"I'm not so sure. Think about it. First, he brings that couple to you. Why?"

"Because he's been dying to get an interview with me."

"Exactly. And he had you right there. But then he left? Have you ever seen a reporter give up on a story so easily?"

"Good point. He went to all the trouble to make sure the Glenns came to see me. He wouldn't leave like that, would he?"

"And that's another thing that bugs me. How did he know where you'd be?"

"I need to ask my mother if he spoke to her before. I'm thinking he tricked the nurse and prompted her call."

"That's true. And he also told the Glenns about the attack in the woods. How did he know about that?"

Rebecca shrugged. "Who knows how reporters figure things out? Sources, I guess."

"And that could be anybody."

"He might have a contact at the sheriff's office. When we called it in they could've let him know."

"I just wonder what else he thinks he knows. He wouldn't have left here if he didn't think there was a hotter story or lead somewhere else." Brody didn't like the way the reporter had tried to bully Rebecca. He made a mental note to keep an eye on the guy.

The fact that Sheffield seemed to be watching their movements didn't sit well. Then again, maybe he was trying to make a name for himself. Solving the case the sheriff couldn't would be a huge boost to the guy's career.

The ride to Mervin's Eats was quiet. Dawson's black sport utility was parked in the lot.

"The place is busy. I wonder if any of Randy's friends will be here." Rebecca's expression was easy to read. Her wide gaze was more desperate than hopeful.

"There's a slim chance we'll get a hit on the first try, right? Let's get a feel for the place. See if we think it's a good idea to ask around. Someone might know something."

"They wouldn't likely tell strangers, would they?"

"We'll make something up." Brody scratched the scruff on his chin. It was long past dinnertime and had been a full day. He could use a hot shower and a warm bed. Thoughts of the kiss he'd shared with Rebecca edged into his mind. He pushed them away. "Ready?"

Rebecca took in a deep breath and grabbed the door handle. "Let's go."

Ryan hopped out of Dawson's SUV first, followed by Dylan and Dawson.

After hugs and greetings were exchanged, the five of them moved inside.

The place was a decent size and had a nice home-town feel to it. Lots of autographed snapshots of a man who Brody assumed was the owner with professional athletes and musicians lined the walls.

A surprising number of people filled the place given dinnertime had come and gone a good three hours ago. There was still plenty of seating for more. Brody stopped at a sign that read Please Wait to Be Seated.

Music played in the background, but it wasn't loud enough to drown out the buzz of lively conversation. The place was about half-full.

A hostess wearing form-hugging jeans and a Mervin's Eats T-shirt greeted them. She checked them out and smiled. "Just five tonight or are you expecting more?"

Rebecca looked to Brody for a response.

"We're all here," he said.

"Do you want menus? The kitchen's open another half hour," she said, twirling her hair and leaning toward Brody.

He looked to the guys, who seemed about ready to bust out laughing. They shook their heads.

"Just two."

"Well, then, follow me." She pulled the requisite number of menus, flashed a smile and spun toward the grouping of tables to her left. She paused long enough to ask, "Booth or table?"

"We're not picky," Brody responded.

Another smile came and this time her cheeks flushed. Rebecca elbowed him as he let her pass him to take the lead. Her eyebrows pinched together as though she were scolding him.

Now it was Brody's turn to try to hold back a laugh. If she'd noticed, then the hostess was most definitely flirting.

And, if he was being honest, his reaction would've been much worse if the tables had been turned. Even so, he put up his hands in the universal sign of surrender and whispered, "I didn't do anything."

The others jabbed him in the shoulder and arm as they walked past.

Ryan was last. "How's Rebecca?"

"Strong. I don't have to tell you what she's been through."

Ryan nodded as they approached the round corner booth. Each one filed in to the right.

Brody slid left, so he could sit next to Rebecca. He liked having her positioned in between him and one of the guys. Anyone wanting to get to her would have to go through one of them first. Brody also liked the idea of having backup. The light dose of pain medication from the hospital was wearing off and a freakin' jackhammer pounded the spot between his eyes.

A waitress stopped by to take drink orders. Brody ordered chicken-fried steak with iced tea and smiled when Rebecca did the same. The others ordered an appetizer of chicken wings and a round of beers. Normally, Brody would join them, but tonight he wanted a clear head. Whoever was after Rebecca could strike at any time. Brody figured the guy wouldn't be stupid enough to try anything with the others around, especially since they were all big guys and this creep only struck like a coward. He didn't fight head-on. He hid in the trees, in the brush, the element of surprise his only advantage. His preferred target had been a child.

The thought of the Sunnyvale boy going missing last year near the anniversary of Shane's disappearance weighed heavily on Brody's mind.

When the waitress had thanked them and disappeared, he clasped his hands and intentionally kept his voice low. "It means a lot to both of us that you guys are here. We're hoping to connect with the whole group, but the girls have spread out so that's a bit trickier on short notice. Samantha's in Dallas."

"And Lisa moved a couple of counties over," Ryan added. "Anyone know where Melanie is?"

Dawson nodded. "I ran into her sister the other day. She moved to Houston, and never comes back to visit. I think she stays in touch with Samantha and Lisa, though. I can check with one of them."

Brody thanked Dawson for helping out with the horses earlier.

"Do you guys still hang out?" Rebecca asked.

Most shook their heads.

"That's such a shame. We were all so close when we were little. Remember how long we used to play outside?" Rebecca asked.

"Remember Red Rover?" Dylan chimed in.

Heads nodded and smiles returned.

"Sad that we didn't stay that way. It's my fault," Rebecca said.

"Everyone's to blame, not just you," Dawson quickly interjected. "We were kids. No one knew what to say or do. We were all scared. Looking back, I feel like we let you down."

"You didn't," Rebecca said. "I was out of school for a

year and my parents didn't let me see anyone. I missed you guys, but everything was so crazy for such a long time. I think I forgot how to have friends."

The waitress arrived with drink orders and the appetizers, momentarily stopping conversation.

"All our parents flipped out after that. Everyone changed. *Everything* changed. And none of it was your fault, Rebecca. We wish we would've gone searching with you that night. If we had, things would've been different." Dylan lifted his mug. "The reason stinks, but we're together now. So, glasses up."

How many times had Brody had the exact same thought? Too many, he thought, as he lifted his glass.

Ryan leaned forward, his serious expression returned. "Justin is grateful for everyone covering for him that night. I don't know if I ever thanked you guys for that."

"Sheriff Brine really had it in for your brother after he got caught breaking into school," Brody said.

"My brother was stupid back then," Ryan said. "He learned his lessons the hard way. Besides, the sheriff couldn't hurt Justin any worse than what he got at home."

Brody remembered that Justin had stayed out of school beyond his week's suspension when he'd been caught. The beating he'd received from his father had left permanent marks on the backs of his legs. "We all knew covering for him was the right thing to do."

"I appreciate it," Ryan said.

"Speaking of the sheriff's office, my friend gave me a copy of the Mason Ridge Abductor's file. According to the FBI profiler, he would most likely have had a job that required him to travel around the state."

"Like a festival worker?" Dawson asked.

Brody nodded. "They ruled out local bus drivers, shop owners, and everyone else with a stable job."

"I remember how adamant the sheriff was about this being a transient worker. Didn't they check out everyone connected to the festival?" Dylan asked.

"They did," Rebecca said. "But there are so many people who come through town this week for the activities. The RV park by the Mason Ridge Lake is completely booked. Has been for months. And it's like that every year. There are workers but then also tons of people who come just for the festival. It's impossible to keep track of everyone."

"So, they're saying it was most likely someone here for the festival and not necessarily someone who works there," Dylan clarified.

"Right," Brody said. "But here's the thing. The Mason Ridge Abductor was smart enough not to get caught, which took some doing. But then lower-IQ offenders are the ones who tended to spend time in jail. This guy has avoided capture for fifteen years. He didn't have to be especially brilliant, just smart enough to cover his tracks. He could be one of us."

"Are you saying you don't think law enforcement had it right before?" Dylan asked.

"The more I think about the facts in this case, the more I believe someone right here could've been involved." Seeing Rebecca's brown eyes look weary and pained caused Brody to clench his hands. He hated everything about this case, except the part about seeing Rebecca again. Even so, watching her expression, knowing how much she was hurting, felt like a clamp around his heart. "There's a reporter who is hot on the case. You guys remember Peter Sheffield?"

"He's a jerk," Ryan said. "But harmless. I heard he's trying to make a name for himself at the paper."

Brody had figured as much. He hoped the guy didn't get in their way.

Rebecca turned to him, a wishful look in her eyes. "Should we tell them about Randy?"

The others exchanged looks.

"Rebecca has been searching social-media sites and she came across someone who looks a lot like Shane. There are pictures online of him hanging out with friends here," Brody said. He fished his phone from his pocket and pulled up the social media site. He located the pictures and passed his phone around the table.

"He has the same chin as Rebecca," Dawson observed.

"That why we're meeting here?" Ryan asked, studying the photo.

Brody nodded.

"Good idea," Ryan said, his gaze shifting to the hostess. "Friendly place."

Brody knew that his friend was referring to her flirting. In fact, she'd kept her eye on the table and a smile on her face ever since. Rebecca seemed to notice, too.

Chapter 8

Rebecca didn't realize she'd been holding her breath until Ryan returned. He'd offered to fish for information from the hostess, giving Brody an out so he wouldn't have to be the one to do it. "What did she say?"

He slid inside the booth. "She recognized him but didn't know him personally. Said he hasn't been in for months, though."

"Did she have a guess as to why?" Rebecca asked.

"I'm afraid not."

"What about his friends? Do they still come in?" she quickly added.

"Negative, but she wasn't surprised. Said groups of young people come and go, many of whom head off to college. A lot of them find jobs in bigger cities after school since professional jobs are scarce around here. Others go into the military."

Her chest felt like a balloon with a hole in it, slowly leaking air—and hopes of finding Shane along with it.

Brody perked up with the news. "The first place we'll check is the military. It'll be easy to find him if he enlisted."

Dylan nodded. "I have a contact, too."

A burst of optimism spread across the men's faces.

Rebecca, on the other hand, felt she was back at square one.

The food arrived, stalling conversation once more. After hearing the disappointing news, she was grateful to be able to fix her attention on eating.

It was probably too good to be true that Shane had grown up a couple towns away, safe, in a good home. If he couldn't be with her and her mother, she'd at least wished he'd be well cared for and happy. He was so young when he'd been taken she wondered if he would remember her at all. She'd read in an article a few years ago that people retained very few memories before age ten. Shane had been seven, well below the age of retention. Her own memories of him had faded over the years. If she hadn't had photographs of him everywhere, would she remember him at all? Being the oldest, she had to believe she would.

A strange thought struck. What if she found him and he rejected her? What if he didn't want to go back? What if he was perfectly satisfied with his life?

Could he be completely happy without ever knowing about his past? Was it selfish to want to force that on him if by some miracle she found him alive?

One thing was certain. Rebecca had to know what had happened to her baby brother. She prayed he was thriving. And if he was, when she saw him, knew he was fine, then she'd decide if she had any right to intrude on his life.

Dealing with her mother complicated the situation. On the one hand, her mother had a right to know about her son. On the other, Shane or Randy or whatever his name was deserved to live in peace, if that was the case.

Rebecca took a bite of chicken-fried steak and chewed.

Brody leaned toward her, his arm touching hers. He seemed to realize she'd gone inside her thoughts, gotten lost there. In barely a whisper, so only she could hear, he said, "This is good. We're making progress."

In difficult times she'd learned that it was best to focus on the here and now. Besides, he was right. They knew more than they had in years. And even if Randy wasn't Shane, at least they could rule him out. Progress. They were making progress. Progress would be her new mantra. She'd already learned the hard way that dwelling on the negative only brought her down further.

And with the guys back together, she was beginning to believe that anything was possible.

When the plates had been hauled away, she thanked them for coming.

"Is there anything else you recall from that night? Anything we need to be on the lookout for?" Dylan asked.

"The thing I remember the most is strange," she said. "It's a smell. Apple tobacco."

"That was never in the papers," Ryan said quickly.

Something flashed in his expression that sent a chill scurrying up her spine. Recognition? She carefully studied him. "The FBI wanted to keep it out of the news. They were already bombarded with leads and they said the more information we gave the bigger chance we had of copycats and false leads. Why?"

"It would've helped people to know what they were searching for," Ryan said, regaining his casual composure with what looked like significant effort on his part.

"Or tipped off the abductor on what we were looking for," she said.

"I thought law enforcement was focused on transients."

"The sheriff's office was. Brine refused to believe someone in town could've done this. The FBI wanted to cast a wider net," Rebecca supplied, still eyeing Ryan.

"What else did they keep out of the news that might've helped?" he asked, and she realized he was most likely just as frustrated as they were.

"That was it." Time had faded so much of her memory. The FBI had also told her that she'd been in shock, and forgetting details was her brain's natural way of protecting her. Not even a hypnotist could pull any more information out of her then. Fifteen years had surely eaten away at anything that might have been left.

With a full stomach, exhaustion set in. Her bones were so tired they ached. She leaned back against the seat, not wanting to interrupt the conversation that had turned to what each of them had been doing lately.

Brody concealed a yawn and that kicked off one for her, too.

"We should probably head back. It's an hour's drive to Mason Ridge and Rebecca hasn't slept in a day and a half," he said.

"Don't break this up because of me. It's nice to see everyone again." She couldn't remember the last time she'd sat around with friends she trusted and had a drink. College had been a blur of classes, her job as a waitress and all-night study sessions just to keep up.

Heads nodded in agreement.

"Then I think we should barbecue at the ranch next Friday night. I'll have plenty of cold beer and beds to crash on so no one has to drive," Brody said.

"I'd like to reach out to Samantha, Lisa and the others," Rebecca added. "It'll be like old times." She stopped short of saying *like when she'd been happy.*

"Until then, promise you'll get some rest. The both of you," Ryan said. "And take care of that gash on your head."

Dylan added his agreement. "We'll keep digging and let you know if anything comes up. Forward a copy of those social-media links. Maybe I'll make a few new friends between now and then."

"Will do," Brody said.

The bill came and Dawson covered it with his hand. "I got this. You two get out of here. We'll stick around a little while and chat up the locals. See if we can dig around a little more while we're here."

Brody argued over paying the bill, lost and then thanked his friends as Rebecca hugged each one.

She wanted to talk to Ryan about his reaction earlier but tabled it. *For now.*

Night had descended around Rebecca and Brody by the time they reached the ranch. The truck's headlights cut through the darkness, lighting a path down the drive before moving across the large ranch house as Brody pulled into his parking spot.

Rebecca tried to shake off the fog that came with drifting in and out of sleep on the way there and then waking too fast. Twelve hours underneath a warm comforter would do her good.

She blinked her eyes open and glanced at the clock. It was eleven-thirty on a Friday night. Normally, she'd be doing laundry. How lonely did that sound?

As if her past hadn't been scarring enough, the few times she'd tried to date in college hadn't worked out. One of her most distinct memories was of her first boyfriend. He'd had too much to drink one night and thought slipping her a roofie would be fun so he could "experiment." Thankfully, he'd passed out before he could do anything sick to her, but the feeling of being vulnerable had shocked her back into protective mode.

Opening up, trusting again, had been next to impossible after that. She'd met a few men in Chicago. She'd watched her drinks like a crazed person whenever she was on a date. Taking her glass of wine or cup of coffee to the bathroom with her had solicited more than a few odd looks. She didn't care. They could judge her all they wanted, but she planned to be fully alert and in control. She involuntarily shivered at the memories and the all-true thought that Brody was the only man she'd ever felt safe around. No way would he try anything funny if her back was turned. Heck, she'd kissed him twice already and he hadn't tried to push for more even though she sensed that he wanted it as much as she did.

Since moving back to Mason Ridge three years ago, the dating well had dried up.

"Hey, beautiful. You're awake." Brody's voice wrapped around her, the rich timbre sliding through her, warming her. Being near him made her want things she knew better than to consider. Things like a real man to wake up next to, to feel secure with.

He turned off the engine, cut the lights, and put his arm around her after they exited his truck.

The porch light came on unexpectedly as they approached, lighting up the front of the expansive one-story brick ranch.

Rebecca froze. "Does someone else live here with you?"

"No. It's one of those motion-sensor lights." He moved his arm from around her neck and she immediately missed the weight of it, the warmth, the feel of Brody's touch.

"You okay?"

"Yeah," she lied. How did she begin to defend just how little it took to completely rattle her nerves?

He made a move toward the front door but stopped short. Instead, he turned, captured her face in his hands and pressed his lips against hers, hard, kissing her.

She opened her mouth enough for his tongue to slip inside, where she welcomed him. The taste of sweet tea still lingered on his tongue. She tunneled her hands into his thick hair and kissed him back, matching every stroke of his tongue. And she didn't want to stop there.

He managed to pull back first. Again. "There. I've been wanting to do that again ever since we left your mother's."

She didn't immediately speak. Couldn't. Not while she could still taste him. Besides, she'd probably just say something to ruin the moment, anyway.

He mumbled an apology before sliding the key into the lock.

"Don't be sorry. I'm not."

He turned, smiled and offered his hand. She took it, electricity and awareness zinging through her. Brody was the excitement of an electrical storm blowing right through her. It was strange how safe she felt with him even though he turned everything inside her upside down.

In the porch light, she could see his face clearly. A face she'd thought about so often over the years. Remembering his features had calmed her when she woke from nightmares.

"I missed you, Brody," she said softly.

He responded by hauling her against his chest. So close, her body flush with his, she could feel his racing heartbeat against her breasts. Awareness trilled through her. She reached up on her tiptoes and wrapped her arms around his neck.

He blew out a warm breath as his hands looped around her waist. "The problem isn't how much I want you, Rebecca. You know that, right? I'm sure sex would blow both of our minds."

This close—her breasts against his muscled chest—her nipples beaded.

"I haven't done casual sex since returning from my first tour, and I have no plans to start now. Especially not with you."

Those last words stung. She pulled back, embarrassed that she'd given in so freely to her feelings. Rather than analyzing that to death, maybe Rebecca should be relieved she felt that way at all. If Brody could unlock those feelings, then surely someone else could. "I think you misunderstood. I wasn't suggesting—"

"You might not have been, but it's been on my mind ever since I saw you this morning. And I think it's been on yours, too."

Or maybe Brody was and would always be the one

she felt secure enough with to let go. And look how that had turned out, two broken hearts.

She didn't want to look into his eyes while she felt so vulnerable. He lifted her chin and that's exactly what she did—looked into those blues. Why was it the only time she felt home was when she looked at him?

Hope of another man igniting those same feelings inside her fizzled. Brody was her weakness, her hot-fudge sundae when she was supposed to be on a diet, and maybe it was time to admit he would never be more to her than a temporary treat.

"Doesn't mean we have to act on it," she said.

"Nope. Sure doesn't." He didn't immediately move.

They stood there holding each other in the moonlight, staring for long moments as though cast in stone and neither could move if they'd wanted to. She wanted to lean further into the feeling, into him, and stay there as long as she could in his arms.

"We should probably go inside," she said, losing herself in his crystalized blue gaze.

Everything about Brody reminded her of being a woman, which was something she'd neglected for so very long.

She rose up on her tiptoes and pressed a kiss to his cheek. "You've done a lot for me, Brody. More than you'll ever realize. I didn't know what to do with that when we were kids, so I pretended breaking up with you was to save you. And part of it was. The other part, the part I still don't want to admit, has to do with me. I'm trying to get over what happened, and I get close. Then, he just reaches up and takes me back down. Whether it's in a nightmare or like now, he's always going to be there, holding me back, unless I do something to change it."

His body tensed as though every muscle was fighting against the words forming in his thoughts.

"I understand," he said. "I'm sorry for what happened to you. But when this case is over, we'll go back to the way our lives were before. Yours involves taking care of your mother and working at the radio station. Mine's here on this ranch. The horses. And we need to keep that in mind before we do something that'll burn us both. No use going down that path again, wasting time."

So many objections charged through her mind, but she couldn't go there. He was right. This case would be over soon, one way or the other. That jerk would end up where he belonged, in the ground or in jail. She refused to believe he'd get to her. And they would each go back to their respective lives. Rebecca would care for her mother in her final days, and Brody would go back to his business.

And all that was going to happen whether she wanted it to or not.

She couldn't control the future. But they had now, this moment, and she didn't want it to end. She shifted her weight to the other foot, stared him directly in the eyes, and said, "I hear what you're saying and I won't argue. But I do object to one thing you said. Time spent with you is never wasted."

"I didn't mean—"

"I know exactly what you meant and I understand where you're coming from. I'm grateful for your help, so I won't push for anything else." Even though she wanted him more than she wanted to breathe. She also recognized what a huge mistake they'd be making if things went any further. As long as her mother was alive, Rebecca was tied to Mason Ridge. From the looks of her mother's condition and refusal to take medication that could save her, that wouldn't be long. Rebecca had every intention of leaving and not looking back when her mother's long battle came to an end. Whereas Brody's life was right there, doing something he loved. Everything he was building for his future was inside that county. And she admired him for knowing where his place was, where he fit. Chicago had been wonderful, mostly because it was far away from Mason Ridge. She had yet to figure out where she belonged.

Rebecca turned toward the door, easing out of Brody's grip. "I love that you bought this place. It suits you. The work that you're doing is amazing. You seem happy here."

"It's been good for me." He led her into the house and turned on the light. "No one's here and my housekeeper doesn't show up until Tuesday so we won't be bothering anyone by being here. Make all the noise you want."

The open-space living room was massive. An oversize log fireplace anchored the room on one side, and the image of a fire, glasses of wine and a bunch of throw pillows on the floor in front crossed her mind. She shook it off, instead focusing on the wood beams across the ceiling. The place was comfortable and masculine. It had that warm lodge feel to it with comfortable furniture she could sink into. Everything about the space was a true reflection of Brody. She clasped her hands together, trying to conceal her overflowing pride. Brody had done good. Better than good. "It's perfect."

His smile shouldn't make her heart flutter, and yet that's exactly what it did.

"The place has two wings, one is made up for guests and the other's mine. You can stay in the guest bedroom unless I can convince us both one night in my room would be worth it." He grinned his sexy little smile where barely the corners of his lips upturned.

She hoped he didn't notice the flush of excitement those words brought. Because right here, right now, if he seriously invited her into his bed she'd say yes.

"I'll grab a towel so you can shower." He motioned toward the long hallway to the right.

A shower sounded like heaven about now. She suppressed another yawn. "I doubt I'll be able to sleep."

"There isn't much more we can do until morning, anyway. We'll be fresh and ready to go after a good night's rest," he said.

"I don't know."

"I'll grab your suitcase, so your clothes will be waiting." He stopped long enough to give her hand a reassuring squeeze. "We'll figure this out, Rebecca."

Brody had always been able to see right through her. "I know you're right, it's just…"

"You want so badly to give your mother good news."

She nodded. "I want to give her something to fight for."

"You already have. She has you." He paused. "Besides, anything happens tonight and I promise to wake you. But you're sleepwalking at this point and you need a few hours of shut-eye before you make yourself sick."

He had a good point. And when she really thought about it, exhaustion weighed heavily on her limbs. Thoughts of a shower and sleeping in a bed were almost too good to be true. She stood and followed him down the hall. He stopped in front of a linen closet, pulled out a fresh towel and pointed toward the first door on the right.

"You'll have all the privacy you need in there."

Probably more than she wanted about then. "You going to bed, too?"

He'd already started toward the front door when he stopped and turned, sexy smile securely in place. "After a long, cold shower."

Brody had been awake for three hours. He'd tended to the horses, eaten breakfast and polished off a cup of coffee. He'd wanted to go inside Rebecca's room to check on her a half dozen times just to make sure she was okay but didn't. He knew better than to trust himself with her while she was vulnerable. She needed some reassurance about life, and that's most likely why she'd made it clear last night she wouldn't mind a little fooling around.

He, on the other hand, couldn't risk it. His heart couldn't take another hit.

Brody made another cup of coffee, using one of the individual cups from the single-serving machine that his housekeeper had practically forced him to buy. He settled in at the kitchen table, studying the file again. Surely something was there he could work with.

His phone vibrated. He checked the screen, found a text from Ryan wanting to know if he could stop by.

Brody responded with a yes and said the front door would be unlocked.

Ten minutes later, Ryan showed. Tension radiated from him in waves.

"That was quick." Brody glanced at the time. It was almost noon and still no sign of Rebecca.

"I was in the area," Ryan said, heading toward the kitchen. "Mind if I grab a cup of coffee and join you?"

Considering Brody lived twenty minutes from the nearest store, Ryan couldn't have been close. Brody didn't need to see the worry lines on his friend's forehead to know something was up. "You know where everything is. Make yourself at home."

"What is this? Almond mocha?" Ryan wrinkled his nose as he picked through the little pods.

"My housekeeper forced me to buy the variety pack. Said it was good to try new things. As it turns out, I'm not so much of a flavored-coffee guy. I like mine straight up and strong." Brody finished the last of his, noticing the dark circles under his buddy's eyes.

Ryan made his own cup, joined Brody at the table and took a sip.

This close, his features looked haunted. An ominous feeling settled over Brody.

"We need to talk about something Rebecca said last night. Is she up yet?" Ryan asked.

"No. She's still asleep. At least I think she is. I haven't seen her yet this morning." Brody glanced toward the guest hallway. He didn't like the way Ryan's face muscles tightened when he'd asked about Rebecca. This was disturbing.

Ryan stared into his cup for a long moment. Then, he looked up at Brody. "Are you okay?"

"You want to talk about how I'm doing?" Brody asked, surprised.

"That's not what I came here to talk about but bear with me for a sec."

Brody checked his watch. "Good. Because I have a lot to do today and I don't like where this conversation is headed."

"Fair enough," Ryan obliged. "How are you doing with all this?"

"Fine. Why? Do I seem like something's wrong?" Brody finger-combed his hair.

"Thought I picked up on something last night and you look tired this morning." Ryan shrugged.

"So I tossed and turned a little last night. I've gone days without sleep on missions. This is nothing." Brody swirled the rest of the contents in his cup. "And the reason I didn't sleep last night is because the Mason Ridge Abductor is back."

"I'm not talking about that kind of okay and you know it," Ryan said plainly.

Brody didn't immediately defend himself.

Ryan took a sip of coffee. "I'm not trying to get you riled up or dredge up the past."

"Then don't."

"It's already here. What kind of friend would I be if I didn't speak up when I thought I should?"

"I know what you're about to say and I appreciate your concern." Brody could almost hear the next words spilling out of Ryan's mouth and he hoped to preempt them.

"Because I don't think you do, I'm not going to shut up yet." Ryan gripped his mug. "Things were bad before."

"I lived it. You think I've forgotten?"

"That's not what I meant. I'm not trying to put you on the defensive. I'm offering to help. We can find a safe place for Rebecca to stay without her staying here."

"You think I can't separate my emotions long enough to take care of business?"

"I saw the way you two looked at each other last night." Ryan rubbed the day-old scruff on his chin. "Everyone noticed."

Brody had already admitted to tossing and turning all night. He'd told himself it was because of this case and not because she slept under his roof. "She was special to me a long time ago."

"And an elephant doesn't forget. Tell me something that I don't know."

"I don't feel the same way toward her anymore. Whatever we had between us died when she walked out. You know what I'm about."

"Loyalty," Ryan said without hesitation.

"Exactly. If someone can't stick with you during the tough times, then you gotta keep walking, because life is going to dish more than you can handle sometimes. Last thing I need is to be with someone I can't trust to be there when it all goes south. You know that about me." Brody's tone was a little more emphatic than he'd planned for it to be.

Ryan nodded. "Even so, there's a connection between the two of you. And that kind of link doesn't listen to reason."

Didn't Brody already know that. Last night had been a prime example of hormones trying to take control, but he'd been strong. Of course, another few seconds of her body flush with his, her heart beating against his, and he knew the story might've turned out differently. And that would've led to all kinds of awkward today. He didn't want to think about what might've happened if he hadn't practiced restraint. He didn't want to talk about this. He wanted to focus on the case. And he knew Ryan had shown up to discuss more than just *this*. Brody figured he needed to throw his friend a bone. "I'd be lying if I denied having feelings for her. Believe me when I say that I know what's good for me in the long run. And the woman sleeping in the other room is not it."

He pointed toward the hallway where she slept and his gaze followed.

She was standing there, chin up, defiance in her stare. The exact look she gave when the pain was more than she could process.

Damn. Damn. Damn.

A few other choice words flashed through his mind. Brody hadn't meant for her to hear what he was saying. Truth was that he didn't know exactly how he felt about her. Yes, he had feelings. Yes, they were strong. Yes, he wanted to take her to bed more than he wanted air. But he had to consider the possibility that this need could be nothing more than residual hurt from a wounded teenager. He'd been destroyed when she'd broken it off with him.

At eighteen, he couldn't think of a future without her. His plans to go into the military, to come back and buy the ranch, all of this, had been to create a life for her. He could see the fault in that plan now. Both parties needed to be on board. He had never shared his ideas with her. And he was still asking himself why he'd returned to Mason Ridge when those plans had been blown to high heaven. He told himself that it was to be close to his father, but Brody could've gone anywhere after the military. When the time came and his father couldn't take care of himself, Brody doubted it would matter where they'd settled.

Rebecca had wanted to be out of Mason Ridge as soon as she came of age. She'd said that she'd broken up with him to save him from himself. Had it really been to free herself so she could get out of this town and not look back just like his mother?

Plus, it wasn't like she'd come back for him. She hadn't reached out once since she'd gone. The only reason she was here now was to be near her ailing mother in her final months. Mrs. Hughes looked to be barely hanging on. As soon as death took her, Rebecca would disappear again. Just like his mother. And there Brody was, just like his father, waiting for a woman who could walk away so easily.

There was no denying that Brody and Rebecca shared feelings. There'd be no point fighting the fact that those feelings, whatever else they were, were strong. But it was probably just unfinished business between them. And even if it wasn't, no good could come from acting on it. Period.

Rebecca hadn't even stuck around for graduation. The last day of school, she'd gone home, packed her bags and caught a flight north to go to school.

Brody knew because he'd stopped by, lovesick, about to ship out but unable to go without seeing her one more time, without being sure that's what she wanted.

She was long gone. No goodbyes.

It had hardened Brody in a good way. Made him suck it up and endure basic training. Falling into his bunk every night exhausted had been a welcome relief to the living hell of realizing the one person who was everything good in your life didn't blink an eye about boarding a plane without a backward glance.

In some ways, he owed his elite status to her. It was because of Rebecca he'd worked his tail off, preferring to punish himself day after day in training so he could fall into bed numb every night. She was the reason he'd maintained focus when others couldn't wait for leave to see their loved ones. Because of Rebecca, he'd kept everyone but his father at a safe distance ever since.

No distractions.

And all those feelings dissolved as she stood there for a long moment, in the hallway, not speaking. Brody's oversize T-shirt long enough to hit midthigh. Then she said, "That one of those pod coffeemakers?"

Ryan's gaze bounced between Brody and Rebecca, stopping long enough to relay an unspoken apology to both. "I better head home. There's something else I'd like to discuss with you, Brody. I'll give you a call later."

"No, please don't leave because of me," Rebecca said, crossing over to the kitchen. "I'll join you both for a cup of coffee."

Ryan nodded.

She made a cup and took a seat at the table, pulling the shirt over her knees as she hugged them into her chest. "What's the plan for today?"

Ryan stared into his cup again for a long moment.

Tension was like a wall between them.

"You said something last night that I can't get out of my mind." His jaw clenched as he looked up at Rebecca.

The knowing look she gave Ryan when she nodded had Brody almost thinking she'd been expecting this conversation. What had he missed that she'd picked up on?

"You mentioned apple tobacco. I didn't know about that before." Ryan paused, his gaze returned to the cup. "Before I say anything else, I just want to say that I'm sure my brother wasn't involved. I know him."

"What exactly are you saying, Ryan?" Brody asked.

Rebecca didn't budge and she looked small, sitting there. Brody fisted his hands to stop them from reaching for her.

"My brother came home smelling like that sometimes. I'd know that scent anywhere, Rebecca. The one you're talking about is distinct."

"I know it wasn't your brother, Ryan," Rebecca said reassuringly. "It couldn't be him. Your brother's tall and stocky like you. You guys have a football build whereas this guy is tall and slim. Plus, I think he's older than Justin."

Ryan didn't look relieved. "He'd smoke it with my uncle when they'd get drunk together back in Justin's troubled days. So, I lay awake last night asking myself if Justin didn't have anything to do with this, and I know in my heart he didn't, then who could it be? What are the chances a transient smokes apple tobacco. It's not exactly a common thing. If we stop looking at random people who could've been in town for the festival and set our sights on people right here, then that changes everything. And right now the evidence points to my uncle."

"What's his build?" Brody asked.

"He's tall and thin."

Chapter 9

Rebecca touched Ryan's hand to comfort him. "Doesn't mean it was him."

"I hope not. But I gotta look at the facts and be honest with myself, with you," Ryan said, his anguish written all over his face. "He's been in trouble with the law, but I can't believe he would do something like this."

"We can see if he was a suspect." Brody studied the police file.

"Do you know where he lives? We can go talk to him," Rebecca offered.

"I haven't seen him in a while. Last I knew he was living in Garland."

"That's half an hour away from Mason Ridge at the most," Brody said. He stopped suddenly.

Rebecca didn't like his expression. But then, she was still reeling from Brody's words while she'd stood in the hallway. They stung, even though she knew he was just speaking the truth. Stuffing those feelings down deep, she took another sip of coffee.

"Turns out, your uncle Gregory was a suspect," Brody said, flashing an apologetic look toward Ryan. "He worked as a delivery driver for a Texas nursery chain around the time of the abductions."

"Which would put him on the highways," Rebecca said.

"The sheriff would've been able to match up his delivery schedule," Brody said quietly. He kept skimming the file.

"My uncle did stupid things when he drank, but he wasn't violent."

"There isn't much more in the file that I can see. Think we can speak to him?" Brody asked.

"No other kids have gone missing in the area since Shane. If his uncle was somehow involved, wouldn't there be others?" Rebecca asked.

"The Glenn boy last year in Sunnyvale," Brody reminded her.

"True." She nodded.

"I thought about that, too. My uncle moved to Garland two years after the disappearance," Ryan said. "Last time I saw him a few years ago his hands shook if he didn't have a drink by ten o'clock in the morning. He's done other stupid stuff, illegal. Been in jail a couple of times. My heart doesn't want to believe he's capable of such a heinous act and yet I can't ignore the facts. What if he did this?"

"I hear what you're saying. It's probably not even him, but it's smart to check into every possibility. I appreciate you coming forward. This must be really hard for you," Rebecca said. A man who couldn't go a day without drinking most likely wouldn't have the strength to subdue both her and Shane, could he? There was another way to solve this. She remembered that her attacker had spoken the other morning in the parking lot. If it had been Ryan's uncle, she would be able to recognize his voice. "I might have a way to resolve this. Does your uncle have a phone?"

"I believe so. Why?"

Brody was already nodding. He'd caught on to what she wanted to do.

"Call him and put it on speaker."

"Justin might have the number." Ryan pulled out his cell. After a quick call to his brother, he punched in the digits. The line rang three times before rolling into voice mail. Ryan's thumb moved over to end the call.

"Don't hang up. Hold on a second before you do that," Rebecca said, stopping him.

This is Greg. You know what to do at the beep.

Brody's gaze was intent on her, studying her.

"Doesn't sound like him," Rebecca said on a sigh of relief. She wanted to find Shane's abductor more than anything but not at the cost of one of her friends. "At least I don't think."

"We can't ignore the possibility that he might know something or be connected in some way," Brody said, looking to Ryan. "Does your uncle have any enemies?"

"My first thought would be Alcorn. He hates all of my family members. You think someone else might try to set him up?" Ryan asked, his voice hopeful. He deflated a second later. "Why would someone do that after all these years? And why to him? It's not like he's rich or powerful. There's nothing to blackmail him for. Even Alcorn has given up."

"The word about apple tobacco might have gotten out. This is a small town, and after running into Peter Sheffield last night I started thinking how hard it can be to keep secrets. All it would take is one leak. Someone had to have seen something."

"I'd like to chat with your uncle," Brody said.

"I'll arrange something and get back to you." Ryan's face muscles were tight.

Brody checked his phone. "I just got a text from Samantha. She's trying to pull together the other girls to swing by tomorrow afternoon. She's already in town to see her father, anyway."

Samantha had moved to Dallas after college for a job in the textile industry.

The reunion with the guys had gone well, so Rebecca was hopeful this would, too. Was it possible to pick up friendships after everything that had happened? Rebecca hoped so. It was a nice feeling to be with people she had so much history with. They were the few people who didn't look at her awkwardly anymore, as if seeing her reminded them horrible things could happen at any moment. "I can't wait to see her and the others. It's been such a long time. In the meantime, we'll keep following leads, right?"

"The festival rolls up the tents tomorrow. I'd initially hoped to wait and see if things calmed down after they leave. But then I checked online this morning and the Glenns' son, Jason, who disappeared in Sunnyvale last year, did so while the festival was packing up," Brody said.

Ryan perked up. "That's a strange coincidence."

"I'm not so sure that timing is accidental," Brody agreed. "Who's in charge of the festival?"

"Charles Alcorn heads it up every year," Ryan supplied.

"Isn't the festival too low-brow for him to be involved?" Brody asked.

"You'd think so," Ryan said. "But they use his land and he makes a fortune every year."

"I wonder if we can get a list of vendors from him? Names?" Brody asked.

"Doesn't hurt to ask," Rebecca said with a quick look toward Brody.

"He has offices downtown in the building next to the mayor's office, doesn't he?" Brody asked with a slight nod.

"He does. Nice building. I saw in a magazine that he renovated the whole inside before moving in a couple of years ago. Only the finest quality furniture. The best finishings. He donated the other half of the building to the city."

"How convenient for him to be right next door to the mayor."

"Easier to line Mayor Garza's pockets when he only has to walk four steps," Rebecca said. It was common knowledge he had a do-what-it-takes-to-get-the-job-done philosophy. It was half the reason she was tempted to take him up on his offer of help.

"In the meantime, we'll keep poking around until we figure this out." Ryan pushed his chair back from the table. "I have a few things to take care of. Keep me posted on what you find out. I'll let you know as soon as I arrange a meeting with my uncle. Stay close to your phone."

"Will do," Brody said, turning to Rebecca as soon as the door was closed.

"You noticed that, too, didn't you?" she asked.

"Yep. Ryan sure got out of here quick when we started talking about Alcorn." Brody stood, walked to the sink and rinsed out his coffee cup. "There's no love lost between their families. Ryan's dad wouldn't give Alcorn something he wanted years and years ago when he was still alive."

"That wouldn't have gone over well. Guess I wasn't around much to notice." She'd been so wrapped up in her own family's issues she hadn't once stopped to consider her friends' problems. "I remember bad blood from when we were kids now that I think about it."

Brody crossed to the back door. "Some old wounds don't heal."

Brody exercised the horses, taking care not to overtax his newest arrival, Storm Rival. The owner didn't have any use for the chestnut Thoroughbred when he developed shin splints after his last race at Lone Star Park. Brody just called him Red. Red had been a promising two-year-old until this happened. Now his future was uncertain. He had a true splint, the worst-case scenario for a racehorse, as evidenced by the bulge just below his left knee and on the inner side of his leg. The problem was all too common in young horses entering heavy training. Bad cases had ended plenty of promising careers.

His owner had been kind and this guy was going to get a second chance in life, a different life. The hefty donation would help keep things running, too.

Being in the barn, away from Rebecca, was a good thing. Her lips were too full, too pink, too damn tempting.

Work was the best distraction.

After he'd arranged care for the evening, he cut across the yard and back to the house.

Rebecca was still at the table, studying the screen on Brody's laptop.

On Brody's phone was a text from Ryan. "Ryan may have found something interesting and he wants us to come check it out. He isn't far from here. Are you good with that?"

Rebecca nodded.

"We can be out of here in fifteen minutes. I just need to get dressed," she said, disappearing down the hall.

Brody forced his gaze away from her backside. Self-discipline was the biggest difference between a man and a boy. While he waited, he took pictures of the suspect list so he'd have it with him in case they came across a name.

She returned ten minutes later, fresh-faced, hair pulled back in a ponytail. Her jeans, low on her hips, fit her curves to perfection. The material of her light blue blouse was just thin enough to allow a peek at her matching lacy bra. "Ready?"

For more than she knew. "Yep."

"I checked the news while you were taking care of the horses." Rebecca moved to the driver's side.

"I'm okay to drive."

She gave him the look that he knew better than to argue with, so he didn't. He held his hands up in surrender. "Okay. Fine."

Taking control behind the wheel, she held out his

keys. "Didn't figure you'd get far without these, anyway. And your head is still healing."

"I've taken worse blows than that and survived." To his ego, for one.

"Can you give me directions? His position should be on your phone, right?"

Brody pulled up Ryan's location using the GPS tracker on his phone. He raised the volume and set the phone between them on the seat.

She cranked the ignition and backed out of the parking spot. "This has all been so crazy I don't think I stopped to thank you for what you did for my mother yesterday afternoon."

"Not a problem," he said casually, and meant it.

"I'm serious. She can be difficult to deal with and I think she was shocked to see you."

"Nah. She was fine. Plus, there was a lot going on. Under the circumstances, I thought she was rather nice."

"And if I admit to being wrong about something, will you promise not to rub it in?" she asked.

"Depends on what it is."

She stopped at the end of the drive long enough to jab his arm. "Be serious."

"I am. Scout's honor."

"Like you were a Boy Scout." She rolled her eyes and made a right turn toward town. "Fine, then I won't tell you."

"Oh, come on. You know I was just kidding." He used to love making her laugh in high school. Her smiles were rare, laughter even more so, and he figured that made them all the more special.

"So you think I'm going to tell you now that you've done a little begging?" She didn't hold back her laugh.

"Any chance it's working?"

"Okay, fine. What's it going to cost me?" He paused long enough to listen to the next instruction from the GPS.

She turned right, as instructed, then nodded. Her serious expression returned.

"You plan to tell me, or did you bring it up just to torture me?" he asked, trying to bring the lighter Rebecca back to life. She was inside there. He knew it and he wanted more of her.

"Fine. I lied to you before to trick you into seeing my mother. You were right. She didn't like you." She cracked a shy smile.

"I believe I won her over."

"Agreed. I wasn't sure what to expect, but you broke through to her." She paused. "I feel so bad for the Glenns."

"They've been through the ringer. It's obvious on their faces."

Again, she nodded.

"You rarely ever talk about Shane. Is that subject off-limits?"

Rebecca neither spoke nor nodded.

"You don't have to now. I just thought maybe it might help or some—"

"Don't feel bad about asking, Brody."

"I don't," he reassured, but she was dead-on. He felt bad for bringing up Shane.

"I should talk about him more. About what happened. Maybe it'll help us figure things out. You say we're down to a couple dozen names aside from Ryan's uncle, right?" She paused long enough to receive and follow GPS directions.

She didn't need to tell him about her pain. He felt it, based on the heaviness in her words, the determination in her features.

Brody leaned forward in his seat and stretched his arms.

"All I can really remember about my brother came from stories from my mom and pictures she showed. Other than that night, of course. I can't seem to forget that. All I keep thinking is who would do something like this to an innocent boy? I mean, the guy has to be a monster, right?" Rebecca's body shuddered just talking about it. "Or, maybe he's crazy."

"You won't get an argument out of me that the man's crazy or needs to be locked up with the key tossed away for good. Hell, give me five minutes alone with him and the bastard won't hurt another child for the rest of his life."

The GPS interrupted, stating that the destination was two blocks up on the right. The distraction gave Brody a minute to regroup as Rebecca drove to the spot and then pulled into a parking space.

"Odd. I expected to see Ryan's SUV here," he said.

"I did, too," Rebecca agreed.

"Something doesn't feel right about this." Brody surveyed the area. He phoned Ryan, but he didn't pick up. "I think you should let me drop you off in town so I can investigate."

"And leave you alone with those bumps and bruises? Not a chance."

"I'm better today. I'll grab Dylan or Dawson. It's the weekend. One of them should be around. On second thought, I'll call Dawson. Dylan will be with his little girl today." He prepared himself for a fight.

"Take me to Angel's. That way, when you come to pick me up, we'll be able to get a decent piece of pie," Rebecca said.

Grateful she didn't put up an argument, he palmed his cell and fired off a text to Samantha. He had no plans to leave Rebecca alone. "Mind if I arrange a little company for you? I don't want you to sit there by yourself going crazy worrying until I get back."

"What makes you think I'll do that?"

"Because I've met you before, remember? It's me, Brody."

"Okay, funny man." She paused, looking resigned. "But you're probably right. Samantha did say she'd be in town this weekend. Maybe we'll get lucky and she'll be available. It would be nice to see her."

Lucky. There was that word again. "Done. She just texted back to say she'd meet us there in fifteen. Okay if she brings her father?"

"All right by me."

The extra fifteen minutes it took to drop Rebecca off at Angel's had Brody's gut tied in knots. He sure as hell hoped Ryan wasn't lying in the woods somewhere, helpless. The image didn't do good things to Brody's blood pressure. He phoned his friend again. Same result.

Bringing Rebecca into those same woods where they'd been attacked felt all kinds of wrong. No way could he take a chance with her safety. And he had the very real feeling they could've been lured into a trap.

Rebecca had downed another full cup of coffee and was feeling much more awake and alert by the time Samantha arrived with her father. Mr. Turner had aged quite a bit since Rebecca had last seen him. His entire head was covered in white and his frame was thinning. The hardware store he owned in town most likely still kept him in shape.

Throwing her arms up, Rebecca waved at the pair. She was greeted with a huge smile from Samantha, but Mr. Turner hesitated. He said something to his daughter, but they were too far away for Rebecca to make it out.

When Samantha pointed at Rebecca and nodded, Mr. Turner looked downright uncomfortable. Not an unusual reaction from people in town, but it reminded Rebecca just what an outcast she was in her own hometown. And as much as she'd love to keep her mother around for many more years, healthy, Rebecca was eager to move back to a bigger town. Chicago had been kind to her. And best of all, no one knew about her past there. She didn't get those same wide-eyed stares and behind-the-back whispers when people passed by her in the streets as she did in Mason Ridge. Don't get her wrong, she loved her hometown more than anything, just not some of the baggage that came with it.

Samantha led her reluctant father to the table and plopped down. He did not. "It's so good to see you, Rebecca. You remember my father."

"Of course. Mr. Turner, it's so nice to see you again." With her mother in long-term care and Rebecca herself living in a rental, she hadn't had much need to stop by the hardware store. She stood and stuck out her hand.

He obliged, shaking just long enough to be polite.

Rebecca noticed his palm was warm, sweaty. Since when did her presence start making people so nervous? She was used to seeing sadness in everyone's eyes. Some were upset even and she figured they didn't want to be reminded of that summer. But nervous? She'd moved into a whole new category. *Great.*

Maybe she had always made people feel that way and she'd been too trapped inside her own head to notice.

"I'm sorry I can't join you two," he started.

"Daddy saw some friends at the counter. He asked if we'd mind if he ate lunch with them."

"Not at all," Rebecca said, figuring he didn't look too sorry. In fact, he looked like he might jump out of his skin if she said, "Boo!"

He scurried off to join a couple of older men seated at the bar stools at the breakfast counter.

When he was out of earshot Samantha leaned in, embarrassment flushing her cheeks, and said, "Honestly, I don't know what's wrong with him lately. Getting old, I guess."

Rebecca figured she had a good handle on his sudden need to eat lunch with someone else, anyone else. The man looked like he'd seen a ghost, which was par for the course for her and another reason she didn't mind working the graveyard shift. She figured most parents didn't want to be reminded what could've happened to their child instead of Shane. "It's fine. This will give us a chance to really talk. We'd bore him to death with our conversation, anyway."

Samantha flashed a grateful look and then summoned the waiter. "I swear he's starting to get senile. And the man doesn't sit still anymore."

"He's fine. Don't worry about it."

The waiter interrupted their conversation. Samantha ordered a club sandwich and sweet tea.

"I should have a salad, but I can't resist the burgers

here," Rebecca confessed. "Looks like I'll be hitting the gym later."

"It's so good to see you. How long has it been?"

Rebecca didn't want to try to reach back too far. "I know I haven't seen you since we headed to different colleges."

"Our ten-year reunion is like next year." Samantha's look of horror brought a smile to Rebecca's face.

"Already? Man, time flies."

"I somehow got hooked with planning duties. I'm on the attendance committee, which basically means I'm responsible for finding everyone and making sure they show up."

Rebecca gave a full-body shiver. "Count me out."

"You have to come. If only to support me," Samantha said on a laugh.

"Do you stay in touch with Lisa or Melanie?"

"Mostly just Melanie. She moved to Houston after college so we don't get to see each other as much as we'd like. Lisa's not too far, though. I've run into her a few times at the grocery with Pops. I meant to call her today."

"I'd love to see both of them again. I work deep nights, so even though I live nearby I never see anyone." She decided not to share just how on purpose that was. But seeing Samantha was nice. Rebecca hadn't realized just how much she'd missed having this kind of friendship. Ties that ran deep.

"Melanie never comes back." Samantha rolled her eyes. "Says her work keeps her too busy and she doesn't get a lot of vacation time. When she does, she likes to see someplace new."

That last bit of information came out a little too

quickly. Samantha practically stumbled over the words in her rush to explain.

Rebecca had no intention of making anyone else uncomfortable, not on purpose. Most people didn't want anything to do with her anymore and she understood on some level. They couldn't help, so they'd wanted to forget. She was just a big old fat reminder of the worst summer in the history of Mason Ridge, of every parent's worst nightmare. Plus, everyone had known and loved Shane. She couldn't blame them for not wanting to be reminded of the horrible incident that took him away from them. If it hadn't happened to her family, she might be able to look the other way, too.

"Okay, you got me. I'll come to the reunion," Rebecca said, mostly to redirect the conversation.

"Seriously? You will?" Again, her friend looked grateful for the change of subject.

"If I'm in town." She wanted to add, *and still alive.*

Chapter 10

Brody picked Dawson up at their meeting point on his way to find Ryan, regretting the extra five minutes it took.

"Have you heard from Ryan at all today?" Brody asked, checking his phone again after pulling into the spot he and Rebecca had occupied nearly half an hour ago. He'd brought his friend up-to-date on the short ride over.

"Nope. Not a word. But then that's not unusual," Dawson said, shoving the last bite of a burrito into his mouth.

Having along a guy as big as Dawson, with almost twice Brody's strength, was a good thing, Brody figured.

"Let's see if we can figure out what's going on." Brody didn't like how Ryan had looked earlier. The edge to his tone hadn't sat well with Brody. After the revelation about Ryan's uncle, he looked even more determined to figure out what was going on. Brody sent another text to Ryan and then waited.

There was no response. Again.

"Here's the most logical place to park, but Ryan's vehicle is nowhere." Brody checked the navigation system's map. If he could believe what was on the screen then Ryan was fifty feet or so off the road.

He and Dawson got out of his truck and headed toward the dot on the screen. As they moved, he thought about the missing Sunnyvale boy, the timing. There had to be a connection. What were they missing? But then, getting inside the head of a man who'd abducted a child wouldn't be easy. What about the age of the Glenn kid? He was seven just as Shane had been. Were there other cases in Texas of seven-year-olds going missing? Did the abductor live in Texas? Brody had to think so.

This far, they didn't have squat to go on except a vague description. The hoodie and sunglasses blocked his face and Rebecca had not been able to get a good view of the guy during either encounter, which was frustrating. No more so than the blow to Brody's head. Having his skull traumatized didn't make for the best recall. Brody made a mental note to run a search for crimes connected to seven-year-old boys in Texas.

The phone vibrated. Brody checked the screen. He had another email from the feed store. Still no word from Ryan.

Cell coverage would become spotty the closer he moved into Woodrain Park. On the other hand, the fact he hadn't heard from Rebecca was good news. Even so, a bad feeling crept up his spine. Call it instinct, intuition or a sixth sense, Brody didn't care. Whatever it was had kept him alive in more than one dicey situation in the military.

For Ryan's sake, Brody hoped like hell Greg hadn't been involved. Brody vaguely remembered the guy hanging around Ryan's house in the summers. Even then Brody knew the guy was no good. Did that mean he was a kidnapper? A murderer?

Rebecca had dismissed it, but Brody couldn't stop thinking about the apple tobacco. What was the chance that was a coincidence?

"I know this area," Dawson said. "These woods connect to Mason Ridge Lake on the south side."

"Which means the RV park where most of the festival workers stay is just on the other side of the lake," Brody agreed, now that he was getting his bearings. The workers pretty much stuck to themselves when they came through town, unlike the winter carnival crew, who would show up in restaurants, chat up locals and walk the town square. The only times he remembered seeing festival people were early in the mornings at the grocery when he'd had occasion to go. And, sometimes, late nights at the Laundromat, although they hung most of their clothes to dry near the lake. If one of their machines needed a part, they'd show up at the hardware store, but that was a rare sighting. The nearest auto shop was in Sunnyvale. If one of their vehicles had trouble, they'd have to go there or be towed. Brody hadn't thought much about their habits before.

Being a Renaissance Festival, people walked around in sixteenth-century costumes. There were horse games played and turkey legs for sale. The workers kept to themselves. He figured the lack of workers in town had more to do with them sleeping in mornings and the fact there wasn't much to do in Mason Ridge.

Dawson followed closely behind as Brody led the way through the thicket.

The lake was coming into view by the time they reached the spot where Ryan should be. "This is it."

"He has to be around here somewhere." The day was in full swing and Brody could see festival workers from across the lake. They looked to be gathered in a circle. Were they having a meeting? "What's going on over there?"

"Hard to tell from here." He moved out of the tree line and to the water's edge. "It looks like they're sitting around having lunch."

Brody moved next to him. Kids ran around, kicking and chasing a ball. A woman was hanging clothes on the line she'd set up from a lamppost to her RV. Nothing suspicious appeared to be going on. It all looked like pretty normal stuff to Brody.

A text came through. Brody checked his phone. It was from Ryan. "He wants to meet at the picnic tables." Branches broke to their left.

Brody whirled around. The trees were thick enough to block his view. He locked gazes with Dawson and then motioned for him to break to the left. Brody broke to the right, his steps so light they made no sound. Dawson's hunting instincts must've kicked in, because he didn't make a noise, either.

The sound Brody heard might have been an animal and that was the most logical answer. No one, and especially not the Mason Ridge Abductor, would be dumb enough to attack them in broad daylight. Then again, he'd just tried that with Rebecca.

Let him pick on someone his own size, Brody thought, stepping ever so softly through the underbrush.

He and Dawson would come at whomever or whatever was making the noise from opposite sides. It was the best way to surprise him.

Another noise sounded, indicating more movement. Brody tracked farther to the left, hoping Dawson was correcting his position as well and that he wasn't being lured into a trap. This scenario had stink bait written all over it.

What if it was Ryan?

Brody reminded himself that cell coverage was spotty in the woods. Or…

A bad thought hit Brody. Ryan would answer his phone if he *could*.

Whatever was making that sound was on the move. And that had to be a good thing, because if it was Ryan that meant he was capable of walking.

Brody picked up a rock the size of his fist and hurled it toward a tree ten feet away to see if he could stir up more movement. An animal would react instantly to the sound and scatter.

He stilled.

Sounds of children's laughter floated across the lake. No bolt from an animal.

Meaning the noise was being made by a person.

A muttered curse followed a grunt and a thud. Then a call for help shot through the trees. Dawson.

Brody broke into a run toward the sound, branches slapping him in the face and underbrush stabbing needles in his shoes.

A large man was hovering over Dawson, who was

on his side on the ground. Brody dove straight into the guy, knocking him off balance.

Dawson immediately rolled away and then jumped to his feet. He moved so quickly the guy didn't have time to react. Brody had already pinned the guy with his thighs. "You like sneaking up on people in the woods?"

"I was just thinking the same thing about you," the guy ground out. "What are you doing over here, sneaking around, watching my friends?"

Hope that this could be The Mason Ridge Abductor died instantly based on this guy's size and general stature. He was big and powerful. Not thin, like Rebecca had said.

"We're looking for our friend."

"Get off me and I'll help."

Brody nodded to Dawson, who eased off the festival worker. He was a big guy with a ponytail. He was a bit older, his white hair streaked with gray.

"If your friends are over there, then what are you doing sneaking around on this side of the lake?" Brody asked.

The man dusted the dirt off his jeans and then took the hand up Brody offered. "My name's Lester Simmons."

"We heard a woman was attacked at the grocery nearby and we didn't want to take any chances. We travel with our wives and children to a different city every week. We've seen and heard just about everything. No one wanted to risk it so we set up watch," Lester said. His deep-set brown eyes and permanent smile lines softened what could have been an intimidating figure. One phone call and he could have a dozen men bolting around that lake. The tables would be turned. Brody and Dawson would be completely outnumbered.

Brody gave a nod of understanding and provided a description of Ryan. "According to GPS on his phone, he should be in this area."

"Hold on." Lester pulled his cell from his back pocket.

"Whoa. Not so fast."

"I already have guys on their way. I'm not dumb enough to investigate a sound alone. Figure I'll give them a heads-up so they can look for your friend." Lester went to work on his phone.

"Thank you," Brody said. "Sorry about before."

"It's cool. Tensions are high around camp, too." Lester pocketed his phone. "Where'd you leave off?"

"The last message I received from him said he'd be near the picnic tables," Brody said, remembering the area.

"There's a set right over here. We come over sometimes for dinner because the barbecue grills are less crowded on this side." Lester led them to the tree line."

Sure enough there was a set of picnic tables nestled near a cove. No sign of Ryan.

None of this made sense.

Brody fired off another text to his friend and moved to the location Ryan said he'd be.

No response. No luck.

More men arrived, coming from every direction, and offered the same response when asked if they'd seen anyone else.

The area had been thoroughly searched and there was still no word from or sign of Ryan. It wasn't like him to pull a prank or do something like this. Brody didn't like it one bit.

"Think we should check his place?" Dawson asked. "Maybe he gave up waiting and headed home."

"That's a good idea. There's no sign of him here and we've been searching for more than an hour." Brody had an idea. He called Ryan's phone and then listened. The buzzing sound came a few seconds later. Brody moved to it, located the device.

"Looks like he was here. I'll take this back to him." Brody swiped his finger across the screen. Sure enough, the texts were there. He scanned the log for any others that might give a clue as to where Ryan could be. There was nothing. Brody turned to Lester. "Your help is much appreciated. I apologize again for the misunderstanding earlier."

Lester's friends looked over at him in confusion.

"Not a problem. Like I said, everyone's on alert around here." Lester smiled and took the hand being offered in a hearty shake.

On the way back to the truck, Brody filled Dawson in on the phone's contents. Dawson double-checked the logs and didn't find anything that stood out, either.

At least they'd made a contact within the festival ranks. Having an ally there might come in handy later. There were so many of them around town for the festival, which wrapped up tomorrow. The more eyes and ears, the better. And it was also helpful to know his family and friends were as concerned as the rest of the town.

Turns out, the festival crowd wasn't so different from the people of Mason Ridge.

Finding Ryan had just become top priority.

The drive to his house took another twenty minutes. Brody parked across the street and then texted Rebecca to find out if she was doing okay.

Rebecca replied that she and Samantha were catching up and he could take his time getting back to the restaurant.

As Brody opened the door to get out, his phone rang. The name of the caller was Rebecca.

Odd.

He quickly answered.

"Brody, I thought you'd want to know that Ryan just walked in."

"He's okay?"

"Not a scratch on him," she replied matter-of-factly.

"Hold on to him for me, okay?" Brody stopped Dawson and ended the call. "False alarm. He just showed up at Angel's in town."

"That's strange."

"Isn't it? At least we know he's not lying in a ditch somewhere." Relief settled over Brody and he realized how clenched his shoulder muscles had been. "Want me to drop you off at your house?"

Dawson nodded as he got back in the truck. "It's been a crazy few days, hasn't it?"

It was more statement than question.

"Sure has." Brody gripped the steering wheel tighter, readying himself for more warnings about his relationship with Rebecca.

"You have everything covered out at the ranch?"

"Thanks for the other day. My neighbor helped out last night and my part-time help pulled an extra shift this morning. So far, so good."

"Call me if you need more help."

"Will do."

Brody shot Dawson a look.

"What?" Dawson asked.

"Nothing. I just thought you were going to warn me about spending time with Rebecca," Brody said, easing his grip on the wheel.

"Sounds like something Ryan would do."

"He already did."

"Then you don't need to hear it from me."

"No. I don't."

"Besides, I got a different opinion about that, anyway." Dawson chuckled. "And you know what they say about opinions and how much they stink."

"I sure do," Brody agreed. "I'd like to hear what you have to say, anyway."

"The two of you together is a good thing in my book. It's natural."

"Us being together has never been the tricky part. It's when she leaves that does me in."

Dawson nodded. "I get that."

"The last time wasn't exactly a trip to the state fair."

"I remember. You were a mess."

"Thanks," Brody said sarcastically.

"Anytime," Dawson shot back, clearly trying to work off the tension they'd both felt. "How do you know she'll do it again? I mean, give her some credit. She's a grown woman now, not some young kid scared of her own shadow."

"True," Brody agreed. "In my experience, when people tell you who they are, it's smart to believe them."

"And actions speak louder than words."

"Most clichés are rooted in truth. That's why they're repeated over and over again."

"Except that she's not the same person she was before. Not in my opinion. And I don't remember her making any promises she'd stick around before."

"Tell that to a kid. Here's another problem you might not have considered." Brody pulled up in front of their meeting place. He lived a few towns over. "Don't both parties have to want to be in a relationship for it to work?"

The door was open and Dawson was half-out when he turned. "Had your eyes checked lately? Because I'm starting to think you're going blind."

Was his vision impaired when it came to Rebecca? He felt the heat between them—there was no questioning their attraction. Could there be more?

It took more than good chemistry to make a relationship work.

Dawson held on to the door. "You remember to call me if you need a hand around the ranch. You hear?"

"I plan to take you up on that offer. And thank you."

"Good. Consider the other stuff I said, too."

"You bet." Brody obliged his friend and appreciated his point of view. Ultimately, relationships came down to loyalty.

And he was grateful for Dawson's.

Rebecca didn't realize that she'd been in the booth for almost three hours by the time Brody walked through the door of Angel's. She waved him over, thinking how fast time had zipped by.

By the second hour, Mr. Turner had excused himself, telling Samantha he could walk home from the restaurant.

Of course, she'd tried to talk him out of going. He'd

told her that he wanted to stop by some of the shops in the square, anyway.

Reluctantly, Samantha had let him go. She'd mumbled another apology, which was unnecessary, and had said that he never got over the abductions. He'd said that he wished he could help in some way but had felt as helpless then as he did now. Some people got over the past better than others. Since Rebecca and Samantha had been friends all those years ago, the whole ordeal most likely hit a little too close to home for Mr. Turner. With the loss of his wife the previous year, it might've been too much for him.

Rebecca understood and had assured her friend there was no harm done.

Those thoughts washed away as Brody opened the door and made a straight line to Rebecca. His head was down, but his gaze was intense and a little part of her wondered if he'd missed her, too.

Ryan, who had been seated next to her, stood as Brody approached the table. The two shook hands and then he leaned over to hug Samantha.

When Ryan sat down again, he moved across the table, leaving the spot next to Rebecca free.

"My phone's missing," he repeated, this time saying it to Brody.

"When did you notice it was gone?"

"Not until she asked me about the text message I sent." He motioned toward Rebecca. "Thing is, I didn't send it."

"You couldn't have," Brody said.

Chapter 11

Brody held out Ryan's phone. "There were all kinds of festival people in the area where someone told us to meet. They were trading watch."

"One of them must've lifted my phone at the gas station earlier when I stopped to get gas. I keep it in my pocket and hardly think about it until I need it. I've never been one of those people glued to the screen." Ryan took the offering. He should look relieved that his uncle might be innocent. Instead, he looked even more worried. "You think one of them tried to isolate you? Get you in the woods?"

"Makes me think someone's watching. Whoever's behind this is most likely still trying to get to Rebecca. But now I may have a contact inside the Renaissance camp." Of course, the guy could have been covering for one of his own. "I met a guy named Lester. He seemed like a good person albeit protective of his people. We might be able to get more information from him."

"We still need to circle back and talk to Uncle Greg," Ryan said.

Brody's coffee arrived.

"I stopped by Alcorn's office and caught a break when his admin was there working. I wasn't sure she would be given this is Saturday. I used Rebecca's name. She turned over a list of vendor names. We can check them against the suspect list to see how many hits we get. We'll focus on those first." Sitting so close to Rebecca had Brody's pulse racing again.

"I think we should speak to my uncle first," Ryan said.

"We can always drive to Garland and check his last-known address," Brody offered.

Rebecca touched his arm. He ignored the heat exploding through him. Everything inside him wanted to haul her in his arms. He picked up his coffee instead of reaching for her. This seemed a good time to remind himself of the fact that most high school sweethearts who went on to marry didn't make it to their third anniversary, or so he'd been told. He already knew how much it hurt when a relationship didn't work. His friends had offered all kinds of unsolicited advice and encouragement when she'd walked out before.

Dismissing the notion of him and Rebecca still together before it could gain traction and make him miss something he shouldn't want he said, "Ryan, you could drive."

"Or we could go back and rest first. I doubt you slept much last night," she offered.

If the Renaissance people were leaving tomorrow,

then he'd rather go now. She was right, though—his head pounded and his eyelids were starting to feel like hundred-pound bales of hay sat on them as the adrenaline wore off from his earlier scuffle. "It's probably better not to wait until morning to follow through on this."

Ryan agreed, looking as if he might explode if he didn't get answers soon. His nervous tick of chewing on a toothpick had already surfaced.

"I hope you guys find him. This is scary," Samantha finally said. She reached across the table and squeezed Rebecca's hand.

"He won't surprise us this time," she said. "You be careful, too. Take extra precaution if you're out somewhere alone, day or night."

"I will. Speaking of which, I'd better get back to Dad. He's had a lot on his mind lately with the store. I guess the pressure of owning a business is getting to him more as he ages." She shrugged. "I'm so happy we got to see each other."

"Tell Melanie hello for me."

Brody picked up on a flash in Samantha's eyes. When he really thought about it, Melanie hadn't been back to Mason Ridge since college. "Tell her we'd love to see her sometime."

"Any chance she'll be coming back for the reunion next year?" Rebecca asked.

Samantha flinched, only for a brief moment. If Brody hadn't been watching her, he would've missed it.

"I doubt it," Samantha said. "Melanie doesn't like to come back. She doesn't have great memories from high school and her parents are almost always on the road now. They go see her in Houston."

Brody figured a small town like Mason Ridge wasn't for everybody.

Everyone stood and said their goodbyes. Brody requested the check and covered their lunch and drinks.

"You haven't eaten anything yet," Rebecca said stubbornly when he tried to usher her out the door.

To appease her, he ordered a club sandwich to go. He tried not to think about how nice it was that someone was looking out for him for a change. Experience had taught him being dependent on others could backfire and the burn left a permanent mark.

Brody had always taken care of himself, especially after his mother had pulled her disappearing act. His father had buried himself in work, so Brody learned his way around the kitchen in order to eat. There wasn't much ceremony to it at first, mostly opening cans of soup and making sandwiches. He'd gotten better over time and once he was old enough to man the grill, his dinners got a lot more interesting.

Conversation flowed easily while they waited for his order. Later, he wanted to double check the social media messages and he still hadn't worked through all the threatening letters to see if anything was there. They had a list of suspects, sure, but he needed something to narrow it down. It was too much to hope for a name but that's exactly what he needed. Then, he could fit the rest of the pieces together.

"I'll drive," Ryan said. "We can leave your truck here."

Brody nodded, thanked the waitress and settled the bill. His left hand instinctively reached for the lower part of Rebecca's back as they walked toward the door.

Pulling it back, he held the door open and followed the others to Ryan's SUV.

* * *

"My uncle usually leaves his door unlocked when he's home," Ryan offered, trying the handle. It turned, so he opened the door. "He's most likely out back, drinking, if he still lives here."

Brody followed, linking his fingers with Rebecca's. To hell with what Ryan thought. Why did Brody feel guilty about holding her hand? Wasn't like he was making a move on her. And yet, having that link kept his heart from racing. It still pounded for a different reason. The vendors hadn't matched any of the names from the suspect list Brody had checked on the drive to Garland. That trail had gone cold.

He didn't have a list of all vendor employees, so festival workers couldn't be ruled out altogether.

Rebecca took two steps inside and froze. Brody immediately knew why. It was the smell of apple tobacco.

He squeezed her hand, urging her forward. Her hesitation disappeared as she powered ahead.

Inside was dark and sparsely furnished. Blinds were closed, only allowing a smidge of light to push through. An old couch with a couple of mismatched chairs pretty much covered the decor in the living room. There was an old TV with a protruding back sitting on an industrial wooden wire spool. The kitchen was on par with the rest of the place. Greg's house was what most people would call a dedicated bachelor pad. It would work for someone in college, but for a man Greg's age most people would consider the place sad.

"This has to be my uncle's place," Ryan said. "I remember this furniture."

Brody looked for any sign there could've been a child there. Of course, Shane had been gone for fifteen years, so whatever Brody saw wouldn't belong to him. If Greg abducted kids, there should be some evidence.

Nothing stood out.

The door to the back porch creaked as Ryan pushed it open.

"It's me, Uncle Greg." Ryan quickly added, "I brought company."

Uncle Greg was a tall and slight man, and it wasn't lost on Brody that he fit the description of the Mason Ridge Abductor. His easy smile faded when his gaze stopped on Rebecca.

"What brings you and your friends all the way out here?" he asked, shifting his weight from one foot to the other, looking uneasy. He held tightly to a beer can as he took a swig. "You folks want something to drink?"

"Nothing for us, thanks," Brody said, noticing the tension around Ryan's eyes as he came up beside him. Play this wrong and his uncle might not talk at all.

Rebecca had eased behind Brody a little more, clearly uncomfortable being around Ryan's relative. Her discomfort wasn't full-on panic and Brody took that as a good sign to keep going. If her fingers stiffened any more, he'd excuse them both. There was no reason to put her through anything she didn't want to be part of and he'd wait with her in the SUV. Since she was doing okay, and he really wanted to stick around to see Uncle Greg's reactions to Ryan's questions, Brody stayed.

Ryan continued, "I need to ask you a few questions."

"Take a seat while I refresh my drink," Greg motioned to a mixed grouping of mismatched plastic chairs.

To be polite, Brody did.

"You remember my friends, Brody and Rebecca?" Ryan asked.

"Nice family, the Hughes." Greg popped open a fresh beer from the cooler, took a gulp and sat down next to Ryan.

Brody noted it was the farthest seat from Rebecca. He also noticed that Greg didn't mention anything about his own family. And that was probably for the best.

Rebecca had a death grip on Brody's fingers. He glanced at her to get a read on whether or not he needed to take her to the SUV. Her gaze was intent on Greg. The creased lines on her forehead indicated she was carefully studying him.

The pulse at the base of her throat beat rapidly but that was her only tell. Otherwise, she looked surprisingly calm. Then again, she had the most to gain from this interview.

No reason to leave yet.

"Tell me everything you remember about the night her brother was taken," Ryan pressed.

"I've already told the law everything I knew." Greg's expression dropped to frustration and despair. "Did they believe me? No. They hassled me for months after that boy went missing. I couldn't walk to the corner without being hauled in for loitering."

His expression was genuine. He had the worn look of an innocent man who'd suffered horrendous abuse at the hands of law enforcement. Brody could see Sheriff Brine pulling something like this.

Greg turned directly to Rebecca. He said, "I'm sorry for your loss, ma'am, but I want you to know that I had nothing to do with what happened. I've told the sheriff the same thing. But he didn't listen." He took another gulp of beer and Brody noticed Greg's hands shook. "I don't want to talk about it no more, either. Isn't it enough I moved out of town to get away from all the harassment?"

Brody hadn't thought about the fact that Greg might've been targeted all those years ago. Everyone knew Sheriff Brine disliked the Hunts. Guess he'd taken full advantage of what happened to demonstrate his power.

Ryan comforted his uncle, who was clearly shaken up just remembering.

"I'm the one who's sorry," Rebecca said, rising from her seat. She walked over and hugged Greg. "The sheriff shouldn't have taken advantage of what happened to my family to hurt you."

Greg blinked up at her, clearly stunned by her kindness. "I've done a lot of wrong things in my life but I would never hurt no child. I cried like everybody when that boy went missing."

She patted his shoulder. "I know."

He crossed his legs, the look of surprise still on his aging features. "If you ask me, the sheriff knew more than he let on back then."

Angry words from a man who'd been scorned. Brody couldn't blame the guy for lashing out. It was no secret that Brine didn't like any of the Hunts.

Rebecca thanked him for his time and turned to Ryan and Brody. "We should head back and leave this poor man alone. He's been through enough already."

Brody rose to his feet ahead of Ryan.

They said their goodbyes and moved toward the house.

Brody stopped and picked up the pipe on the plate

being used as an ashtray. He turned. "Can I ask you something?"

"Shoot," Greg said, still visibly shaken at the memories of what Sheriff Brine had put him through.

"Why apple tobacco?"

"That's easy. Picked up the habit from an old drinking buddy who used to come to town with the festival." The man didn't flinch.

Greg took another drink and Brody tried his best not to look too interested in the answer to his next question. "Do you remember that guy's name?"

"Sure do. Thomas…oh, what's his name. Something. It's right there on the tip of my tongue." He banged his knuckles on his forehead. "I remember now. Last name was Kramer."

"Thank you. You've been a big help today. We appreciate you being honest with us."

"I do what I can."

"You don't happen to know where Thomas is now, do you?"

"Nah. I don't get to the festival anymore. I try to stay clear of that town with Brine breathing down my neck every time I walk on the sidewalk."

One look at Rebecca said she'd caught on.

They had a name.

"Any chance you can still describe him?" Brody asked.

"Sure," Greg said. "He was my about my height and build. Had brown eyes."

Find Thomas Kramer and they had a shot at finding out what had happened to Shane.

Brody thanked Greg for his time.

By the time the trio reached the SUV, Rebecca

looked about to burst. She held it in long enough to open the door and slip inside.

"We have a name," she said.

"We sure do. And he matches the description, too."

"Thomas Kramer. Wasn't he one of the suspects?" Rebecca asked.

Ryan started the SUV, put the ignition into Drive and pulled away from his uncle's house. His worst fears put to rest, he looked relieved for the first time since this ordeal had begun.

"It's familiar." Brody checked his phone. "Sure is."

They owed the encampment a visit. He checked his watch. The festival wouldn't start for hours. It would be more difficult to find Lester with those costumes on. Brody wished he'd asked what job Thomas Kramer had at the festival.

With this being the last night, Brody had very little time to work with. He wasn't sure it was safe for him to go on his own to the RV park where festival workers kept a close watch.

Based on the protection details they had going, it wouldn't surprise Brody if they carried guns for night duty.

Did they know they'd had a kidnapper among them? Were their efforts to keep out locals like they'd said, or were they protecting their own from a threat within? Lester had said that they'd started patrolling based on the grocery store attack.

In hindsight, their efforts seemed larger than the crime. A local woman was mugged at the grocery store and suddenly they're setting up patrols, attacking anything that moves in the woods?

Seemed like on over-the-top reaction to what the sheriff's office had said was a random occurrence.

Chapter 12

This was the closest Rebecca had been to a break-through in the case in years—she could feel it. Energy hummed through her at the thought they could be getting close to solving a fifteen-year-old puzzle and possibly finding her brother.

Thoughts buzzed around in her head. If Kramer had been a suspect, why would they have let him go? Wouldn't the sheriff have interviewed him? What about the FBI?

Of course, there were more leads than people to handle them back then. Even at twelve, Rebecca had known that much.

Ryan had been quiet for the entire half-hour trip so far. "My uncle is a drunk. It's possible he's remembering the name wrong."

"I thought about that," Brody said, flashing a knowing look toward Rebecca. "Never hurts to take it seriously, though."

Rebecca knew both men were trying to soften the blow if this turned out to be a nonlead, and she loved them for it.

By the time Ryan had dropped them at the restaurant where Brody's truck was still parked, Rebecca's thoughts ping-ponged from Thomas Kramer to Brody.

They had a name, Thomas Kramer, and the very real possibility he would lead her to the truth.

For the rest of the ride to Brody's place, she vacillated between excitement and fear. Questions assaulted her. What if they'd found him? What if they hadn't?

What if they wrapped this case and she and Brody walked away from each other for good?

The truth was that she liked being close, having him depend on her. Making sure he ate and didn't overexert himself were things that made her ridiculously happy.

There was something so right about taking care of Brody.

He'd barely set his keys on the table in the foyer when she said, "I'll grab the letters to see if one of them is signed by Kramer."

"While you do that, I'll see if I can find any news about him or an address," Brody said, moving to the laptop in the kitchen.

When he came back into the open-concept room, he brought the laptop with him and moved to the sofa. "It's more comfortable over here if you'd like to join me."

She did, tucking her foot under her bottom as she sat down. They had a name. And she had a feeling this all would be over soon. "We're getting close."

"We don't know if Thomas Kramer is our guy yet. If not, this isn't the end."

Tears rolled down her cheeks despite her best efforts to hold them back. She hadn't expected to get so emotional with him, dammit.

"You told me something the other day and it made a hell of a lot of sense," he said.

Wiping a few tears away, she said, "What was that?"

"Holding in emotion is dangerous. Not talking about the things that bother us, bottling them up, doesn't lead to anything good. And I think you're putting on a brave front right now."

His words hit home and the floodgates opened. Tears streamed and she couldn't hold them back if she'd tried.

"Get over here," he said.

Rebecca was in his arms before she could recount all the reasons this would be a bad idea, her face buried in his strong chest.

"You're scared and there's nothing wrong with that," he said, his voice a deep, steady timbre. His quiet strength was like the river that cut through granite.

This was the closest she'd been to figuring out the past.

Rebecca pulled herself together. "I'll be okay."

She picked up the stack of letters and set them on her lap.

Brody kissed her forehead before opening the file on his laptop.

It didn't take long for him to say, "Look here."

Her heart skipped a beat as she read the screen. "Are those notes from his interview?"

"Looks like it," Brody said. "Did you notice this?"

"He had a child who died at age seven," she said, horrified. "Wouldn't that make him a prime suspect?"

"I would think so," Brody said quickly, his eyes skimming the file. "Here. It says that his alibi checked out and that's why he was cleared of suspicion."

"It says he was caring for a sick aunt that weekend," Rebecca said. "She could've lied for him."

"I'd put money on it."

"Any chance we can find his address?" she asked.

Brody minimized the window on his screen and then pulled up a search engine. He tapped the keys on the keyboard. "Nothing. Although, his address might not be listed."

"Or he could live with someone else. Another relative," she said.

"True." Brody rocked his head.

"Any chance his aunt's name and address is in that report?" Rebecca's pulse raced in her chest.

Brody pulled up the file and scrolled through the entire page. "It's not here. When we go to the festival tonight, I'll ask Lester about Kramer."

"I feel like we should be doing something more right now," she said, feeling antsy. Answers were close. She could feel it.

"We are," he said. "And we will. I know patience is difficult right now, believe me, but the truth will come out soon enough."

"I want to talk to this Kramer guy."

"We will," he reassured. "Right now, there's not much more we can do until we talk to Lester tonight."

"You're probably right." Her heart trilled against her rib cage and she needed to slow down her breathing, find a way to calm herself.

Looking around Brody's place, at the comfortable decor, she could see herself living in something like this with him. In fact, this was exactly the kind of place she'd live in if she had a ranch. She loved the open space of the landscape, and the Texas sky was nowhere brighter in the day or more majestic at night than in Mason Ridge. Chicago had been wonderful, too, for different reasons. And mostly, it had been different.

Walking down the street there she could be anyone. She was no longer "that girl." No one whispered.

And yet, Mason Ridge would always be home in her heart.

Was it because Brody was there?

"I didn't leave you all those years ago, Brody, so much as run away from here, from everything I felt. I needed to sort out my emotions, but I hurt you in the process. I'm so sorry."

Brody lifted her chin until her face was raised and she looked into his clear blue eyes. She'd expected to find pity in them, but instead she saw something hungry, something primal. Need?

"What time should we leave?" she asked.

"We have a little while. The festival workers will be setting up for opening soon so I doubt we'd get in without a warrant, which we don't have."

"We have a little time to kill?" Rebecca ran her finger along Brody's strong jawline. Neither looked away.

Chapter 13

Brody felt Rebecca's heartbeat pounding against his chest. The rapid rhythm matched his own. With her in his arms, he felt an emotion that was foreign to him—intimacy. And an overwhelming need to pick her up, take her to his bed and show her just how much a woman she'd become overtook him.

He'd experienced need but nothing matching the intensity of this feeling.

Somewhere in the back of his mind, he realized being this close was a bad idea. Staring into her honey-brown eyes, the smell of her shampoo drowning his sense, and all reasoning flew out the window.

Just when he thought he might be able to stop this from going any further, she shifted position enough to pull her shirt over her head and drop it on the floor.

"You can tell me no if you think this is a bad idea,

Brody." The way his name rolled off her tongue made him want to hear her say it again and again as his tongue moved down her neck.

She stood and shimmied out of her jeans. Underneath, she wore matching lace panties.

Blood pulsed toward his already uncomfortably stiff length.

He tugged her toward him until she was standing in front of him, his hands to either side of her hips. Leaning forward, he rested his forehead on her stomach. "You have no idea how badly I want to do this."

He looked up at her as she stood there with defiance in her stare.

"But?"

"No buts. I want to make love to you, Rebecca. Now it's your turn to take an out, because I've already made up my mind. If you have any doubts about what we're about to do, you're going to have to be the one to stop this. In about two seconds, I won't be able to so I need to know that you want this. Me."

"It's always been you, Brody. I've always wanted you."

That was all the encouragement he needed. Standing, rising to his full height, he dipped his head down and claimed her mouth. Their lips molded together as he slid his tongue inside her mouth, the need to taste her overtaking every rational thought.

Her hands traveled across his chest, moving upward until they tunneled in his hair, pulling and tugging as her tongue swirled inside his mouth. She tasted so sweet.

His shirt joined hers on the floor.

By the time he reached for the zipper of his jeans,

her hands were already there, so he let her do the honors. A second later, his pants were tossed on top of hers.

There in his living room wearing nothing but a bra and panties was the most beautiful woman he'd ever seen. She needed to hear it. "Rebecca, you're gorgeous, sexy."

Thoughts of the innocent kisses they'd stolen in high school were a world away. High school was a world away. And Brody couldn't say he was especially sorry they weren't those same two people they'd been.

He'd grown up, become a man.

His Rebecca, still sweet, had an incredibly sexy side. He'd noticed the way men looked at her. He didn't like it.

"I missed you, sweetheart."

"I'm right here, Brody," she said.

Standing now, he felt an all-too-familiar tug at his heart. Rebecca was the only one who affected him in that way, who reached beyond the mask of strength he wore. With her, he felt a strangely comfortable sense of vulnerability.

This time, he kissed her.

Their mouths moving together, the heat between them rose as his hands moved along her stomach, her breast. He palmed one and her nipple beaded against his palm.

It was her silky bra that hit the floor next. She was all curves and soft skin, and his groin tightened when he really saw her.

Brody took her by the hand and led her to his room.

By the time she was on the bed, all of their clothes littered the floor. *Rebecca on his bed.* He liked the sound of those words more than he should.

"Do you have protection? There hasn't been a need for me to be on the pill," she said.

"That can wait."

On his knees, he ran his finger along the tender flesh of the insides of her thighs. Her body quivered along the stroke of his hands.

"Brody, I want you *now*."

"I have no plans to rush this." It had been a long time since Brody had been interested enough in a woman to take her to bed. He'd stopped doing casual sex.

Looking at Rebecca, at the perfection that was her, everything in his body begged for quick release, but self-discipline was his middle name and he had every intention of enjoying this to the fullest.

"Brody, are you planning to torture me by making me wait?" She sat up, took his arm and tried to urge him toward her. Her face was flush with need, and he felt her body humming with anticipation. "Because I can't."

He smiled at her, moving just out of her reach. She was everything he wanted in a woman—beautiful, intelligent, sexy. And not one female had lived up to the standard she'd set so many years ago.

"As a matter of fact, I had something different in mind." He leaned forward and kissed her to disarm her.

Tucking his hands underneath her sweet round bottom, he tilted her until her head rested on his pillow again.

"No fair…" She pouted until she seemed to realize what he was doing.

She was already wet for him when he inserted three fingers inside her and so he was the one who groaned.

He worked her mound with his thumb as he dipped

his fingers again and again, loving the way her body moved and the sensual moans she made.

Pulsing faster, deeper, harder, her muscles clenched and released around his fingers.

"Brody," she whispered breathlessly.

He would never get tired of hearing her say his name.

Rebecca should be embarrassed at how quickly she'd climaxed. She wasn't. Everything with Brody seemed right and the sexual tension between them had been building since they'd met up at the coffee shop the other morning. If she were being totally honest, it had been building long before that. In high school, they were too young to really know what it was or do anything about it.

Even though he'd tipped her over the edge once already, she wanted more. She needed to feel his weight on top of her, pressing her into the mattress. Him moving inside her.

She pushed up on her elbows, watching as his shaky hands managed the condom. "You need help with that?"

"I think I got it." He rolled it over his tip.

She reached over and guided it down his large shaft.

His guttural groan at her touch nearly drove her crazy. She wanted him to feel everything he'd just given her and so much more.

Pulling him over her, opening her legs to welcome him, he released a sexy grunt as he drove inside her. She opened her legs more, adjusting to his length.

Her hands mapped the lines of his back, memorizing everything that was Brody, and he thrust deeper, reaching her core. She matched his intensity, craving, needing more and more as they rocketed toward the edge.

He pulled out a little, his tip still inside, and tensed.

"What is it, Brody? What's wrong?"

"Nothing. It feels a little too right and I'm already there. I want this to last."

"Don't stop now. We can always do it again."

His smile faded as he reached the depth of his first thrust. She bucked her hips, needing to fly over the edge with him.

Harder. Faster. Deeper.

More.

Their bodies, twined, exploded with pleasure. A thousand bombs detonated at once, sending volts of electricity and pleasure rocketing through her. She could feel him pulsing inside her as her muscles clenched around his length.

When he'd drained her of the last spasm, he pulled out and folded on his side next to her. The weight of his arm over her, his touch, quieted any protest trying to tell her that this might have been a bad idea. His heart raced, matching her tempo, as he leaned over and pressed a kiss to her temple. And then another to her forehead as he pulled her in closer. His body was soft skin over powerful muscle, silk over steel.

She wanted to say the three words roaring through her mind but stopped herself, refusing to think about the fact that he had built a life in Mason Ridge and she was a temporary resident.

Being with Brody was dangerous but far from wrong, even if it wouldn't last.

Brody woke with a start. He'd only dozed off for half an hour and yet it had felt like so much longer. No doubt the result of a satisfied sleep that came with the best sex of his life. Rebecca lay still in his arms, the scent of her citrus and flowery shampoo filling the air around him. He could get used to breathing her in, lying next to her all night. Part of him wished they could stay right there.

The window of opportunity to track down Lester and, therefore, find Thomas Kramer, was closing.

In a few hours, it would be dark outside and the fireworks show would begin over the lake, signaling the end of the weeklong festivities.

The workers would scatter as the break-down crew went to work. By morning, there'd be nothing left of the festival but memories. He slowly peeled her arm off him, careful not to disturb her.

There was enough time for him to make a cup of coffee and he wanted to let her sleep as long as possible.

It took all the self-discipline he possessed to disengage himself from her soft, warm body. Drawing on what was left of his willpower, he slipped out of the covers, located his boxers and put them on.

One last look at her while she lay there, her shimmering chestnut hair splayed across the pillow, and everything in his crazy world seemed right.

How long would it last?

Rebecca had been clear. She would leave town and not look back the minute she could.

He turned and walked out of the room.

The coffee was ready in a couple of minutes. His housekeeper had given good advice about stocking the shelves. And he was all right living by himself, wasn't he?

Didn't Brody prefer to do things his way, like keeping his shoes inside the door and not cleaning up the mud right away when it rained? He knew how to take care of himself, how to cook. Weren't those things important to him? He didn't have to explain where he was on a Friday night or defend having an extra beer while he watched the game.

After serving in the military, he'd wanted nothing more than to come home and be part of the community again. He figured he needed to get his bearings first before he tried to build onto his life.

Someday he planned to find the right woman and make their relationship permanent. Kids didn't seem like the worst idea at some point. He didn't care if he had boys or girls so long as they were healthy. Of course, if he had a daughter, he'd want her to look just like Rebecca.

Brody sighed sharply, ignoring the pain in his chest, and booted up his laptop, sipping his fresh brew.

Assessing how far he'd come should make him feel a sense of gratification. The house was comfortable and nice. He had land. His work rehabilitating horses was important and made a difference. He had enough money to be happy but not so much it was all he cared about.

So, why did he suddenly feel there was a gaping hole in his life?

A still-sleepy Rebecca shuffled into the room. "I can't believe I conked out."

"Come sit down. I'll make you a cup of coffee." He'd had time to reach out to a friend in the military about Randy the other morning and had been hoping to hear back. There was no response, which wasn't surprising. It had only been a day. *Give it time, Fields.*

He'd enlisted Dylan's help, as well. Brody would ask for an update when he saw his friend later. Patience racked right up there with second chances. Brody didn't care for either.

"Do we have time?" she asked, stretching. She looked sexy as hell standing in his living room.

"It'll only take a sec." He moved to the kitchen, popped a pod into the coffeemaker and returned a minute later with a fresh cup. "Here you go."

She thanked him with a kiss and a smile. "How's your head?"

"Better." He motioned for her to join him at the table.

"This coffee is fantastic." She was sitting on the edge of the seat, looking nervous.

Did she regret sleeping with him? He almost laughed out loud. That would be a new one. Wasn't he always the one keeping one foot out the door in every relationship since her? High school crushes hardly counted. Maybe he'd held everyone at a safe distance since his mother had ditched him. Brody hadn't had a horrible childhood. He and his father had been close, two bachelors under the same roof. His father had worked long hours to dig them out of the hole created by his mother.

Brody shoved those thoughts aside as he rose. "I'm going to hop in the shower before we leave. Care to join me?"

The smirk on Rebecca's lips was sexy as hell as she took his hand. "I'd love to, Mr. Fields."

After making love again, Brody dressed, thinking twice wasn't nearly enough. Could this, whatever *this* was, morph into something more permanent? He couldn't go there yet. What he could manage was enjoying what they had for today.

And he didn't have a whole lot of time to consider much of anything else considering time ticked away on finding Thomas Kramer. Brody's internet search had turned up unlucky. Then again, he hadn't expected to find Kramer easily. This guy had avoided capture for fifteen years. He traveled with a festival that was on the road forty-five weeks out of the year and could live anywhere.

Dawson texted that he was already at the festival with Ryan looking for Lester, and that Dylan was coming with Maribel. Said that Dylan had some news for Rebecca that he wanted to deliver in person. Brody hoped he knew what that meant. He wanted to keep a smile on her beautiful face.

"Think we have time to swing by and see my mother on our way? I spoke to her nurse earlier and Mother's having a good day. She had a great visit with Chelsea and Kevin this morning and they promised to stay in touch. They left their information with Mother. I guess having company did wonders for her," Rebecca said, entering the room. She'd dressed in a light blue tank top, jeans and sandals.

"It's on the way to the festival grounds, so that's not a problem." He withheld the information about Dylan's news. No sense getting excited about it before they knew what it was. Dawson had been tight-lipped so far.

"I'm ready if you are."

He nodded as her ringtone sounded in her purse. She retrieved her phone and checked the screen. "It's my dad. Do you mind if I take this?"

"Not at all." Brody smiled. From all he'd known, Mr. Hughes was a good guy. He deserved to know his daughter.

"Hi, Dad," she said into the phone, moving to sit on the couch in the next room. "I'm good. Thank you for calling." A beat of silence passed. "I'd love to come see you and the boys." Another hesitation. "Next Sunday? Barbecue?" She glanced toward Brody.

"Good idea," he whispered, just loud enough for her to hear.

"Would you mind if I brought someone?" Her eyes flashed toward Brody again. "Good. See you at six. Sure, I'll bring a swimsuit."

There was a moment of silence followed by, "I know I haven't said this in far too long. I love you, Dad."

She closed the phone and turned to Brody. "What are you doing next weekend?"

"Taking you to a barbecue." If she needed him there to ease her way back into her father's life, Brody didn't mind helping out. It was the right thing to do and he felt good about encouraging the reunion. Not everyone had a relationship with a parent worth holding on to. If someone did, they needed to grab hold with both hands and hang on for the ride. Those first steps toward the starting gate were often the hardest to take. "For what it's worth, I'm proud of you."

"You probably don't want to hear this from me, Brody." She glanced down to the floor and then back up at him. "I think you're a great man."

His heart skipped a beat because he thought she was going to say something else, the three words he wasn't ready to hear. Because when this was over, he had every intention of walking away.

Rebecca was happy she didn't have to coax Brody to go inside with her to see her mother. Panic had engulfed Rebecca when they'd gone to her room only to find it empty. Turned out, her mother was in the recreation room playing a game of chess with another patient, looking pleased she'd made a friend.

They'd cut their visit short, promising to return the following day. Her mother had made Brody vow he'd return soon, too. Then she'd thanked him for looking after her daughter so well.

Since the festival was a short drive, Rebecca didn't argue when Brody made a move to drive again.

Neither said much on the ride over. Tensions rose the closer they got. Brody parked near Main Street and then texted the others to let them know he and Rebecca were there. It didn't take long to find Ryan and Dawson.

"We found our friend, Lester, from earlier," Dawson said. "He said Thomas Kramer was part of the breakdown crew. Or at least he had been until last year when they'd found him peeking through windows of the workers' RVs."

Rebecca couldn't help but think Kramer would have to be strong to do that job.

A text came from Dylan saying he was delayed with Maribel and would join them as soon as he could.

"Another reason their guard has been so high?" Brody asked.

"Exactly. Lester was up-front with us, but we both got the impression he was uncomfortable talking about one of his own," Ryan added.

"If they fired him last year, why come back? Why follow them here?" Brody asked, taking Rebecca's hand.

She wondered if the sudden urge to keep her close by came with knowing Kramer could be right next to them and they wouldn't know it. "Good question," Ryan said.

Dawson nodded. "I told Dylan I'd stick around the midway area. I'll keep watch. You guys should check the perimeter and see if he's hanging around, watching for another target."

Brody agreed.

Rebecca looked around, remembering the timing of Chelsea and Kevin's son's disappearance. "I wonder if they suspected him of the Sunnyvale kidnapping and that's why they beefed up their own security. It had happened on the last day of the festival last year."

Brody nodded. "There have been reports of him showing up in other places, but our guy says he hasn't seen Kramer," Dawson said.

"I ran a search of abductions of seven-year-old boys in the area and there haven't been many in the past fifteen years," Brody said.

"Maybe those are the only ones here." Rebecca didn't want to think about the truth in front of her. If Kramer had been the one to take Shane and he was still hurting boys, then it stood to reason that Shane was dead.

Chapter 14

"I keep wondering why he'd come back. He had to know he'd be figured out eventually," Rebecca said as she, Ryan and Brody walked the perimeter of the festival while Dawson waited on the midway.

Brody didn't like the answers he came up with. "It's been a long time in between abductions here. Plus, he's bold because he's done a great job of hiding his activities so far. He knows this area, the woods. He's been able to slip under the radar all these years. But his time is up. We know who he is. He's going down and it's only a matter of time before we find him."

She paused, releasing a heavy breath. "Do you think it's possible that Shane's still…"

"I do. And you have to believe it, too." He didn't want to tell her what he thought Dylan's news would be just in case he was wrong. Brody and Ryan exchanged knowing glances.

Brody checked the surroundings. They were stopped near a farm road toward the back of the festival grounds. There were no residential developments for a good two miles on either side of them. He only had one bar on his phone.

Ryan pointed to a fresh trail that had been cut through the brush. "Someone's been here. Could be teenagers looking for a party spot, or…" His gaze bounced from Rebecca to Brody.

Teens were known for searching out good places to build a bonfire and drink near the county line. And this had all the right markings for it.

"Except this trail has been trimmed and they don't normally use anything sharp," Brody pointed out, examining the marks.

"This might be another wild-goose chase, but it's worth looking into," Ryan said.

"Let's check it out. We can notify the sheriff if it's worth his time. I'm sure his office has been inundated with leads since the sketch hit the air."

Ryan nodded. "True."

Rebecca, on the other hand, remained perfectly still. Her face had gone pale. Brody didn't like having her along, but he didn't figure she'd let him go without her. He linked their fingers and took a step forward.

She followed until they moved into the tree line. She stopped, refusing to budge, except to grip his hand like death.

"Hold on a second, Ryan." Concerned, Brody turned his full attention to her. "What is it, Rebecca?"

She stood frozen for a long moment. "Do you smell that?"

"What?"

Ryan moved to Brody's side.

"I know that smell." Fear widened her eyes; the color drained from her face, and her fingers were icy cold.

"What is it, Rebecca?"

"Apple tobacco." Her moment of hesitation dissolved like salt in boiling water. Her gaze narrowed and her lips thinned as determination replaced fear. She stalked toward the woods.

Brody and Ryan kept close beside her, flanking her, as the sun kissed the treetops. She needed space and Brody intended to give it to her. Enough to work out her anger, but not so much as to leave her exposed.

Rage burned through Brody with each forward step. Even though the light was beginning to fade, he saw a small building positioned in the trees ahead coming into focus.

Rebecca had to have seen it, too. She didn't stop charging ahead. In fact, she increased her pace. Not a good idea. He couldn't let her be the first one to see what was inside that place.

Everything inside Brody wanted to stop her, to protect her from what he feared would come next. They could be walking up on a body, even Jason's from last year.

That there was no stench in the air was the only positive sign this might not go south.

He squeezed Rebecca's hand for support and exchanged a look with Ryan. She seemed to understand the need to move slowly and quietly, just in case Thomas Kramer was inside. Or watching from somewhere in the woods, setting another trap.

Brody would've liked time to gather intel before storming into the building, set a perimeter.

Instead, he signaled for the others to stop and listen.

There was no noise coming from the broken-down old shed.

A chill raced up Brody's back as he surveyed the area. The trees were thick enough to conceal the building, which was large enough to house a few people and supplies. "Hold position while I try to get a visual."

Rebecca and Ryan nodded.

This was exactly the kind of location Thomas Kramer would use. An abandoned shed in the woods that had been long forgotten. Unfortunately, there were far too many places like this in and around Collier County.

The suburban sprawl spreading from Dallas had not reached this place. And that was a large part of the reason Brody had returned. The other incentive had been to stay close to his father.

A little voice said he came back to be close to Rebecca, but he shut that down.

That same irritating voice said he came back because he still had feelings for her.

Was there any possibility that was true?

No.

Did he feel something when Rebecca was around? Yes.

Love?

Brody shoved the word down deep as he moved stealthily through the woods. *Loyalty* was better.

The shed door had a place for an outside lock, which meant the original owner most likely had kept small farming equipment inside at some point. Brody inched closer without so much as snapping a twig. He didn't want to give away his location should Kramer be inside. Surprise was the best advantage and Brody had a lump on the back of his head to prove it.

There was no lock. Either the place was clean or they were about to walk into a trap.

Brody's need to protect Rebecca overrode his rational mind, because his first thought was to breach the building alone. No way did he want her within five feet of that shed. He circled back to her and Ryan.

"You sure you want to do this?" he asked.

She nodded. "Did you find anything?"

"There's no lock on the door. We shouldn't have any trouble getting inside." He hesitated. "I do want to remind you this could be a setup. Or you might end up seeing something you can't erase from your mind. I'd prefer to go first."

"I thought about that," she said ominously.

"And you still want to go in with me?" He looked her straight in the eyes. Any fear, any hesitation, and he'd go on his own. "Ryan can stay here with you."

Her head was already shaking, and Brody noticed that her body was, too.

"I can't live my life afraid anymore," she said.

As much as he wanted to stop her, to talk some reasoning into her for staying back, he couldn't. He understood her need to face her fears. Hell, he'd done the same thing. When his Humvee had been hit by an RPG, he'd volunteered for the next mission just so he'd have a chance to climb back in one and drive down that same street. He knew if he didn't, he might as well go home. In his eyes, being useless to the men who depended on him would be far worse than dying.

Brody linked his fingers with Rebecca's and led her toward what could be her worst nightmare. If she was ready to face her past, could they think about starting things up again? The thought caught him off guard. Did he want another chance with Rebecca?

Up to now, he'd convinced himself that he'd accepted this assignment for unselfish reasons, for her. Had he done it for himself all along?

Not ready to process that information, he tucked it away and moved to the door. He'd give her one last chance to reconsider. "Ready?"

Brody and Ryan moved like a well-rehearsed team, Ryan against Brody's back, insuring no one could surprise them from any angle. The two barely needed words between them to know what to do, their connection was so strong.

It wasn't so long ago that she and Brody had shared the same unspoken communication link. Had the years changed him or was he holding back with her because she'd hurt him? She'd felt the sparks between them, they'd made love, and she wondered if that could grow into anything more.

And yet, she knew that wasn't possible.

Good relationships were based on trust and communication. Without trust, good communication was impossible.

And above all, Brody valued loyalty.

She stood in front of the shed, her body trembling, and she wondered if it had anything to do with Brody as much as her fear. Yes, she was scared of seeing what was on the other side of that door. But the determined part of her kicked in and all she could see were Chelsea and Kevin's faces, their pain. The same expression had haunted her mother for so long.

Rebecca knew firsthand how devastating not knowing could be. Shane's disappearance, the years spent searching for him, had branded her. The situation had become worse when her father decided it was time to give up and move on. He'd said he didn't want to live in the past any longer. The same hadn't been true for her mother. She'd sworn she wouldn't rest until she found her son alive or brought his body home. On some level, she must've seen her husband's willingness to put the past behind them as a betrayal to their son, to her. Whatever love had existed between them had fractured. Her mother's relentless dedication to putting up new signs year after year had worn her father down even after their split. He'd said her activity was a slap in the face. He'd cry and say he was sorry that he couldn't bring their son back.

Rebecca didn't blame her father. She figured he was surviving the best he could under the circumstances.

Kevin and Chelsea's love for each other seemed to run deeper. Instead of standing on opposite sides of the room, they stood together. He'd been ready to catch her when she'd fallen. No matter the outcome of their case, Rebecca believed that couple would survive.

They were strong.

It was a safety net she'd never known as a child. Up to now Rebecca had believed relationships couldn't stand the test of time, not when something really bad happened, because of what had materialized with her own parents. And that made it harder to trust in her relationships.

Maybe there was hope for real love, a true connection.

Brody slowly opened the door. What was left of daylight filled the empty space.

That there was no stench had been a comfort. She knew they weren't going to find bodies.

Was anyone inside? It was too quiet. Another piece of her heart broke off that this would be another dead end.

Brody and Ryan stood in front of her, blocking her view. No doubt they felt the need to shield her from whatever horror might be inside the building.

"What's in there?" Rebecca asked as she tried to brace herself for whatever waited on the other side of that door.

"I'll keep watch out here in case he decides to come back to check on this spot," Ryan said, turning to place his back against the wall.

"Someone's been here." Brody took a deep breath and stepped aside.

There was just enough daylight left to see clearly. Bugs flew around her. She slapped her left bicep and then her leg. Mosquitos seemed to be everywhere, poised to take advantage of a quick meal. Dusk was a feeding frenzy.

Flies buzzed around her ears. Rebecca scarcely noticed. Her gaze was intent on the space she'd just stepped into. There was rope on the floor and empty juice boxes in the corner. Her legs almost gave when she took a step closer as horrible memories assaulted her.

"Yes, he has," she said through chattering teeth.

Brody palmed his cell and checked his screen. "According to my map, Mason Ridge Lake isn't far from here. He most likely wouldn't walk there and back, so there might be a source closer. Hold on, let me zoom in. Okay, we have a farmhouse about forty yards from here. Maybe they saw something."

"He was freaked out by me being there. Kept mumbling that I wasn't supposed to be around." Shivers rocked her body just thinking about it. She'd worked to erase those memories for so long.

Before she could ask, Brody was beside her. His arm around her waist steadied her.

"Ryan, call it in. There might be DNA evidence that can positively identify him," Brody called out. He turned to her and said, "Step lightly out of here. The sheriff won't be happy we've trampled all over their evidence."

"They've never been able to find his DNA before," she said. "He's clever."

"These aren't fresh. But, he might not have had time to wipe the place clean." Brody pointed to the empty juice cartons. "And they should be able to identify the child based on those."

Good point. Identifying a child and possibly Kramer would go a long way toward making sure this never happened again.

Brody helped her outside and held on to her while they waited for the sheriff to arrive. "That bothers me."

"What?" Rebecca asked.

"That they weren't able to find DNA evidence before."

"He's too smart," Rebecca said.

"Which doesn't exactly jibe with the theory of a transient. Kramer's tricky. I wonder what else he's has done."

"None of it has to make sense to us. We're normal people and this guy is a calculating monster," Rebecca said. "But the other issue I have is whether or not the sheriff will believe us. He could brush us off and say this could be from anyone."

"Unless the DNA on the juice boxes matches a missing kid in the database," Brody said.

Rebecca nodded, thinking about Jason and his parents, the agony of waiting.

Ryan's gaze moved from Brody's arm to his face. "You sure that you two waiting around here is a good idea?"

"We should head back to the festival. He could be there right now," Brody said.

"Absolutely not. I don't want to leave. Not until we have answers," Rebecca argued.

"Ryan makes a good point. There's nothing we can do to help. In five minutes, the place will be crawling with law enforcement, and we need to give them space to do their jobs."

As much as she wanted to protest, that made sense. Ryan's head was rocking back and forth in agreement, too. Plus, the sheriff didn't exactly believe her most of the time, anyway. Maybe it would be best if she was out of sight. "Okay, but let's walk the woods. Maybe there's another place nearby he stashed someone."

Brody shook his head. "He's gone. He wouldn't stick around."

"But we're so close. He was here. What if he—"

Brody's arm tightened around her waist. He leaned down and said, "I can only imagine what you must be going through. I'm so sorry."

He whispered other reassuring words—words that steadied her racing pulse.

"It's just that we're so close. I can feel it. He was here at some point, which means he comes back."

"He doesn't know we're onto him. And he won't have time to disappear before we find him this time. We're closing in. Plus, others are looking for him. He can't hide with the festival workers anymore. If he's around, we'll find him."

True. She knew that. But everything inside her wanted to keep looking for him in the woods.

She could hear footsteps and radio noise getting louder. "They're coming."

"I didn't think it would take long since they're close by, watching over the festival," Brody said.

Ryan gave Brody a bear hug first and then hugged her. "I'll stick around and give them a statement. You two get back to the festival."

"You sure?" Brody asked.

Seeing the exchange between close friends struck her in a place very deep. She thought about what Brody had said a million times about some families being made from the heart instead of shared tissue. He was right about that. And a lot of other things, too. Most of all, he was right that no matter how much her heart ached to be close to him again, it was impossible to go back. Even though her pulse still raced with every brush of his arm against her.

And her heart beat heavy in her chest.

Because she also knew she would never feel like this toward another man for as long as she lived.

By the time she and Brody had finished walking the perimeter of the festival grounds with no luck Ryan had texted to say he was on the midway with the others.

Dylan walked up to the group with his daughter in tow as they arrived.

After hugs and greetings, Rebecca focused on the little girl to take her mind off Jason, Shane and the horrors that lay in the woods. Maribel had Dylan's bold green eyes. She also possessed his dark hair with curls.

Maribel beamed up at Rebecca and her heart literally melted.

Bending down to eye level, Rebecca said, "I've known your daddy since I was this tall." She held her hand up around four feet off the ground.

"Really?" Eyes wide, rosy round cheeks, Maribel was a cherub incarnate. Her *r* came out as a *w* and it was about the cutest thing Rebecca had ever heard.

"It's true. You look a lot like him."

Maribel took a step toward Rebecca and threw her pudgy little arms around Rebecca's neck.

Rebecca hugged the little angel back. She heard Dylan say something about Maribel normally being shy with new people.

Dylan inclined his chin toward the cotton-candy stand. Ryan took the little girl's hand and led her out of earshot.

Wiping away a loose tear, Rebecca said, "She's beautiful, Dylan. You did good."

"I'm lucky," Dylan agreed, but the look in his eyes said he was ready to change the subject. "You want to sit down over there?" He motioned toward a bench.

"No. I'm fine. What is it?" The seriousness in his expression tightened a coil inside her stomach.

A look passed between Dylan and Brody, causing an ominous chill to skitter across her nerves.

"Tell me," she said.

"It looks like I found him."

"Shane?" Surely her ears were playing tricks on her. Dylan couldn't possibly mean her brother.

"We believe it's him." Dylan nodded.

Brody was by her side, his warmth and his touch the only things keeping her upright.

"I have a contact in the military who found the name Brody gave us, Randy Harper. I had an idea which branch he might be in because Dawson took me back to that restaurant outside of town, Mervin's Eats. I brought Maribel, figuring we could gain the hostess's trust easier if my daughter came along. It worked. The hostess started talking about a friend of hers who'd dated him up until the time he left for the service. She couldn't remember his name or which branch, so I asked her to call her friend, and she did."

Air whooshed from Rebecca's lungs as she tried to let his words sink in. Could they have found Shane? Was it even possible after all these years? Tears were already streaming down her cheeks and she didn't bother to wipe them away. They were glorious tears of release. Tears that had been held inside far too long. Tears that needed to be set free. "Where is he?"

"All we know right now is that he's alive. He's in the army out on a mission. I'm told he's a great soldier."

"How can you be sure it's him?"

"We won't know for sure until he takes a DNA test but she said he had a birthmark that looked like Oklahoma on top of his right foot."

"That has to be him. What are the chances someone else would have that?"

"He doesn't remember much of his younger years. She said it bothered him because he'd been told his whole life that his parents had been killed in an accident, that he'd been sent to live with his Uncle Kramer on the road, and that he was an only child but he could swear he had an older sister."

Rebecca dropped to her knees, put her face in her hands and cried.

Everyone gave her space, even Brody. He seemed to know she needed a minute.

The release was sweet as she finally let go. *Shane, my baby brother, you're alive. You remember me. I've missed you so much.*

When she could stem the flow of emotion, she wiped her face and stood. "What else?"

"That's all I know for now. We're waiting for DNA confirmation, but that could take a little while since he's deployed. My contact says we can make contact when he returns to base."

"Do we know when that will be?"

"Sorry. That information is classified. My contact had no idea. My guess is a couple of days to a week at the most."

Rebecca threw her arms around Dylan's neck. "I don't know how to thank you. All of you."

"Us finally helping you has been a long time coming," Dylan said, hugging her back.

Maribel ran up with a big pink cloud-like puff on a stick. "Da-da!"

Rebecca took a step back and laughed as the little girl plowed into her father's legs with her cotton candy. He picked her up, not paying any mind to the pink splotches left on his jeans. Brody was right. Seeing Dylan with his daughter, the tenderness in his eyes, made her believe people could change for the better. She'd always loved her friend, but he was the last person she'd expected to see with a baby on his arm. "Seeing you with your daughter makes me think about life a little differently."

Dylan smiled one of those wide and genuine smiles. "Guess I never knew real love before."

Rebecca had. "You hold on tight to it."

"Yes, ma'am."

The little girl wiggled out of his arms and squealed as she ran through her dad's legs.

Brody and the others formed a protective circle around Maribel. He pulled Rebecca closer as his gaze surveyed the area. He had to know what she was thinking...*he's still out there.*

Chapter 15

"We need to find Lester. Maybe we can pin him down for information about Kramer's whereabouts," Brody said, his frustration outlined in his sharp sigh. "He might know where his aunt lives and I have a feeling Lester didn't tell us everything."

"All I keep wondering is if his aunt lied to authorities before."

Brody's lips thinned. "I want to know why she would do that."

"It's a good deception. Places him away from the scene, gives him an alibi, and he gets free rein. Heck, he could've given her something to knock her out without her even knowing. I wouldn't put anything past a man like that."

Brody stopped suddenly. "That's him. That's Lester right there."

"The guy with the white streak in his hair?"

"Yes. Come on." Brody clasped her hand tighter, as though he knew she needed the extra support. Every step closer to finding Kramer tightened the coil in her stomach. How could the man who'd taken away her brother and ripped her family apart so easily slip through the system?

She wasn't crazy and she was so close to being able to prove it. The man who'd haunted her for fifteen years was real and he was right there in Mason Ridge. "Kramer was ruled out as a suspect too easily back then. We have to find that bastard and bring him to justice." Dare she hope they would find Jason? That Shane seemed to be alive and well was an encouraging sign. Rebecca said a prayer that the little boy was out there, somewhere close by, safe. She tried not to think about the fact that he'd missed a birthday with his family, or how many her brother had. A thought struck her. "I must've gotten too close when I found Shane—Randy online. That's why Kramer came back for me."

"Makes me think he won't leave until he finishes the job," Brody said. "We can't risk it, though. If he figures out we're this close, he could disappear."

Brody touched Lester's shoulder. The guy spun around a little too quickly, his eyes wild.

"Sorry, it's just me," Brody said.

Relief washed over Lester's features, but he tried to play it off. "No problem. We're all a little jumpy with this being the last night. So far, so good, though."

"This is my friend Rebecca," Brody said, introducing her.

After they'd shaken hands, he continued. "Thomas

Kramer abducted her and her brother fifteen years ago. She got away, but they never found Shane."

Was Brody intentionally putting names and faces to the story? Lester's expression softened.

"I wish I could help you out, man. No one knows where he is."

"So you're saying that you haven't seen him at all?" Brody pressed.

Lester's gaze moved from Rebecca back to Brody. "Not me personally. One of the guys believes he did."

"Here?"

"Yeah. Earlier, though. I've been watching out ever since," Lester continued. "We put extra eyes on the campsite, too."

"That's smart. Just in case."

"Sorry to hear about your family," Lester said to Rebecca.

"My mom took things really hard. She never recovered." It was true. Rebecca also wanted to play the sympathy card in case this guy was holding back information.

"Kramer's aunt lied for him. Do you have any idea where she lives?" Brody kept pushing.

"I have a kid of my own, a little girl. I can't imagine." Lester paused. "His aunt Sally doesn't live far from here. She's in Brighton. It's why we're extra careful here and in Sunnyvale."

"You must've heard what happened last year," Brody said, glancing at Rebecca.

She made the connection, too. Randy Harper was from Brighton.

Lester nodded.

"Did you know Kramer very well?" Rebecca asked.

"We thought we did. Apparently not."

"According to the police report, he had a son who died," Brody said.

"We didn't know until years later about that. Way after the fact. It all started to make sense then."

"When exactly did you figure this out?" Brody asked.

Lester shrugged. "Not sure exactly. Heard it through the grapevine and couldn't be too sure of the source."

"And you didn't think to go to the police with it?" Rebecca fired back.

"No," he said with a look of apology. "We thought it was all hearsay. Plus, if we don't run a tight ship then we don't get invited to places. None of us wanted to be associated with a person who abducts children. We couldn't afford to have that hanging over our festival. None of us would have a job."

"Even so, why didn't anyone come forward?" Rebecca asked. "That kind of information is pretty damning, don't you think?"

"We didn't know for sure it was him. Besides, we believed that he was caring for his aunt."

"Didn't you suspect anything when he suddenly showed up with a kid on the road?" Rebecca asked, mustering the kindest voice she could under the circumstances. The coil was tightening and it was becoming unbearable.

"That's the thing, he didn't. Not for a few years, anyway, and we didn't put it together back then. All of a sudden he would talk about his kid going to school, or playing some kind of sport. We figured we just didn't know him well enough to get personal before," Lester said.

"If he didn't take the kid on the road, then where'd he keep him?" Brody asked the question that was on Rebecca's mind.

"Must've been with his aunt Sally," Lester said. "I actually know her address. It's where we used to send his checks."

He pulled up her name on his contacts list from his phone.

Brody entered the information into his cell, and then thanked Lester as he and Rebecca made a run for the truck.

"Now that we have her address, we need to pay her a visit," he said.

"Do you think it's best to investigate without involving the sheriff?" Rebecca asked.

"Even if I trusted his judgment—and I'm not saying I do—the sheriff has to work within the law. We don't. And I have every intention of using whatever means necessary to make her talk. If that's where Kramer took Shane, then it stands to reason he'd take Jason there, too."

"You think we'll find Kramer there?"

"It's possible. If not, we might find a clue as to where he's hiding. All we need is a receipt or motel bill."

She didn't want to think about how relieved she was that the bogeyman who'd haunted her for a decade and a half had a face and a name. No longer was he a larger-than-life figure in a young girl's imagination. He was flesh and blood. Evil, but a man, nonetheless. And men could be taken down.

She glanced up and was startled to realize Brody was watching her as they ran. No doubt, her concern played out on her features.

"I know what you're thinking and we'll get him." Brody's words were spoken with a silent promise as they made it to the truck.

"We find him, we might find out what exactly happened to Shane. I have to think Kramer didn't do anything to hurt my brother, not now that I know he's grown and in the military. Plus, he seems to be taking these boys in an attempt to replace the son he lost."

She paused, trying to let that sink in.

"It makes sense. We don't have the details yet but it wouldn't surprise me to learn that he cared for Shane in the way he wished he could've for his own son."

"I hope DNA confirms that it is Shane for more than selfish reasons. I'd like to give that to my mom. She's been holding on so long. I want her to know what happened to her son, that he's alive." Tears welled in Rebecca's eyes. One broke free and spilled down her cheek. "I need so badly to tell her we found him, but I want to wait until we're one hundred percent sure. Otherwise, we'd break her heart again and she can't take that."

"Shane's alive. Believe it. And we'll get confirmation soon enough."

Brody climbed into the driver's seat and programmed his GPS with the address of Kramer's aunt.

"There isn't a day that goes by that I don't wish he'd kept me and set Shane free." More tears fell as she buckled her seat belt. She needed to tell Brody everything she remembered, to let it go. "We were so scared, but somehow I figured out that my bindings were loose. Shane was upset, crying, so Kramer was in a hurry when he put me back into my shed and he didn't tie me securely. It took me a minute to realize what had happened. He'd taken Shane to another building to calm him. It was dark outside and I remember my legs giving out as soon as I left the shed. I went looking for Shane. I thought if I could get to him, then maybe we could both get away. I was in shock. I couldn't believe I was free." She paused to stop the sobs. "When I couldn't find him, I thought if I could get away and go get help that we'd get back in time."

A few more tears flooded her eyes. She didn't realize she'd been squeezing her hands together until her fingers hurt.

"It's okay. You don't have to talk about this now," Brody soothed, guiding the truck onto the main road.

"I need to do this, Brody. I've been holding it in far too long. It feels good to finally let it out, to really breathe."

"Take it slow. Stop if you need to." He kept his steady gaze on the road in front of them.

"I got lost in the woods. I remember wandering around, afraid to make noise, stop or sleep. By the time they found me, I was dehydrated and delirious. The sheds had been cleared. Everything had been moved. Shane was gone. The monster who took my brother had disappeared." Sobs racked her, so she didn't fight them.

Saying the words made everything real. Being with Brody was different. He made it safe to open up those old wounds. He made her want to let go of the pain and finally talk about it.

She needed to hold on to the feeling while it lasted because as soon as this case was over, he'd be out of her life again. When she could return Shane to her mother, Rebecca would move away from this town and start a new life for herself.

Talking about the past was the first step toward letting it go.

Brody reached out to her with his free hand, patting hers but saying nothing. His touch was more reassuring than any words ever could be. His hand quickly returned to the wheel.

"And you already know we never found out exactly what happened to my brother until now. He was declared dead ten years ago but it felt so hollow. There was no body. No memorial service. Even after the declaration, my mom refused to accept it. She kept vigil. She talked about him like he'd walk through that door any minute and surprise us all. She made a birthday cake for him every year and brought out old photos."

More sobs came.

Brody just sat there, silently reassuring her.

"For years after she'd see him places—on the playground, driving away in the backseat of cars at the gas station, on a school bus. With every anniversary of his disappearance, those news articles would run, and she'd relive what had happened all over again. And yet, she never gave up hope of finding him. Now, he's alive and she deserves to know what happened to her son."

Sitting there, listening to Rebecca as she told her story, without being able to take away her pain or make the jerk who'd hurt her pay for his sin, was a knife stab to Brody's chest. Justice was coming, though. Even if this lead didn't pan out, Brody would find a way.

Hearing the words, the raw pain, seeing how Rebecca kept the weight of the world on her shoulders frustrated him to no end. He'd told her before but it was worth repeating. "None of this was ever your fault."

"I know."

"You were just a kid. We were just kids. You did the best you could to survive. That's all any of us can do."

She mumbled something else in agreement and he had to grip the wheel from wanting to reach out and touch her again. He was on a slippery slope with Rebecca, sliding downhill fast. There were no branches to grab on to, nothing to save him. His heart was falling down that sinkhole called love and nothing inside him could gain purchase to stop it on the way down.

They'd driven straight for an hour and a half when the GPS indicated they were getting close to their destination.

Brody slowed the vehicle when he entered the cul-de-sac. He parked two houses down as he watched a tall, thin man exit the ranch-style house.

Kramer?

Rebecca reached for Brody's hand and then squeezed.

The man took the driver's seat of a green sedan.

He was too far away to be able to tell for certain that it was Kramer.

Until the sedan slowed as it neared them and the driver saw Rebecca.

His expression said everything they needed to know. And then he accelerated, his tires squealing as they struggled to gain traction.

"It's him," Rebecca said, her voice no longer shaky with fear. "I saw his face."

Pride filled Brody as he banked a U-turn in the cul-de-sac and sped to Kramer's bumper.

Dark eyes stared at them from the rearview mirror.

"He makes it onto the highway and there's a good

chance we'll lose him," Brody said. "Make sure your seat belt is secure."

"Catch him, Brody."

Kramer turned onto a farm road.

Brody maintained a safe distance without allowing Kramer too much leeway.

A few turns and they were following him onto a gravel road.

"He knows this area," Brody said. And Kramer was using it to his advantage as he maintained break-neck speed.

Brody's truck was heavier. He floored the gas pedal, trying to keep up.

Kramer must've panicked because his car veered left and then right. He cut through a corn field and then circled around toward the street they'd been on before.

Any number of innocent people could get hurt if Kramer was allowed to get back on a main road.

Brody gunned the engine, pulling beside Kramer, trying to force him off the road.

In response, Kramer drove his speed up past the hundred-mile-an-hour mark.

The two-lane road was empty, save for Brody and Kramer. That could change any second. Brody had to decide if he should keep pushing the limit, or drop back and follow. But then what? Allow this man to get away? To reach the highway?

Brody gunned the engine, keeping pace with the sedan, and then nudged the wheel right.

Kramer twisted his, jerking the vehicle away from Brody a second before their side panels collided. Then, Kramer overcorrected and his vehicle flew out of control. He sideswiped a tree and was sent into a death spin.

Another tree brought a sudden stop to the deadly rollover. The sound was deafening. The blaze ignited instantaneously.

By then, Brody's truck was at a complete stop.

"Stay here," he said to Rebecca, who was already barreling toward the inferno.

She kept going.

All he could do at that point was try to catch up with her.

The blast that came next caused them both to freeze.

Brody reached for Rebecca's hand. She spun around and buried her face in his chest as they both fell to the ground.

"It's over," she said, tears streaking her cheeks. "It's finally over."

They stayed long enough to give statements to law enforcement and learn that an officer had been sent to the aunt's house. No one was said to be home.

Once in the truck, Rebecca put her hand on Brody's arm as he cranked the engine.

"Can we go there?" she asked. "I need to see for myself that Jason isn't there."

Brody nodded.

Twenty minutes later, he pulled into the familiar cul-de-sac.

Rebecca made it to the door first and knocked. Lights were out and everything was completely quiet. It didn't appear that anyone was home, just as the officer had reported.

"We can ask the neighbors who lives here. Maybe one of them will know something," Brody offered.

"That's a good idea actually. Surely, someone has

seen something," she said, spinning around and heading toward the opposite house.

A middle-aged woman answered on the second round of knocking. Rebecca introduced herself and Brody. He hung back a little so as not to intimidate the woman.

"We're sorry to bother you, but we're trying to reach our friend Thomas Kramer. Is this still his address?" Rebecca pointed to the house in question.

The woman gave an odd look. "Do you mean Thomas Harper?"

Harper? Brody made the connection to Randy's last name.

Rebecca must have, too, based on the way her shoulders stiffened.

"Right, sorry. Having one of those days," Rebecca hedged, recovering her earlier demeanor.

"I'm Patricia and yes, that's his house," she confirmed. "Doesn't look like anyone's home. He travels most of the time for work. His little boy comes to visit sometimes."

"And his aunt?" Rebecca asked.

"Never saw a woman around." She shrugged. She had a solemn look on her face, completely unaware that her neighbor was a monster.

"How long have you lived here?" Brody asked.

"We moved in a couple of years ago," Patricia responded.

Brody wondered if the aunt was still alive. He gripped his phone in one hand and gently squeezed Rebecca's with the other as he thanked Patricia and told her to have a good night.

On closer appraisal of the house, a few of the side

windows were boarded. The front room had a window AC unit. The door would be easy to breach. "His aunt might live somewhere else," he said. "She could be nearby. I'm guessing she keeps Jason when Kramer is on the road."

"I can't leave until I know for sure," Rebecca said.

"I know." Brody took that moment to kick the door. It flew open.

Stepping inside, he called for Jason.

There was no response.

It was dark and Brody had no idea what waited inside.

He clicked on a light. The room looked like something out of an episode of *Hoarders*. Stacks of papers and magazines were everywhere. Old pizza boxes and fast-food bags were piled on the coffee table.

Brody caught movement out of the corner of his eye, so he tracked it to the kitchen. "Jason. We're here to help. Your mommy and daddy are looking for you."

A whimper sounded from inside the pantry.

Opening the door slowly, Brody repeated the boy's name.

As light filled the little room, he saw the boy huddled in the corner. His clothes were dirty and he was frightened. "It's okay, Jason. Take my hand."

The little boy started crying harder.

Rebecca dropped down to her knees. "Hey, Jason. My name is Rebecca and I'm here to take you home. I know a very bad man took you away from your family. He did the same thing to my little brother. It's going to be okay. I know you're scared. But you didn't do anything wrong."

In one swift movement the boy sprang into her open arms, buried his face and cried.

She soothed him, stroking his hair, and when she smiled up at Brody there was a deep sense of peace in her features.

"I'll call his parents first and then the police," he said.

She nodded, moving carefully as if trying not to disturb the boy clinging to her. "Have his parents meet us here. I want to stay until they arrive."

"Absolutely." Brody wouldn't have it any other way.

The Glenns made record time.

As soon as the little boy heard his mother's voice, he broke into a full run toward her. Brody watched Rebecca, witnessed the emotions playing out on her face as each parent thanked her and gave her a hug.

Brody stood back a little, taking it all in. The thought struck him that he'd believed Rebecca to be disloyal. What an idiot he'd been. She was the most loyal sister and advocate that anyone could hope to have in their corner.

As soon as the family walked away, Brody hauled her close to him.

"It all makes sense now," she said, looking into his eyes. "The timing of why Kramer attacked the other morning. He was getting desperate because he must've known I'd found Shane."

"You threatened to expose his lies and uncover the truth. He couldn't have that happen. His life would've been over."

She nodded.

"Are you ready to get out of here?" he asked.

"Yes. Get me away from this."

Brody didn't let go of her hand as they walked away from the house.

She glanced toward the house one more time. "He can't hurt anyone else, Brody. It's over."

The ride back to town seemed to zoom by even though neither said much. Brody didn't mind. Silence was comforting as she sat in the middle seat, snuggled next to him, and there was something very right in the world.

Rebecca. *His Rebecca.*

There was a fork in the road ahead. Go left and he'd be taking Rebecca back to her bungalow. Make a right and he'd be heading to his ranch.

The road was split, but his heart knew exactly what it wanted, *if* she wanted him.

He stopped the truck in the middle of the farm road, put on his emergency flashers and opened his door. "Will you step outside with me?"

Surprise was written all over her face, but she did as he said. "Is it safe?"

"Should be at this hour." It was just past midnight. A new day had dawned. Could they make a fresh start?

He met her at the front of the truck, the headlights lighting a path, his heart pounding against his chest. "Rebecca, we can't change the past."

She dropped her gaze to the ground. "I know. And you don't have to say anything, because I already know how you feel."

"Do you?" He lifted her chin until her eyes met his, those intense honey browns vulnerable. "Because I don't think you do. As much as I loved you, I needed to grow up. I had too many wounds from the past, from my mother."

"I'm so sorry about the past, Brody, but I can't change it."

"I wouldn't want you to. We let go of what we had in high school and maybe that was a good thing. Life is crazy and it's uncertain. I'm only sure of about one thing. I love you."

Her eyes sparkled as soon as she heard the words. "I love you, Brody Fields. Always have and I always will. It's only ever been you. But you need more than my words."

He placed his hands around her neck and guided her lips to his, to home. "You're all I need, Rebecca. You're enough."

She kissed him slowly, sweetly; that shy smile had returned.

"I just have one question," he said.

"Which is?"

Right there in the middle of the road, he bent down on one knee, preparing to ask the woman he loved to marry him.

He didn't touch ground before she'd dropped into his arms and said the one word he needed to hear before he had a chance to ask.

"Yes," she said. "I'll be your wife."

Scooping her up, taking her to the passenger side, he asked the other question on his mind. "You belong at the ranch with me. Are you ready to come home?"

Tears streamed down her beautiful face as she said, "You're home to me, Brody. I'm already there."

Epilogue

"Whatever will I do with one of those things?" Her mother's face screwed up as she motioned toward the laptop Rebecca was setting up on the side table next to her bed. Beside it, she placed Shane's Spider-Man watch.

"Believe me when I say that you're going to want to keep this close," Rebecca said, motioning toward the laptop.

"Tell her I don't know how to use it," Mother said to Brody. Her gaze stopped on the keepsake.

He smiled and his clear blue eyes sparkled. "Trust her. She knows what she's doing."

The past few weeks had been good to her mother after hearing news of Thomas Kramer's death and his aunt's arrest. Her mother had started leaving her room to play chess every afternoon and stopped resisting physical therapy. Every day she was getting stronger and the doctor was hopeful, especially following the initial results of how well her body was adjusting to the new medication.

Rebecca hadn't told her about all the events that had transpired. She'd been waiting for the right moment to talk about Shane. And this was it.

"I'd rather help make wedding plans than dicker around with one of those," Mother protested. Again.

"Just a second." Rebecca pulled up the program she'd installed to allow an overseas face-to-face chat. "There's someone who wants to talk to you."

"What's wrong with the phone? I know mine still has a cord, but people do use it from time to time."

"Nothing. But this call can't be made using one of those." Rebecca checked the screen, her heart thumping in her throat. "Are you there?"

Static and blur were all she had.

Then, the screen cleared up and she saw his face. It was Shane, her baby brother. She'd found him—tests had confirmed it—and she was about to share him with her mother.

Rebecca shifted the laptop so her mother could see. "Mother, it's Shane. He's alive. Your son is alive. And he has something he wants to say to you."

"I heard what happened. How you never gave up on me. I love you, Mom." He looked good, strong.

Her mother clasped her hands together and tears streamed down her face as disbelief transformed into joy. "How could I? You're my baby boy. I love you."

"There's so much I want to know, but I only have a few minutes to talk," Shane said. He had that proud Hughes chin and determined gaze.

"It's okay, son. We have the rest of our lives to get to know each other again." And from the looks of her, her mother planned to stick around to enjoy every moment.

* * * * *

Prologue

The tears leaked out of Kay Duvall's eyes, even as she tried to
focus on what she had to do. *Had* to do to bring Ben home safe.

She fumbled with her ID and punched in the code that
would open the side door, usually only used for a guard taking a
smoke break. It would be easy for the men behind her to escape
from this side of the prison.

It went against everything she was supposed to do.
Everything she considered right and good.

A quiet sob escaped her lips. They had her son. How could
she not help them escape? Nothing mattered beyond her son's
life.

"Would you·stop already?" one of the prisoners muttered.
He'd made her give him her gun, which he now jabbed into her
back. "Crying isn't going to change anything. So just shut up."

She didn't care so much about her own life or if she'd be
fired. She didn't care what happened to her as long as they let
her son go. So she swallowed down the sobs and blinked out as
many tears as she could, hoping to stem the tide of them.

She got the door open and slid out first—because the man holding the gun pushed it into her back until she moved forward.

They came through the door behind her, dressed in the clothes she'd stolen from the locker room and Lost and Found. Anything warm she could get her hands on to help them escape into the frigid February night.

Help them escape. Help three dangerous men escape prison. When she was supposed to keep them inside.

It didn't matter anymore. She just wanted them gone. If they were gone, they'd let her baby go. They had to let her baby go.

Kay forced her legs to move, one foot in front of the other, toward the gate she could unlock without setting off any alarms. She unlocked it, steadier this time if only because she kept thinking that once they were gone, she could get in contact with Ben.

She flung open the gate and gestured them out into the parking lot. "Stay out of the safety lights and no one should bug you."

"You better hope not," one of the men growled.

"The minute you sound that alarm, your kid is dead. You got it?" This one was the ringleader. The one who'd been in for murder. Who else would he kill out there in the world?

Guilt pooled in Kay's belly, but she had to ignore it. She had to live with it. Whatever guilt she felt would be survivable. Living without her son wouldn't be. Besides, she had to believe they'd be caught. They'd do something else terrible and be caught.

As long as her son was alive, she didn't care.

Don't miss
Hunting a Killer *by Nicole Helm,*
available February 2021 wherever
Harlequin Intrigue books and ebooks are sold.

Harlequin.com

HARLEQUIN

Heartfelt or thrilling, passionate or uplifting—Harlequin is more than just happily-ever-after.

With twelve different series to choose from and new books available every month, you are sure to find stories that will move you, uplift you, inspire and delight you.

SIGN UP FOR THE HARLEQUIN NEWSLETTER

Be the first to hear about great new reads and exciting offers!

Harlequin.com/newsletters

Love Harlequin romance?

DISCOVER.

Be the first to find out about promotions, news and exclusive content!

f Facebook.com/HarlequinBooks

y Twitter.com/HarlequinBooks

Ⓞ Instagram.com/HarlequinBooks

Ⓟ Pinterest.com/HarlequinBooks

You Tube YouTube.com/HarlequinBooks

ReaderService.com

EXPLORE.

Sign up for the Harlequin e-newsletter and download a free book from any series at **TryHarlequin.com**

CONNECT.

Join our Harlequin community to share your thoughts and connect with other romance readers! **Facebook.com/groups/HarlequinConnection**

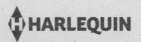